Catching LADY THEO

ELLA QUINN

KENSINGTON PUBLISHING CORP.

kensingtonbooks.com

KENSINGTON BOOKS are published by

Kensington Publishing Corp.
900 Third Avenue
New York, NY 10022

Copyright © 2025 by Ella Quinn

All rights reserved. No part of this book may be reproduced in any form or by any means without the prior written consent of the Publisher, excepting brief quotes used in reviews.

Without limiting the author's and publisher's exclusive rights, any unauthorized use of this publication to train generative artificial intelligence (AI) technologies is expressly prohibited.

All Kensington titles, imprints, and distributed lines are available at special quantity discounts for bulk purchases for sales promotion, premiums, fundraising, educational, or institutional use.

This book is a work of fiction. Names, characters, businesses, organizations, places, events, and incidents either are the product of the author's imagination or are used fictitiously. Any resemblance to actual persons, living or dead, events, or locales is entirely coincidental.

To the extent that the image or images on the cover of this book depict a person or persons, such person or persons are merely models, and are not intended to portray any character or characters featured in the book.

Special book excerpts or customized printings can also be created to fit specific needs. For details, write or phone the office of the Kensington Sales Manager: Kensington Publishing Corp., 900 Third Avenue, New York, NY 10022. Attn. Sales Department. Phone: 1-800-221-2647.

Kensington and the K logo Reg. U.S. Pat. & TM Off.

ISBN: 978-1-4201-5698-0 (ebook)
ISBN: 978-1-4967-6014-2

First Kensington Trade Paperback Printing: December 2025

10 9 8 7 6 5 4 3 2 1

Printed in the United States of America

The authorized representative in the EU for product safety and compliance
is eucomply OU, Parnu mnt 139b-14, Apt 123
Tallinn, Berlin 11317, hello@eucompliancepartner.com

Praise for Ella Quinn

A WORTHINGTON WEDDING

"Quinn keeps the plot moving swiftly as her refreshingly forward-thinking characters navigate these challenges. It's a joy to watch this perfectly matched couple fight for each other."
—*Publishers Weekly*

THE MOST ELIGIBLE VISCOUNT IN LONDON

"Georgie and Gavin are very appealing leads in Quinn's fun romance."
—*Booklist*

THE MOST ELIGIBLE LORD IN LONDON

"Quinn creates a richly detailed traditional Regency world."
—*Kirkus Reviews*

"With a love triangle, a protective Great Dane, and meddling mothers, this new Regency series launch brings on the drama but is filled with tenderness. Readers who recognize characters from Quinn's earlier 'Marriage Game' series (*Enticing Miss Eugenie Villaret*) will be especially rewarded."
—*Library Journal*

THE MARQUIS AND I

"Quinn's delightful Worthington series is uniquely enjoyable for its humor and network of characters in large families, even as, here, she addresses the serious subject of women being forced into sex work. Amid the busy plot and social concerns, romance builds in this satisfying, memorable read, perfect for fans of Grace Burrowes and Tessa Dare."
—*Booklist*

Books by Ella Quinn

The Marriage Game
THE SEDUCTION OF LADY PHOEBE
THE SECRET LIFE OF MISS ANNA MARSH
THE TEMPTATION OF LADY SERENA
DESIRING LADY CARO
ENTICING MISS EUGENIE VILLARET
A KISS FOR LADY MARY
LADY BERESFORD'S LOVER
MISS FEATHERTON'S CHRISTMAS PRINCE
THE MARQUIS SHE'S BEEN WAITING FOR

The Worthingtons
THREE WEEKS TO WED
WHEN A MARQUIS CHOOSES A BRIDE
IT STARTED WITH A KISS
THE MARQUIS AND I
YOU NEVER FORGET YOUR FIRST EARL
BELIEVE IN ME

The Worthington Brides
THE MARRIAGE LIST
THE HUSBAND LIST
THE GROOM LIST

The Lords of London
THE MOST ELIGIBLE LORD IN LONDON
THE MOST ELIGIBLE VISCOUNT IN LONDON
THE MOST ELIGIBLE BRIDE IN LONDON

Here Come the Grooms
A WORTHINGTON WEDDING
CATCHING LADY THEO

Novellas
MADELEINE'S CHRISTMAS WISH
THE SECOND TIME AROUND
I'LL ALWAYS LOVE YOU
THE EARL'S CHRISTMAS BRIDE

Published by Kensington Publishing Corp.

To my granddaughters, Josephine and Vivienne

CHAPTER ONE

Stanwood Place, June 1823

Leo, Duke of Chandos reached for his mistress while her friend kneeled between his legs. Having her friend with them was a present for him. It was good that she didn't know he was going to dismiss her by next week. Pamela climbed on top of him, she reached back to adjust his pillow. Why was the pillow so flat and rough? The linens he kept at the villa were always soft and the pillows plump. Suddenly he was drowning in cold water. How did he fall into the water from a bed? And where were the women?

"Wake up."

What the devil? Women never spoke to him in that tone of voice. He opened his eyes and drops of water flowed into them. "What is going on?"

A young lady stood over him with her hands on her hips. "You are supposed to be helping Charlie, not lying there as if you crawled into a bottle of brandy and forgot to crawl back out."

He stared at her, trying to get his eyes to better focus. "You are shouting."

"I am not. I am not even speaking loudly." An evil look entered the lady's lapis-blue eyes, which was all he could seem to see. "However, I will do if you do not get up. Immediately."

"No!" Leo's head was already throbbing. He didn't need more pain. He pushed himself into a sitting position. "I'm up."

She crossed her arms over her chest and her foot began to tap. He'd imagined a dainty foot encased in silk. But this one was shod in sturdy leather. "Not. Good. Enough."

It was then that he noticed her chestnut hair flowed down her back in curls. "A schoolroom miss?" Finally, the rest of her came into focus. "You're the one who beat me at cards."

"And you are that duke." Lady Theodora Vivers pressed her rosy lips together. "It does not matter. Rise now, or I will take other measures."

Concerned over what "other measures" could mean, Leo scrambled to his feet. "Where am I needed?"

She regarded him as if he was a worm. "I will have a bath sent to you. You have half an hour to make yourself presentable and meet the rest of us in the drawing room. And brush your teeth. You smell like a still."

Turning on her heel, she strode away. He'd never been treated like that in his entire life. He'd never been spoken to in that manner. And certainly not by a young chit. God help the gentlemen of London when she came out. She'd stand everyone on their collective ears. An image of fribbles standing in line to ask for her attention appeared in his mind.

No! She's mine.

Blast it all. He was going to marry her.

He dragged himself to his feet and chased after her. "Lady Theo!"

She stopped and turned to face him.

"You could marry me." He hadn't planned to propose. It had just popped out. It must be his desire to make her his wife. "When you come out next year, of course."

Her eyes widened, and she laughed. "You would hate being married to me."

Leo hadn't expected that. He crossed his arms over his chest. "I don't know why."

Lady Theo held up one finger. "You would no longer be able to drink to excess."

She had a point, but he was becoming tired of the hangovers.

She held up finger two. "You would not be allowed your high-flyers, widows, or bored wives."

He had a feeling if he had her it wouldn't matter. But how the hell did a schoolroom chit know about that?

"Three." The third finger came up. "You would have to actually do something with your life."

"I do do things with my life. I'm a duke."

"That is a rank with the possibility of an avocation. Not an occupation."

It was a damn good thing he was now sober, or he'd never be able to work out what she meant. He was having a hard enough time as it was. "What else. You have two more fingers left."

He rather enjoyed seeing her hands without gloves. "Oh, Good Lord grant me patience." But she held up her fourth finger. "You would have to rise early."

Not if he could keep her in bed. "Go on."

"You are being ridiculous. Those are all my fingers. The other digit is called a thumb."

She turned her back on him and left. He must speak with her brother, Stanwood, about her. Surely a match could be arranged.

Chandos Hall, Late March 1824

Leo opened his eyes. He could almost feel the water dripping down his face. Another dream of Lady Theo Vivers dousing him. He'd been having the same dream for close to a year. During that time, he'd become more and more determined to marry her. To ensure he was correct in his choice of bride, he'd haunted the house of his friend Charlie, the Earl of Stanwood and Theo's brother-in-law, when their enormous family met there and finagled invitations to Worthington Place, where she lived with her brother, also her guardian, Matt, the Earl of Worthington and his wife, Grace, the Countess of Worthington and children. All the while biding his time until she had her come out. And today was the day he'd go to Town and begin to court her. "Matson, what time is it?"

Leo's valet poked his head from the dressing room into the bedchamber. "Just past five in the morning, your grace. We will depart at eight. The trunks have been packed; her grace, your mother, is prepared to depart. Everything is in order."

For the first time in his life, Leo felt as if his being finally had purpose. He'd stopped drinking to excess, stopped gambling, although he'd never done much of that, and had not had a mistress since he'd left Town last June. He was ready to be the type of husband Theo deserved and her family demanded, and the type of man he wanted to be. "Excellent. I will break my fast in a half hour. Is Turner following us?"

Leo's father's secretary had changed his mind at least twenty times about whether to depart before or after Leo. "Mr. Turner will not be coming. He has decided to retire and left at sunrise. He said that he had prepared all the documents you required."

"Damn." Perhaps Leo didn't need a secretary. Still, he couldn't be bothered with it now. He trod to the wash basin. He didn't think he'd ever been this excited to go to Town.

Precisely thirty minutes later, he entered the breakfast room to find his mother and her companion, a cousin, Mrs. Merryweather, already at the table. Mama glanced up. "Constance and I have decided to depart shortly. We will see you in Town. I have a great deal to do if you are to select a wife and wed this Season."

Leo went to the sideboard, putting eggs and beef on his plate. Toast was already on the table. He took his customary seat. "Vouchers for Almack's?"

"One of many things to which I must attend. I have heard from several of my friends, two of whom are Patronesses of Almack's." She chewed on a piece of toast and swallowed. "There is also Lady

Bellamny's soirée for young ladies just out. I will attend that to gather an idea of which ladies might be most suitable."

Leo had debated whether to tell his mother about his decision regarding a bride, then decided against it. He'd come to know Theo over the past year and understood he must approach her with care. She would not fall into his arms simply because of his rank and wealth. He'd have to court her properly. He would attempt a shortcut via her brother Worthington, but that was likely to fail. "An excellent idea."

"When we attend Almack's do not forget that you can ask one of the Patronesses for permission to waltz with a lady who has not yet been approved."

"What do you mean *approved*?" It was the oddest thing he'd ever heard. "I'll wager that all of them have waltzed at country balls and assemblies as well as private balls. How else are they to become proficient?"

"Yes, my dear." She cast an exasperated look at the ceiling. "This is only for permission to waltz at Almack's. Not other venues."

That made more sense. In that case, he'd ask for Theo. He'd be damned if another gentleman would have the pleasure of securing her waltzing privileges with his soon-to-be wife. "It seems like an idea someone invented to make the Patronesses more powerful."

His mother shrugged lightly. She was the most discreet person he knew. Not even in private would she be coaxed into a dangerous conversation. She patted her lips with a serviette and rose. "We will see you in a few days."

Leo had jumped to his feet the second she pushed back her chair. "I will see you then. I intend to stop by Stanwood Place on my way."

"Of course, dear." She bussed his cheek. "Have fun."

"I will. You as well." He inclined his head to her companion. "Have a pleasant journey."

Theo tried not to bounce in her seat, she was eighteen now, as they approached Stanwood Place. Since the former Lady Grace

Carpenter, Theo's sister-in-law, and Matt, her brother had married ten years ago. The Carpenter siblings and Theo's siblings had become one large family. From the beginning they had decided to be brothers and sisters without distinction of blood. Stanwood Place was the main estate of Charlie, the Earl of Stanwood, the head of the Carpenter side of the family, and his countess, Oriana. Theo, Grace, Matt and their children, Gideon, Elizabeth, nine and eight years old, Edward and Gaia who were almost five-year-old twins, arrived shortly before luncheon. Mary, Theo's closest sister, had been visiting Charlie, and Oriana, and their new babies for a month now. Theo hoped Mary would be ready to travel to Town with them instead of waiting for Charlie and his family to make the journey.

Charlie's Great Dane Apollo met them at the door and glanced at the carriages. Soon a bark from either Daisy or Zeus emitted from a carriage built especially to carry them, and Apollo dashed to it.

Grace planned for her, Matt, and Theo to stay here a few days before continuing to Worthington House which was situated in Berkeley Square, Mayfair, London.

"Theo!" Mary rushed to them. "I am so glad to see you. You would not believe how much the twins have grown."

Charlie and Oriana greeted Matt and Grace while Mary took Theo into the house.

"They are so adorable," Mary continued.

A feeling of dread trickled down Theo's spine. She smiled brightly. "Are you ready to go with us to Town?"

Her sister stopped walking and faced her. "I have decided to wait until Charlie and Oriana depart."

"But it is my come out." Theo tried to keep the desperation she was feeling from her voice. She and Mary had been inseparable since they were eight and five respectively. Ten years ago.

"I know." Her tone was so kind Theo's heart sunk. "It is *your* come out. I cannot participate. We both knew this would happen someday." Mary linked her arm with Theo's. "You will have fun shopping for your wardrobe. I will be in Town before your first events. And the rest of the family will be there as well. We have heard from the twins and Madeline, as well as Charlotte, Louisa, and Dotty. We will all be there for you." Mary smiled. "Surely you know I would not abandon you in your time of need." She led Theo upstairs. "Chandos was here for a few days. He left yesterday." Mary was the only one Theo had told about her reaction to him when he waltzed with her during the Christmas ball. "He asked about you."

"I am sure it was only to be polite." As much as she wished otherwise, the Duke of Chandos had a reputation for eschewing any interest in young ladies. He would also make a truly horrible husband.

Mary lifted one shoulder and dropped it. "He didn't say anything to me, but he was with Charlie for hours."

"Perhaps I should delay my come out until you are able to be out as well." No one in the family would be happy about that, but Theo felt as if she was being left alone.

"No. You will not." Mary firmly shook her head. "We have discussed this before." She hugged Theo. "It is your time. Everything will work out the way it is supposed to."

"I suppose you are correct." She tried to summon another smile and failed. "Let us go see the babies." As was so common with the Carpenter side of the family, Oriana had given birth to twins. A boy and a girl, Lady Olivia Elizabeth Prudence and Charles Robert Edward, called Robin, Viscount Carpenter. Both of them had the Carpenter blond hair, but while Olivia had the same sky-blue eyes as her father, aunts, uncles, and many of her cousins, Robin had his mother's amber eyes. Theo could not help but think that if she wed this Season, she too would have a child by this time next year. A vision of Chandos crossed her mind. Tall, broad shouldered, wavy black hair and moss-green eyes. He probably made all the ladies in Town swoon when they saw him. Yet as handsome as he was, he was not for her. She would be shocked if her brother would even allow the match. She must find someone eligible who met the qualities she wanted in a husband, and a rover was not one of them.

"Matt," Charlie greeted his brother-in-law and former guardian. Due to some ridiculous law that married ladies could not be guardians of children, after Grace married Matt she could no longer have guardianship of her brothers and sisters. That was when Matt took guardianship. Charlie had been sixteen at the time. "You and I must speak."

Matt glanced at Grace, who was now headed to the stairs with Oriana. "Lead on. I suspect they will be occupied with your children for a while."

Charlie strolled to his study and waved his brother-in-law to one of the chairs in front of the fireplace. Tea was served almost immediately. Once he'd poured, he fixed his gaze on Matt. "Chandos visited me recently. He wishes to wed Theo."

Matt choked and reached for a serviette. "Did you have to tell me that after I'd just taken a drink? What the devil is he up to?"

"He says he's in love with her."

"Indeed?" Matt raised a skeptical brow. "I know he's a good friend of yours, however, I do not think his is an eligible parti for Theo."

"In the past I would have agreed with you." Charlie would have even warned his old friend off his sister. "Yet, he has changed. He's healthier. When he was here, he drank moderately. His conversation consisted of his estates and the improvements he was making. You've seen him over the winter. You must have noticed the changes?" He waited for Matt to take all that in. "And he has not had a mistress or any other woman since the main Season last year."

"I can't say that I have. He's your friend after all. If what you say is true, that is a change." Matt gave Charlie a hard look. "Did he do all of it for Theo? I have found that when changes are made for someone else, they rarely last."

"I believe that's part of it." Charlie drained his cup. "Still, I got the strong impression that he did it more for himself. It was time for him to act like a responsible adult." He selected one of the small sandwiches from a plate. "He plans to approach you when we arrive in Town."

"Very well then. I will hear what he has to say." Matt finished his tea and ate a sandwich. "Does Oriana know about Chandos's intentions?"

"Yes. I told her after he departed. Strictly from her own observations, she believes he has matured."

"Speaking of Town, when do you plan to arrive?"

"A day or two before Easter. The children will be almost six weeks old by then. Mary has expressed a desire to wait and come with us." Charlie picked up a ginger biscuit. "Unless you have an objection?"

"Not at all. Theo won't like it." Matt's lips formed a thin line. "But it will encourage her to engage with other ladies who are making their come outs."

Charlie nodded. "Mary has been concerned about that as well."

"She has always been an old soul." Matt smiled. "I remember when she was five years old. She told me I'd made a mull of it with Grace and demanded to know what I was going to do about it."

"I heard she'd been speaking with you." Charlie chuckled. "I'm glad you were able to convince Grace to marry you. She planned to never wed."

"That was the first time I had to work for something I wanted." Matt blew out a breath. "I knew I'd never be happy unless I married her." He grinned. "And then I learned that the rest of you came with her."

"Thank God, it's all worked out." Charlie had been away at school, but his siblings had written to him expressing their support for the match. "Come. It's time for you to see my twins. I'm a very proud papa."

Matt stood. "I'm happy for you."

"I am too." In fact, Charlie had never been happier. They strolled to the hall and up the stairs. "Theo will make the right choice, whomever she picks."

"Intellectually, I agree. The problem is that she was so young when my father died, I've been more a parent to her than a brother. I hope I can stand back and trust her."

"You'll do what's right." Charlie motioned to the nursery door. "You always have done."

CHAPTER TWO

Theo, Grace, and Matt spent four days at Stanwood Place and gave in to the pleads of their two older children to be allowed to remain until their Uncle Charlie and Aunt Oriana came to Town. Mary insisted on staying in order to help with the new babies.

She hugged Theo as their brother and sister entered the coach. "I almost forgot to tell you that Sarah Pettigrew is looking forward to seeing you in Town." Mary gave Theo one of her "significant looks." "You are the only other lady making her come out whom she knows."

"I will make sure that she feels comfortable." Tears pricked Theo's eyes, and she blinked rapidly to dispel them. Mary took care of everyone. This was the first time they had not traveled to Town together. "I cannot wait until you join us."

"I am looking forward to it." Mary hugged Theo again. "You had better go. I will see you soon."

Theo glanced out the back window as they left the drive. Mary stood there watching until Theo could no longer see her sister.

Grace leaned over and patted her knee. "I know you miss her, and she will miss you. However, you must remember that this is your Season. She still has three years before she can make her come out."

"I know." Theo took out a handkerchief and blew her nose. "And I knew this was coming. I just did not expect it to be so hard."

"In some ways it is much like the time when Madeline and Eleanor wed before Alice," Grace said.

Theo had forgotten about how unhappy Alice had been when her twin, Eleanor, and their sister Madeline had wed and left home. It seemed a very long time ago. Alice was so miserable that she almost married the wrong gentleman. At least, Theo was starting out alone. That had to be a little easier. "You are right." She should have hugged Mary again and smiled. "Sarah Pettigrew will be there. That is one person I will know."

Grace nodded. "I am certain you will become fast friends."

"Yes." Theo thought back to how Lord Pettigrew had attempted to deny Sarah a Season by claiming that she was betrothed to Charlie. Fortunately, it turned out that it was a lie. That was when Theo and Sarah had met and become friendly. "I believe you are correct. We must find Sarah's address. When do we visit Madam Lisette? And when is Lady Bellamny's soirée for young ladies?"

"I have their direction." Grace grinned. "Fortunately, they have leased a house not far from us. You have your first fitting in two days, and Lady Bellamny's soirée is in a week. That will give you time to have at least one suitable gown. I sent your measurements ahead. I also ensured that Sarah was invited to the soirée."

"Excellent." Theo was starting to feel better. Grace had thought of everything. Leaning back against the plush squabs, Theo resolved to have the best Season she could. She would find a gentleman who loved her and whom she loved in return. This *was* her Season, and she would enjoy it.

They spent that night at the inn they normally used, then continued on to Town in the morning.

The day after arriving Theo and Grace called on the Pettigrews.

"The Countess of Worthington and Lady Theodora Vivers," the butler intoned as he led them to the parlor.

"Theo!" Sarah jumped up and ran to Theo as Lady Pettigrew admonished her daughter for her exuberance. "I am so glad you are here. I do not know anyone else and some of the other ladies I encountered have not been welcoming."

Humph. That was not at all acceptable. "I am happy you are here as well." Theo twined her arm with Sarah's. "Let us make plans." Theo recalled all the places she saw during her times in Town. "There are so many things to do. Before the Season begins, we should visit the Tower, and some of the museums, as well as Burlington Arcade. My older sisters said it is the best inexpensive shopping for items such as fans, hair combs, and so many other things. Pin money"—she raised a brow—"only goes so far."

"That is so true." Sarah clapped her hands together. "It seemed to last forever at home, but I imagine London is much more expensive."

"That is exactly what my sisters said. And you require more things. We are no longer in the schoolroom." Theo was glad she had come, and she was determined to discover who the unkind ladies were. "And we must visit Davis's Amphitheatre where they have trick horse riders. We shall have so much fun!"

She turned to Grace. "What else do we have to look forward to?"

"We must not forget the theater and opera. However, Vauxhall will wait until later," she said. "To which modiste are you giving your custom?" she asked Lady Pettigrew.

The lady heaved a sigh. "That is a question we have not resolved." She pulled a face. "Apparently, the one who made my gowns is no longer in business, and the others to which I have been recommended do not have time."

Grace pressed her lips together. "Allow me to see what I can do. I will notify you soon."

As their fifteen minutes was at an end, she and Theo rose. Theo took Sarah's hands. "Would you like to ride in the Park tomorrow morning early? Did you bring your hack?"

"Yes, thank you, and I did. At what time should we meet?"

"Very early." Theo was grateful that she could have a good ride in the Park. Unfortunately, they must leave no later than daybreak. "Be ready just before sunup. I will come by for you."

Sarah nodded excitedly. "I will be ready. If I am not, feel free to roust me from my bed."

"I will do exactly that. I love a good ride in the morning." Theo hugged her friend again.

Grace addressed Lady Pettigrew. "Theo will have a groom with her."

Her ladyship's lips tilted up. "Thank you. I will send one with Sarah as well."

"I will escort them to the door," Sarah said. "I look forward to tomorrow morning."

"As do I." Theo patted her friend's hand. "We will have an excellent Season."

"Yes. We will." Sarah smiled broadly.

When they reached the door, a Worthington footman was waiting to escort them to the carriage. Once they had been handed inside, Theo turned to Grace. "Why would other young ladies be cruel to Sarah?"

"I have never understood the reason some people cannot be kind." She slowly shook her head. "What is more important is that you befriend other young ladies who have been made to feel badly."

"I will do that." Theo knew it was what her family expected of her. "I am glad we visited them."

"I am too." Her sister smiled. "I want you to know that there is no reason to think you must marry. We all expect you to wed the right gentleman for you, even if it takes more than one Season."

Theo did know that. All her siblings had reinforced that opinion. Yet, other than Grace, who had not really had a Season, all of them had found their spouses in their first Season. Theo would as well. She had a feeling that she would. When they arrived home, she sent a message to the stables that she wanted Epione, her mare, ready early the next morning. Theo took a deep breath. Mary had been right. All Theo had to do was to enjoy her Season. All would be well.

Leo had been taking care of the accounts when his butler knocked and entered the study. "Your grace, Lord and Lady Worthington, and Lady Theodora have arrived in Town."

"Thank you, Hoover. Please ascertain if Lady Theo plans to ride tomorrow morning. If so, have Asclepius readied at daybreak." Her sisters had all ridden at dawn when they'd been out. It stood to reason Theo would do the same. Thankfully, Leo did not need to wait for an introduction before approaching her.

"Yes, your grace." His butler bowed and left.

It was now time to start planning his campaign. During the past year, in addition to ensuring that Theo was the right wife for him, he'd spoken with her brothers-in-law about their courtships. Worthington ladies, whether they were Carpenters or Viverses, were notoriously difficult to court. From the Marquis of St. Albans, who was married to Alice, Leo had learned to discover her favorite flowers and other things. The Marquis of Montagu, wed to Eleanor, told Leo not to pretend about who he was. He must be himself. The Duke of Rothwell, married to Louisa, said not to lie to her. At. All. The Marquis of Kenilworth, wed to Charlotte, explained in a wry tone that she would not be compromised into marriage. That seemed strange to Leo, but the ladies were all extremely strong-willed and supported by their family. Harry Stern and Phinn Carter-Woods, married to Madeline and Augusta respectively, had been no help at all. The only problem Stern had was his future mother-in-law, which difficulty had been easily overcome, and Carter-Woods had chased Augusta across Europe because she wanted a university degree. Which she now had. Yet, despite all the advice, Leo still felt as if he was not exactly sure what his future bride wanted or how to pursue her. And that was not a feeling a duke liked to have. Surety had been bred in him. He was to always know what was needed. He lifted the one glass of brandy he allowed himself and sipped. He was missing something. What the devil was it? And he'd promised Charlie that Theo would have her come out ball before Leo courted her in earnest.

The next morning, he rode out to the Park and searched for Theo. Finally, he found her in the company of another lady returning from the Serpentine. Drat. He'd been late. Trotting up to them he lifted his hat. "Ladies, good morning."

Theo gracefully inclined her head. "Your grace. What a surprise to see you up at so early an hour." Turning in her saddle, she addressed the other lady. "Sarah, you remember the Duke of Chandos? You danced with him last year at Lady Stern's ball." Theo raised one dark brow. "Chandos, you, of course, will recall Miss Pettigrew."

Theo was good. She'd make the perfect duchess. He had a vague memory of being made to dance with multiple ladies at an assembly of some sort and later at the ball, but he never would have remembered the chit's name. He bowed. "Indeed, I do." Good Lord, she was making her come out. With Theo. He cut her a look, then smiled and bowed to Miss Pettigrew. "Naturally, I remember. I hope you are enjoying your time in Town."

The lady giggled. Lightly. But it was still a giggle. "It is delightful seeing you again, your grace."

"Ah, yes." He kept his smile in place. A groom rode up, and Theo inclined her head. "You must excuse us. We are due home."

Backing his horse up, he nodded. "I look forward to our next meeting."

"As do I." There was a challenge in Theo's lapis eyes.

He forced himself to slowly incline his head. He was a duke, drat it. Not merely some gentleman hoping to be deemed acceptable. "Ladies, I wish you a good day."

Theo's lips tilted up, and she rode off followed by Miss Pettigrew, who appeared rather confused.

"Do you not like him?" Sarah caught up to Theo. Well, she supposed she had been riding rather quickly.

"I do. He is one of Stanwood's friends." She took a breath. "I simply do not trust him."

"But why not?" Her friend was obviously confused. "He is a duke."

"A duke who is not looking to wed."

Sarah's lips formed a perfect O. "I understand. He is a rake."

"In short, yes. However, he has never been connected to the ruination of a lady. Quite frankly, I am shocked that he will be at Almack's. Perhaps his mother is pressuring him, and he has decided to stand up with ladies who will not assume he is in search of a wife."

"That makes sense," Sarah said. Although it was obvious that she did not understand at all. "Dancing with us will only show that he is being kind to the sister of his friend and her friend."

"Indeed." As tangled as that was, it was the truth. "I suppose we must assume he will dance with us." Theo started to roll her eyes and turned it into a head shake. "You did notice that he failed to say which sets he wanted."

Sarah understood that difficulty at once. "Oh, dear. That would be most awkward if one has already accepted another for the same dance he wants."

"It would." Theo took another breath. "I suppose he must be prepared to be disappointed."

"How sad," Sarah said. "I can only assume that dukes expect to be placed before all others."

"I believe you are correct." Chandos was not stupid, but he was oblivious. She clearly remembered having to throw water on him at Stanwood Place. "Unfortunately, for him."

"Yes, of course." Sarah displayed a rare sense of resolve. "If a gentleman asks me before he does, I must accept the first gentleman."

"Exactly." Spurring her horse, Theo rode toward the gate. "Despite that, it should prove interesting."

"You are, of course, correct," Sarah agreed.

Suddenly, Theo had a sense that her friend considered her an oracle of a sort. Then it occurred to her that, although she had older sisters who had gone through a Season and wed, and Theo had spent several Seasons in Town, her friend had not. She must be very careful not to guide Sarah in the wrong direction. Theo doubted that her friend's father would allow her a second chance to find a husband before arranging a match. Perhaps she should ask Charlie and others in her family, maybe even Chandos, who they would recommend for Sarah. Yes. That was exactly what she would do. Help her friend find a husband.

They rode first to Sarah's house, as she did not, for some reason, have a groom. That being the case, Theo decided to take care of the matter. When Theo arrived home and dismounted, she turned to Mick, her groom. "Can you please bring one of the other grooms to attend Miss Pettigrew tomorrow?"

"Yes, my lady. I'll see it done."

She smiled at him. "Thank you."

Theo washed, changed, and went to break her fast. When she entered the breakfast room, she was surprised to see most of her sisters there. "I am so happy to see you!"

Madeline, Alice, and Eleanor surged forward, followed by Louisa and Charlotte. Augusta, her husband, and son had gone back overseas.

"We are so glad to see you," Madeline grinned. "You have become such a beautiful lady."

"She was always beautiful," Eleanor said as she hugged Theo. "And intelligent, and wise. Come to us if you feel unsettled. That is the reason we are here. Men can be very strange."

"And difficult to understand," Alice said as she hugged Theo too. "Trust me. I am surrounded by men who have no idea how to behave around a lady."

"Unless you have a desire to be carried off by a Highlander," Alice's husband, St. Albans, quipped as he strolled into the room.

Theo narrowed her eyes at him. "No, thank you. I do not wish to live in the Highlands. I believe I will choose someone closer to home."

He gave a great guffaw. "I suppose I must tell my male kin to stay in Scotland then." His eyes took on the look of a sad puppy. "They'll be verra sad."

Alice, his wife, slapped his arm. "Get on with ye now. Ye great fraud."

"Scots?" Theo stared at her sister. "When did you pick it up?"

Alice gave herself a shake. "It is my mother-in-law's fault. It's catching."

Theo wanted to roll her eyes but knew better. "That is an interesting excuse."

Her sister shrugged. "It is the only one I have. Other than I do like to be heard, and they tend to ignore anyone who speaks the King's English."

Theo's other brothers-by-marriage ambled into the room and greeted her. This might be an excellent time to address prospects for Sarah. Once everyone was seated and the children had been served, she addressed the adults. "Do you remember Sarah Pettigrew?" They all nodded. "She must find a husband this Season. Otherwise, I have a feeling her father will choose for her."

"We need a bit more than that," Kenilworth said. "What is her temperament? What does she like?"

"What does she want in a husband?" Charlotte added.

"She is easy to get along with." Theo recalled how distressed Sarah was about the unkind ladies. "Someone kind, who will be devoted to her. Naturally he must be able to support a wife and family."

The gentlemen nodded, and Kenilworth put his cup down. "We will look around."

"As will we," Charlotte assured her. "We will all be at Lady Bellamny's. There are bound to be ladies who wish to marry off their sons."

"Excellent. I am certain among us we will find the perfect husband for her." The dishes were making their way around the table. Theo added shirred eggs and rare beef to her plate. She would be busier than she had thought.

CHAPTER THREE

Leo strolled into the breakfast parlor and was surprised to see his mother at the table. "What brings you down so early?"

"Good morning to you too." She glanced up from a stack of cards at her elbow. "There is too much to organize for me to lay about."

His mother was the only person, other than his father, who could give him a set-down without raising her voice. Well, there was one other. Theo. "Good morning. What are your plans for the day?"

"I considered taking you on morning visits but decided against it."

Thank God for that. He addressed the dishes on the sideboard. "Did you not think I would enjoy them?"

"I thought the young ladies would drive you back to your clubs." A footman placed a plate on the table in front of her, which consisted of a soft-boiled egg, toast, and marmalade. "I am attending Lady Bellamny's soirée for young ladies this evening. I will be able to discover there who are the best prospects for you."

Leo carried his plate to the table, taking the chair across from his mother's. "That sounds much better than parading me around Town."

"Indeed." Mama poured him a cup of tea from the pot on the table. "Gentlemen are not allowed at the main event. However, you may come for supper. By then I will have formed my opinions."

He wondered if he should tell her that he had already made his decision, but she appeared to be more animated than she had been since his father's death three years ago. "Tell me when to arrive and I will be there."

She finished eating her egg and toast then swallowed the rest of her tea and rose. "Be there at eleven for supper. I will see you at dinner."

He'd planned to dine at his club, but something in her tone made him reconsider. He must find out more about this event. Who could he ask? "Until then."

Leo donned his coat, hat, and picked up his walking stick. Once he reached the pavement, he almost immediately saw the Marquis of Montagu, one of Theo's brothers-by-marriage. "Montagu, I'm glad I met up with you." Leo fell in alongside the man. "What can you tell me about Lady Bellamny's soirée this evening?"

"It is an event for young ladies to meet other ladies making their come outs. As well as for mothers of marriage-minded sons to look over the crop of young ladies and see their friends that they might not have seen lately. My mother met Eleanor at the event and thought that she'd be perfect for me. Not that Mama gave herself away."

"Of course not." Leo was going to have to tell his mother he had made his choice. He didn't want her trying to find another young lady for him. "Will you be there this evening?"

"Only to fetch Eleanor. She and the rest of the sisters are going to support Theo."

"Excellent. I shall see you there." Leo tipped his hat. "I have a few things to do before this evening."

"I do as well. I say, when are you going to become more involved in the Lords? We could use another Whig vote."

That was something he had planned to do. It was also something Theo would expect him to do. "Soon. Very soon."

"Good. I'll see you this evening." Montagu strode off.

"Yes, you will." Even if Leo wasn't able to start courting Theo formally he could be with her.

Theo studied herself in the cheval mirror for any flaws in either her gown or her hair. She must look and act perfectly this evening. Even though Lady Bellamny had known Theo since she was a child, the Grand Dame would expect perfection. Theo would not be the first of her sisters to fail.

"My lady, it is time for you to go down," Payne, Theo's maid, said.

"Thank you. I must not be late this evening."

"Yes, my lady. I was told." Theo held still while her maid placed a Norwich silk shawl over her shoulders, then handed her a reticule, and fan. "Have a good time this evening."

Theo pulled a face. "I am not sure this evening is meant to be fun."

Grace was descending the stairs when Theo arrived at the landing. "Will everyone else be there this evening?"

Everyone else being her sisters.

"Yes. Except for Oriana. She and Charlie will not arrive until Friday."

Theo would not have blamed her sister-in-law if she had decided to remain in the country after just having had the twins not more than two months ago. "I expect that she will not go around much."

Grace nodded. She had counseled both Oriana and Charlie to remain in the country, but they insisted on being in Town for Theo.

Matt came out from his study. "I'll see you at eleven along with the rest of the gentlemen. Rothwell told me that Louisa is arranging to have a table put together so that we can sit as a family."

Theo was glad they would all sit together. "We need to go before I become more nervous than I already am."

"You will be fine." Grace twined her arm with Theo's. "You know exactly what to do."

Matt accompanied them to the coach and helped them in. "Have a good time and meet other young ladies."

"I will try." Theo had never been so happy that Sarah would be there as well.

Several minutes later, they pulled up to Lady Bellamny's house on Upper Brook Street. As Theo had been told, the footmen expeditiously moved the ladies into the house so that the line was kept short. When she was announced, she presented herself to Lady Bellamny, curtseying to the proper degree then rising. "Good evening, my lady."

"Good evening, Theo." Her ladyship nodded. "Perfect. Just as I expected. I predict you will make a brilliant match." Lady Bellamny sounded like she knew something that Theo did not. Then her ladyship glanced at Grace. "My dear, you have done it again. I congratulate you."

Smiling slightly, Grace inclined her head. "Thank you."

"You have only Mary left until your girls are old enough to make their bow."

"Yes. In three years, she will come out," Grace responded easily.

Her ladyship nodded and addressed Theo again, "Mingle. This is the only event you will have without gentlemen."

"I will, my lady. Thank you." She and Grace stepped aside for the next young lady to be presented. Theo watched as the lady's curtsey verged on insulting. Lady Bellamny's black eyes seemed to bore into the girl. "Well, Philomina," her ladyship said to the older woman accompanying the young lady, "I see you have your work cut out for you."

"Unfortunately." She curtseyed, took her charge by the arm walked off.

"But I do not understand," the girl complained. "I am the daughter of a marquis. I outrank her."

The woman huffed. "Come and I shall explain it to you. Your prospects for the Season have been reduced."

"Who is she?" Theo whispered to Grace.

"A young lady who was not properly prepared, but who should

know better. Come, let us stroll. We are bound to find someone we know."

"There are Sarah and her mother. I should ask how her introduction to Lady Bellamny went."

"Invite them to join us for supper." Grace glanced around. "I see Louisa. I shall apprise her of the change in numbers."

"I will." Theo went directly to her friend. "Good evening. Did Lady Bellamny terrify you?"

"Yes." Sarah laughed. "My knees were shaking, but she told Mama that I would do."

"Excellent." Theo was happy for her friend. "Let us introduce ourselves to some of the other ladies. I see Lady Lana standing with someone else. We first met when we were both in Town a few years ago."

Sarah came to a stop. "Which one is Lady Lana?"

"Red hair, pale green gown." Sarah had a strange look on her face. "Why?"

"The lady next to her is one who was cruel to me."

That would not be allowed to stand. "We will greet Lady Lana and find out who the other female is."

"If you think we should." Sarah sounded dubious.

"Indeed, I do." Theo firmed her jaw. "I wish to know why she believes she is better than others."

Lady Giselle Darnel stood beside her dear friend Lady Lana Grant at Lady Bellamny's event. "I have decided whom I will wed."

Lana's eyes widened. "Already? We have not even been to a ball or Almack's, and there are no gentlemen here."

"I saw him this afternoon in the Park. It is the Duke of Chandos. He will do quite nicely."

"The Duke of Chandos?" She sounded out of breath. "Giselle, you cannot. He is a rake. My mother told me I was not to accept a set from him if he was bold enough to ask without an introduction. Which she said she would not allow."

Lana was a dear, but Giselle was sure her friend was not the sort of lady who would attract a great deal of attention from gentlemen. In fact, she was certain Lana would need help in acquiring a husband in one Season. "He is a duke. A wealthy, young, and handsome duke. And I have a desire to be a duchess."

Lana's forehead wrinkled. "There is that, I suppose."

"Do not frown. You will get lines." Giselle was constantly having to remind Lana to keep her face as calm as possible. "I will think of something to gain his attention. I heard he received a card for Almack's. He has never before attended. That must mean he is looking for a wife."

"Perhaps his mother is pushing him to have an heir," Lana said. "I would not want to marry either a rake or someone who does not truly wish to wed."

Giselle shrugged lightly. "That only matters if one wants a love match." She glanced across the room where her mother was in conversation with another lady. "I wonder who that is."

"That is the Dowager Duchess of Chandos," Lana said helpfully. "Mama pointed her out to me earlier."

That might mean his grace was going to attend the supper. "We should try to find a table close to her at supper."

"Oh, look. There is Lady Theodora Vivers coming this way." Lana smiled. "She was very nice to me when I met her a few years ago and again at a store selling hats earlier this week."

Giselle groaned. "She has that ninny Miss Pettigrew with her."

"Whatever you do, do not take against Lady Theo. Her family is extremely well connected."

That was odd, Lana never spoke to Giselle in such a firm tone. "You make her sound as if she is related to the royal family."

"She might as well be." Her friend appeared as if she would faint. "One of her sisters is the Duchess of Rothwell. Another is the Marchioness of St. Albans, he is the heir to—"

"I know, I know. Just remain calm."

When Lady Theo reached them, she smiled at Lana. "It is good to see you again." Her hard blue eyes cut to Giselle. "Please introduce me to your companion."

"It is very good to see you too." Lana looked a bit panicked. "This is Lady Giselle Darnel. Giselle, Lady Theo Vivers."

"Lady Giselle, I believe you have already met my friend Miss Pettigrew."

Lady Theo emphasized the word *friend*. For the first time, Giselle was unsure of herself. "Er. Yes. We were at the modiste when we met."

"This is Miss Pettigrew's first time in the metropolis." Lady Theo smiled sweetly, but her gaze remained hard. "It would be horrible if anyone were to be unkind. After all, not everyone has had the benefit of visiting Town with their family during the Season when they are young. We who are more familiar with being here must assist the others. Do you not agree?"

How dare she think to chastise me? Giselle opened her mouth, when another lady came up to them. A lady who looked very much like Lady Theo.

"There you are." The lady smiled tightly at Giselle. "I am the Duchess of Rothwell. And you are?"

Giselle straightened her shoulders. "Lady Giselle Darnel."

"Hmm." The duchess regarded her for several moments. "Allow me to give you some advice. The *ton* is very small. Once one gains a reputation for being difficult, or rude, it is hard to rid oneself of that reputation." Her grace gathered Lady Theo and Miss Pettigrew with a glance. "Come. There are some other ladies I would like you to meet."

Giselle kept her lips tightly closed as they ambled away. "I have never been so insulted in my life. How dare they?"

Lana bit her bottom lip. "I think because, as I said, they are well connected and are sure of their positions. My understanding is that although Lady Theo is making her come out, she has known the Patroness of Almack's for years, as well as other notables."

"I do not care how *well connected* she is. She will not get away with speaking to me in that manner." When Giselle wed Chandos, no one would look down on her.

* * *

At eleven o'clock sharp, the gentlemen who had been gathering in front of Lady Bellamny's house were allowed to enter. Leo had joined the Worthington family men and was determined to remain with them. That way, he had a chance of sitting with Theo at supper. He supposed he would have to find his mother and bring her as well. If she had not already decided to sit with one of her friends.

Matt Worthington let them in and went directly to his wife. "My dear, we have Chandos in tow. Can you send someone to find his mother and ask if she would like to join us?"

Lady Worthington chuckled softly. "Let me see who I can trust with the task."

"I know who she is," Rothwell's wife said. "I will find her."

As Louisa Rothwell glided off, Leo started to search for Theo, but it wasn't necessary. His gaze seemed to immediately be drawn to her. Lord, she was beautiful. Her chestnut hair was piled on top of her head and threaded through with pearls. A few loose curls framed her face. He wanted to twist the curls around his fingers. Her bodice was low enough to be fashionable, but not too low. Still, he wanted to cover her with a shawl. Her gown was of the latest style in a buttery silk that clung to her curves and showed her small waist. A single thin gold chain with a pendant adorned her throat. He'd give her rubies when they were wed. His mouth went dry. She was easily the most poised and beautiful lady here.

Theo started toward them as soon as she noticed her brothers-in-law and sisters gathering together. She looked up at him. "What are you doing here?"

Suddenly, Leo's cravat was too tight. "I came to fetch my mother."

"Oh." For the first time she seemed to be at a loss for words.

"I do have a mother." Leo used a teasing tone.

"Of course you do." She fixed him with a look. "I met her this evening. She is lovely. I simply could not understand why she had decided to attend."

Meaning that Theo didn't think he was looking for a wife.

"There is no accounting for what my mother will decide to do or which events she will attend. It surprised me as well."

Theo's gaze softened as if she was in sympathy with him. "I suppose that is true." Her dark, well-arched brows drew together. "I have never before met her. Does she usually come to Town?"

"She has not been here for a few years. I'm pleased that she decided to make the journey this year."

This time Theo gave him a curious look. "Well done. I honestly did not believe that you thought about anyone other than yourself."

Leo was so shocked he couldn't think of an immediate response. He'd spent a year proving himself to her, yet she knew nothing about it. Most of the time he'd spent with her family had been observing her. Not engaging with her. Except for family card games, which he invariably lost to her. Now, he'd have to show Theo who he was. How could he have been such a fool? "I think you'll find you don't know me as well as you think you do."

She tilted her head to one side, and her eyes narrowed slightly. "I suppose we shall see."

Leo offered her his arm, and she lightly placed her hand on it as they made their way to the supper room. Once he'd held out a chair for her, she sank gracefully into it. He turned to go to the buffet table, then stopped. If he brought back what *he* thought she would like, Leo would just be confirming what she thought she knew about him. "Are there any special dishes you would enjoy sampling?"

"More than anything I would like a savory ice if there are any." She grinned, and Leo's heartbeat increased.

That was telling. Now he knew not to send sweets to her. "Do you in general like savory over sweet?"

"Yes." She smiled. "As a matter of fact, I do."

"I will do my best." After bowing slightly, Leo followed the other gentlemen. Convincing Lady Theo Vivers to be his wife was going to be much more challenging than he'd thought, and he hadn't expected it to be easy.

CHAPTER FOUR

Sarah slipped into the chair on Theo's other side. "I wanted to thank you for what you said to Lady Giselle."

"You are welcome." Knowing how much one's reputation mattered, there was really nothing else Theo could have done. "I hope it made her think twice about being mean to another lady, or gentleman, for that matter."

Sarah leaned closer to Theo. "My mother told me that the duke is a rake."

"Oh, indeed he is, but he is harmless enough." At least for her he was. Chandos knew better than to try to seduce her. "You might remember that he is also a close friend of my brother Stanwood. It would not surprise me if he was recruited to watch after me this Season."

"Oh." Sarah's brows slanted down. "I never thought of that. Does this occur often in your family?"

Theo let out a sigh. "Indeed, it does. If you pay attention, you will see that all of my brothers-by-marriage are here. They will also, along with my sisters, be at most of the events I attend, if not all of them."

"I wish I came from a large family." Theo knew that Sarah had an older brother, but he was out of the country on his Grand Tour.

"You may take advantage of mine." Theo smiled. "I am certain they will be happy to help." Which reminded her that she must also request Chandos's assistance in finding a husband for her friend. Sarah's father was not to be trusted.

Chandos returned to the table with the rest of the gentlemen. He was followed by a footman carrying a tray with three plates and glasses of champagne. "I selected every savory item I could find." His lips tilted up as he placed the dish in front of her. "I also brought some things that I hope will tempt Miss Pettigrew's palate."

Sarah blushed bright red. "Thank you, your grace. You really did not need to go to all the trouble."

He appeared taken aback. "If you wanted to eat I did. No one else knew you had joined us. Rothwell has a plate for your mother."

"Oh, dear." She fanned her face. "Thank you again."

He was being exceptionally kind this evening. Once Chandos had taken his seat Theo leaned toward him. "That was very nice of you. Both for the food and for noticing she was sitting with us."

"I notice many things." His tone was deeper than it had been. Almost intimate. "At times I get the feeling there are so many of you, the occasional addition goes unremarked."

That was perceptive. The back of her neck tingled, and she gave herself a shake. What else could she expect from a rake? Theo glanced over to see Sarah in conversation with Rothwell. "I have something to ask you. I think Miss Pettigrew might require some help in finding a suitable husband." In fact, Theo might make that her mission this Season. She had met a number of ladies this evening with sons. "Do you have any ideas as to who might be a good match for her?"

He looked at Theo with open curiosity. "You want me to play matchmaker?"

He sounded astonished. "Yes. If you would not mind. After all, you know more single gentlemen than anyone else I know."

He stared at her for a few moments, then said, "What does she want in a husband?"

This time she was prepared to answer that question. "He must be genuinely nice and kind. He must be loyal to her after the marriage, and he must not be a rake."

The corners of his well-formed lips tilted up. "I have the feeling rakes are not *au courant* this Season."

Theo wanted to roll her eyes. "Are they ever in fashion?"

"Occasionally. I will consider her desires." His green eyes narrowed a bit as he regarded her. "It might be of help if you explain to me exactly what you believe a rake is."

"A man who cannot be trusted with an unmarried lady, and who will keep a mistress after marriage." That should be obvious.

"Ah." He raised his chin a bit in understanding. "In that case, I agree that they are never *au courant*. At least not to anyone who wants a love match."

"Why do you ask?" Was there more than one way to be a rake?

"Well, there were some who would have considered both Kenilworth and St. Albans, indeed, even Worthington, to have been rakes. Not your definition of a rake, but men who kept mistresses and so forth when they were single."

Theo had heard things about Kenilworth and St. Albans, but Matt? "Really?"

"I prefer the term 'a gentleman about Town' over rake." Chandos finished one lobster patty and started on another one. That reminded her she should taste what he had brought her before supper ended.

"Hmm." She picked up a spoon and sampled the ice. "This is delicious! How does one know the difference?"

"I believe it is champagne." He smiled. "For one thing, a gentleman who is used to being on the Town does not ruin young ladies. Ergo, once he decides to wed, parents of young ladies are more likely to encourage a suit than not."

"That makes sense." She finished her ice and licked the spoon.

"I agree with your assessment that it is champagne." Next, she tried the lobster patty.

He stared at her with an intent expression in his eyes. "In addition to rakes, fortune hunters and those who cannot support a family are also to be avoided."

"Naturally. I do not believe Matt would allow either of those types of gentlemen to be introduced to me." The problem was that Sarah did not have anyone like Matt to protect her. "How am I to stop them from being introduced to my friend?"

Leo was still trying to recover from seeing Theo lick her spoon clean. His body had immediately reacted. Still, he had to focus on her questions. She was determined to take care of her friend. "I will help. You should ask your family as well. I am certain that if Worthington doesn't already have a complete list of eligible gentlemen, he soon will."

Theo appeared to consider his words and nodded. "Yes, you are correct. From what my sisters have told me he is very strict about that sort of thing."

"There is one more matter." Leo really should not tell her this, but she had already mentioned mistresses. In fact, she had known about them before she was out. "A gentleman looking for a wife will not keep a mistress."

Theo's lips formed a perfect O. "That is good to know. How would one discover if he was keeping one? Who would one ask?"

He'd done it now. He knew her. Why had he not considered that she might just question gentlemen or others. "You cannot ask. I know your family is quite progressive, but it's not done for an unmarried lady to admit she knows certain things."

She gave him a look that clearly said he was being an idiot for thinking she might do something so inappropriate. "I was not going to go around asking just anyone."

Leo needed to end this conversation before he got himself into trouble. "Your sisters would be the best people to query. They will be privy to the information."

"You are probably right." She gave him an approving smile. "From what I understand, married ladies discuss everything."

There. That was settled. Now to begin the almost courting process. "Would you like to accompany me on a carriage ride tomorrow afternoon?"

"How nice of you to ask." Theo's eyes sparkled. "If Grace approves, I will be happy to go with you."

Leo resisted a smug smile. He had already gained Lady Worthington's approval. "I look forward to her answer."

Theo glanced down at her plate and her expressive brows came together. "What is this?"

"Scalloped oysters. I find them quite tasty." He hoped she liked them. They were one of his favorites.

She speared one of the oysters with her fork, popped it in her mouth and swallowed. "Excellent choice. These are very good."

He was more pleased than he thought he'd be. "I'm glad you like them. In France, raw oysters are served on ice."

"That sounds interesting." She finished the dish then began on the lobster patty. "I would like to go to Paris, but not in the summer. I have been told it is unpleasant."

"I believe you are correct. Like London, most people flee to the country. I was fortunate enough to be there in early autumn. It was quite enjoyable." He'd take Theo there on a wedding trip.

"It is a shame that ladies do not make Grand Tours." Her fork hovered over a piece of cod in sauce. "Although, my nieces are discussing visiting the Continent when they are older."

Good Lord. What put such an idea in their heads? "They are eight and nine. What made them think about that?"

"Augusta. She has told them a great deal about what she saw during her travels." Theo finished the fish and started on the asparagus.

"I had forgotten about that. I heard that she and her husband are back in Europe again. Something to do with their son."

"Yes." Theo nodded. "It is the stupidest thing imaginable. Phinn's sister-in-law has taken it into her head that she wants to raise their son."

"So, they are stopping her by departing. Interesting." A bit extreme but effective.

"Well, that and a colleague wrote to them asking for her expertise in languages and Phinn's in ancient architecture."

Leo wanted to turn the conversation to what Theo wanted. Granted, taking care of several houses and helping with the estates took up a lot of time, but knowing her, as he thought he did, she would want to do more. "I know your sisters are involved in charities of different sorts. Is that something you're interested in doing as well?"

She dabbed her serviette against her rosy lips and took a sip of champagne. "I have already started working with my sisters in their various charities and donating to them. I want to be able to continue their work as well as to help the dependents on my future husband's estates."

Whether her spouse agreed or not, obviously. He couldn't hide his smile. He would let her do whatever she wished. "That sounds like a superb plan."

"Thank you." She returned his smile. "I will, naturally, have to ensure that the gentleman I marry will not attempt to stop me."

"I am sure I would not want to try to stop you from anything you wanted to accomplish." Leo didn't want to move too quickly. But he did need to make sure she knew how he thought about her ideas.

She wrinkled her adorable nose. "I must admit, I am not very malleable once I have decided on a course of action."

That was most definitely true. "No, but I have always found you to be reasonable."

"Yes. I am that." She fell into silence while she finished the offerings he'd brought to her. When she was finished, she glanced up. "That was all excellent."

An accolade. He inclined his head. "Thank you. I am happy to be of service."

Miss Pettigrew leaned over and whispered something to Theo. She looked across the table at Lady Kenilworth and mouthed something. When her ladyship rose, so did Miss Pettigrew and Theo. "Excuse us."

He touched her arm before she could leave. "Please tell me if there is anything, a task I can perform for you or favor you need. I will be happy to assist."

"Thank you, Chandos. That is very kind. I hope to see you soon."

"You will. Do not forget we are riding tomorrow at five."

Theo glanced around. "Will you please ask Grace for me? I really must go now."

"With pleasure." As he watched Theo follow her sister and friend out of the supper room, Leo wondered if he had made any progress at all with her. He understood and had been told by all her brothers-in-law that being her friend was the first step. Still, he wanted much more than that and wasn't sure how to move from friend to lover. He'd never had this problem before. In fact, most of his romantic dealings weren't even romantic. They were transactions for conjugal relations.

Kenilworth slid into the seat next to Leo's. "The ladies are saying their farewells to Lady Bellamny. How is it going with Theo?"

"I'm not sure." He shook his head. "I have no way to judge how she feels or even thinks about me." He chuckled lightly. "She asked me to help her find a husband for Miss Pettigrew."

Kenilworth seemed to ponder that for a second or two. "I believe that means she thinks of you as a friend. You're much further ahead than most of us when we were courting her sisters. That was the part that took the most time."

"I'm taking her for a carriage ride during the Grand Strut tomorrow." Leo hoped to make more progress then.

"Don't expect much to occur then. You'll be too busy managing your horses and the traffic. You could take her for ices at the end of the ride."

"That's a wonderful idea." She'd enjoyed the ice this evening. "Thank you."

"I must go. I trust you are riding early."

"Not early enough. I saw her leaving the Park this morning."

Kenilworth stood and slapped Leo on the back. "She'll be going even earlier every day."

"I know." Leo almost groaned. "If a lady wishes to gallop, she must be out before everyone else."

"Think of it this way. You will no longer be greeting the dawn at the end of the night, but at the beginning of the day. You should know. Worthington has a strict rule that they leave straight after supper."

Why hadn't anyone else told him that? No wonder she could awaken with the sun. Leo rose. "I had better go. I must find my mother. She's my excuse for being here."

"Indeed. I will see you later." Kenilworth held out his hand. "See if you can get Theo to invite you to break your fast with the family."

"I will." Leo shook the offered hand. "Thank you again."

"My pleasure. We all want to see her settled well."

Kenilworth strode off, and Leo searched for his mother. He found her speaking with another lady that appeared to be the same age. "Mama."

"Chandos, there you are. I was told you joined the Worthington party for supper. The Duchess of Rothwell asked if I would like to join you, but I had already been invited to dine with Lady Bellamny." Mama turned to the lady with whom she was speaking. "Lady Carlisle, allow me to present my son, Chandos. Her ladyship has a daughter out this year. Lady Patricia."

Her ladyship curtseyed. "It is a pleasure to meet you, your grace." Lady Carlisle glanced around. "Unfortunately, my daughter is not here at the moment. She met so many lovely ladies this evening she is probably with one of them."

"It is a pleasure to meet you as well." He held out his arm. "Madam, I would like to depart. I have an early morning."

His mother's brows rose. "Of course." She turned back to her ladyship. "I hope to see you soon."

"Yes. I hope so as well."

Leo escorted his mother to another lady to bid her good evening. Fortunately, she was still speaking with the Worthington ladies.

Her ladyship smiled at his mother. "Your grace, have you met Lady Worthington and her sisters?"

Mama smiled politely. "Except for the duchess, I have not had the pleasure."

Once the introductions were made, Leo stepped over to Theo. "May I escort you to your carriage?"

"Yes, if you wish."

Once he handed her in, he went to his mother and helped her into his coach. He gave her the forward-facing seat, then leaned back against the squabs. "There is something I must tell you."

In the lamplight he could see her surprise. "What is it, my dear?"

"I have decided to marry Lady Theo Vivers."

Mama leaned forward a bit and stared at him. "Are you certain? I thought Lady Patricia might be more to your taste."

"I am absolutely sure. She is the lady I want."

"Well, then," Mama huffed. "I do not know why you could not have told me before. When will you announce your betrothal?"

"Not for a while. She doesn't appear to know I'm interested in her." That was a lowering statement to make.

"I see." His mother started to chuckle, then stopped. "Well, this is not a problem you have had before. From what I have seen, females seem to think you are interested even when you are not. This should be diverting."

"I'm glad you think so." If he had his way, he'd just carry Theo off, but she'd probably stab him with her knife.

CHAPTER FIVE

A line of pink streaked through the antelucan sky as Theo rode with her groom, Mick, and one other groom to the Pettigrews's leased house. Sarah's mare was standing with a footman in front of the short set of stairs.

As soon as Theo stopped, Sarah came down the steps. "Thank you for your loan of a groom. Mama discovered that Cook has been sending our groom to the market with one of the maids."

It never occurred to Theo that the Pettigrews had brought only one groom. Although, considering Lord Pettigrew remained in the country, it was not surprising. "This is Straw. He can act as your groom when you require one."

"Thank you. That is very kind of you." Sarah glanced at the servant. "Straw?"

He tugged on his cap. "It was better than Berry, miss."

Understanding dawned on her face. "Well, then. Let us go, shall we?"

The groom cupped his hands, and she mounted her hack.

Theo headed down the street toward the Park. Two shadowy figures on horseback approached them from the right as they reached the gate.

"Good morn."

Chandos? Who was the other man? "Good morning to you. You are up early."

"As you know, the only time one can gallop without creating a commotion is early morning." He turned to the gentleman next to him. "Please allow me to present Lord Marrow."

Theo quickly placed him as the Earl of Marrow, heir to the Marquis of Carlisle. He had a sister, Patricia, who had just come out. "It is nice to meet you." Theo glanced at Sarah. "This is my friend, Miss Pettigrew."

"Ladies, my pleasure." His lordship smiled politely and fell in beside Sarah.

Chandos joined Theo, who glanced at him. "I had no idea riding this early in the morning was so fashionable."

"I beg your pardon?" His eyes widened a bit. "Marrow?"

She nodded.

"Ah, well. I returned home last night to find he'd left a card. I thought an early ride would be just the thing to recover from a long coach ride to Town."

"That was nice of you." She might have to revise her view of the duke.

He gave her a rueful look. "Despite your obviously poor opinion of me, I am considered to be a good friend and an excellent all round fellow."

Theo raised her brows to express her doubts.

"Lady Theo, I realize that we got off to a bad start, and you tolerate me only because I am Stanwood's friend, but I would like to be your friend as well. I can be very useful."

She was not quite sure what to make of his offer. Then again, he had agreed to help find her friend a husband. "Let us see how this goes, shall we?"

"I will endeavor to prove myself to you." He glanced up. "Race you to the large oak tree."

She urged her mare into a trot. "Go!" Her horse started to gallop. Chandos quickly caught up to her, but did not draw ahead.

They reached the tree at the same time. "Did you not want to win?"

"It appears that my horse did not wish to." He gave his hack a disgusted look.

"That is the silliest thing I've heard." Horses not wanting to win a race.

"What can I say?" He lightly shrugged. "Stallions have their own minds at times, especially when a pretty mare is present."

Theo had not actually been around that many stallions. Most of her brothers rode geldings in Town. "You might have a point." She turned in her saddle to look for Sarah and found her with Marrow cantering toward the Serpentine. "Shall we join Miss Pettigrew and Lord Marrow?"

Chandos inclined his head. "If you wish."

What was that about? He was the one who brought the viscount. Theo started toward her friend and his lordship, and the duke followed. "I know she has a groom with her, but I would feel better if I did not leave her alone too long. She has never been in Town before."

"Ah. I understand. Playing gooseberry."

"Well, someone has to. She is not what I would call up to snuff."

"This from a lady just out?" Chandos said teasingly.

"I might be in my first Season, but I have a great deal of experience gained from watching my sisters." Theo fixed him with a look. "Who do you think helped St. Albans convince Alice to wed him? And that is just one example."

"I wasn't aware he'd needed help."

"Indeed, he did. Mary and I came up with a scheme. We also assisted our sister Madeline be able to wed Harry Stern."

Leo had no idea Theo had been so busy. No wonder she was confident beyond her years. Not at all like some of the other ladies just out or even in their second year. It was her self-assurance that had originally drawn him to her. If Theo hadn't had her hair down until just recently, he would have thought she was older than eighteen. "I will take you at your word."

She gave him one of her suspicious looks. "How exactly?"

"By helping you, of course." He had to show her that he was dependable. It was clear she would not be enamored by any of his rakish charm. "I will also have a word with Marrow."

Her eyes flew wide. "Do not tell me he is a rake."

"No. No. Not at all. But he is a man. And by the way he is paying attention to Miss Pettigrew, he finds her interesting."

Theo's eyes narrowed as she stared at the couple. "You might be correct." Miss Pettigrew laughed at something Marrow said. "She certainly seems to be having fun talking with him."

"There you see." Leo mentally congratulated himself. "I might have found a suitable match for her."

"That remains to be seen." She brought her mare to a halt. "How are his finances? Is he able to support a wife and family?"

Good Lord, she was strict. "I've never heard either he or his father is under the hatches, but I will discover anything you want to know."

"Well, we must make sure. Alice was on her way to falling in love with a scoundrel before Mary and I interceded."

This was it. Falling in with Theo's schemes was how he'd become part of her life. Once he did that, he would convince her to marry him. "We should make a list of what I need to find out."

She graced him with one of her wide smiles. "Perhaps you should join us for tea."

"I would be delighted." They rode on a little further, keeping watch over her friend and his as they did. "Are you attending the opening of Almack's?"

"Yes. Grace received the vouchers shortly after we arrived. She arranged for Sarah and her mother to be approved as well."

"Would you honor me with a set?" He tried to breathe, but it was harder than he'd thought.

"Yes." He filled his lungs. "That would be delightful. You are an excellent dancer."

"You are as well. Shall I ask Miss Pettigrew?"

"Please do. I am certain that after you stand up with her, other gentlemen will find they want to dance with her as well."

Apparently, Theo was not at all concerned about whether she would be asked for other sets. "I'm sure Marrow will ask both of you as well."

"How as your ride been?" she asked as they reached their friends.

"Very nice." Miss Pettigrew smiled. "His lordship has been exceptionally kind."

Marrow kept his gaze on her as he smiled as well. "I am being nothing of the sort. Mad dashes across the Park are not as enjoyable as meandering around. I almost feel as if I'm in the country again."

"Do you prefer the country to Town?" she asked.

"I make a habit of coming in order to keep an eye on matters for my father. He prefers the country. But I'm also happy to be home." His smile widened. "As for you never having been here before, if you allow me, I would enjoy showing you the sights."

She slanted a slightly panicked look at Theo, who gave an imperceptible nod. *What was that about?* "If my mother allows."

"I have an idea," Theo said. "Sarah, you and your mother should join us for tea this afternoon, and his lordship could join us as well. If no one has other plans that is."

Miss Pettigrew's smile blossomed again. "What a perfect idea." She looked uncertainly at Marrow. "If you would not mind."

"Not at all. I am completely at your disposal for tea. Thank you for the invitation, my lady."

Leo got the distinct impression that Marrow was more than merely interested in Miss Pettigrew. "While we're on the subject of entertainments. Miss Pettigrew, might I beg a set of you at Almack's."

A light blush colored her cheeks. "Yes, of course."

"I must not be behind Chandos." Marrow bowed. "Would you honor me with a set as well?"

The blush deepened. "That would be lovely."

He turned to Theo. "My lady, I would ask you as well."

"Of course." Her lips curved up. "I would be delighted."

Leo caught Theo's twinkling eyes. "This has been a productive and enjoyable morning."

"It has indeed." Her eyes indicated her agreement. She glanced at her groom, who nodded. "I believe we should go home now."

"Oh, yes." Miss Pettigrew started toward the gate. "My mother will wonder what is keeping me."

Leo wanted to ask if he could join Theo for breakfast, but he needed to speak with Marrow to ascertain the information she desired of him. Fortunately, she rode next to Leo, leaving Marrow to accompany Miss Pettigrew. "That was neatly done. Inviting them to tea."

"It seemed as if it was the most expeditious way for Lady Pettigrew to meet his lordship and form an opinion of him."

"Thus, clearing the way for him to be allowed to not only stand up with Miss Pettigrew, but accompany him, chaperoned, of course, to some of the sights."

"Yes. Astute of you."

He dipped his head. "I do my poor best."

"You are doing very well." She gave him a look of approval, and he wanted to preen.

Marrow and Miss Pettigrew stopped before going through the gate.

"I thought I would escort Miss Pettigrew to her house," he said.

That did not help Leo at all in his plan to have his friend join him for breakfast.

"Why do we not all go together. The Pettigrews' home is not far from Berkeley Square," Theo suggested.

She was brilliant. That would give him time to invite Marrow to break his fast with Leo. "I agree."

"Very well, then." Marrow inclined his head. "We shall all go together."

Leo noticed that the groom accompanying Miss Pettigrew appeared relieved. Why was that?

Marrow kept up a steady stream of conversation about the places Miss Pettigrew should see while in town, volunteering, again, to escort her. She seemed to agree with all his ideas. By the time they reached the house on Upper Grosvenor Street, plans had been made to visit the Tower, the museum, the opera, the theater, Vauxhall, rides in the Park, and various other places. Leo didn't know when his friend was going to do anything else but accompany Miss Pettigrew around Town. Was Marrow actually attempting to ensure that he had no competition for her hand? If so, that meant Leo had best get busy making sure everything was as Theo wanted it.

They bid adieu to the lady, and he was surprised to find a different groom take Miss Pettigrew's horse, and the original groom ride off toward Berkeley Square. "Why does it look as if the groom is going to your house?"

"Because he is," Theo said. "They only have the one here for the Season. Therefore, when we ride together, she will use one of our grooms."

Marrow started to ride off, and Leo called out to him. "Wait a moment if you will." He glanced at Theo. "I am going to invite him to break his fast with me so that I can speak with him alone."

"What an excellent idea."

He could die happily if she would look at him like that more often.

His friend joined them. "What is it?"

"If you will go with me to escort Lady Theo home, I thought you could join me for breakfast."

"Thank you. That's a wonderful idea. My mother wants to speak with me, but she will not be down for a few hours yet."

"Well, then. Let us go."

They fell in on either side of Theo as they continued their way. They were almost at the square when it occurred to Leo that one possible problem with his plan to wed her might exist. He separated them a bit from his friend. "Are you thinking of finding a suitable mate this Season?"

She appeared a bit surprised. "That *is* the purpose of a come out."

As unhelpful responses went, that was one of the most unaccommodating. "Meaning?"

Her dark brows slanted down. "If I find someone, then yes. But I am in no hurry."

Bloody hellhounds! He'd really not expected that answer. For a second, he wished she was more like other young ladies, but then he wouldn't be interested in her. He'd simply have to find a way to make her want him for a husband.

He helped Theo down from her horse and walked with her to the door. "Until tea."

"Yes. Until then." The door opened and she stepped inside.

Leo joined Marrow and rode to his house on Park Street. "You seemed interested in Miss Pettigrew."

Marrow was quiet for several moments. "I am. Do you know, Chandos, I never believed in love at first sight, and I still might not, but she attracts me as no other lady has. I feel at home with her. She is not silly or interested in my rank. It was an oddly comforting feeling being treated like a man and not a title."

"In that case, you had better get your financials together. You can afford a wife, can't you?"

"I can." He laughed. "Even without the allowance I receive from my father, I can afford to marry."

"What about the estate? Is it in good condition?"

"It is." Marrow stared at him. "You sound like you are her brother or father."

"No, no." Leo waved his hand. "I am considering marriage myself and getting ready for any questions of me." He urged his stallion into a trot. "Come along. I'm famished."

He should arrive at Worthington House early this afternoon to speak with Theo.

CHAPTER SIX

Theo rushed through her toilette and arrived in the breakfast room just as her married sisters were arriving. Although, describing them as married was unnecessary. At the moment, Mary, the only unmarried one aside from Theo, was still at Stanwood Place.

Interestingly, her brothers-by-marriage had already assembled. "You are here early."

They all glanced at her, then Matt said, "They brought the children."

"I saw Chandos riding away from this direction as we were on our way," Kenilworth said. "Did he accompany you on your ride?"

She slid into her seat at the table. "Yes. He and a Lord Marrow."

Rothwell frowned. "Did you not ask him to break his fast with us?"

Why were they all so interested? "I considered it, but he wanted to speak with his lordship." She placed the serviette on her lap and poured a cup of tea. "I might as well tell you what happened."

"Yes. Please do." Eleanor placed her elbow on the table and her chin in her palm.

"As you probably know, Sarah Pettigrew is riding with me in

the morning. Today Chandos brought Lord Marrow. During our ride, it appeared that he had formed an interest in her. I asked his grace to look into his lordship's finances and other things. Just to ensure that he was a suitable parti for Sarah. He said he would and asked Marrow to join him for breakfast. They will all be here for tea this afternoon. Including Lady Pettigrew."

Theo spooned shirred eggs onto her plate from the dish a footman held, then added ham. A small rack of toast was already on the table next to her.

"You could have asked one of us," Montagu said.

Theo swallowed a bite of the eggs she had taken. "You are all busy with the Lords. Chandos needs to make himself useful."

Kenilworth barked a laugh, as Rothwell rubbed his forehead. Their resident duke gave her a look. "Only someone from this family would say that. Did you not think that perhaps Chandos has duties such as the Lords?"

She put down the fork as she considered her brother-in-law's statement, then glanced around the table. "Has he ever attended the Lords?" Her question was met by shrugs and shaking heads. "There, you see. Being useful will be good for him." She looked at Grace seated at the foot of the table. "Grace, would you like to inform Jacque that guests will be attending tea?"

"Yes. Please tell Thorton. He likes to know about changes."

"I will." The rest of her sisters were all busy finishing their breakfasts. "What is everyone planning for the day?"

"We gentlemen are having a meeting shortly," Matt said.

"As are we ladies," Louisa commented. "Would you like to join us? We will be discussing our various charities."

That sounded interesting. "I would. It is time for me to decide what I want to do."

Charlotte's gaze focused on Theo. "Dotty, Louisa, and I could use another head and pair of hands. If you are interested, that is."

Dotty, the Marchioness of Merton, was Charlotte's childhood friend who married a cousin of Theo's, the Marquis of Merton.

They had become part of the extended family. They had two children. The oldest was a daughter, Vivienne and a new baby, Samuel.

Louisa nodded. "We already spoke with Dotty about the possibility. She will arrive early next week."

"I just might be." Theirs was one of the more interesting endeavors. They took care of war widows in need and took in former prostitutes and their children. All of whom were trained for positions they would like. Eleanor was involved in making mining and other work safer. Alice and Madeline rescued children from the streets, then educated and trained them. One of the boys had taught Theo and Mary how to pick locks even faster than Charlotte picked them. And one of the girls had taught them how to pass notes and things on without being seen. Both those children had gone on to more schooling. Augusta was the only one not involved with charities, but she was academically minded and translated ancient works for scholarly texts. "Where are we meeting and when?"

Louisa glanced at Matt. "If you are going to be in your study, we will use the library."

"That is fine with me." He placed his serviette on the table and rose. "Gentlemen."

Chairs scraped back as they stood.

Kenilworth patted Theo's shoulder as he passed by. "I am available if you need anything."

"Thank you." He was her favorite brother-by-marriage. Although, St. Albans and Harry Stern were close seconds.

"Why did the children decide to break their fast in the schoolroom?"

"They had not had an opportunity to be together since Christmas," Grace said.

"We even brought Vivienne with us so that she could be with the rest of the cousins." Charlotte rose. "Dotty wanted more time with little Samuel."

Samuel was just three months old. He would be like a cousin to Olivia and Robin.

Theo stood as well. "I am glad to be included."

The gentlemen filed into Matt's study that was already set with additional chairs near a sofa and armchairs near the fireplace. "Before we begin, I want to discuss Chandos and Theo."

There were nods all around.

"I know there is only one girl out this Season, but it already seems like more," Rothwell said.

"That's because it's Theo," Kenilworth said. "She is much more up to snuff than the rest of the sisters were when they came out."

"And all of them knew what they expected in a husband," St. Albans added. "Alice has my father shaking in his boots half the time."

Stern looked at Matt, then the rest of them. "Did Chandos approach any of you for advice?"

"Yes," they each affirmed.

"He's smarter than we were," Montagu muttered.

St. Albans pulled a face. "Definitely cannier than I was."

"Charlie asked us to assist him." Matt wanted to word this properly. "Unless it gets to the point that helping him is harming Theo. However, we are not to mention a word to her."

Kenilworth gave him a dubious look. "I understand the reason. There is absolutely no point in putting up her back. I do think we will pay for this subterfuge at some point." He glanced at the others. "I did tell him in no uncertain terms that she would not be compromised into marriage. I don't believe he would try that path. He has too much pride, but just to warn him in the event he becomes desperate."

"Did you tell your wife?" Montagu asked quietly.

"I learned my lesson about keeping things from Louisa a long time ago," Rothwell said with feeling. "Theo might be irritated with us, but she'll get over it quickly. Louisa can hold a grudge."

Kenilworth nodded. "I wouldn't dare attempt to keep anything like this from Charlotte."

The rest of the brothers-in-law agreed.

"When Mary comes to Town, she will have to be told," St. Albans said. "She and Theo played an important part in me being able to convince Alice to marry me."

"Mary already knows." Matt glanced at the rest of his brothers-by-marriage. "She spoke with Charlie and agreed that Chandos would be an excellent match for Theo."

"What do we do now?" Rothwell looked around the room. "Do we have a plan?"

Matt shook his head. "We play it as it comes. So far, Chandos has become trustworthy enough for Theo to give him tasks. Let's wait and see."

"I have one idea." Harry Stern leaned back in his chair." We need to get the duke to take his seat in the Lords. We can always use another peer on our side."

"Theo would like that as well," Kenilworth agreed. "The only question is will he have time while he's dancing attendance on Theo?"

Rothwell frowned. "That's a good thought. The only other one of the girls to come out by herself was Augusta, and she left for the Continent."

Matt poured tea that had been carried in and handed out the cups. "Enough of this. Kenilworth, I leave it to you to approach Chandos about taking his seat. Now. Let's discuss our legislative agenda."

Leo congratulated himself on letting his valet know to have his cook prepare a substantial breakfast early today. With any luck at all, he would be invited to break his fast with Theo tomorrow. He'd kept the conversation light while he and Marrow were eating; now it was time to ask more questions. "As I said, I have been putting my financial information and estate in order so that I am ready to wed when I find the right bride."

Marrow placed his serviette on the table. "It hadn't occurred to me to do that. On the other hand, I really hadn't planned to wed so soon." He shook his head thoughtfully. "However, I believe I must start. Fortunately, my father's man of business keeps the accounts in order. My father has been gradually handing me more control over the estates. Still, he will have to approve my choice of bride." He picked up his cup of tea and swallowed the rest. "Do you know anything about Miss Pettigrew's family?"

Leo had not even considered that the tables might be turned on him. "Not a great deal. The family lines are excellent." At least that's what he'd gathered at the ball Lady Stern had given. "The father's a bit of a toad. But I got that from Stanwood. His father didn't like the man because he was a hard Tory."

"I don't think my father will care one way or the other what her father's political leanings are. Do you know anything about her?"

"She seems nice enough. That Lady Theo befriended her says more about Miss Pettigrew than anything else. Lady Theo will not abide anyone who is puffed up in their own consequence or false in any way."

"I'd heard that about the Worthington ladies." Marrow poured himself another cup of tea. "Dowry?"

"Respectable. The father is a baron with one estate in the Midlands near Stanwood's main estate."

"I don't see anything to which m'father could object." He took a drink and set the cup down. "I suppose I'll get a better idea when I meet her mother this afternoon."

"There's nothing to be embarrassed about there." Lady Pettigrew couldn't be more different from her husband. "What are you getting up to this Season?"

Marrow shrugged. "I was going to look for a mistress to set up, but I won't if I am courting Miss Pettigrew. You?"

"My days of Seasonal mistresses are a thing of the past. My only goal is to convince Lady Theo to marry me."

Marrow looked surprised. "I can't suppose that will be too difficult. You are a duke and warm enough to keep a wife with the elegancies."

As if that mattered to her. "You don't know Theo. She doesn't care about rank or great wealth. Her brother will make sure no one who cannot support her will be allowed an introduction, but nor will he attempt to influence her choice. Aside from that, I need to be careful in courting her. She's not impressed with my former self."

"You really are taken with her." He shook his head as if amazed. "I actually never thought I'd see the day."

If only he knew. "I would do anything to make her my wife. She is not a perfect person. None of us are. But she's perfect for me."

His friend laughed. "What made you decide that?"

"Last summer not long before Stanwood wed. She found me passed out when I was supposed to be helping. She threw a pail of water on me, then proceeded to give me the best set-down I've ever had. And she wasn't even out yet."

Marrow went into whoops. "Well, that wouldn't suit me, but I can see how she is just what you need. Give me a lady who is calm and steady."

Leo raised his cup. "Such as Miss Pettigrew."

"It seems that might be so." His friend raised his cup as well. "Good luck to the both of us." Marrow gave Leo a narrow-eyed look. "All this talk of finances doesn't have anything to do with your future wife, does it?"

Leo had made a mull out of that. "Theo is very protective of her friends. Especially ones who she considers rather green."

"You, my friend, are going to be led a pretty dance before this is all over." Marrow pushed back his chair and stood.

"Trust me." It was becoming clearer every day. "I am well aware of that fact. I'll go along as long as it gets me what I want."

Theo in his life and in his bed. As his wife and duchess.

Leo arrived about twenty minutes earlier than the appointed time. A footman opened the door. He handed the man his card. "I am here to see Lady Theo."

The footman stepped aside. "Please come in, your grace. I will inquire if she is receiving."

The servant handed the card to a younger footman and the lad dashed up the stairs. A few minutes later, he ran back down them. "Her ladyship said she'll be here in a few minutes." The lad glanced at the older footman. "We're to take him to the morning room."

The servant bowed. "If you will follow me."

Leo was led to a large room at the back of the house overlooking a garden, decorated much more for comfort than for style. It exuded a feeling of warmth. What seemed like dozens of children were running around outside with two Great Danes. Theo's nieces and nephews. He recognized some of them from this past year.

"Good afternoon, Chandos." Theo had entered the room without him hearing her. "The nice thing about having a double house is that the garden is sufficiently large to allow vigorous play. It is important for both boys and girls to exercise."

Interesting. He definitely did not remember his sisters being allowed to tear around either the house or the garden. "I never thought of it. Are they all related to you?"

"No." Her lush lips tilted up at the ends. "Some of them are the children we take in in order to train. They all have academic lessons in the morning and after luncheon. Then, as you see, playtime. After tea, there is practice of some sort for everyone."

Interesting. "Will they all join us for tea?"

"Only my nieces and nephews. The others will have tea in the servants' dining room."

Not completely egalitarian then. "I have spoken to Marrow about his finances. He assures me they are in excellent condition. I'm afraid I was not very delicate about the matter. He asked me if I was asking because of Miss Pettigrew." Leo gave Theo his best innocent look. "I told him that you were very protective of your friends."

She cast her gaze at the ceiling and laughed. "That has the benefit of being the truth."

"I think it helped. He told me that he was quite interested in her and was looking forward to meeting her mother." He wanted to take Theo's hands. "He wants to assure himself that his father will have no objection. I did my best to reassure him. After all, Lady Pettigrew is good *ton*."

"She is indeed." Theo smiled. "We have all got to know them much better over the past year." She glanced out the window. "I hope finding a suitable husband for her is this easy."

Leo wanted to keep the conversation going. "What is her dowry? I told Marrow it was adequate, but I have no idea."

"That's a valid question. I shall endeavor to discover the information. I do know that Matt will act in her father's stead if there is an offer of marriage."

"I suppose he will be the one to give permission for the marriage as well." Even Leo's limited knowledge of Lord Pettigrew led him to believe the man would never trust a female, even his wife, to handle that type of responsibility.

"Well, that's certainly what her father expects. My brother, however, will defer to her ladyship."

"I'm glad to hear that." The respect for the ladies in the family was one of the reasons he had been drawn to first Stanwood and then the whole family. And especially Theo.

She tilted her head and gave him a curious look. "I am not sure I would have thought you were so progressive."

"I wasn't raised that way. But I've learned a lot from Stanwood and the other gentlemen in your family."

"Have you taken your seat in the Lords yet?"

Leo knew that question was bound to be posed. "Taken my seat, yes. Been active, no."

"Matt and the others have formed a group to discuss legislation and gather other peers to vote their way. You should ask him about it."

"That sounds like a good idea. I will." It would also make Theo think better of him. He couldn't regret that she had caught him under the hatches. If she hadn't, he never would have known that she was the one for him. He *had* come to regret that she thought poorly of him because of it.

CHAPTER SEVEN

~~~~~~

Their youngest footman in training burst into the morning room. "My lady, your other guests are here."

Theo forced herself not to laugh at Chandos's expression of surprise. "Please tell her ladyship and show the guests in."

"Yes, my lady." The lad went off again.

"Does he do that often?" he drawled.

"He's better than he was. At least now, he has conquered titles."

"You told him to inform her ladyship. How, pray tell, with so many 'ladyships' in the house, does he know to which one you are referring?"

A burble of laughter threatened to escape. "Grace is the only one called her ladyship. Everyone else is referred to by their titles."

"Ah. I see." He glanced out the window. "The children have gone."

"Yes. They will be here shortly." Almost as if she had called them, the sound of feet clamoring down the stairs could be heard. She looked up at him and smiled. "As I said."

"Is that noise coming from the main staircase? I distinctly remember carpet on them."

"No. I suspect they decided the servants' stairs would be more useful. They will have either been told or worked out themselves that we have guests. Descending the main staircase would mean having to stop and greet our visitors before coming in here."

"I wish I'd known to do that when I was a child. It would have saved me a great deal of time."

This time Theo did laugh. "They are nothing if not resourceful."

Constance, Charlotte and Con's oldest daughter, and Vivienne came into the room, followed by the others. Constance was the first to spot Chandos and curtsey. "Good afternoon, your grace. Do you remember our names, or shall we remind you?"

"Good afternoon, Lady Constance. I believe I have spent enough time around you to recall your names. Unless, that is, you have added anyone."

"No." She screwed up her face in thought. "Not yet. Probably next year."

He glanced at Theo, a question in his eyes.

"The next set of them will be old enough. So far, the babies have been born in batches. One of my sisters announces her pregnancy and the others follow."

Chandos ran a hand though his well-coifed hair. "It almost sounds as if they plan to have the babies together."

She had often had the same idea. "I suppose I will find that out at some point."

Grace entered the parlor next to Lady Pettigrew, followed by Miss Pettigrew and Lord Marrow. "I'm glad you see you are already here." Grace smiled at the other adults. "Please find your seats. Children, sit at the table."

Hugh was Charlotte and Con's eldest child. Theo tilted her head toward Chandos. "If it is only Hugh and Constance, and possibly one or two others, they may sit with us. When everyone is here, they must use the table."

"That is an excellent idea. Shall we find our places?"

Thorton entered followed by two footmen carrying trays filled with tea, biscuits, tartlets, and sandwiches. The children were given milky tea, which the girls practiced pouring.

Theo sat on one of the couches, and, to her surprise, Chandos sat next to her. Across the long, low table Grace and Lady Pettigrew were on the opposite sofa. Theo leaned forward to assist Grace in pouring tea and making up the plates. Once more he surprised her by assisting in handing out the cups of tea and plates. She had had no idea he was so well trained. For some reason, she imagined that he was used to being served at all times. If only he was not a rake, she might allow herself to get to know him better.

"My lord," Lady Pettigrew said, "how are your parents?" Marrow's eyes widened in confusion. Clearly, he had no idea that she might know them. She chuckled lightly. "Your mother and my elder sister were friends. They came out together. As I recall, although your parents' match was arranged, they were very much in favor of it."

"Indeed. My father has often said that if his parents had not agreed to allow him to marry Mama, he would have eloped with her."

Lady Pettigrew grinned. "And she said that she would never have done anything so outré."

Marrow appeared curious. "Is it strange that I have never met your sister?"

"No. She died in childbirth. Her husband lost no time in finding another wife." Her lips twisted. "One must have an heir. Your mother and I correspond several times a year."

"I am sorry for your loss. That cannot have been easy."

Lady Pettigrew blinked rapidly. "It was not. I still miss her."

Theo had the feeling that her ladyship would have said more, but this was not the time or place. "How long has it been since you have been to Town?"

"So long I cannot even remember. Once I had my son, I never visited the metropolis again until this year. Lord Pettigrew comes up for the Lords, but I was never interested in politics."

"Are you interested in politics?" Marrow had turned to Sarah.

"Since spending time with Theo's family, I have begun to form an interest. I find it fascinating how much one can accomplish when one is involved." She glanced at her mother. "Not that I would express my newfound ideas at home. My father is a strict Tory. As you probably know, the Worthington family are not."

Leaving Grace to converse with Lady Pettigrew, and Sarah to come to know Marrow, Theo meandered to the windows to the garden. She almost jumped when Chandos appeared beside her. "I thought you would stay and talk with your friend."

"Not while he is chatting with Miss Pettigrew. What do you take me for?"

Chandos was right. He would have been in the way. Theo was really going to have to reevaluate him. "I did not think about it."

He glanced to the side. "I didn't hear the children leave."

"They know when to be quiet. They are old enough to understand when they cannot become involved in the conversation. Although, I suppose I shall now be teased for matchmaking."

A grin dawned on his too handsome face. It was no wonder that he was a rake. Females of all sorts must fall all over him. He turned to her from gazing out the window. "I will attest that you had nothing to do with it. They found each other all by themselves. I will admit that I was chuffed to discover her ladyship, not Lady Worthington, knew Marrow's mother. If they do decide they would like to wed, it will make it easier."

"Quite true. I wonder what happened to her sister." A frown formed on Theo's brow.

She probably had the same idea as Leo did. "I got the feeling that her parents were not successful in arranging happy matches for their children."

"Yes." She nodded slightly. "That is what I think as well. I do believe she wants a better marriage for Sarah."

He turned and leaned against the windows to be able to look at her better. "Why is it not important for you to marry this Season?"

Theo raised one shoulder in an elegant shrug. "I suppose I am trying to put it off."

That he didn't understand. "Why? All your sisters have successful marriages."

"Oh, no." Her smile was a bit sad. "It is not that. It is just that Mary and I have been best friends for so long, I never thought about not coming out with her."

"She is three years your junior."

"I know. And I know I am not making sense. She told me to come to Town and find a gentleman to wed so that I could help her when she came out."

"But you miss her, and she is not here yet."

"Exactly." Theo blinked rapidly as if to clear tears from her eyes. "I truly believe that if she could avoid coming this year she would. I am half afraid that it is exactly what she will do."

"Because she is worried that you will feel badly for coming out first?"

"You are much too preceptive, your grace." She narrowed her eyes, giving him a suspicious look. "Have you spoken with her?"

"Me?" Leo placed a hand over his heart. "I have not. Although, I will admit to accidentally overhearing her in conversation with Stanwood." Leo could not resist taking Theo's hand. "She loves you a great deal. This is hurting her as well. I think you should honor her wishes and find the best gentleman you can to wed." *Which would be me.* "I'll even assist you."

Even though tears made her eyes more luminous, more beautiful, he liked her smile better. Theo sniffled. "Let us see what happens."

"Very well. I want you to know I will help whenever I can. I am your friend." There, he'd said it. Leo held his breath waiting for her to respond.

"Thank you. That is very kind. Perhaps I will take you up on your offer."

A stir came from the sofa. He glanced over Theo's shoulder. "Lady Pettigrew and company are departing."

Theo started to turn around, then seemed to notice that he was holding her hand. "I must bid them farewell."

Did that mean he should go as well? "Yes. Of course." Reluctantly Leo released her hand. She was riding with him today. "I will walk with you. Don't forget we are riding in the Park today."

"Yes. I will be ready at five." Her tone was thoughtful, then she glanced down at the hand he'd been holding with an expression he couldn't interpret.

He followed her to the front door.

When Marrow and the Pettigrew ladies reached the steps, he said, "My lady, may I take Miss Pettigrew riding this afternoon?"

Lady Pettigrew raised one brow. "You must ask my daughter first."

"I already did. She said it was up to you." He placed his hand over Miss Pettigrew's, and she smiled at him.

"In that case, you may go." Her ladyship inclined her head. "You may also escort us to our house."

"With pleasure." Marrow bowed, and the three of them turned toward Green Street.

Theo glanced up at Leo, her eyes happily sparkling. "That looks to be going well."

"I agree. I will see you soon."

"Until then."

He watched her enter the house and the door close. If only he could tell if he was making progress. Well, he had at least another hour this afternoon. Less than an hour later, he presented himself at Worthington House.

The front door opened as he jumped down from his curricle and strode up the short walk to the steps.

"Good afternoon, your grace," the butler said. He turned to the same young footman Leo had seen earlier. "Please advise Lady Theo that his grace has arrived." The lad started up the stairs at a run. "Walk, if you please. One does not run in the house."

"Yes, Mr. Thorton." Back straight, the young servant continued at a much more stately pace.

Leo considered making a comment, but few butlers would welcome one of his quips. Just as he was wondering if he'd be taken to the parlor off the hall, Theo descended the stairs. Her peach-colored carriage gown and spencer signalized her creamy skin. The wide brim of the bonnet allowed curls to frame her face, drawing his attention to her rosy lips. Few women were lucky enough to have lips that color without using cosmetics.

He went forward and held out his hand as she reached the bottom step. "You are enchanting."

For a moment he thought she would laugh at him. "Thank you, sir. But it is only a carriage gown."

"That may be, but any gown can draw attention to a lady's attributes."

She gave him a stern look. "I am quite sure this is not a proper conversation for us to be having."

He managed a contrite expression. "You are most likely correct. I will have to mend my conversational ways."

Theo laughed as he escorted her to his carriage. "Or keep different company."

"I am very satisfied with the company I am currently keeping. Thank you very much." *Minx.* He handed her into the curricle. "Would you like to visit Gunter's after we have our ride?"

A delighted smile appeared on her countenance. "I would like that very much. Thank you for suggesting it."

He started his pair and drove out of Berkeley Square toward the Park. He'd just feathered the corner onto Hill Street when she said, "I would have thought you would have asked an older lady to go with you to on the Grand Strut."

Leo was absolutely not going to tell her that the only females he allowed to drive with him previously were his ladybirds. "I don't usually attend the Fashionable Hour."

"Did Charlie ask you to do this? To watch over me?"

Fortunately, he had to attend to his pair as a dray decided to stop in the middle of the street, and he couldn't answer her. Not that he had an answer. Not yet. "I thought you might like it. Do you not?"

"Oh, no. I am very pleased you asked me. I simply do not know why you would."

The Park was already crowded when he drove through the gate. "This is going to take a while."

"It always does." Her melodic voice was as dry as it could be.

Leo had thought he'd be showing it to her for the first time. "Why do I have the feeling you've done this before?"

"Grace used to take us. In order to get us used to how it goes." She waved to two older ladies in a landau pulled up along the verge. "Lady Bellamny, Lady Cowper, how lovely to see you."

"I am glad to see you as well," one of the ladies said. The other smiled and nodded.

"Ladies, have you met Chandos?"

The older of the two raised a quizzing glass. "Not since he was in short coats. Your mother seemed to be in good spirits. I trust she is?"

"Better, I think. Now that she's in Town."

"So, Lady Cowper was telling me she appeared well. I understand you have vouchers for Almack's. I expect to see you there."

So, this was the ferocious Lady Bellamny. "I am happy to have renewed our acquaintance, my lady." The other one, the one who appeared to be inspecting him, could only be Lady Cowper. "Lady Cowper, my pleasure."

"I am pleased to meet you as well, your grace." She glanced at Theo. "My dear, should you really call him by only his title?"

"He is a friend of my brother Stanwood, and I have come to know him over the past years. However, if you believe I should call him your grace, or his grace of Chandos, I shall."

"Chandos is fine with me, my lady."

Lady Cowper gave him a put-upon look. "Of course, it is. However, Lady Theo is a lady just out. Not one of your chums. People do not need to get the wrong idea. Address him more formally when in company, my dear."

"Yes, my lady."

"Run along now," Lady Bellamny said. "You will be holding up traffic if you do not."

Leo did as he was told. Although the conversation had given him an insight as to how the Grand Dames of Polite Society thought of Theo. They treated her like one of their own. As to impressions, he wanted the *ton* to know that Theo was his.

CHAPTER EIGHT

"Well, that was embarrassing." Theo had thought, or she had wanted to think, that she would be able to treat Chandos differently than other gentlemen. She supposed she should have known better.

"What was?" He appeared confused.

"Being told that I cannot address you by your title in public."

"Oh, that. Well, if I'd actually given it any thought, I might have suggested you address me with more formality." He shook his head. "But probably not. I've become used to it. It's as if we have to pretend we don't know each other."

"That is it exactly. I might have known if I had been raised in places where there were boys my age or slightly older and was instructed on the matter. I shall have to ask Grace." She wondered, "Were you never told to change how you address a young lady?"

His dark brows furrowed. "I really didn't know any. Other than my sisters that is."

"We are a pair." How could they have both been so ignorant? "Well, we know now."

"You called me the Duke of Chandos when you asked if Miss Pettigrew remembered me."

"Yes, but that was only because I was not certain how familiar she is with *Debrett's*. I am well aware that Ladies Bellamny and Cowper know everyone." Theo might have to have more than one talk with Grace. "I have been being introduced to the *ton* since I was a child. It never occurred to me I would make a mistake."

"Ah. Now I understand the problem." He sounded as if he'd made a discovery. "You know everyone and have for a long time. However, you have moved into a different category and must behave slightly differently."

He really was astute at times. "Exactly. I must be more careful."

"We will both be more cautious." Chandos grinned at her.

They really were getting on quite well. Theo glanced around to see who else she knew was there and noticed a matron staring at them. "Do you know who that lady in the red landau is?"

He glanced quickly to the side. "No. I don't recognize her."

"I wonder who she is and why she is staring at us."

"I have been on the Town for years, but I rarely attend many events." He frowned. "I should say, events that ladies attend."

"You are now. Is it because of your mother?" Other than the fact that Chandos was Charlie's friend, Theo really did not know much about him.

"Partly. I have other reasons as well. This is the first Season she's been here since my father died."

Theo knew his father was deceased, but nothing else about it. "When did he pass on?"

"Shortly after I returned from the Continent." He was silent for a second. "I did not take it well."

"That is understandable. I do not remember my father. I think Matt experienced some form of behaving badly when Papa died. Yet, he has always been more of a father to me than a brother." She wondered if her brother would ever tell her about it.

"I wouldn't be surprised. I think many men do. I suppose it's a way of grieving." Chandos drove forward as the carriage in front of them moved. "For most of us, it is a drastic transition."

"I imagine it must be. Men inherit the title and estates, or business. They are suddenly responsible for everyone. Grace is the only lady I know who experienced that sort of obligation when her parents died."

He nodded. "Stanwood told me about it. He said she kept all his brothers and sisters together instead of allowing them to be divided up among their relatives."

Theo had not understood what a huge accomplishment it was until she was older. "Yes. She is remarkable. I'm glad Grace and Matt married. Before then, he used to go away for weeks at a time. After they wed, he stayed home."

Chandos had been looking ahead at traffic, then he glanced at Theo. "Sometimes there needs to be a reason to change."

Was that what Chandos was searching for? A reason? But to do what? Not be a rake? Perhaps there was something she could do to help. Charlotte might have some ideas. Theo glanced up to see they were leaving the Park. Had she truly not seen anyone else she knew? Or had she ignored them?

"Ices?" he asked in a light tone.

"Yes, please. I hope they have some savory ones. They usually do."

"You mean you hope they have a champagne ice." He grinned at Theo, and suddenly her chest seemed tighter.

"That or perhaps white wine." Yet, the champagne ice was excellent.

A waiter ran up to them when they parked on the verge in front of the building. "Would you like to hear our special ices for the day?"

"We would," Chandos responded. "Please start with your savory ones."

"Lavender, white wine, Parmesan, and ambergris."

"All of them sound interesting." Theo seemed so fascinated Leo wanted to laugh. "I will try the Parmesan."

"For you, sir?"

"The lavender." He glanced at her. "If you like, we can each taste the other's ice."

"Yes. That is what Mary and I do. Although, she likes the sweeter ones better." Theo's expression saddened.

He was starting to consider writing to Stanwood and asking when he planned to come to Town. Leo hated to see Theo in distress. In the meantime, he had to find ways to cheer her. "The ices in Italy are called gelato. They're wonderful. I hope you can try them someday."

"I do as well. Maybe I will be allowed to visit Augusta." Theo clapped her hand to her mouth. "Forget I said that. No one is to know where they are."

Leo had heard about the problems Phinn and Augusta were having with his sister-in-law, the marchioness. The couple's location was a closely held secret in the family. "I'll not tell anyone."

"Thank you. I must guard my tongue more carefully." Theo looked so guilty that he decided to take pity on her.

"I was there when the plans were made."

Her eyes widened. "You knew?"

"Yes. I believe I am the only outsider to be aware of their location." Leo was about to take her hands when the waiter returned with their ices.

"Let's try these." She scooped some onto her spoon and took a bite. "It is different, but tasty. It reminds me of a cheesecake I once ate. What of yours?"

He'd been concentrating so much on her, he'd forgotten to sample his own. He ate a spoonful. "Very good. Do you want to taste it?"

"Yes." Smiling, she nodded. He held the spoon to her lips, and almost groaned as she took it into her mouth. "It is very good. Here, taste some of mine."

This was going to kill him, but he'd die a happy man. She touched the spoon to his lips, and he opened his mouth and ate the ice. Although, he'd rather be tasting her lips. "Excellent."

They were finishing their ices when Leo remembered to look at the time. Her family generally dined early. Flipping open his pocket watch, he saw it was shortly after six o'clock. "I must take you home for dinner."

Theo's eyes widened and the guilty look was back. "I completely forgot about the time."

"It's no matter. I'll have you there in a trice."

"Would you like to join us? There is always room for one more."

Some of the best times of his life were when he dined with her family. "I would be honored."

Giselle scowled as she turned away from watching the carriage from a window in Gunter's. "I cannot believe she is riding with the Duke of Chandos! How would he even know her? There have not yet been any balls or other events where she could meet him. This has to be stopped."

"It is strange." Lana peered out the window where the carriage was stopped. "I wonder if he is a friend of the family. That would explain it."

"It would." Giselle tried to calm herself. The duke *would* be hers. "If that is the case, once there are other things to do, he will see that he no longer needs to spend time with her."

"The first assembly at Almack's is next week," Lana said. "I have heard that his mother received vouchers. He will most likely escort her."

"Yes." Giselle smiled at her friend. "Of course, you are correct. I will find a way to have him introduced to me. And he will ask me to stand up with him."

"Exactly!" Lana clapped her hands together. "That should not be difficult."

Not at all. "I will enlist my brother's help. He will do it for me."

"Oh, look! Miss Pettigrew is driving down the street with Lord Marrow."

"Where?" Giselle tightened her lips as his curricle drew up next to Chandos's carriage. "How did she meet him, and why did he offer to drive her in the Park?"

"I have no idea." Lana shook her head. "They appear as if they are enjoying one another's company."

"Be that as it may, I do not like her." Giselle rubbed her forehead. She would have a headache if she did not calm herself. "You should be with Lord Marrow." He would be perfect for her friend. And take him away from Miss Pettigrew.

"He is handsome." Lana appeared worried. "But how would I ever meet him?"

"The same why I am going to have the duke presented to me. My brother."

"If you think he would do it." She sounded unsure.

"I know he will." Mama expressly wanted him in Town to do just that. And to help watch over Giselle. "He will arrive within the next day or two. Before Almack's first assembly at any rate."

"Very well then. If you think it will work." Her friend's smile faded when she glanced out the window again. "If he has not already formed an attachment to Miss Pettigrew."

"I do not know how it would be possible. After all, there are not many opportunities for them to meet until next week. But if he has, I shall think of something."

Just as Leo picked up the reins, Marrow drove up with Miss Pettigrew. "I see we were not the only ones with a good idea. Lady Theo and I can attest to both the Parmesan and lavender ices."

"Indeed," Theo chimed in. "They are both excellent. We would stay, but I have to go home. We dine early because of the children."

Marrow glanced at Leo. "I must take Miss Pettigrew back soon as well. Where are you going afterward?"

"I'm dining with Lady Theo and her family." He could not help but to grin.

Marrow glanced at Miss Pettigrew and smiled. "I am dining out as well this evening. But a bit later I believe."

Her lips curved up. "Yes, at seven. Although, I have to admit that dinner at my house will not be nearly as entertaining as at

Worthington House." She glanced around and her smile faded. "Lady Giselle and Lady Lana are in Gunter's watching us. They just looked away."

"They know that they were caught staring." The only time he'd heard Theo's voice be harder was after she'd thrown water on him.

Leo stopped himself from glancing at the shop. "Lady Giselle?" Both Theo and Miss Pettigrew nodded. "My mother told me to be careful around her."

Theo glanced at Leo, her brows forming a line between her eyes. "She is just out. How could she have gained a reputation of any kind so soon?"

He shook his head, trying to remember the exact conversation. He'd been much too distracted by thinking of Theo at the time. "Something about her mother wanting her to make a brilliant match. Or was it her mother that had made an excellent match in some way?"

"That sounds ominous," Marrow said. "In that case, I'd keep my distance from her friend as well. Birds of a feather and all that."

"To be forewarned is to be forearmed." Theo placed her hand on Leo's arm, making him even more aware of her than he already was. "We must be going."

"Yes, of course." He started forward. "Enjoy your ices."

A groom was waiting when they arrived at Worthington House, but he got to Theo before the servant did. "Allow me."

She looked at him in confusion and held out her hand. Instead of taking it, he placed his hands around her waist and lowered her to the ground. She sucked in a breath that was music to Leo's ears. She might be the least green of any young lady coming out this year, but she was still an innocent. Before she could speak, he held out his arm. "Shall we?"

Her answer was a silent nod.

They reached the open door and Thorton bowed. "I take it you are joining the family for dinner. Please follow Jeffers to a chamber where you can refresh yourself." The butler looked at Theo. "My lady, your maid is waiting. Dinner will be announced in about twenty minutes. Please join the family in the blue drawing room."

"Grace must have held dinner back," Theo murmured. "I'll wait for you on the landing."

"Thank you." Leo imbued his voice with feeling. "I have no idea where the blue drawing room is located."

She grinned like he knew she would. "I will show you. But only this time."

"Then I'm on my own. I see. No special treatment for dukes."

Theo chuckled. "As if you did not know that already."

Leo rushed through his toilet and tried to reach the landing before she arrived, but she made it there before him. "Lead the way, my lady."

She took his arm as they descended the stairs then turned to the right as if they were going to the morning room. They had only taken a few steps when he heard voices from an open door. It appeared as if the children were already down. As they entered the parlor, it was clear that all their parents were there as well.

"Good evening." Theo seemed to float into the room.

"I pushed dinner back a bit. Fortunately, Jacque is used to it this time of year."

"We saw you going to Gunter's," Hugh said.

Theo accepted a glass of sherry from Worthington, and Leo was handed one as well.

"That would explain how you knew we were going to be a bit late coming home," Leo answered the lad.

"Chandos." Kenilworth clapped Leo on the back. "Welcome. I've wondered how you've been doing."

He slid a glance at Theo. "I'm not quite sure yet."

"Well, it can take time." Kenilworth looked at his wife, who was conversing with Louisa Rothwell and Theo. "Some roads are harder than others."

That was nothing Leo didn't know. "I was glad to be invited. I just wish I knew if it meant anything."

Kenilworth shrugged. "I wish I could tell you."

CHAPTER NINE

"What made you decide to invite Chandos to dinner?" Charlotte asked.

The reason Theo had asked him had not entered her mind. "I do not know. He is easy to converse with and took me for ices. I suppose I thought to return the favor."

"By inviting him to a family dinner?" Louisa's brows rose.

"It is not like he has not been to one before. He appears to get on well with the children."

"Very true. He was around a great deal last summer before Charlie and Oriana married." Charlotte glanced at Louisa. "As you know, I spent a lot of time there helping Charlie."

"You make me wish I would have been there as well." Louisa tilted her head to one side and gazed toward where Chandos was speaking with some of the other gentlemen. "He does seem very comfortable with everyone." She glanced at Theo. "You know, he might be an excellent prospect."

"No." She had to nip this in the bud. "I had heard things that made me think he might be a rake, and it was confirmed when I was shopping for gloves before Lady Bellamny's event. I heard some ladies discussing who he might take as a mistress this Season. That indicates two things to me. One, he is not looking to wed, and two, he is a rake."

"I cannot argue with that." Louisa shrugged.

Charlotte slid her a look Theo did not understand. "At least until some gentleman in whom you are interested comes along, Chandos is excellent company."

That was true. "I agree. He can discuss everything." And even understand her feelings. "He also has excellent taste in ices."

"And he is accepted everywhere. Rake or not, he has never crossed the line with the major hostesses," Louisa added.

"I do wish he would be more interested in the Lords." To Theo's mind it was a waste if a peer did not do his part to make the country better.

"I think you might have got that wish," Charlotte said. "Con spoke with him earlier today, and he has agreed to attend the next meeting Con and the others hold."

It was interesting. Charlotte's husband was the only one they called by his nickname. "Excellent." Despite his undesirability as a husband, his convictions were in the right place to help others.

Thorton called them to dinner, and Chandos was immediately at Theo's side. "If I remember correctly, everyone escorts their wives in, leaving only you and me."

"You are correct." She grinned at him. "Although sometimes the boys will decide to escort me."

"Yes, well." He had a sly look on his face. "I made it worth their while to allow me to accompany you this evening."

Silly man. "You did not."

"As you wish." He escorted Theo to her place midway down the table and pulled out the chair. Once she had taken her seat, he lowered himself into the chair on her left.

Hugh, Charlotte and Con's son, sat on Chandos's left. "When are you going to let us practice on your grays?"

Theo could not believe what she was hearing. Had he really promised her nephew that he could use his carriage horses for practice?

"You'll have to arrange it with your father. I cannot take you away from your lessons."

"I had forgotten about them," Hugh said. She doubted he actually had forgot, he but probably wanted to. "We'll work out a time and let you know."

On Theo's right, Constance, Charlotte and Con's daughter said, "I heard Papa say that your phaeton will arrive by the end of the week."

Chandos turned his head toward her. "Phaeton?"

"Yes." Constance nodded. "A high-perched phaeton. Just like all my aunts have."

He glanced at Theo, mirth brimming in his green eyes. "All of your sisters have them as well? How did that come about?"

"I am not exactly certain how it started, but my two eldest sisters received a phaeton that they had to share. If there is more than one sister making their come out, the last one to wed gets to keep it."

"It's an interesting view on how ladies think compared to gentlemen." He grinned. "I can guarantee you that if I had a brother and we were in that situation, neither of us would choose marriage. Especially not at eighteen."

She could understand that. "I cannot see two young gentlemen agreeing to share a carriage."

His forehead creased as he seemed to think about what she'd said. "I believe you're right. It would be a continuous squabble as to who had the rights to use the vehicle."

"Ladies are more civilized," Constance responded sagely. "And more mature."

He looked at Theo again. "They must be. No one in their right mind would allow a gentleman to wed at eighteen."

"I know." Constance nodded. "They are supposed to become knowledgeable about crops first." She frowned slightly. "But no one has told us the reason."

Theo had never seen Chandos's eyes that wide. She was hard-pressed not to burst out in whoops.

Around them, lips, tightly pressed together, were trembling as the other adults tried not to laugh.

"Right then." Con rose. "You children need to get ready to go home and to bed."

Hugh stuffed a piece of bread into his mouth and jumped up. The rest of them pushed their chairs back and filed out of the room. Once the door was closed and they had given the children enough time to reach the hall, everyone started to laugh.

"This wouldn't have anything to do with sowing wild oats, would it?" Chandos glanced around the table.

"Exactly that." Con rubbed his forehead. "My mother in her infinite wisdom told my daughter that I needed to sow my wild oats before marrying."

"And she thought it meant actual farming." Chandos chuckled. "It's a very reasonable explanation to a child or children who are in the country for much of the year."

"Yes, well," Charlotte said. "Now they all think that is what it means."

"I'm trying to remember when I first heard the term." Leo thought it must have been when he developed an interest in females.

"The boys will discover the meaning long before the girls do," Rothwell said.

His duchess gave him a dubious look. "Somehow, I doubt they will be able to keep it to themselves. And I do not believe that they should. Girls deserve to have and should have more knowledge than society believes."

"Exactly," Charlotte chimed in. "It is unfair and actually harmful to keep it from them."

"To be forewarned is to be forearmed." Theo gave a firm nod. "I heard of a girl who had no knowledge at all who was harmed by a man. All she knew was that he had hurt her. It was not until her mother called a doctor that they knew she had been raped."

Leo had never thought of that. Although, he did know men, he refused to call them gentlemen, whom he would not put past that kind of behavior. "I'm glad that you are aware of what can happen."

Grace stood. "Let us resume our conversation in the drawing room."

Leo rose as did the rest of the gentlemen. He was not surprised when they joined their wives to stroll out of the room.

Theo placed her hand on his arm, and he wanted to keep it there. Forever. He needed to make plans to be with her again. They soon gained the parlor, and glasses of wine for the ladies and brandy or port for the gentlemen were passed around.

Theo accepted a glass of claret. "Has anyone heard from Charlie?"

"I had a letter from Oriana," Charlotte said. "They plan to travel down next week with Dotty and Merton.

It seemed as if Theo had let out a breath of relief. Leo hoped she'd feel better once her younger sister was here. "Excellent. It will be good to see them and the little ones again."

"It will be." Theo smiled slightly. I cannot believe it has been almost a year since the wedding."

"I remember when he won that card game from Oriana's cousin Ognon." Stanwood's skill with cards never ceased to surprise Leo. Yet, Theo's talent outshone even her brother's. "Do you ever have card parties while in Town?"

Rothwell groaned and Kenilworth had an evil grin on his face.

Lady Worthington shook her head. "Only if it is just family. Usually, the Season is so busy we do not have the time."

"Will you take Lady Theo to a card party?" Leo asked.

Her eyes brightened. "I would love to attend a card party."

"And fleece everyone present." Worthington's tone was as dry as dust.

She lifted one shoulder and dropped it in an elegant shrug. "They should learn to play more proficiently."

"We shall see." Lady Worthington smiled at her husband. "I cannot remember the last time I was invited to one. They took place all the time when I had my shortened Season."

"I have to admit, it is mostly the older crowd now." In Leo's mind it was a lost social event. "Most of the gentlemen, and even ladies, want to gamble for higher stakes than those at a card party."

"Well, I think it would be fun." He could see Theo's mind working on how to get one up.

"Wait until you have gone through your first two weeks of balls and other entertainments before you start planning one," Lady Kenilworth advised. "You will be exhausted."

"Speaking of balls and entertainments," Lady Worthington said. "Lady Thornhill sent an invitation for a private viewing of some artifacts that they brought back from Italy recently as well as other objects they have collected."

Lady Kenilworth appeared interested. "That should be fascinating. I have attended her salons but have never seen all the items they have displayed in their house."

"Yes, indeed," the Duchess of Rothwell agreed. "When is it?"

"On Saturday." Brows raised, and Lady Worthington gave those gathered a questioning look. "Shall I accept for all of us?"

Everyone nodded, the ladies more emphatically than the gentlemen. Why was that? It really didn't matter. If Theo was going to be there, Leo wanted to be there as well. "I have never been."

"It is so interesting," Lady Montagu said excitedly.

"Other than having to watch those artist chaps trying to get your lady's attention, it was enjoyable." Montagu scowled slightly.

"I wholeheartedly agree." St. Albans huffed. "About the artists."

His wife practically rolled her eyes. "We were not even married." She fixed him a look. "In fact, I had told you I was not interested in marrying you."

He opened his mouth. "Nevertheless," the duchess said, neatly interrupting what could have become an argument. "She is very well traveled, and it is a joy to visit with her."

Lady St. Albans raised a brow at her husband. "If you had been paying attention the invitation is for a private viewing."

"She'll still probably invite the artist chaps."

If a bunch of damn artists were going to be there Leo was definitely going, if only to take care none of them made overtures to Theo. "Is sounds like a wonderful time." He glanced at Lady Worthington. "My lady, may I invite myself to go with you?"

She graciously inclined her head. "Chandos, I would not have mentioned it if you were not allowed to accompany us."

"Thank you." Well, that was stupid of him. Of course she would not have spoken of it. He really did have to become used to being around polite company instead of a group of heathens. He finished his brandy. "I should be going now. I have some work to do before I can rest, and an early morning tomorrow." He turned to Theo. "My lady, would you walk me out?"

"I will." He rose before she did and offered her his hand. "Allow me."

"It is amazing how I was always able to rise myself before I was eighteen, but now I must need help." She had muttered the sentiment more to herself than anyone else.

Lady St. Albans gave Theo a sympathetic look. "All too true."

Theo took his arm as they strolled to the hall. "I do hope you can manage to rise early."

He wasn't even going to ask what she thought he'd be doing instead of the pile of correspondence he had to answer. "I have ordered my valet to have me up and out of the house before the sun rises."

She smiled at him but shook her head. "Everyone needs their rest."

"As you will discover next week when the Season starts in earnest." He wanted to twit her at least a little for not trusting him.

"From what I have heard, Matt will insist that I leave the entertainment after supper, or at midnight."

Leo seemed to remember that being mentioned. "Then you will be able to have several hours before riding."

"That is what I hope." Theo removed her hand from his arm, and the footman opened the door. "Have a good evening."

"You as well." He didn't want to leave. Or rather he wanted to kiss her before he left. No. Actually he wanted to kiss her and take her to bed. Instead, he strolled out the door to where his curricle waited. The streets were still busy with wagons and drays making deliveries, maids bringing children back home from the park in the middle of Berkeley Square, and patrons headed to Gunter's. In the past, he would have been preparing for an evening out at his club, at some hell, or with his mistress. But not tonight, and not any night again. He resisted glancing toward the door until he'd climbed into the carriage. Theo was still there. Speaking to the footman. He waved and she waved back. If only he could take that as a sign that she was interested in him.

The next morning, he arrived at the Park so early he had to wait for the rest of their little group to join him. Marrow was the first to come, followed by Theo and Miss Pettigrew.

"Good morning." Theo smiled.

"Good morn to you." Leo returned her smile. "Shall we race?"

"Absolutely." They started their horses and quickly moved from walking to trotting to a full gallop. She beat him by a nose. Her mare pranced around clearly proud of herself. His stallion snorted as if to say, "I let you do that."

Her mare tossed her head in answer.

"What is her name?"

"Epione. It means soothing." She leaned over and patted the horse's neck. "What is your stallion's name?"

"Asclepius. The name means healing. I got him just after my father became ill. I suppose in my way I'd hoped it would help heal him." Did she know that in myth, Asclepius married Epione and had several children? Was that a sign that Leo and Theo would wed? "She's quite pleased with winning the race."

"She always is when she wins." Theo patted the mare again. "Let's walk around and cool them off."

"A good idea." They searched the Park. "I see Marrow and Miss Pettigrew have decided to visit the Serpentine again."

Theo stared in that direction. "I wonder how dinner went last night."

"Let's meander over and ask." Leo hoped his friend was making more progress than he was. That meant Theo would have less to take up her thoughts. Giving her more time to think about him.

A devilish look entered her eyes. "Who is playing gooseberry this time."

"Me?" He placed his palm over his heart. "Never, I am merely overly inquisitive."

She laughed out loud. It was from her stomach, and he would only hear it in moments like this when no one else was near them. They started toward their friends.

"Do you think they will tell us?" Theo whispered as they drew closer. "What if they have two different ideas of what happened?"

"We'll soon find out."

CHAPTER TEN

Theo slid a look at Chandos as they joined their friends. "I forgot to ask. How did your evening go last night?"

The couple glanced at each other, and Sarah responded, "It was very enjoyable."

"Er, yes. Very enjoyable. I am going to escort Lady and Miss Pettigrew to a private viewing this weekend."

Theo slid Leo a quick look. "At Lady Thornhill's?"

"Why, yes!" Sarah was clearly surprised. "How did you know?"

"We have been invited as well. Apparently, the viewing will have a number of participants."

Chandos's forehead wrinkled briefly. "I was about to ask how your mother knew her ladyship, but naturally, they would have kept up a correspondence."

"They have." Sarah's expression was wistful. "I am glad they did, but it is a shame it has been so long since they have been able to visit."

Suddenly, Theo had a thought. "Did your mother receive an invitation?"

His brows shot up. "I have no idea. It didn't even occur to me to ask. However, I shall do so when I see her today."

Mick took his watch out and glanced at it. That was the signal to go home. "I must be going."

"We will all go," Sarah said and smiled shyly at Lord Marrow, who returned the gesture. That was a good sign.

As they rode toward the gate, Theo sidled her mare up to Chandos's stallion. "Would you like to join us for breakfast?"

"I would, but I'll smell like horse."

"That is nothing to worry about. Thorton will send for your valet while you bathe." Fortunately, Matt had had pipes run to the two bathing chambers they now had in the house.

"Thank you." Chandos appeared uncertain. "If you are sure it's no trouble."

"None at all. It has been done before." She almost said that most of her brothers-in-law had broken their fast with them, but he was not looking to marry, and she did not want him to think that she was interested. They had started a good friendship. There was no need to spoil it with misunderstandings.

A short while later, she showed him where the breakfast room was. Her sisters and their husbands, and her nieces and nephews were just taking their seats.

Hugh watched Chandos as if the boy was trying to work something out. He opened his mouth, but Con put a hand over Hugh's lips and shook his head. It did not stop the looks he was casting the duke, but it did stop him from talking. Theo would have to explain to the children that Chandos was just a friend and nothing more. All of them were completely capable of asking if she was going to marry him. They had, after all, been through this scenario before.

"Chandos," Matt said. "We're having a meeting to discuss legislation later this morning. Would you like to join us?"

"Thank you. I would. It's high time I became an active member of the Lords."

"Excellent. We will meet at eleven. We generally have luncheon here as well."

"That sounds good. I'll tell my staff not to expect me."

That was odd. Theo thought he would go to his club for luncheon.

"We plan to be here for luncheon as well," Charlotte said. "There are some things I must see to this morning."

Theo drank the last of her tea. "Charlotte, if you are visiting the charity in Richmond today, I would like to accompany you."

"Yes, I will be happy to have you join us." She patted her lips with the serviette. "I will be back to pick you up within the hour."

Chandos stood. "I should be on my way as well." Theo started to push her chair back. "Allow me."

"Thank you." She smiled. "I shall walk you out."

When they reached the front door, the butler opened it. Chandos looked as if he would take her hands, then he bowed. "I suppose I'll see you at luncheon."

"Yes, I suppose you will. Did you like breaking your fast with us?" For some reason, she was sorry to see him go.

"Yes, indeed. I had a lovely time."

"I will see you later."

He strolled out the door and down the steps. Instead of his horse, his curricle had arrived. Well, that made sense. He would not want to ride after having bathed and changed. She turned and walked back into the house as the children were making their way up the stairs. "Wait. There is something I want to tell you."

They all stopped and turned to face her.

"Chandos is just a friend. Nothing more. So, there is no reason to ask if we are going to marry. We are not."

Constance gazed at Theo. "We will not say a word." She poked her twin's side. "Will we, Hugh?"

"No. Now that I know, I won't mention it."

The other children nodded in agreement, then resumed their way to the schoolroom.

"Thank you." Theo sighed softly. "Have a good day of classes."

Once they had attained the first landing, she went to her chamber to change into a carriage gown. She had not been to the Richmond house since last year. Would anything be different?

Probably only the faces. As soon as they could, the residents who wished to leave were placed in jobs and suitable housing found.

Leo tooled his curricle out of the square. If he was going to begin taking an interest in the Lords, he had to find a secretary. It was a damned shame his father's secretary had retired. First, he'd ask his mother, then the gentlemen with whom he was meeting at Worthington House. Leo pulled up in front of his house on Park Lane, and a groom came running to take his equipage. The door opened as he went up the steps.

Hoover, his butler, bowed as he strode in. "Is her grace at home?"

"I believe she is still in the breakfast room, your grace."

"Thank you." That was one thing about Mama, she did not remain in her chambers to dine. A footman stationed at the door opened it. It had never before struck him how many servants he had opening and closing doors for him. "Mama."

She glanced up from a newssheet. "Yes, dear. Good morning."

"Good morning. I must find a secretary. Do you have any ideas of who would be suitable?"

"That was not something I expected to be asked. Let me give it some thought. I am certain I must know of someone. How was your breakfast?"

"Thank you. Breakfast was interesting. I have been invited to a meeting with Worthington and his brothers-by-marriage concerning some bills. I intend to take my seat in the Lords."

Her eyes widened in approval. "I am glad. It is what your father would have wanted."

It's what Theo would expect as well. "It occurred to me that if I'm going to be doing the political work as well as attend to my estates, I'll need help."

"I agree. It's a shame your father's secretary decided to retire."

Exactly what he'd been thinking. "Mother, he was older than Father."

She shrugged. "That's true. I will go up now and see what I can do."

"I'll also ask at my meeting. One of the gentlemen must have an idea." At least Leo hoped they did. "I'll be in my study."

Mama rose. "If I find anyone, I will send a note to you."

"Thank you." He walked over to her and bussed her cheek.

Striding into his study, he sighed at the amount of work to be done. Unlike in previous years, he'd ordered that he be consulted on all decisions. He might have taken on more than he could reasonably handle from here. He sat behind the large oak desk his father had used and his father before him. And probably more than that. Some enterprising lad had carved his initials into the top corner. Leo had been promising himself that he'd find out who it was, but he hadn't had an opportunity.

He was finishing up what he could do before his meeting, when his butler knocked on the door.

"Come."

Hoover handed him a note. "Your grace said to give you this."

Leo opened it.

Chandos,

There are two young men who might be suitable. The first is Mr. Robert Howard, He is the son of Lord Howard. Mr. Howard was supposed to have gone into the church and completed the education, but found it was not to his taste. He is in Town now looking for tutoring positions. The second is Mr. Horace Whiting. He is the son of Viscount Whiting. He was acting as a secretary to one of the Foreign Office ministers, but did not want to leave England at this time because of his grandmother's health. They are, apparently, very close.

Mama

Whiting sounded promising. Experience was helpful. Leo would ask at the meeting if anyone knew him or the other gentleman for that matter. He made neat stacks of the papers he still needed to read and tugged the bellpull for Hoover to send out the others and to bring his carriage around. Then again, he could walk faster, and it might clear his head.

Hoover entered the study. "Your grace?"

"Thank her grace for me and post the letters. I am having luncheon out."

"Dinner, your grace?"

"I'm not certain." He wanted to be invited to dine with Theo. "I'll be at Worthington House."

"I shall inform her grace."

"Ask her if she knows Lady Thornhill." Perhaps Mama received an invitation as well. It would be an excellent time for her to come to know Theo and her family better.

"Yes, your grace." His butler bowed.

Leo came across St. Albans on Park Lane. "Are you going to the meeting?"

"As a matter of fact, I am. As my father's emissary. He's not in Town yet, and he wanted to know what Worthington was thinking when it came to legislative efforts."

That was interesting. "I thought he was a Tory."

St. Alban's grinned. "Not after Alice got done with him. He has been inching closer to the other side very year."

"All the sisters are impressive. I'm surprised they don't join the meetings."

"That is what luncheons and dinners are for. We thresh out the broad strokes and they fill everything else in."

Leo had listened to Theo expound upon legislative details. "That sounds like an excellent idea."

"How is it going with Theo?" St. Albans glanced over quickly.

"I have no idea. I think I am a friend. Whether I'm anything else is hard to guess."

"We're all on your side. That said—"

"I know. It's up to her. How do I get her to see me as an eligible parti?"

"The first thing you're going to have to do is rid yourself of your image as a rake." St. Albans grimaced. "It's not easy."

"I have not taken a mistress and will not. That part of my life is over." Leo didn't know what else he could do.

"The problem, old chap, is that she heard some ladies talking about you and your mistresses."

That wasn't good. "When? I haven't been anywhere. The only lady anyone could have seen me with is her."

"At Lady Bellamny's event." St. Albans shrugged. "It will take time. It's a damn shame we can't have those kinds of conversations with our intended wife. It would have saved me a world of trouble." They turned the corner onto South Street. "Stay close to her. Make sure you have sets reserved for Almack's and any balls."

"I've already asked to stand up with her at Almack's. I plan to have my mother approach one of the Patronesses to recommend me as a partner for the waltz."

"That's a good first step." They crossed over to Hill Street. "You're doing better than I did. I refused to acknowledge how different Alice was from other ladies."

"I learned that when Theo won every penny I had."

St. Albans looked surprised. "When was that?"

"When I got back from my Grand Tour." Leo smiled at the memory. "Stanwood left with his sister and her husband and came back. I arrived after the Season and visited him. As luck would have it, the family was there helping him settle into his home. Theo must have been about fifteen."

"Is that when you made your decision about her?"

"Good Lord no! She was just a child. An impressive girl but completely out of bounds. I made that decision over the past year."

St. Albans cleared his throat. "Ah, you are in love with her. I know she won't marry without that. It was on their list."

Love? List? Leo's cravat was suddenly too tight. "What list?"

"Alice, Eleanor, and Madeline had a list. I assume Theo must have one as well. It's normal things. For them. But I do know that none of them will wed unless it's a love match."

Love. Leo hadn't thought of being in love. He wanted her and admired her and would not wed another. Was that being in love? Who could tell him?

"I had to ask my mother about it." St. Albans flushed as if he was embarrassed. "She called me a great fool for not knowing."

Leo might have to ask his mother as well. "Once that's established, I suppose the only other hurdle is the settlement agreement."

"Don't bother. Worthington has an agreement he uses for all the sisters. He won't diverge from it."

That was odd. "How is that possible? Everyone has different assets and levels of wealth."

"It works on percentages. Trust me when I say that he will have a very good idea of your holdings and liabilities."

He understood. "His man of business."

St. Albans nodded. "And that's not all. My father almost choked when he discovered that if we had a child and anything happened to me that Alice would have guardianship."

As much as Leo's father trusted his mother, he knew for a fact that she would not have had guardianship over him. From what Stanwood had said, Worthington's father had not given his sisters' mother guardianship over them. "How did that come about?"

"From what I've been told, it began with Merton and Dotty."

"Dotty?"

"Lady Merton. I forgot that you aren't in the habit of calling the ladies by their first names. At any rate, Merton is a cousin and he and Worthington didn't get on well at all. Her father was still in the country, and Worthington was designated to draw up the agreements. With Sir Henry consenting to certain parts." They turned a corner, and St. Albans stopped talking.

"Go on."

"Worthington wanted to make sure that Dotty would be treated well. So, Merton had to sign the agreement if he wanted to wed Dotty. That is how it's been ever since."

"And in order for you to be able to wed your wife your father had to agree?" Leo couldn't see it. St. Albans's father was as difficult as they came.

"Had to if he wanted me to produce an heir. Alice and I made a decision that we'd present a united front. Along with Worthington, of course."

"Interesting." If Leo could win Theo, he didn't care what was in the damned agreements. It was the love thing that bothered him.

Fortunately, they arrived at Worthington House and the conversation ended. Or was it fortunate? Leo still didn't know if what he was feeling was love or not. He'd better work it out damned soon.

CHAPTER ELEVEN

Theo and Charlotte arrived back at Worthington House before the gentlemen's meeting broke up. They divested themselves of their hats, gloves, and coats, then repaired to the morning room.

"So, tell me." Charlotte lowered herself onto one of the smaller sofas. "What are you looking for in a husband?"

Theo shrugged. "I do not really know. I suppose what we all look for. Love. Kindness. Someone who is interested in being a partner and will listen to me." She sat on a chair next to the sofa. "How did you know Con was the one?"

"I had my first glimmer when he offered to drive me to fetch a young woman who was in trouble. He also told me I was correct about an issue we had been arguing about. And he corrected his behavior."

"Was he a rake?"

Charlotte tilted her head as if she was considering the question. "He was very much like Chandos. He had mistresses. That is what we were arguing about. And he was not interested in marrying. Not then. However, young ladies were safe around him. No. I do not think he could be called a rake in the sense that he would harm an innocent."

What she had said about Chandos struck Theo. "You do not believe Chandos is a rake."

"He is definitely a man around Town, but not a rake. When he gets ready to wed, he will make the changes that he must." Her sister stared at her for a moment. "I have come to believe that all men must make changes even if they are not rakes. Take Montagu. He originally wanted a wife who would leave all the decisions to him and simply make his life more comfortable." Charlotte tapped her finger against her thigh. "Or Rothwell. He had a secret. One he kept from Louisa. He almost lost her before he realized he had to change."

"Matt did not have to change."

Charlotte smiled. "He had to make the most change. He had to decide to take on all of us and be a full-time parent figure."

"I suppose you are right. He was always like a father to me, but he did come and go a lot until he met Grace." Theo nodded to herself. "I do not really know what I want. I suppose I will feel an attraction to some gentleman at some point."

"There is no rush. I am sure you will put it all together."

The sound of a door opening and male voices reached into the room. "I think the meeting is over."

"Come then." Charlotte rose. "Let us find out what they have been discussing."

The front door opened, and feminine voices could be heard. "I think everyone else is here as well."

They strolled up the corridor to the hall where their sisters were removing their coats and hats.

As the sisters greeted their husbands, Chandos approached Theo. "I felt like a dunce. I have a lot to learn."

She shook her head at his rueful expression. "Everyone has to start somewhere."

"I will guarantee that you knew more about legislation when you were in the schoolroom than I do now."

"Probably." Theo almost felt sorry for him. "But we, Mary and I as well as my nieces and nephews, were encouraged to learn.

And St. Albans too. His father did not allow him to have any responsibility until he was married."

His dark brows drew together as if he disapproved. "That's odd."

"That is what Alice said." Theo took the arm he had offered to her. "You will learn."

"I must, and quickly."

They took their seats, and, once again, he sat next to her. The children joined them, and the conversation ranged from repealing the Corn Laws—that was taking years—to investing in steamships, to private laws, and what could be done to help the rights of married women.

"We have been publishing pamphlets explaining to women their rights and what can and cannot be done in settlement agreements," Charlotte said.

"Can they all read?" Chandos appeared stunned.

"The women in business are able to read," Madeline said. "At least for the most part."

"The three of us are running a clinic to help women who require legal help before they marry," Eleanor added.

Chandos turned to Theo. "How did your trip to Richmond go? Have you decided to assist in that way?"

"It went well. As I suspected, the faces had changed, but the results have been excellent. We have only had one or two per year return because they were not ready to be on their own."

Another thing Leo wished he knew more about. "How do they find you?"

"There is a sort of whisper network. If necessary, they can contact someone who will go to them and assist."

That sounded dangerous. "Are you involved in that part as well?"

"No." She shook her head. "The closest anyone came is Dotty's sister, Henrietta, and that was not supposed to have happened."

"And Dotty, herself," Grace said. "It was before she and Merton wed."

Worthington groaned. "I do not wish to discuss that. Thankfully, it has become a safer enterprise to run since then."

"What happened?" Little Constance asked.

"Nothing that you need to know about now." He cut Lady Kenilworth a look. "You get to explain this one."

Her ladyship laughed lightly. "I will when the time comes."

Now, Leo really did want to learn more. Perhaps he'd ask Merton when they came to Town. Leo placed his lips as close to Theo's ear as he could without drawing attention. "Would you like to ride with me this afternoon and go to Gunter's?"

Her lips curved into a definite smile. "I would. Five o'clock?"

It was then he remembered to ask about a secretary. He had not wanted to interrupt the conversation during the meeting. "I find that I am in need of a secretary. My mother suggested Mr. Horace Whiting and Mr. Robert Howard. Have any of you heard of them? Or do you have other recommendations?"

"I would not suggest Mr. Howard. He does not know what he wants to do at all," Louisa said. "His mother was complaining about him recently."

"Whiting?" Montagu said. "Did he just leave a position?"

Leo nodded. "That is what my mother said."

"The minister who lost him was not pleased." Rothwell grinned, making Leo wonder at the reason.

"But it was because Whiting did most of the work," Kenilworth added. "I understand he is extremely competent."

"That's what I have heard as well," Rothwell confirmed. "Much more so than the secretary for whom he worked."

Leo was pleased that both men were known. "I will find out how to contact him for an interview."

"I believe he has rooms on Jermyn Street," Montagu said. "If not, someone at Whiting House will be able to direct you."

"Thank you." Leo would write a letter when he got home and let his butler take care of the rest.

A clock chimed, and the children rose from their chairs. It must be time to go back to their classes. Lady Worthington stood as well, and Leo and the other gentlemen rose as did the ladies.

He glanced at Theo. "I'll see you at five."

"Good luck with your secretary search."

"Thank you. Hopefully, the information I have will do."

"I hope so too." She smiled. "I will see you later."

"I'll walk you out," Worthington said. Leo had the feeling he was going to be questioned.

They got to the front door and Worthington stepped outside with Leo. "How is it going with Theo?"

He shook his head. "To be honest, I have no idea. She seems to like my company, but she's not given me any indication that she thinks of me as anything other than a friend. I'm not sure how or if I should press her."

Worthington stared across at the park. "It's early days yet. Continue as you are for a while."

That wasn't helpful. "Thank you. I'll take your advice."

"Tomorrow we're meeting at Brooks's for luncheon at one. Please join us."

"I will. Thank you again." Leo climbed into his curricle.

"Oh, there's one other thing. Theo's phaeton will arrive on Wednesday morning. You might want to suggest that she take you for a drive."

Now, that was a wonderful idea. He knew she was an excellent whip. "I'll do that."

Worthington left, and Leo started his pair. He had to find a secretary. Otherwise, either the estate was going to suffer, or his courtship of Theo was. Neither outcome was acceptable. When he arrived home, he went directly to his study and penned a note to Whiting and called for Hoover.

"I was told Mr. Whiting has or had rooms on Jermyn Street. If he cannot be found there, his father is Lord Whiting. This must be delivered as soon as possible."

"We'll find him, your grace. Should the footman wait for a response?"

"Yes. If he agrees to meet with me, have him come by either immediately, or tomorrow morning at ten."

Hoover bowed and left. Leo began to sort the mail he'd received into piles. Ones from yesterday. Those received today. Work. And social events. He came across a card from Lord Fellows inviting him to a gathering at his house on the river in Greenwich. Leo had attended a few events there since he'd returned from his Grand Tour. The first time he'd brought his mistress, but his tendency not to share what was his had created some difficulties. After that, he'd gone alone. He threw the card in the fireplace and watched it burn. That was his past life. This was the year he began anew.

Sometime later, as he wrote an answer concerning a tenant issue, a knock came on his door. "Enter."

Hoover opened the door. "Your grace, Mr. Whiting is here to see you."

Thank God! Leo prayed this went well. He inclined his head.

"Sir, his grace will see you now."

A tall, slender gentleman entered the room. He had sandy hair and wore glasses. To Leo, he looked exactly like how he pictured a secretary would appear. Coming from around his desk, he held out his hand. "Welcome. I'm glad you had time for me today."

"I was pleased to receive your letter."

This sounded promising. "Have a seat."

Leo took his chair behind his desk again. "I have heard some of your qualifications, and you came highly recommended by friends."

The man looked curious. "May I ask who?"

"Indeed. The Duke of Rothwell and Lord Kenilworth."

"I respect both of them a great deal," Whiting said. "Can you tell me exactly what the position would entail?"

"Correspondence." Leo resisted a shudder. "During the past year, I fully took control of my holdings. When I was at home, everything was manageable. Now that I'm in Town and looking to wed, it has become more difficult."

"Courting is interfering," Whiting observed.

"In a word, yes. It's dashed hard to attend even the few events I have gone to so far and keep up with the questions I receive from my estate managers."

Hoover brought in a tea tray and Leo served. Once Whiting had a cup of tea and had taken a sip, he put down the cup. "You said you had recently assumed full control. Who was managing before?"

"My father, but he died about three years ago. I did not take it well and continued on with my life as it had been before. Then I had a revelation. You could describe it as being doused with a bucket of cold water. It was made clear to me that there was something I wanted more than a life of frivolity."

"Were your estate managers pleased with this turn of events?"

That was an interesting question. "I would have said they were. In the beginning. Then I followed the lead of a few gentlemen who were testing new methods, and they became not surly, but they had a great many reasons why the old ways were better."

Whiting tented his fingers. "Now you are inundated with minor problems."

"Exactly. How did you know?" Leo had not even considered how trivial some of the requests were.

"People in general don't like change. From what I understand, you hadn't been involved when your father was living and left everything to them after his death. That is not as unusual as you might think. It might be a way to put you in your place, as it were. Or to make you throw up your hands and let them have at it again."

"I will not do either of those things. My father believed a landlord should be actively involved in his estates." Leo wished he'd done that from the beginning. On the other hand, he'd had a lot of fun for a few years. Perhaps he'd needed to do that to realize how empty that life was.

"I can see that you will not. My suggestion is to allow them to continue on during this Season. When you return you can make changes."

"I could fire them all." That seemed like an excellent idea.

"Unless you wish to return to your main estate and do a tour of the rest, it would be difficult to let them go now."

"You're right. What should I do?"

"If you decided to hire me, I would handle all the correspondence." Whiting raised his brows. "You would still have to make the decisions, but you won't be required to take the time to respond. That will provide you with the courting time you need."

And when Leo returned to his estate, he'd have Theo with him. She, he knew, had a great deal of knowledge about estate management and dealing with dependents. The question was should he consider this until tomorrow or just hire Whiting now? It suddenly struck Leo that he'd never hired anyone. Except a mistress, that is. He should speak with someone. Like Theo.

"Thank you for your insight."

Whiting rose. "Shall you need some time to consider my suggestions?"

"Yes. I will get back to you no later than tomorrow."

He bowed. "Your grace. I hope we can work out a mutually acceptable arrangement."

"As do I." Leo came out from around his desk and shook Whiting's hand. Leo escorted the secretary to the front door. "I will be in touch."

"Your grace," Hoover said. "You are riding with Lady Theo at five. You must leave now if you do not wish to be late. The carriage is being brought around."

A humorous look entered Whiting's eyes. "I take it your staff has been with you for a long time."

"A very long time." They strolled outside and Leo saw the curricle being brought around. "To be honest, the position of secretary is the first one I will hire."

"I understand. My father tells stories of when he first took the title."

Leo had heard the tales as well. "It can be a bit of a trial with servants and employees who have known you all your life."

"Indeed, it can be." Whiting walked to the street and turned.

Leo definitely needed to speak with Theo about him. He also had a feeling she would like being asked for her opinion.

CHAPTER TWELVE

Constance burst into Theo's parlor with a wide smile on her face. "Charlie, Oriana, Mary, Gideon, Elizabeth, the little ones, and Dotty are arriving tomorrow! Is that not wonderful?"

"It is indeed!" Payne helped Theo into her spencer, then placed her bonnet on her head and inserted the hat pin. "Are you excited to see all the babies?"

Theo would be glad to see her niece Elizabeth and nephew Gideon again, but especially Mary. "I am." Constance bounced on the balls of her feet. They will grow up with Timothy."

Timothy was Charlotte and Con's son born last December. "They will. I must say, it's almost as if the babies are planned to have cousins."

Constance shook her head. "They cannot be. Charlie did not even know he was going to have a baby when Mama knew."

"Very true. Maybe she started it. Because then Dotty found out she was going to have a baby."

"And Charlie and Oriana were next!" Constance bounced again.

Theo glanced at the clock. "As much as I would like to stay

here and talk about all of it, I have an engagement in just a few minutes. Chandos is taking me for a ride in his carriage."

Her niece suddenly became serious. "Yes. I know. Aunt Grace said I could not keep you." Then Constance smiled again. "You should invite him for a ride when your phaeton gets here. Papa said that would be on Wednesday."

She was certainly well-informed. Then again, Constance was the same age as Theo had been when she had started paying a lot of attention to what everyone in the family was doing. And when Grace and Matt met and married. "That is a very good idea."

"I thought so. That is why I suggested it. I like him. He's always nice to us." Constance dashed out as quickly as she had arrived.

"Well, that was interesting."

Payne chuckled. "She has a great deal of energy."

Theo laughed lightly. "That she does. I had better go down. If I am going to insist that gentlemen who come for me are on time, I must be as well."

The new doorbell chimed. "He is here." She strode out of her parlor and down the stairs. Theo had reached the first landing when she saw Chandos standing at the foot of the stairs gazing up.

"Good day." He smiled at her, and something fluttered in her stomach. That was strange. She descended the rest of the way. He held out his hand. "I live in hope that the Park will not be too crowded."

"I am afraid you will be disappointed." She placed her gloved hand in his.

"I can't be too disappointed when I'll be with you." He smiled.

That sounded . . . What? Practiced? No. Different. She gave herself a shake. "Let us be on our way. The sooner we can get around the Park the sooner we can have ices."

"Never let it be said that I stood in the way of you and an ice." Chandos placed her hand on his arm as they strolled out of the house.

Instead of assisting her into his carriage like he normally did, he picked her up and placed her in it. Theo's breath caught. No one had ever done that before. At least not since she was a child. "Goodness."

The corners of his lips rose. What had got into him today?

The carriage rolled forward as he started the horses. "I need advice."

Ah. Now it all made sense. He wanted her in a good mood. "About what?"

"As you know, I must hire a secretary."

"Did you meet with Mr. Whiting?"

"Yes." Chandos glanced at her in surprise. "How did you know?"

"It stands to reason that you would not require advice unless you had already met with him." She now understood what Eleanor had been talking about when Montagu had little knowledge of estate management. "What about the interview concerns you?"

He told her what he and Whiting had discussed and his recommendations.

"I think he has an excellent grasp of the situation. What concerns you?"

Chandos appeared a bit embarrassed. "I have never hired staff before. You have, haven't you?"

"Yes. Just tell me what you want to know." Why did gentlemen always seem to beat around the bush?

"Were you afraid to hire the wrong person?" He cringed.

Now they were getting somewhere. "Everyone hires the wrong person at some point. It could be that the person presents well but does not actually have the skills. Or perhaps they cannot manage to get on with the other staff. However, a well-written employment contract will smooth things over. Unless they are untruthful or they steal, or something like that, a good recommendation also helps."

"Employment contract?" He sounded stunned.

Considering he had never engaged someone before, it was not surprising that he did not know a contract was required. "Yes.

You write down all their duties, the salary, additional things such as, for servants, the amount of fresh tea they receive and cloth for gowns, livery. That is more for servants. An employee should be paid enough to be able to support himself and his family if he has one. You must decide if he is to live at your house or if he will have his own dwelling. You might want to discuss that with him." Theo glanced at Chandos to ensure he understand what she had said. "Do you need to know anything else?"

"Is he the right person?" He looked so concerned her heart went out to him. He really was afraid of making a mistake.

"Only you can answer that question. However, I will attempt to help you. How does he make you feel? For example, did he ease your mind about how to handle the difficulties you are having that made you decide that you needed a secretary?"

He nodded. "He did. I was irritated that my stewards would play those sorts of games, but he did seem to know what to do."

"Good. Did you have a good rapport with him? Did you get the feeling you can trust him? I should think that would be very important. After all, he will know about most of your personal and other business."

Leo could trust her. He never really thought of his feelings for an employee.

When he didn't answer, Theo frowned. "Do you not get ideas about people? I will give you an example. When you first met Charlie, what did you think of him?"

That was easy. "He was a good fellow that I'd like to know better."

"There you are." She nodded her head once. "What was your impression of Mr. Whiting?"

The way she smiled at him made Leo feel as if she'd given him a gift. "Competent. He has a dry sense of humor. Very focused on the matter at hand."

"And he has a good reputation."

"Yes." Leo was finally beginning to think he could do this. "You're right. He knew what should happen, but also made me know it was my decision." All he had to do was hire him. There was only one problem. "Do you have a contact I could use?"

"I do."

He'd expected Theo to look as if she was going to roll her eyes or do something like that, but she didn't. She just gazed at him as if she was proud of him. No one had done that in a very long time. "Can you give me a copy when I take you home?"

"I will work on one with you." She gave him a sidelong look. "After ices."

"Naturally." He had to laugh. "After ices." He glanced around and was not pleased to see Thanet riding toward them. "We are about to be imposed upon."

She glanced in the direction Leo was looking. "By whom?"

"The Earl of Thanet. Worthington would murder me if I introduced him to you."

Theo raised one imperious brow. "He is a friend of yours?"

At least she made it a question. "No. Merely an acquaintance."

"How do you know him?" There was more than a hint of censor in her tone.

"How does a gentleman know any other gentleman? School, clubs, that sort of thing." House parties Leo was no long attending. "Do me a favor, and if you have to look at him, give him your coldest and most imperious look."

A lewd smile appeared on Thanet's face. Good Lord. Of course, he thought Theo was Leo's latest mistress. With whom else had he driven in the Park before? Leo steeled himself.

"Chandos," the man hailed. "Care to introduce me to your friend?"

"No." He thought for a very brief moment that Thanet would leave it at that, then he opened his mouth. "I would like to keep my head on my shoulders. However, if you want to risk yours then you may apply to her brother."

"Her brother, eh?"

That was when Theo gave him a look of such disdain that Leo was extremely glad he was not on the receiving end.

Then Lady Bellamny, accompanied by Lady Cowper, drove up and stopped. "Lord Thanet, go away. Even you should know better than to accost young ladies. You are not welcome in polite company."

He gave Leo an odd look, backed up his horse, and left.

"And you, your grace." He knew he was in trouble when she used that tone. "How could you even think of—"

"My lady," Theo said quickly. "He was not. In fact, he told me my brother would be upset if he introduced that man to me and told that person he would not provide an introduction."

"Just as well." Her ladyship's tone bit, and her black eyes bored into him. Her message was clear. If he wanted to spend time with Theo, he would ensure something like this never happened again.

He gave a quick nod indicating that he understood. He would have to get the word out that he no longer had mistresses.

"Very well then," Lady Bellamny said, sounding somewhat mollified. "Have a good ride."

Theo smiled brightly. "Thank you, my lady. I am sure we will."

"It is amazing the types of men some of the gentlemen seem to know for no good reason at all," Lady Cowper opined as they drove away. "I am glad you stopped and let 'that person' know he was not wanted."

"He really is bad." Theo's look of amazement made Leo feel even more guilty than he had been. "What did he do?"

"Among other things, almost ruined a young lady." And refused to support a child he'd got on his mother's maid. That he'd not tell Theo.

"We should probably tell Matt before he finds out some other way."

"I'll do it when we get to your house." Leo had the feeling that Worthington would have a great deal to say on the matter and none of it would be good.

"It will be all right. After all, you cannot be held responsible for what other men do." She patted his arm.

It was Leo's fault that he knew those types of people in the first place. "I hope you are correct."

"I am." Her tone was assured, but he was not at all looking forward to the conversation.

They finished their ride greeting those who stopped. One of them was the Earl of Rochford, a friend of Leo's and Stanwood's. "When did you get into Town?"

"Last night." Rochford turned to Theo. "Good afternoon, my lady. I see you are finally out."

"I am. How have you been? We have not seen you since New Year's."

"Well. I've been well. My father had a bout of the influenza, and I was afraid we'd lose him, but he's hale and hearty now."

"I am glad to hear that. It's hard to lose a loved one."

"When is your come out ball? I expect an invitation."

"Goodness." Theo seemed surprised. "I do not even know. I'm certain Grace has the date planned. I will make certain you are on the guest list. Although, I am sure you already are."

Rochford backed up his horse and bowed. "I hear Stanwood will be in Town soon."

"Indeed." Theo grinned. "I was told by my niece, Constance, that he, Oriana, the babies, and Dotty Merton are arriving tomorrow."

"Excellent." Rochford waved. "I'll see you soon."

They were headed to the gate, when Theo said, "Who are those ladies staring at you?"

The traffic was heavy, but Leo took a quick look. Damn. Ladybirds. "I don't know."

She shook her head. "There is something strange about them, but I cannot put my finger on it."

He knew. They wore paint and were not dressed quite right to be ladies. Still, they weren't his problem. The only female he wanted was Theo. "I don't know either." Fortunately, they were passing through the gate. "On to Gunter's."

This time he had white coffee, and she had bitter orange blossom.

"This is excellent. It has a certain bitterness." Theo licked her spoon, and he almost groaned again. This was going to kill him. "Would you like a bite?"

"I would." He'd pretend he was licking her. "Here, have some of mine."

Her adorable nose wrinkled. "I am not sure I will like coffee."

"Take a smaller taste at first." Leo could imagine sitting with her naked in his room trying different types of ices.

She dipped her spoon into his cup, and took an almost infinitesimal piece, and sampled it. "Oh, this is much better than I thought it would be. I wonder if I would like real coffee."

"You'll have to try it someday." Preferably with him.

Theo took a larger bite. "I will. This is sooo good."

He tried hers and it was surprisingly fresh, and it had a hint of the orange peel he'd tasted in Italy. "This is as well."

They finished their cups, and he signaled for a waiter. As they were waiting, he glanced around, looking for Marrow and Miss Pettigrew. Instead, Leo saw the same two young ladies that had been here before. And, as before, they were staring at him and Theo. He almost thought he had spilled something. The waiter finally arrived, took the cups, and he started the carriage. "Those two young ladies were staring at us again."

Theo lifted one shoulder in a graceful shrug. "They obviously do not have anything better to do."

"I suppose I had better ready myself for Worthington's wrath."

"You will simply explain to him what happened." She grinned. "It will not be that bad. I'll join you when I find a copy of the contract I want."

Leo hoped she was right but knew how he'd feel if someone like Thanet had tried to approach one of his sisters. He pulled up to the house and a footman and groom ran to the carriage.

"Your grace, Lord Worthington would like to speak with you."

Theo's jaw dropped and she snapped it shut.

"I'll be there immediately." Leo went to the other side of the curricle and lifted her down. "Wish me luck."

"I will hurry." Her tone was brisk. "I refiled all the contracts. It will not take me long to find it."

They parted in the hall. A footman escorted him to Worthington's study. He held up a small piece of paper that looked as if it had been torn from a pocketbook. "I received this from Lady Bellamny."

"I can explain."

He sat behind his desk without even offering Leo a seat. "Go on."

"As you no doubt know, I attended events which no lady would grace with her presence. I met Thanet at one of them. We were never close. But it was not a secret that I had a mistress for the Season and would drive her in the Park. He obviously assumed Lady Theo was my latest. He asked for an introduction, and I denied him . . . I'm sure you heard the rest from Lady Bellamny."

"Indeed." Worthington dragged a hand down his face. "You have spent the last year proving what a good man you are. You'll have to tell your former acquaintances that you are no longer running with their crowd."

"I thought by not frequenting the hells and clubs they would get the hint." And the fact that he didn't have a mistress.

"My advice is to write to Fellows refusing his invitation. I assume you received one"—Worthington's brow rose, and Leo nodded—"telling him the reason. He will inform the rest of them. You might also mention the encounter today and emphasize that as you will not be taking a ladybird any longer, not to approach you."

This time it was Leo's turn to be shocked. "You know Fellows?"

Worthington smiled. "I was not always married or in the market to wed. However, Thanet is particularly despicable."

"I'll do as you say." Leo was just thankful that he was still allowed to spend time with Theo.

CHAPTER THIRTEEN

Theo found the contract she wanted, went to Matt's study and knocked.

"Come."

She opened the door. "I hope you have worked things out. It was an unfortunate encounter, but that is all." She held up the document as she turned to Chandos. "Shall we go to the morning room so that you can review this?"

He had turned to look at her when she entered the room. He now glanced back at Matt. "I interviewed Whiting yesterday and, after discussing it with Lady Theo, decided to make an offer of employment to him. However, I have never hired anyone before."

"Exactly." She smiled at her brother. "I explained he would need an employment contract and offered to show him a sample."

The two gentlemen exchanged a look she did not understand. Matt cleared his throat. "I will send a servant to join you."

"Very well." To Theo's mind it was a waste of a servant's time, but proprieties must be observed. She raised a brow at Chandos. "Are you ready?"

"Never more so." He smiled at her. She had seen him do that

hundreds if not thousands of times before, but, for some reason, it caught her attention.

She shook it off.

Thorton entered the room. "My lord?"

"A servant to sit in the morning room with Lady Theo and his grace."

The butler bowed and left.

"Well then. Let us get to it." She walked out of the parlor and Chandos followed.

When they entered the room, a tall, dark-haired footman who was standing next to the bellpull bowed. "My lady, your grace."

"Good morning." A thought struck her. "Are you to act as my personal footman?" All her sisters had one during the Season, but hers had not yet been assigned.

"I am, my lady. I hope you will be pleased."

He had a lilt she was certain she recognized. "Welsh?"

"Yes, my lady. I served in the Sixteenth Royal Carnarvon Rifle Corps."

"What is your name?"

"Jones, my lady."

"Excellent. You may have a seat while his grace and I do our work."

She led Chandos to the rectangular table so that he could sit next to her while they reviewed the contract. "As you can see, this is the contract for Charlie's secretary."

Chandos appeared surprised. "Did you draft this?"

Theo wished she could have said yes. "No. I did sit in on the meeting when it was drafted. I made copies of all the contracts from Stanwood and anyone else who would give them to me. When we attain the age of sixteen, we begin visiting our married sisters to learn how different estates are managed and the challenges in different parts of the kingdom."

"It almost sounds like an apprenticeship. How did it come about?"

"I suppose it is, in a manner of speaking." She was surprised he was interested. "I was quite young when the system developed. As I understand it, after Louisa, Charlotte, and Dotty wed they were writing to and meeting with Grace about running the different households and estates. At some point early on, they decided it would be helpful to the rest of us to be able to have practical experience on something other than our home estates."

He leaned back in the chair. "Have you gone to Scotland?"

Theo resisted a chuckle. "Indeed. Unlike with my other sisters, who just had to establish that they knew what they were doing, Alice had a more difficult time. They called her a Sassenach, which means English in Gaelic, and it is not meant in a good way. She had to prove she was much stronger than she looked and more stubborn than they were. At one point, one of the servants—" No, that was not technically correct. "You have to understand that everyone who works in the house is actually a family member of some kind. So, they are not the usual type of servant. In any event, one of them was rude to her, and she took him by the ear and marched him to where she wanted him to be and told him he'd not get dinner if he did not finish the chore to her satisfaction."

Chandos raised a skeptical brow. "And did he?"

"Not to her satisfaction, no. She refused to allow him in the hall to dine and told the kitchen staff and others that if they fed him, they would receive the same treatment. That did the trick." A different footman brought a tea tray and Theo poured. "The man was one who, apparently, challenged everyone."

"I gather she is now established."

"Yes. They treat her as if she is one of them." She glanced at the contract. "Let us go through this."

They spent the next hour poring through the terms.

Chandos's black brows pulled together as he read. "When the period of employment ends, is it usual for the salary to remain the same?"

Theo was glad he was paying attention. "I suppose some do. In our family we like to keep our servants and employees. Therefore, we raise their wages. For the regular servants there is an increase built into the contracts. When it comes to employees, it is negotiated in the new contract.

"It is?" He put his elbow on the table and cradled his chin in his hand. "Why? Why not do it with the servants as well?"

That was an excellent question. "My understanding is that one reason is there are many more servants than employees, and employees have more agency. They are, after all at the very least gentry. Some, such as Mr. Whiting, are part of the aristocracy. Also, their duties are more likely to vary from employment period to employment period."

Straightening, he nodded. "I can see that. Such as, at the present time, I will have my secretary do what I perceive are the most necessary tasks. Yet, as time goes on, he will take on more assignments."

"Exactly." This was surprisingly enjoyable. She never actually considered that Chandos thought about anything but himself. Yet, Theo had been wrong. He was, in fact, rather impressive. "An example is when Charlie had his secretary come to Town to obtain the special license."

"I remember that." Chandos pulled a sheet of foolscap over to him, picked up a pencil and made several notes, then slid it over to her. "This is what I believe I will need immediately and in the near future."

Open, read, and sort correspondence.
Discuss with me the contents.
Reduce to writing my responses.
Keep my calendar, send copies to my mother, valet, butler, and anyone else I designate.
Become familiar with the senior staff and employees at the various estates.
Travel with me as required. Travel alone as needed.

"Do you have anything else to add?" Leo watched as Theo read the list.

"I would include whether or not you wish him to take his meals with you. Due to his status, he will not dine with the staff."

That was a good point. "I will state that it is up to him. If he wishes to dine with me then he can."

She appeared to think about it for a moment or so. "That will be satisfactory. Do you want to add the discretionary clause? I would advise it."

It would protect him from his secretary talking about him. Although, he couldn't imagine the man would. The punishment was quite severe. The loss of the remainder of his salary. "Yes. Just to be on the safe side." Leo straightened in the chair. "Where is the most efficient place to have this drawn up quickly?"

"We can ask Matt's secretary to do it. He has a clerk."

"Very well then." Leo stood and held out his hand for Theo. "I want to get this done as soon as possible. I really am drowning in correspondence."

Instead of walking ahead of him, she took his arm. "I hope he is in."

"When is Stanwood arriving?" It had to be soon. The last letter Chandos had received stated her brother et al. would be in Town for the first Almack's assembly. That was in less than a week.

Theo glanced up at him and grinned. "Tomorrow. Constance came to tell me just as I was dressing to ride with you."

"Excellent." He hoped Mary would be with them. Leo had heard talk that she might remain with Lady Stern to take classes with the lady's daughter. Not that he would tell Theo that. She was so ambivalent about having a Season it could very well make her decide to leave Town or, at the very least, cause the blue devils.

They arrived at a door next to Worthington's study, and she knocked.

"Come, please."

The man behind the desk looked to be in his middle forties. He had thinning light brown hair and spectacles. "Lady Theo, how may I help you?"

"Do you have time to draft an employment contract for his grace?"

The man glanced over at his clerk, a younger man sitting at a much smaller desk. "Louis?"

He glanced up. "Yes, sir. It should not take long."

Theo handed him the papers. "Thank you. When should we return?"

"Can you give me an hour? That will be sufficient time to make two originals and a copy."

Leo inclined his head. "Yes, thank you. I greatly appreciate this."

"We will return in about an hour." She took his arm, and they left the room. "What shall we do until then?"

That was the wrong question to ask him. What he wanted to do was find an empty room and kiss her senseless. "I'm not sure." The sound of horses galloping came from the main staircase. "It is time for dinner?"

Theo opened her brooch watch. "Not yet. Grace pushed back the time until seven."

They strode to the hall as the children reached the last landing. Hugh led the charge.

"Carriages!" one of them called as they raced across the hall to the door a footman had fortunately opened.

Theo's normally smooth forehead wrinkled. "Who could it be?"

Leo wanted to know too. "Let's go see."

They waited as the girls dashed across the hall, then followed. *Carriages* had been the correct description. There were three. One for baggage, one for babies, and a third for the adults and one almost adult.

"Mary!" He sensed Theo struggling to walk and not run to the coach. Fortunately, the path was short. She wrapped her arms around her sister. "I am so glad you are here!"

A footman handed down another girl about Mary's age. She hugged Theo back and turned. "You know Martha Stern." Mary pulled the girl forward. "She is staying with Dotty for the Season. We will be sharing classes and such."

At first glance, Leo could see Martha definitely had the look of Lady Stern, girl's mother as well as her sisters, Dotty, the Marchioness of Merton and Henrietta, Viscountess Fotherby.

Theo hugged Martha as well, yet he could feel the tension or maybe disappointment in Theo. She had wanted Mary to be here for her. "I am very glad to see you! Welcome to London."

"The last time I was here was when Dotty and Dom married." The girl smiled. "This is going to be so much fun. Dotty told Mama that as Mary and I would come out together, we should spend more time together."

Theo nodded tightly. "That is an excellent idea. She is right."

Lady Worthington and Worthington joined them. Leo took Theo's arm, drawing her away. "You know that this is what Mary needs. She cannot wait around until you have the time to spend with her."

"I know." Theo rapidly blinked her eyes. "Thank you. I was being selfish."

"Not selfish." He lightly brushed away a tear that had fallen on her cheek. "You simply didn't want anything to change. That's normal. Most of us like to keep things the way they are."

"Yes." She nodded and gave a watery smile.

Leo handed her his handkerchief. "Dry your tears before she sees them."

She dabbed her eyes and blew her nose, then started to hand it back to him. "I will have this laundered first."

"Thank you." He chuckled and was surprised to find her joining him.

"I feel much better. I do not know how you did it, but you seemed to know just what I needed."

"I know how close you are with your sister, and how much you've missed her. You had no knowledge that she would bring a friend. It had to have been an unwelcome shock."

"It was." Theo slowly shook her head. "It is good for her to have someone with whom to spend time."

"Someone her own age, who is engaged in the same activities as she is."

"Yes. I think Mary was concerned that she would be left alone." Theo gazed over his shoulder. "No. I know she was. She has been spending more time with Charlie and Oriana. And, I suppose, Martha. The Carpenters and Sterns have been neighbors for years."

He took Theo's cold hands and felt a jolt. "Perhaps they need each other."

"You are right. She nodded sharply. "It is time we make our own way like our other sisters have."

"While remaining close. I've noticed that about your family."

"It is something on which we have prided ourselves. Our family just grows. No one goes away."

It was a family he hoped to enlarge by his presence. "Are you ready to face everyone again?"

"I am." She gave him a real smile this time. "I imagine Grace will order tea and dinner will be put back. Would you like to dine with us?"

His cook was going to be upset, but he couldn't miss the opportunity to stay with Theo. "I would be delighted."

When they turned to follow the others into the house, Worthington caught Leo's eye and gave a slight nod. He had to think that was a good sign. Then Mary glanced at him and her lips rose at the ends. Was she happy with him too? Did she know he wanted to marry her sister? What was he thinking? Of course she knew. And, apparently, she was on his side. If only Theo was.

Dinner was so entertaining that Leo decided his children would be allowed to dine at the table when they were of an age. He returned home to find a missive from his mother requesting he attend her. But first, he wrote a quick note asking Whiting to meet with him in the morning.

Leo climbed the stairs to his mother's apartments, knocked and entered.

Her companion greeted him. "She is waiting."

"Chandos." Mama's tone took him by surprise. "When am I going to meet this paragon you have decided to wed?"

"I thought you met her at Lady Bellamny's."

She flipped her hand dismissively. "An introduction and a few pleasantries only."

"Have you been invited to Lady Thornhill's viewing?" That would make it much less fraught. He was not ready for Theo to come here.

"I have and shall attend." His mother gave him a sharp look. "As will she and her family. That will do nicely." Mama waved him away. "You may go now."

Wonderful. Now he had to worry about what she would say to Theo. He didn't need more complications. But it looked as if he was going to get them.

CHAPTER FOURTEEN

Before Theo went into dinner, she and Chandos had stopped by the secretary's office and reviewed the contract. As she knew it would be, it was exactly as he wanted. The secretary assured him the document would be sent to Chandos House immediately.

She was interested that during the meal, he held conversations with the children, ranging from their favorite games to what they were studying in class. He even got into a conversation with the girls on their plans to go on a Grand Tour and what they should visit. Theo had never seen this side of him before.

Later, she and Mary met in Theo's chamber.

"I am so glad you are here." It finally struck Theo how lost she had been without her sister.

"I am happy I came as well." Mary's countenance was solemn. "I almost remained in the country. Then Dotty had the idea to bring Martha to Town."

"You would have deserted me?" Theo did not know what to think about such an idea of abandonment.

"Theo, both of us have to work out a way to go on with different lives."

How did she continue to forget that? Perhaps because she was not seriously looking for a husband. "You are right. I just do not like it."

"It is the way of life." Mary was quiet for a few seconds. "I like Chandos a great deal."

"He is becoming a good friend." Until the Season began in earnest, and he too went his own way. "Unfortunately, he has a number of habits I will not abide." Then she remembered that her sister and the others were not supposed to have arrived until later. "What made you come today?"

"Oriana and Dotty originally thought it would be easier to travel more slowly." Mary grinned. "But neither of them really like slow travel. We were going to stay at Alice and St. Albans's estate, but by the time we were at the turnoff, they decided to continue to Town."

"Will you be allowed to attend Lady Thornhill's viewing tomorrow?"

"No." Mary shook her head. "Grace said that it will be more like an afternoon salon or soirée, and it would not be proper."

And that was it in a nutshell. Mary would be allowed to participate in very few, if any, of the activities which Theo was attending. Chandos was right. "I am very glad Martha was able to come to Town."

Tears filled Mary's eyes, but she nodded. "I am as well. It will make this Season much easier."

Theo reached over and embraced her sister. They stayed that way for a long time. "I will always be here for you. Even if I do find a gentleman and wed."

Mary wiped her eyes. "What do you mean 'even if you do wed'? You will find the right gentleman and you will marry him."

"I shall try." More than that, Theo could not promise. Other than Augusta, Theo did not believe any of her sisters had been so pococurante about marriage.

Mary yawned. "I am for my bed. It has been a long, tiring day."

"I agree." It had been an emotionally exhausting day. "Will you be allowed to ride with me in the morning?"

She shook her head again. "No. As you and I did, Martha and I will ride ante-noon." She smiled. "Sedately and properly chaperoned."

"Ugh. I will see you at breakfast."

"You will." Mary jumped off the bed and went to the door. "Good night."

"Good night to you."

Payne entered as Mary left. "Let's get you to bed. The sun is rising earlier each day, and you need your sleep."

Theo supposed she should start taking the Season more seriously. Dark circles under her eyes would not be acceptable.

The next morning, Theo was mounting Epione when Chandos rode up and executed the most elegant bow she had ever seen from the back of a horse. "Good morning, my lady."

"Good morn to you. That was nicely done." She turned her mare toward Hill Street.

"It occurred to me that using the social graces I possess would be useful." He caught up to her and rode by her side. Mick and the other groom followed behind.

Useful for what? What did it matter? "Yes. I came to something of the same conclusion last night after Mary and I spoke."

Chandos directed a sympathetic look toward Theo. "What did you talk about?"

"She made it clear that our activities this Season will not often cross paths. She also told me that it was my duty to find a gentleman to marry."

That was excellent news. One of his major difficulties with her was that she hadn't been certain that she wanted to wed. "What did you think about that?"

"Augusta was the only other of us who had not wished to marry."

"Because she wanted to attend university." Leo watched as Theo bit her bottom lip, and he wished he could kiss it.

"Yes. I, on the other hand, do not have that excuse. In fact, the only reason I had was that Mary would not be able to come out with me." Theo shrugged lightly. "It was rather silly, actually."

"I don't believe that." He infused his voice with as much certainty as he could. "I think what you have been feeling is understandable. Every time I visited when you and she were there together, you were like two peas in a pod. Always together. Always whispering." She glanced at him, and he grinned.

"You were right when you said it was good that she has a friend with her."

"And so do you. Isn't that the reason you befriended Miss Pettigrew? Deep down you knew you did not want to be alone?"

Theo's rosy lips formed a thin line, but her expression was thoughtful. "Charlotte was the one who suggested it, but yes. I agreed because I thought we could help one another."

They were in sight of the Pettigrew residence. "Look who is here before us."

Theo's eyes widened. "Marrow. Did you know he would be here?"

"No. However, it doesn't surprise me." They slowed their horses. "It also wouldn't surprise me if there is a betrothal announcement soon."

"That would be lovely." Theo's smile was a bit wistful. Whether it was for her friend or for herself he didn't know. Still, with Sarah taken care of, Theo could turn her talents to another lady or perhaps a gentleman who required help.

"I think so as well." If only it could be the same with her and him. Then again, he'd agreed that she needed to have a Season. "Let's join them."

They rode to the gate together and were happy to find the Park empty. As before he and Theo raced to the oak tree. Asclepius still showed no disposition to race ahead of the mare. "My mother received an invitation to the viewing today."

Theo gave him a droll look. "This private viewing is becoming larger and larger. Will you escort her?"

"I thought I'd come to Worthington House, and we could

travel over with your family. I wonder if Oriana has received an invitation."

"I do not know." Theo tilted her head to the side. "I rather doubt it, but the card Grace received instructed her to bring the family. That includes Charlie and Oriana."

"I suppose it must." They walked their horses toward the Serpentine. "Almack's is this week. Is there anything else?"

"The first ball of the Season at Lady Harrington's."

Leo hoped he had received a card. If not, he'd contact the lady's husband and request one. Then he remembered a piece of advice he'd been given. "May I have the supper dance?"

Theo gave him an odd look. I was a combination of curiosity and disbelief. "Yes, you may."

"Excellent." He wanted to pat himself on the back, but this was a small step. They reached Marrow and Miss Pettigrew. "Are you attending the Harrington ball?"

Her face lit up. "We are. Lady Worthington has been so kind in informing her friends that we are in Town."

Marrow glanced at Leo. "I'll have to see if I've received an invitation." Marrow directed his attention to Miss Pettigrew. "If I have been invited, I would be honored to stand up with you."

A blush rose to her face. "I accept."

He glanced at Theo. "And you as well, my lady."

Theo appeared pleased. Even though she must have known it would be offered. "You may have any set but the supper dance."

"The first country set." Marrow waited for her assent, then turned to Miss Pettigrew. "The supper dance sounds like an excellent one for us."

"I agree."

Leo was bound to request a set from the lady as well. "May I have your first country set?"

"You may, your grace."

By the end of the rather inane conversation, they were all smiling. Gone were the days when he could simply tell a whore that he was her next partner. When he and Theo were betrothed, he'd be able to commandeer all her dances. Albeit with her permission.

The four of them headed for the gate.

Theo leaned over. "Are you joining us for breakfast this morning?"

"I wish I could. But Whiting is coming over at ten, and I must prepare for that."

"Yes." She gave him an encouraging look. "That is more important."

Leo wouldn't normally agree. But he did need a secretary. "When are you leaving for the viewing?"

"After tea. You and your mother can join us."

"I must ask her. I will send a note."

They left Miss Pettigrew and Marrow at her house, and Leo rode on to Berkeley Square with Theo. Instead of allowing her to dismount herself, he clasped his hands around her waist, and she slid down so close to his body that it was hard to let her go. "I'll see you this afternoon."

"Until then." He thought she sounded slightly out of breath, but it could have been his imagination.

Bloody hellhounds. Was he grasping at straws? How could he know what she thought? He remounted his horse and glanced over to where she stood. Above her, movement in a window caught his attention. Had someone been watching them? If so, who? And did it matter? He didn't have time to be distracted. What he needed to do was to discover if he had been invited to the Harrington ball and find out how to ensure that he'd receive cards for all the events to which Theo was invited. Would his mother know? Of course she would. Still, this was the first time she'd been in Town since his father died. For a moment, the pain of that death seized Leo's heart, and he had trouble breathing. God, how he missed him. The one thing Leo did know was that Papa would approve of the changes Leo had made, and of his intended bride.

He arrived home and threw the reins to a groom. The door

was opened when he reached the steps. "Is her grace still in her chambers?"

"Yes, your grace. She has asked to be informed when you arrive home."

"Please tell her that I will bathe and join her for breakfast."

Hoover bowed. "Yes, your grace."

Taking the stairs two by two, Leo reached his apartments and was pleased to find a bath being drawn in the bathing chamber his father had added.

Matson assisted him with his coat and boots, and Leo stripped off his clothing. "How did you know I'd be home?"

"You have an early meeting."

That made sense. "Excellent man." Leo sank into the large bathtub. Scrubbed himself. And waited for his valet to pour water over him. "I'm joining my mother for breakfast."

No sooner had he spoken the words when a bucket of water sluiced over him.

He arrived in the breakfast room at the same time as Mama. "Good morning."

"Good morning to you, my dear." She held several cards. "I have invitations to discuss with you."

"Have you received one from Lady Harrington?"

A line formed between his mother's eyes. "Let me look. The name does not sound familiar."

"If not, I'll speak to Lord Harrington."

Mama frowned. "Harrington, Harrington. That is Lady Markham's son, is it not?"

Leo, having taken a bite of eggs and ham, chewed quickly and swallowed. "Yes."

"I am going to her at home today. I will ask her if I can procure an invitation." She shuffled through the cards. "Actually, it appears as if I must make the rounds. I renewed my acquaintance with several ladies at the soirée, but clearly, not enough of them." She smiled at him. "Perhaps I should speak with Lady Worthington about which events she is planning to attend."

"Will that not be obvious?"

His mother's chin rose. "Not the way I will ask."

He could only nod. This really was her milieu, not his. "I'll leave it to you. Whiting is arriving in"—Leo opened his pocket watch and looked at it—"less than an hour." It was amazing how quickly time passed when one was busy. "I hope we can come to terms."

"You must have a contract," Mama said.

"Theo helped me with it yesterday. It's in my study."

"I am growing more and more interested in meeting her."

That's what Leo was afraid of. He hoped his mother didn't scare Theo off.

Mary turned from the window to find Grace behind her. "He is very attentive of her."

Grace nodded her agreement. "We all think it would be a good match."

"You mean everyone except Theo." Mary understood Theo's concerns about Chandos's past behavior. It was a shame Chandos could not have approached her earlier, giving him more time for Theo to get to know the man he was becoming. That he could not was making his path much more difficult. On the other hand, he had agreed that he must wait until she was out.

"Indeed. I am afraid she will listen to the rumors surrounding his reputation and prior actions."

"I am sure she will." Mary turned to go downstairs. "I will help where I can." This was not going to be easy.

Her sister put her hand on her shoulder. "I know you will. I simply do not know if any of our assistance will work."

Neither did Mary. Theo had very definite ideas about what she wanted in a husband. And about what she did not want. Chandos would have to tread carefully but firmly if he wanted to win her hand.

CHAPTER FIFTEEN

Theo waited in the hall, dressed in what she had been assured was a very stylish carriage gown in pale yellow with a matching spencer.

"Are you excited?" Mary asked.

"I am." Theo could not hide how much she looked forward to the viewing. "It will be my first adult event."

Grace entered the hall from the corridor to her study. "Are you ready?"

Surely this was not everyone. "Where are the others?"

"Your sisters and the gentlemen will meet us there." Grace pulled on her gloves.

The doorbell chimed, and Thorton opened the front door. A footman stood there. "His grace of Chandos and the Dowager Duchess of Chandos have arrived. His grace would like to know if you would do him the honor of riding with him."

Theo glanced around the footman at the large town coach standing in front of the house.

Her sister appeared to be in thought. "Yes. We will be happy to ride with him and the duchess." She turned to Thorton. "Please inform the stables that I will require the carriage to arrive at Thornhill House in two hours."

"Yes, my lady." He bowed.

Theo did not understand. "Why two hours?"

"That will be sufficient time to view the artifacts and converse with the other guests." Grace raised a brow. "One does not wish to be the last to depart."

"I suppose that makes sense." In a strange way.

"Good afternoon." Chandos had replaced the footman. "Allow me to escort you to the coach."

Normally, Theo would simply take his arm, but she had to wait for her sister.

"Thank you." Grace took one arm, Theo took the other.

Naturally, he assisted Grace into the vehicle first, then Theo. Grace took the seat next to the duchess and Theo sat next to Chandos.

"Mother." He motioned with his head to the duchess. "May I introduce you to Lady Worthington and her sister Lady Theo Vivers?"

Turning slightly, her grace smiled politely at Grace. "I believe I knew your mother, Lady Stanwood. She was a few years older than I, but I remember her being very kind to a girl just out."

"Yes, I have been told that." Grace returned the smile. "I only hope that I am half as good-natured as she was."

Then the duchess glanced at Theo. "Good afternoon. I suppose this must be your first real event. I trust you are prepared for it."

"It is a pleasure to meet you." She had the distinct feeling that Chandos's mother did not like her for some reason. Theo assumed a polite smile. "I am, your grace." She would have thanked the duchess for inquiring, but it had been a statement, not a question.

Chandos caught her attention, cut a look at his mother, and almost rolled his eyes. "Well, then. Now that the formalities are out of the way, I propose we enjoy the rest of the afternoon."

"I understand the viewing will be well attended," the duchess said as she adjusted her shawl.

"That is my impression as well," Grace responded. A small smile played around her lips. "I believe we will all know several of the guests."

The faint crease between the duchess's brows deepened. "Including your sisters?"

Once again, Theo pasted a polite smile on her countenance. "Indeed, your grace. My married sisters and their husbands are attending as is my brother Stanwood and his wife."

"As well as Marrow, Miss Pettigrew, and Lady Pettigrew," Chandos added. A twinkle entered his eyes. "I would be surprised if we did not see Lady Bellamny and Lady Cowper."

Was he teasing his mother? "I would be as well."

"I have not seen Emily Cowper for years," his mother said. "I do hope you are correct." Then the duchess's eyes narrowed at Theo. "How do you know Lady Cowper?"

"My sister knows all the Patronesses," Grace inserted smoothly. "Although she is just now out, all my younger sisters were with us during the Seasons. I made certain to take them out for rides during the Fashionable Hour. Lady Bellamny has been a family friend all my life."

"I see." The duchess appeared not confused, but as if she had the wind taken out of her sails.

This had been a strangely stilted conversation. Fortunately, it was over. They had arrived at Thornhill House.

A footman opened the door and bowed. Chandos jumped down and handed out first Grace, then his mother, and Theo. Grace and the duchess linked arms and proceeded up the steps.

Chandos took Theo's arm. "Don't allow her to worry you. She can be a bit of a dragon."

"She does not bother me at all. Although, I do have the feeling that she does not like me for some reason. Does she give that impression to most younger ladies?"

"I have no idea." He pulled a face.

"When you decide to wed, I suggest you warn the lady you choose."

His lips were suddenly too close to her ear and a shiver ran down her neck. "If she can frighten a lady, then that lady is not meant for me."

Theo shook off the feeling. "I suppose you are correct. She will, after all, be a duchess."

"The first thing she has to be is a strong woman who is true to herself."

Theo's jaw almost dropped. She had never thought to hear such a sentiment from him. Yet, there was no time to respond. They had just reached Lady Thornhill, and Grace was waiting.

"My lady." Grace motioned Theo forward. "Please meet my sister, Lady Theo Vivers."

Lady Thornhill was a tall, slender woman dressed in a long red robe covered with flower embroidery. Her silver hair was apparently held up with sticks. She looked very much like some of the paintings Theo had seen on Chinese vases. "I am delighted, my dear. You looked very much like your sister Rothwell."

"Thank you, my lady." Theo was happy to be able to give a genuine smile. "I am looking forward to seeing your artifacts."

Lady Thornhill laughed lightly. "I must admit some of them are quite old, other things are what we thought interesting without regard to age." She glanced at Chandos. "You must be the Duke of Chandos. Your mother said you were escorting Lady Theo."

Smiling, he bowed and took her ladyship's hand. "It is my privilege to be allowed to escort her, my lady. I am also delighted to meet you."

Pink colored Lady Thornhill's cheeks. "You, sir, are making me blush."

Lord Thornhill, who had been silent until now, chuckled, and put his hand on his wife's arm. "No flirting with my lady. You save that for the young, unmarried ones."

She tapped his arm with her fan. "Reginald." Before Theo and Chandos left, Lady Thornhill leaned over to Theo and whispered, "Keep that one."

If they had had time, Theo would have assured her ladyship that she had no designs on him, but Grace was motioning for them to move along.

Leo had caught what Lady Thornhill said to Theo. And he'd seen her expression of surprise. She really did not know he intended to make her his wife. He'd suspected it, but that look of surprise impressed it upon him as nothing else had been able to. His mother, who was speaking with a matron who was accompanied by a young lady, attempted to get his attention. He'd told her he wasn't interested in meeting other women, and, it appeared, she had decided to ignore him. He inclined his head to acknowledge her, and moved on, staying close to Theo and Lady Worthington.

Footmen carried around various drinks and foods. He secured Theo a lemonade and himself a glass of claret. Shrimps that had been coated with some kind of batter and held together by sticks were offered and they both accepted. He glanced around. The large hall reminded him of a medieval castle with rooms and corridors off of it. Each room was decorated differently. "Where shall we begin?"

Theo chewed and swallowed. "These shrimps are excellent. I wonder what the batter is. It is very light."

"I don't know." He shook his head. "I suppose we could ask. Does one parlor speak to you over another?"

A footman arrived, and she deposited the stick on his tray. "Let us start at the first room and visit them in order."

That was his Theo. Ever organized. "The blue room it is." As they walked in, he was immediately transported to Greece. "I can't believe this."

"What?" Her lapis eyes gazed up at him.

"The mural on the wall looks exactly like some of the villages I visited in Greece." He strolled around, amazed that the inside of a house had been brought to life. "The pots and textiles, the floor and wall tiles. They are all authentic."

Theo's eyes widened as she scanned the room. "They really made a room that replicates a Greek house?"

He nodded. "The furniture. Everything."

The expression of amazement on her beautiful face made him want to hold her in his arms. "I would love to see this in Greece."

"You should have the opportunity." Leo had, of course, heard about her nieces' plans for a Grand Tour. He now wished she'd had the opportunity. "Shall we visit another country?"

"Yes." Her face was bright with excitement. "Let us."

It was as if they were moving around the Mediterranean countries. Then they left Europe and moved to Egypt, India, and Asia. From what he could see, the most complete parlors were of Japan and China. When did the Thornhills do all that traveling?

Leo and Theo were in India when Kenilworth and his wife found them.

"We have been searching for you," Lady Kenilworth said.

Kenilworth raised a brow at Leo. "Your mother's been looking for you as well."

Of course she was. "She can look to her heart's content. Where did you last see her?"

"In Portugal," Lady Kenilworth replied. "Why are you avoiding her?"

"She keeps trying to introduce me to young ladies." The words were out before he'd thought about them.

"You must know that Chandos does not wish to wed," Theo said nonchalantly as she studied a little statue of a goddess with three breasts.

Her sister gave him a look that clearly asked, now what are you going to do?

"What do you think she does with three of them?" Theo mused.

Leo shrugged. "Maybe she always has twins or three babies."

"No." She shook her head. "If she wanted to feed twins by herself, she would need four breasts."

Kenilworth turned his back to them, his shoulders shaking.

His wife gave him a disgruntled look. "They are probably meant as symbols. When you see Lady Thornhill, you should ask her."

"Good God!" Kenilworth blurted out. "Not in company. Write her a note."

Theo stared at him as if he'd lost his mind. "I am quite up to snuff enough to know not to say something like that in public. Thank you very much."

Behind them someone coughed. "Excuse me, but I couldn't help overhearing. She is the goddess Meenakshi. She was a Hindu warrior goddess. It was said that the third . . . er . . . breast would disappear when she met a man worthy to be her husband."

"Thank you." Theo beamed. "Now my brother-in-law does not have to worry about me saying something embarrassing in public."

The gentleman bowed. "I am happy to be of help." He glanced at his watch. "I must go. I hope you enjoy the rest of your visit."

"Thank you," Theo said. "It has been fascinating."

"Please tell my aunt. She is always a bit concerned about what the young ladies think."

He bowed again and left the room.

"That was strange," Lady Kenilworth said. "I wonder why he did not introduce himself."

Leo had no answer for that but decided to venture a thought. "Shy?"

"Or embarrassed that he was explaining a statue with three breasts to a young lady," Kenilworth said.

Theo nodded. "That is much more likely. If he was shy, he would not have said anything."

She was right. As usual. Leo looked at her sister. "Why were you looking for us?"

"To tell you that we will take you home. Grace received a message and had to leave."

Theo glanced at him. "Have we seen everything?"

That was a good question. "I have no idea." He looked at Kenilworth. "We have been all around the Mediterranean, Egypt, China, Japan, and here."

"And been fed food and drink from each area," Theo added.

"Russia," Lady Kenilworth said. "That was my least favorite. There is a great deal of gold and not much else."

"And dozens of young ladies," Kenilworth whispered to Leo.

Theo lifted one shoulder in a shrug. "In that case, we can go if you wish."

"I shall leave a note to my mother to take the coach." They made their way to the hall, where Leo was provided with pen and paper. "Please find the Duchess of Chandos and give this to her."

"Your grace." The butler bowed. "She left you a message that she went home and took the coach."

Theo covered her mouth and laughed lightly.

"I am glad we were in agreement." Leo held his arm out for her.

She took it. "We still need to find Lady Thornhill and tell her we are leaving."

"If you please, my lady. Her ladyship said that she does not expect anyone to search for her. I will pass on the message."

"Thank you. Please tell her we had a wonderful time, and that her nephew was very helpful."

"Lord Holland, my lady?" The servant seemed surprised. "I shall indeed tell her."

A footman entered from the front door. "Lord and Lady Kenilworth's carriage is waiting."

Leo didn't want to give Theo up. Riding with her in the mornings and seeing her at other times during the day was not enough.

"You forgot to tell me how your discussion with Mr. Whiting went."

"Well." Leo had forgotten all about it. "He is moving into quarters in my house for the nonce. We'll see how it works out for both of us. Today, I left him hard at work on the correspondence that arrived."

"Excellent." She smiled as he handed her into the coach and followed. "Did he want to make any changes to the contract?"

"Not at all. He was very impressed by it." He grinned. "Thank you. It always helps to have one's employees and servants have a good opinion of one."

"I have never heard that vocalized before."

Probably because her family were all sensible of what was owed to those who worked for and depended on them. "Would you like to ride with me this afternoon?"

"I almost forgot," Kenilworth said. "Your phaeton arrived complete with a pair of grays. I took the liberty of sending a footman with a message to have them ready when you arrive."

She turned to Leo and smiled broadly. "Would you like to ride with me this afternoon?"

"Yes. Absolutely, I would." All the world would see them together. Perhaps that would stop the idea that he could ever be interested in anyone else.

CHAPTER SIXTEEN

It was all Theo could do to keep from bouncing in her seat as they drew closer to Worthington House. She had worked on the design for the carriage and was excited to see it completed. The high-perched phaeton's glossy, royal-blue body shone in the sun. The trim was in gold, and the wheels were painted deep yellow. The seats were in medium tan leather. Standing hitched to the carriage were two matched grays held by Mick.

Theo sucked in a breath and let it out. "It is even more beautiful than I thought it would be!"

"Look at that pair." Chandos stared out the window of the coach. "Who selected them?"

"I would dearly love to take all the credit," Con drawled." But the truth of the matter is that I merely accompanied Lady Evesham to the gentleman who had them for sale. She was one who approved the purchase."

Lady Evesham knew more about horseflesh than almost anyone. "I am glad she was there. She and Grace have been friends for years."

"You, my dear, did an excellent job with the carriage." Charlotte smiled at Theo. "Is that a place for packages and a fold-down seat in the back?"

"It is." Theo could not wait to try it out. "In the event I wanted to drive it when I went shopping, I knew I would require a place for packages and a groom or footman."

The coach stopped, and Chandos jumped out before the steps could be put down. He offered his hand to Theo, but when she took it, he wrapped his arm around her waist and swung her out. "Goodness." She had to catch her breath. "That was unexpected."

He gave her an enigmatic smile. "It was effective."

Really, he should not have done that. "It must be. I am standing on the pavement."

"Are you ready?" He placed her hand on his arm and led her to the carriage. "I shall help you in."

Once again, the stairs had not been let down, and Theo did not feel like waiting. "Very well."

He lifted her up and her feet found the floor of the carriage. Chandos did not let go until she was seated. "Thank you." She hoped her voice did not sound as breathy to him as it did to her. The phaeton dipped as he climbed in. "Are you ready?"

Leaning back, he folded his arms over his chest. "When you are."

The groom, holding the leader, glanced at her. When she nodded, he stepped away and she gave the pair their office. She started slowly then gained a bit of speed in order to feather the corner out of the square. As she knew they would, the grays had excellent action. "They are magnificent."

"Whoever Lady Evesham is, she is an excellent judge of horseflesh." From the corner of her eye, Theo caught Chandos glance at her. "I would like to make her acquaintance."

"She will be at my come out ball."

"Will I be invited?"

"I cannot see why you would not be." She drove through the gate into the Park and took her place on Rotten Row. The first carriage they saw was Lady Bellamny's. Theo pulled up beside her. "Good afternoon, my lady."

"I see you finally got your phaeton." Her ladyship pulled out a quizzing glass on a stick. "Very pretty driving. I saw you enter." She leveled the glass at Chandos. "Are you brave or besotted, your grace?"

Theo was going to die of embarrassment. Why would her ladyship think he was besotted?

He inclined his head. "Lady Theo is an excellent driver, my lady."

That was diplomatic. She gave Lady Bellamny a polite smile. "We will see you later."

"Have a lovely ride." She waved as a landau came up behind them.

"Do they handle as easily as they appear to?" Chandos grinned. "Or are you simply an excellent whip?"

As long as he was going to gammon her, she would respond in kind. "I am an excellent whip, of course." His eyes filled with mirth, and she could understand how women would fall all over him. "Although, to be fair to the horses, they are very easy to handle."

"Not now, but someday, I would like to try them." She did not understand why Chandos sounded wistful.

"Someday you shall." They continued around the Park, greeting and nodding at those they met. Theo was surprised at how many people she already knew.

Sarah waved. She and her mother sat in a landau while Lord Marrow, riding next to them, tipped his hat.

"I wonder how long we'll have to wait before they make an announcement," Chandos commented.

"I would suppose another few weeks." Theo would be surprised if it occurred before then. "At least not until her come out ball."

He furrowed his brow. "When is that? Do you know?"

"In three weeks, I believe." She would have to ask Grace. "It is after mine. They did not make their final decision to come to Town until much later."

"And yours is?" He raised one dark brow.

"In two weeks." The invitations are to go out tomorrow. "Grace's secretary is to insure they are done."

"Everyone seems to have secretaries," he mused.

"Some ladies have companions that perform the same tasks. Yet, I believe, they mostly are widows and poor relations."

"Yes. I think you're right. My mother's companion is a widow and is responsible for responding to all invitations."

They left the Park and Theo headed toward Berkeley Square. "Shall we go to Gunter's?"

"Yes indeed." He rubbed his chin. "I wonder if those two girls will be there staring at us again."

"I suppose we shall see." Theo hoped they had found something better to do.

The waiter ran out when they pulled to the side of the road. He glanced up and seemed to hesitate for a moment before reciting the list of specialties.

"I shall have the Gruyère."

"I believe I will have the Riesling," Chandos said.

"That sounds good as well." She liked Riesling wine.

"You will have to tell me if you enjoy it." He fell silent, his forehead creased as if he was concerned about something.

"Are you having some sort of difficulty?"

"No." He shook his head, but his expression did not change. "Not a difficulty." He turned and looked at her fully. "What I said about not wanting to meet young ladies. I did not mean you."

Was that all? Theo smiled. "I know that. You are already acquainted with me. You know that I do not have any designs on you."

"Indeed." Leo didn't know why he just hadn't kept his mouth shut. Now she was more firmly convinced than before that he was not looking to marry.

The ices arrived and they each took a taste of the other's.

"I cannot decide between the wine or the cheese." Theo took another bite of hers.

"I know what you mean. The cheese has a depth, but the wine is light and has a slightly fruity taste."

"Hmm. Perhaps the cheese now, while there is still a slight chill in the air, and the wine when it becomes warmer."

"Cannot we eat both in both types of weather?" Why did she want to categorize them?

"I suppose." Her forehead wrinkled, and he wanted to soothe it. "I like for things to have their places."

That was interesting. "Does that include people?"

She finished her ice. "I have never thought about it. But it might. It makes it easier to say this person belongs here and that person there. Or this person had this function and that person another."

"Is that not somewhat simplistic?" He did not want to insult her. "Especially for someone as intelligent as you are?"

She gazed at him as if trying to work out a puzzle. "How do you look at people?"

"I believe everyone, or most people, have different facets that they show at different times or with different people. For example, your sister Lady Worthington. At times she is a mother and might be stern or worried or playful. At other times she is an elegant and graceful lady. And she also has large houses and properties to manage or help to manage. She draws on a different part of herself for her different positions." Theo tilted her head to one side and continued to gaze at him. "You also have different facets. You are a younger sister, an aunt, a manager of servants and estates. You must behave differently in each of those roles."

"I understand." Her forehead smoothed. "It is the same with you."

"It is. We also grow and mature." How did he turn this conversation to one where she might understand that he had changed? "What might have been entertaining for a few years no longer has the appeal it once did. Fortunately, or unfortunately, one sees that more with gentlemen than ladies."

"Such as when gentlemen drink to excess, gamble, and do other things?"

"Yes. Most of us must change to have the lives we truly want."

"And will you do that eventually?"

Before he could answer, the waiter came back to collect the dishes and the payment. Then Kenilworth and his lady stopped next to them.

"You will be late to dinner if you do not leave now," Lady Kenilworth said. She glanced at Leo. "You may join us if you like."

"Thank you." He really wanted to spend more time with Theo, but . . . "I must look in on my new secretary. It is his first full day."

"Another time then." Her ladyship picked up the reins.

"Meeting at Brooks's during lunch tomorrow," Kenilworth said.

"I'll be there." Now that he'd made a mull of it with Theo, Leo would definitely require more advice. He turned to her. "I can walk from your house."

"Very well."

It was a short drive from Gunter's at one end of Berkeley Square to the other end where Worthington House was located. Mick was waiting to take the carriage when she arrived in front of her house. Leo jumped down and went around to help her alight by clutching her waist and lowering her slowly to the pavement. "I'll see you tomorrow morning."

"Until then." She smiled before striding into the house.

He was halfway home when St. Albans's carriage stopped next to him, and St. Albans said, "Are you not joining the family for dinner?"

"I must see to some things at home. Another time. Will you be at the luncheon at Brooks's tomorrow?"

"Haven't heard about it yet. But most likely."

"I'll see you then." Leo waved and walked on.

"If you change your mind," Lady St. Albans said, "send a note, and we can hold dinner."

"Thank you." That would solve his problem. "If all is going well, I shall do that." He just hoped Whiting didn't have any difficulties.

He ran up the steps to his house and the door opened. A footman bowed. "Is Mr. Whiting in his study?"

"Yes, your grace. He asked about you not long ago."

That didn't sound good. "Thank you."

Leo made his way quickly to his secretary's office, knocked, then opened the door. "How has it been going?"

The man started to stand, and Leo motioned him to remain seated. "Well, I believe. I wanted you to review the responses I was able to make before I sent them out. I will need to discuss the others with you."

Leo might make it to dinner with Theo yet. "Can it wait until tomorrow?"

"Yes. Absolutely." Whiting removed his spectacles. "Unless you require anything else, I was about ready to leave for the day."

"Nothing at all. I will see you after breakfast." Leo went to his study and penned a quick note, then gave it to the footman outside the door. "Have this delivered to Worthington House as fast as possible."

"Yes, your grace." The man strode quickly toward the hall. The next thing he heard was the front door opening and closing. When he arrived in the hall, his butler was there. "I am dining out."

"At Worthington House, your grace?"

"Yes. I will not be late."

"I shall inform her grace."

"Tell her that I wish to speak with her when I return if she does not have another engagement."

"She and Mrs. Merryweather are dining at home this evening. I have not been apprised of any other plans."

"Excellent. I will see you later." Leo was never more grateful that Theo's family didn't dress formally for dinner.

He hailed a hackney. When he arrived, the family was in the drawing room.

Theo came forward and greeted him, followed by Lady Mary. "I am so glad you could join us."

He bowed. "I am as well. It appears as if Whiting has everything under control. I must review what he's done today and speak with him about some other matters, but that can be done in the morning." He glanced at Lady Mary. "Good evening, my lady."

She made an elegant curtsey and smiled. "It is good to see you, your grace."

"I'm glad you were finally able to make it to Town. Your sister missed you."

Kenilworth's son, Hugh, brought Leo a glass of sherry. "My father said you would want this."

"Thank you. He was correct." Leo took a sip. "Who was ill, or was it something else?"

"Edward, one of the twins, fell and hit his head. The doctor examined him and said he would be fine. He has to be quiet for a few days," Mary said. "He tried climbing the wall."

"How old is he?" He was having trouble placing the younger ones. He didn't see them that often.

"He is four and a half," Theo said. "Next year he and Gaia will join us at the table."

Thorton, the butler, came in and announced dinner. Leo winged out both of his arms, but Hugh came to escort Mary. That was when he noticed that Worthington's eldest son, Gideon, was escorting two of the girls. "Impressive."

"They are." Theo smiled. "We are all proud of them."

Leo could see why. She led them to the seats they had taken before at the table. He held out her chair. A sudden feeling of well-being filled him. He not only wanted Theo. He wanted to be part of this family. Not every gentleman could say that.

Lady Giselle poked Lana in the side. They were sitting across the barouche carriage from their mothers in the backward-facing seat. "The Duke of Chandos just got out of a hackney at Worthington House."

"Do you suppose he is visiting Lady Theo?"

"What do you think? After all, he's been driving with her and today she was driving that high-perched phaeton, and he was with her. It would not surprise me if they went for ices again."

"I thought your brother was going to arrange an introduction."

"He has not seen him at his club. And there have not been any events. Our mothers would not allow us to attend Lady Thornhill's viewing today."

"The first Almack's assembly is this Wednesday," Lana said.

"Yes, but more importantly, there is a ball before then. I will make sure my brother attends."

"I almost forgot. Lady Penchly is having a ball on Monday."

"Yes. Everyone will be there." Giselle smiled. "I shall make sure that he asks me to stand up with him."

CHAPTER SEVENTEEN

When Leo arrived home, he was told his mother had retired with a sick headache, which is what his mother always did when she didn't want to have a conversation. She'd never done it with him before, but she had with his father. He'd have to speak with her after his meeting with his secretary.

Early the next morning, he rode with Theo, Marrow, and Miss Pettigrew, broke his fast at Worthington House, and returned home. He would have lingered, but the Season had now begun in earnest. Theo had final fittings, the gentlemen had the Lords and Commons, and Leo had business to attend to as well before the luncheon meeting.

When he arrived home a groom took his horse, and he entered the house. "Hoover, please inform her grace that I wish to speak with her in an hour."

"Yes, your grace."

Whiting was already at his desk when Leo joined his secretary.

"Here are the letters I wrote yesterday." Whiting handed over a short stack of missives.

Leo reviewed them. "Excellent. It's amazing that knowing nothing about the estates, you were able to give cogent responses."

"The answers were simple common sense. I knew, for example, that if the price of anything had risen, you would want to know the reason." His secretary folded the letters and prepared them to be sealed. "These I was unable to respond to until I spoke with you." Whiting handed Leo one of the missives.

Once Leo had finished reading it, he wanted to consign it to the fire. "This boundary dispute has been going on for years. I believe it is finally time to call in a surveyor. I don't know why my father didn't do it."

"I have a feeling we're going to find out." Whiting's tone was dry. "I will find who normally does the surveys for that area and instruct the estate manager to allow him access."

"Very good." So far, Leo was extremely pleased with his new secretary. "What else do we have?"

They spent the next hour discussing the best ways to settle the other disputes, and Leo left his secretary to respond to the notes.

"Tell me when you are done, and I will seal and frank them." He might have to have a seal made for Whiting. It would save time. Leo went to his study and tugged the bellpull. Hoover answered the summons. "Tell my mother I would like to see her now."

"I believe she is readying herself for an appointment, your grace."

The devil she was. "Then I'll speak to her before she departs."

A few minutes later, Mama entered the parlor. "What did you wish to talk with me about?"

"Please, have a seat." Leo motioned to a chair.

She raised her chin. "I would rather stand. I must leave immediately."

"In that case, I shall be blunt. Do not, under any circumstances, attempt to introduce me to any young ladies. I know whom I want to wed. I have no interest in anyone else."

"Although I am sure she is a very nice girl"—his mother sniffed—"I believe you can select someone more suitable."

"I do not." What was she getting at? "I do not want anyone who is more interested in my rank or wealth than me as a man."

"We all wed for those things." Her chin rose. "You should have a wife you can mold into what you want. That is how your father and I started out."

This could rapidly devolve into a circular argument. "Theo is of the appropriate rank to marry a duke. She has a suitable dowry"—not that he knew or cared what it was—"and the appropriate education and temperament to be my duchess." His mother's countenance assumed a mulish look. "Did you receive and respond in the affirmative to Lady Harrington's ball?"

Mama inclined her head. "I did. I expect you to escort me."

"As do I. I plan to leave after supper. Is that convenient for you?"

"Yes. There is a ball I would like to attend after the Harrington event."

"You may bring me back here and take the town coach." He had to get at least some sleep before riding with Theo the next day.

"I had hoped you would join me." He couldn't believe Mama was actually using a cajoling tone with him.

"I am sorry to disappoint you. Unless something changes, I plan to attend one event an evening for the foreseeable future."

"Indeed. In that case, I shall see you later." Head high and her back straight, Mama left the room. She reminded him of a frigate under full sail. This argument was obviously not over. She was not happy that he wouldn't take her advice.

"I wish you a good day." Leo rubbed his forehead. Why the devil had she taken a dislike to Theo?

He went back to Whiting's office. "I shall require you to perform another task."

"Yes, your grace?" He took off his glasses.

"I'll have all the letters and invitations delivered to you so that I can see them before anyone else in the household does."

"Should I answer them?" He appeared to understand how unusual Leo's request was.

He needed to consider how to handle that. He no longer trusted his mother to accept only the invitations to events he planned to attend. Somehow, he had to find out which entertainments Theo was attending. Would it be as simple as asking Lady Worthington? Theo said her sister made those decisions. "I don't know yet."

"Very well, your grace." Whiting donned his glasses and looked at the correspondence on the desk.

"I have some errands and then a luncheon. I'll have an answer for you when I return."

Whiting nodded and Leo strolled out. It was time to go to meet the other gentlemen. His butler handed him his walking stick, hat, and gloves. "Hoover, I want all of the correspondence to be delivered to Mr. Whiting upon arrival."

"Even those addressed to her grace?"

"Yes. All of it. There is no need to inform my mother. I shall do so." After Leo decided what to do.

"As you wish, your grace."

"I will not be here for luncheon. However, I will dine at home."

"Cook will be very happy, your grace."

As much as Leo paid the man, he should take his meals here more often. "It is always a good idea to keep the cook happy. I shall see you later."

He descended the steps to the drive, then turned onto Park Lane and continued onto Piccadilly. When he arrived at St. James Street, he was hailed by Lord Darnel, an old friend from school.

"Chandos." The man hurried to Leo. "I haven't seen you at the usual haunts."

In other words, the places he used to frequent until last summer. "I've been rather busy."

His chum fell in beside him. "Would you like to have luncheon with me?"

"I'm afraid I have another appointment." Darnel was frequently in need of something. "Is there anything you want?"

"Yes, actually." He smiled. "I would like to introduce you to my sister. I understand you might be in the market for a wife."

Leo had told his mother to keep that quiet. He'd tell the world if he thought Theo wouldn't be upset. Yet, he had to secure her hand first. He wouldn't deny he was looking to wed, but he wasn't going to encourage anyone either. "I'm not interested in meeting any young ladies."

"Oh. Well, then." Darnel appeared confused. "I'm sorry to have mentioned it. She will be disappointed."

Kenilworth strolled up to them. "Are you ready?"

"I am." Leo turned to Darnel. "Perhaps I shall see you another time."

"Are you attending Lady Penchly's ball?" Darnel seemed hopeful.

"Not that I know of. When is it?"

"Tomorrow evening."

"I shall have to ask my mother. She is keeping the social calendar." That was a small lie that would, hopefully, stop Darnel asking about his engagements for a while.

He bowed. "Until the next time."

Darnel left and Kenilworth raised a brow. "I have heard that his father is getting ready to cut him off."

"That's not surprising." He and Leo headed toward Brooks's. "He wants to introduce me to his sister. I assume it would be a way to get back into his father's good graces."

"You're probably correct. How is your new secretary doing?"

"Quite well. I'm very pleased. Now, if only my mother would fall in line."

Kenilworth barked a laugh. "I am not certain any of them are capable of that. My mother was so happy I was marrying that she fell all over Charlotte, and *she* had not yet decided to marry me. Rothwell's mother, on the other hand, wasn't at all happy with his choice of Louisa. And Lady Wolverton—Louisa, Augusta, Madeline, and Theo's mother—was furious when Madeline decided to wed Stern."

"My mother believes I need a wife I can mold. I would rather have one with her own opinions and who already knows how to take charge. To forestall any shenanigans on her part, I have decided to have all the household correspondence delivered to my secretary. I just don't know what to do after that. I only want to accept invitations to events Theo will attend."

"Charlotte will have the list. We are all called upon to support whomever is making a come out. I can arrange to send it to you."

"Yes, thank you. Absolutely." Leo breathed a sigh of relief. "Then I only need to ensure that I'm invited to all of the events."

Kenilworth grinned. "We can help with that as well. Most of the balls and other things we'll attend are given by friends or close acquaintances."

"Thank you." Although Leo didn't fully understand why the family had decided to promote his suit, he was grateful. "Getting her to see me as a suitor is much more difficult than I'd anticipated."

Kenilworth raised a brow. "You didn't help yourself by telling her you didn't wish to meet young ladies."

"I made it even worse this morning." Leo could have kicked himself. "I told her that didn't include her, and she said that of course it didn't. She knew I wasn't looking for a wife."

"The road hasn't been easy for any of us." Kenilworth grimaced. "You'll work out a way to encourage her to come around."

Leo hoped the man was right. Currently, he had no idea how to manage it.

"Theo, that is beautiful!" Mary exclaimed. "I am so glad waistlines are beginning to fall. I was becoming tired of the high waists."

"I was as well." Theo smiled at her new gown in the mirror. "I am also happy that Grace doesn't insist that I wear white or light pink. Those colors make me appear sallow."

"Lady Stern had to talk Lady Pettigrew out of dressing Sarah in those colors for that very reason."

Sarah had light blond hair and blue eyes, yet her skin tone was much the same as Theo's. "She told me about that. I am very sorry for the young ladies whose mothers refuse to relent."

"The girls are excited to see you in your first ball gown." Mary smiled. "Remember when we wanted to see Grace, Charlotte, Louisa, and Dotty in their gowns."

"All of our sisters." Theo and Mary were the last two. "At least I have partners for two dances."

"Chandos and who else?" Mary asked.

"Lord Marrow. He asked Sarah first." Theo smiled. "We, Chandos and I, think they will make a good match."

"I am sure there will be gentlemen lining up to ask Grace or Matt or one of our other brothers or sisters to be presented to you."

Theo hugged herself, then stopped before she wrinkled her gown. "I do hope so. I had not been excited about the Season before. This has changed everything."

"My lady." Payne strode into the room carrying a velvet pouch. "Her ladyship said you are to wear these this evening." The maid smiled. "They are yours."

She spilled the jewelry out onto the toilet table. There was a strand of pearls and matching earrings. "Oh, they are lovely."

It had become a tradition in the family that when one of them attended their first ball of the Season they received pearls. A tradition Theo had forgotten. "Put them on me, please."

She fastened the earrings while her maid hooked the necklace. What was so special about the gift was that they were for a young matron. Not the sets of smaller pearls girls received. She glanced into the mirror again. "They are perfect."

Mary gave her a quizzical look. "Why is Chandos attending?"

"I suppose Charlie asked him to look out for me." It had to be that since he had not been in Town until recently.

Grace tapped on the open door. "You look as beautiful as I knew you would." She gazed at Theo's image in the mirror for a moment and smiled. "We should be going. Matt is starting to pace."

Theo exchanged a grin with Mary. He always wanted to arrive early and return home after supper. "I am ready."

Payne draped a silk paisley shawl around Theo's shoulders and handed her the reticule and fan they had chosen for this gown.

Mary accompanied them down the stairs. "Have fun."

"I will." Theo returned her sister's smile. "I will tell you all about it in the morning."

"I will look forward to it."

She and Grace each took one of Matt's arms. He helped them into the Town coach before climbing in himself and giving the order to depart.

"You have been told the rules," he said. "But I'll repeat them. No dancing with anyone who has not been introduced to you by me or one of the family. If you have to go to the ladies' room, take someone with you. No leaving the ballroom with a gentleman. We will depart after supper."

"I remember." Theo knew they were to keep her safe. Too many things could happen to a young lady who wondered around alone.

There was only a short line of carriages when they arrived. Elizabeth, the Countess of Harrington was friends with her older sisters. They had come out together.

"Theo!" her ladyship exclaimed. "You are just beautiful. I knew you would be. Congratulations on your first Season." Elizabeth took Theo's hands. "Louisa, Charlotte, and Dotty arrived a few minutes ago." She peered down the short set of stairs to the ballroom. "They and their husbands are speaking with the Duke of Chandos. I understand he has become a friend of the family."

"He has. I am very glad to see you." Theo curtseyed, then joined Grace and Matt. Footmen circled the room with glasses of champagne, lemonade, and wine. No food would be served until supper.

When they joined their family, Chandos took her arm. "You are a vision, my lady."

He was probably saying that to be kind, but, nevertheless, heat rose in her cheeks. "Thank you, your grace. You are very handsome." He was dressed in a black evening suit with white striped stockings and black pumps. His cravat was white and tied into a Mathematical secured with an emerald pin. The only fobs were his quizzer and a pocket watch. He would probably be the most elegant gentleman here this evening. "Thank you for requesting a set. Other than you and Lord Marrow, I do not know if I will dance again." She glanced around. "Is your mother here?"

"No. She decided to spend the evening at another ball given by a friend."

A gentleman came up to them. "Chandos, will you introduce me?"

"I will not." He raised his quizzing glass and pointed it at Matt. "You must apply to the lady's brother. Lord Worthington."

"Thank you." The man bowed and strolled away.

"Coward." Chandos tucked his quizzer away.

It did not matter. Three gentlemen were standing in front of her brother.

"Worthington was right," Chandos said. "If they cannot request an introduction through him, they have no reason to dance with you at all."

Con brought one of the gentlemen to her. "Lady Theo, may I present Lord Hereford?" Mentally, Theo placed him as an earl. She curtseyed. "My lord, Lady Theo Vivers."

She held out her hand. "It is a pleasure to meet you, my lord."

"The pleasure is all mine." He kissed the air above her hand. "May I have the honor of the first country set?"

"That set is taken. You may have the first dance."

"Thank you. I will look forward to it." He walked away toward a footman carrying drinks.

Chandos laughed lightly. "You do know that the first set is usually a minuet?"

Theo really had not thought about it. "I suppose someone told me at some point."

"Poor chap." He sounded genuinely sad for his lordship.

"Is that why you asked for the supper dance?"

"No. I wanted the supper dance because it's a waltz and then I can have supper with you."

"Oh." She did not know what to say to that. It never occurred to her that Chandos would want to spend that much time with her at a ball.

CHAPTER EIGHTEEN

Leo clenched his jaw as he watched Theo step onto the dance floor with another man. She glowed as the crystals sewn onto her deep cream-colored gown sparkled beneath the chandeliers. The gown's modest neckline barely hinted at the swells of her breasts. The bodice that clung to her form teased him with what lay beneath. This was going to kill him.

"Chandos." He was surprised to see Rochford at the ball. Leo's longtime friend came up to him. "You look like you're thinking of murdering someone."

"Hereford, at the moment." Then it would be her next dance partner.

"The Earl of Hereford? What did he do?"

Leo focused on Theo again. She had just taken her place in the line.

"Ah." Rochford dropped his quizzer. "I see the problem. Have you reserved a set with her?"

"The supper dance." He couldn't tear his gaze from her. The music started. She moved so gracefully. Just like she did everything else.

"That was good thinking." His friend remained quiet for a moment or two. "You're going to drive yourself mad doing that."

"Ask if she has a set left." At least he knew he could trust Rochford with Theo.

He chuckled. "I'll ask, but there's a fairly long line of gentlemen waiting to stand up with her."

Leo glanced toward Worthington. That was a true statement. "You'll have to approach her immediately upon her return."

"Very well." Rochford heaved a sigh. "That won't give you much relief."

Leo glanced at his friend. "Marrow has a set with her as well. That only leaves two more dances before the supper set."

"You really have been thinking about this. What happens after supper? There are still more sets."

"Worthington makes them leave after supper." Thank God for small favors. He focused on Theo again.

St. Albans and his lady joined them. "Chandos, people are noticing."

"What?" Reluctantly, he glanced at the man.

"That you are staring at Theo." Lady St. Albans shook her head. "You must stop. Nothing is going to happen to her on the dance floor. She knows not to go off with anyone."

"I know." Intellectually, he knew. Yet, he couldn't stop some other part of him from wanting to protect her.

"We have all been through it." St. Albans had a wry smile on his face. "You feel like you wish you had a sword to run the bounder through. Or be able to carry her off on your faithful charger."

That was it exactly. "Yes."

"Lady St. Albans gave her husband a fond look. "I had no idea."

He nodded and patted her hand. "I will guarantee you that all your brothers by marriage experienced the same thing."

"I am exceedingly glad to know that." She glanced at Leo. "However, you may not make a scene. This is her first ball. You will have to learn to live with it until she agrees to wed you."

A sharp sense of frustration struck him, and he closed his eyes for a brief second. "How did you get through it?"

"Not well," St. Albans muttered. "You'll feel more the thing during the supper dance. I hear it is a waltz."

"That's what I was told as well." Leo would be able to hold Theo in his arms. That would make him feel better.

"Good evening, Rochford," her ladyship said. "I did not see you there."

He laughed. "I am easy to miss when we have Chandos here looking like he wants to start a war."

"There is that." She poked his arm. "Come away where you are not so noticeable."

He followed her to where a group of the family were standing and sitting. Most of the gentlemen were as tall as he was. Lady St. Albans was correct. He would not stand out as much. Theo wouldn't have appreciated him making a spectacle of himself. "Thank you."

She glanced at Rochford. "Am I to assume you are going to ask Theo to dance?"

"Yes, my lady." His lips twitched. "All for a good cause."

"When she is being escorted back to us, move to the front of the group, bow, and request the set," Lady St. Albans instructed.

He appeared confused. "I would always bow."

"Yes, but doing it first allows you to request the next dance. It is not a formal rule. As a practical matter it will stop other gentlemen from interrupting."

That was excellent advice. Leo would have to keep it in mind. At some point, he would be able to have two sets with Theo.

Kenilworth and his lady joined them. She raised a brow at her sister. "Are we minding him?"

"Yes. He was staring at Theo."

"I am in complete sympathy with him," Kenilworth said with feeling.

"We all are," Rothwell said.

Slowly, with the exception of Worthington and Lady Worthington, who were still being made known to gentlemen wanting an introduction to Theo, the rest of the family joined them. The minuet came to a close, and Rochford, following Lady St. Albans's advice, secured Theo's third set. Leo moved so that he was once more standing next to Theo.

Miss Pettigrew and Marrow came over as well.

"I am not at all unhappy to have missed the minuet," Marrow said.

"It is not my favorite dance," Miss Pettigrew agreed. "But it is very elegant."

"It is," Theo added. "I suppose it is helpful if one does not really wish to speak much to one's partner."

The strains of the orchestra announced the next set, which was the first country dance. Leo bowed to Miss Pettigrew and Marrow bowed to Theo. The four of them strolled to the dance floor. The tension Leo had been feeling faded away as they took their places. Even if he wasn't dancing with her all of the time, at least he could touch her hands and was with her. When the set was over, they returned to their circle.

Another gentleman was given permission by Worthington to be presented to Theo. Leo recognized him as the Earl of Holland, Lady Thornhill's nephew. "My lady." He bowed. "May I have the next set?"

Theo curtseyed. "I already have a partner, however, my fourth set is available."

Holland smiled. "I would be honored."

That left one more set she would dance with another gentleman. Leo didn't have long to wait before one arrived. He'd known the Marquis of Crewe since school. He had only recently come into his title. After Worthington presented Crewe, he secured Theo's fifth set. Leo didn't think Holland would be much of a rival. Crewe, on the other hand, was another matter. He had no known heirs and must be desperate to wed and start a family. The man would bear close scrutiny. Fortunately, the set was a quadrille. Unfortunately, Holland had secured a waltz. Leo's teeth clenched each time they twirled.

"You're going to do your teeth permanent damage," Marrow said as he watched Miss Pettigrew dance with another man.

"I don't understand how you can be so calm." Leo wanted to go to Theo and snatch her away from Holland.

"You must keep this between us." Marrow kept his voice low. Leo nodded.

"She and I have an understanding. However, I have agreed we would not make a formal announcement until her come out ball. Next week, I will be able to stand up twice with her."

Lucky dog. He wished he could have an understanding with Theo. "I wish you both well."

"Here they come." Marrow held out his hand to Miss Pettigrew. Smiling, she took it.

Leo did the same to Theo, but after touching his fingers, she went to one of her sisters and they left the room.

"Are you having a good time?" Alice asked as they skirted the room.

"I am." Theo would not have believed how much fun a ball could be. "Although Lord Holland is not the best dancer, he did make interesting conversation."

"That is important. You will spend much more time talking with the gentleman you wed than dancing with him." Alice wrinkled her nose. "On the other hand, marrying a man who can make conversation and dance is the best option. Even Phinn is an excellent dancer."

Theo did not want to tell her sister that she had not really looked at any of the gentlemen she had stood up with, as prospective husbands. "That makes sense. Even Grace and Matt still like to dance together."

Alice unerringly led them to the ladies' room. Three screens were set up, as was a mirror with extra hairpins and pins for one's clothing if needed. A maid was present to help any of the ladies. Theo went behind one of the screens. Alice selected another.

The door opened and closed.

"I am shocked to see the Duke of Chandos here," one lady with a slightly nasal tone said.

Theo had been about to come out from behind the screen but decided to remain where she was.

"I overheard my brother saying that he refused an invitation to one of Lord Fellows's parties." The second woman had a low melodic voice.

"Humph. He probably did not want to share his mistress. I understand that is a requirement."

"I had no idea." There was a rustling noise. "I wonder who he chose for this Season," Nasally said.

Theo had never even considered that gentlemen might do that. Share a person? As if they were property. She was glad to hear Chandos would not do anything like that.

"It is a little early to know. I heard he has been driving during the Promenade with a young lady, but then I was told he is a friend of her family. I hope the girl does not decide to fall in love with him," the lady with the nice voice said.

It was a good thing Theo had already decided that he would not be a good husband for her.

"Goodness no! I remember when . . . Well, I shall not speak of it. Her mother made sure she made a good match," Nasally said.

"You do not mean to tell me that he—?"

"No, no, of course not. She had merely formed a fascination for him. He is handsome."

Theo let out a slow breath. *She was glad he had standards.*

"Extremely." Pins rattled in a dish. "If I was not so fond of my Gerald, I would consider Chandos," the lady with the low voice said.

"It would not do you any good. He refuses to oblige married women," Nasally commented. "Come to think of it, I have never heard of him being close to a widow."

"It is a shame that only courtesans have his attention." The lady with the low voice sighed.

"Indeed, it is."

Theo was trying to decide if it was a good thing he only went to courtesans or not when the door opened and closed again.

There was movement from the other screen. "Theo. We must return. The supper dance will start soon."

"I am coming." She came out from behind the screen. "Did you hear what they said about Chandos?"

"I could not have avoided hearing. They were certainly not keeping their voices down."

"I wonder who Gerald is." Her sister had linked arms with her and was swiftly leading them back to the ballroom.

"We will probably never know. I do not remember hearing either voice before."

"Did you know about those parties?" One of Theo's sisters must know.

"I have heard something about them." Alice tugged Theo closer and whispered, "I would not believe everything you hear about Chandos. Then again, what they did say was not very bad at all. He sounds like any other unmarried man on the Town."

"I suppose you are right." Theo would like to know when he was planning to acquire a mistress. She could not be seen with him after that happened.

They arrived back to their circle, and Chandos stepped over to stand by her side. Soon the introduction for the supper dance began and he bowed. "My lady, I believe this is my set."

She placed her hand on the arm he offered. "It is, your grace."

As Chandos led Theo to the dance floor, she wondered why she had never before noticed how strong his arm was. It was not as if she should not have known. He had given her his arm numerous times over the past year. And lately, he had actually lifted her into and down from carriages and coaches. She gave herself a shake. It was probably just the conversation she had overheard. Theo would like to ask him when he planned to take a mistress. But he was not in the habit of defiling young ladies, and she did not want to shock him. She supposed that at some point, Matt would tell her she could not ride with him, or Chandos would stop suggesting they ride together. She curtseyed and he bowed, then he took her in his arms as they prepared to dance. She would miss sharing ices with him. The first moment the set started she could immediately feel the difference between Lord Holland's and Chandos's dancing. He made her feel like a feather. As if she was the most graceful person on earth. She knew *he* would never step on her toes.

"We can converse." His deep voice rumbled through her.

"I was thinking that you are a much better dancer than Lord Holland."

Chandos flashed a quick smile, and the corners of his eyes crinkled, making him appear even more handsome. Yet, she had always thought he was handsome. A lady required more from a gentleman in order for him to be a husband. "I can't tell you how happy it makes me to hear that."

Oh, no. He would not. "You are not to tell him."

"Me?" He looked insulted, then he glanced down at her with his lips twitching. "If you insist, I shall not say a word."

"I do insist. He is a very nice person, and I would not want to hurt his feelings."

"You're right. He did explain the three-breasted goddess to you." Chandos appeared as if he would burst out laughing.

Theo stifled her own loud laugh. "And to you as well. Do not pretend you knew."

"And to me as well. Although, I did think some of my ideas were good." He had a smug expression.

"They were ridiculous." That should put him in his place.

He twirled her so that her back was to his chest. His warmth caressed her. "My lady, you wound me."

Even though she knew he was teasing, for a moment, a very brief moment, she almost believed him. "I am sure you will get over it."

"Only if you share your ices with me at supper."

"In that case, you must bring me more than ices that I will like." Theo was looking forward to her first real supper. Well, supper at a ball.

"Have no fear. I trust I know exactly your taste in ices and other foods." He twirled her again so that she was facing him.

"I suppose you do. I almost forgot this is not the first time you have fetched my supper."

"You must acknowledge how useful I am to have around."

"I agree." This time Theo was afraid she would not be able to control a laugh. "You are extremely useful."

The music stopped and, once again, they curtseyed and bowed, and she took his arm. He slanted a look at her. "I am famished."

"You?" She could not believe he had said that. "All you have done is stand around talking. I have danced every set."

"Trust me when I tell you that I expended a great deal of energy talking."

What on earth did he mean by that? "I will have to take your word for it."

Chandos had never flirted with her before. If that is what he was doing. Then again, it really did not matter. Sooner or later, he would revert to his old ways. He was not for her.

CHAPTER NINETEEN

Leo brought back four different ices for Theo and various other foods he knew she liked. This evening was going superbly well. Soon he would be the one to ensure she could dance the waltz at Almack's. Even if his mother refused to assist him, courtesy of his outings with Theo, he now knew most, if not all, of the Patronesses of Almack's at least well enough to ask to be recommended to Theo. While she had been dancing, Lady Kenilworth—Charlotte, as she had given him permission to address her—had provided him with a list of events that Theo would attend. As soon as he returned from his morning ride and possibly breakfast at Worthington House, he would discuss the issue with his secretary. Yes. Leo smiled to himself. Everything was going quite well.

"Would you like us to give you a ride home?" St. Albans asked as they made their way back to the long table someone had requested for the family.

"Thank you. I would. I have no idea when my mother will decide to send the coach for me."

"I thought that might be the case." St. Albans went to his wife, and Leo to Theo.

"Here you are, my lady." He directed the footman who had

followed with a tray where to place the ices, right in front of her; the champagne, to her right; and the other dishes, in a half moon around the ices. "Everything from the table you could desire."

She smiled brightly and even blushed a little. That was, indeed, a gift. They worked their way systematically through the dishes.

"These crab cakes are marvelous. I wonder if their cook is French."

"I think he must be." Leo drew her attention to a small cheese soufflé. "This is something one doesn't see if the cook is English."

"I suppose you are right." She finished the crab cake and dipped her spoon into the soufflé. "Wonderful! I believe I shall have this served at my come out ball."

"As well as ices?" He smiled at her enthusiasm.

"Definitely ices." She finished the soufflé and started on the last ice. "I suppose we will have Gunter's cater them."

"I believe that is what most people do." He remembered Charlotte's whispered words about the next ball. "May I have the supper dance at Lady Exeter's ball?"

Theo swallowed, then took a sip of champagne. "You may."

"Thank you." He had no doubt that by tomorrow morning gentlemen would be lining up at her door and sending tokens to her beauty.

"It is a pleasure dancing with you." A smile formed on Theo's rosy lips. "From my short experience, no one does it as well."

"Thank you. I only hope that you continue to appreciate my skill after you have more experience." That was one thing in his favor. Leo glanced at Worthington, who was pushing back his chair. "I believe you will leave soon."

She looked at her brother. "I suppose I will be."

Worthington spoke to his lady on one side of him and Louisa Rothwell on the other side. Each lady in turn spoke to the person next to her. Long before the message could be repeated to them, the ladies had begun to rise, which meant all the gentlemen were standing.

He pulled out Theo's chair. "That was effective."

"He has had a lot of practice."

When she placed her hand on his arm, he almost covered it with his fingers. "Does this suit you? Departing early?"

"I think so." She lifted one shoulder and dropped it. "Especially, if I wish to ride early."

"I can't imagine many people will be up with the birds as you are." They joined the line of her family making their way out of the supper room. Lady Worthington found Lady Harrington and they all took their leave of her.

Leo escorted Theo to the coach and helped her in. "I shall see you in the morning."

She gave him a curious look and tilted her head. "You will not go to another entertainment?"

"No. I am for my couch." He squeezed her fingers lightly. "Good night."

"Good night to you." She continued into the coach, and he moved aside to give Worthington space to assist his wife.

St. Albans came up to Leo. "Are you ready to depart?"

"Yes. Thank you again for the ride."

"It is no problem at all. Aside from that, my wife overheard a conversation you should know about."

That sounded ominous. Leo was trying not to hold his breath. "My lady?"

"You may call me Alice. We have known one another for some time now." She glanced at her husband. "While Theo and I were in the ladies' room two other ladies entered. Because of where we were, we could not see them. They were discussing your habit of taking a mistress for the Season. The only thing helpful in the exchange was that they agreed that you did not dally with innocents, married women, or widows. However, Theo is well aware that courtesans, even the well-paid ones, often feel as if they have no choice."

Leo was not going to ask how she came by that piece of information. The family did not withhold knowledge from their girls, and Kenilworth had told Leo about the row Kenilworth had with his wife about his ladybird before she agreed to marry him. "I will not be taking a mistress this Season."

"I have been informed of that. I wanted you to know that I believe she has the intention to allow you to squire her around until you find a companion."

That was extremely helpful information. "And when I do not?"

Alice shook her head. "I have no idea. I think she has decided that you are unsuitable to be a husband." She glanced at her husband. "But others of us had made the same decision and changed our minds."

"Perseverance," St. Albans said. "And help from friends."

"I know all about the part Mary and Theo played in helping us." Alice gave him a put-upon look.

"You must admit that they were right. Normanby was a blackguard." St. Albans sat back against the squabs.

"The two of them are very perceptive." Alice's brows slanted down. "When it comes to other people. Somehow, I do not have the feeling that Theo will be the same when it comes to herself."

And that was the rub. "I shall come as close to living in her pocket as I can be without being betrothed to her."

Her sister nodded. "Be her friend."

That is what all of them had said. "I wish I had Theo to help me."

Alice laughed. "That would be helpful." She stared over his shoulder. "Mary might be able to be of assistance. Still, it is early days."

For everyone but Leo it was early days. But he'd been working toward this for almost a year. "You're right, of course. I must be patient."

"Are you attending Dorie Exeter's ball?"

"I am. I have already asked Theo for the supper dance." Being able to be before the other gentlemen was a masterstroke.

"I managed to have the supper dance with Alice. It didn't help," St. Albans grumbled.

"That is because you were irritating the life out of me," his wife pointed out.

Leo hoped that he wasn't upsetting Theo. "Will someone tell me if she doesn't want to dance with me?"

"Trust me," Alice said. "Theo knows you well enough that she will tell you herself. She will be kinder to a gentleman who appears unsure of himself."

It was then that Leo knew his real rival was the Earl of Holland. The man was much too nice and unpretentious. He also had a great deal of knowledge about things Theo might find interesting. The coach slowed and turned into his drive, then came to a stop. "Thank you for the conversation and the ride. I shall see you tomorrow evening."

"I am happy to help." Alice smiled. "I'll give some thought to what more I can do."

"I would appreciate that." It was then he remembered his plan for Almack's. "I was going to have my mother assist in arranging for me to be presented to Theo as a suitable partner for the waltz at Almack's. Would you do it?"

"Yes." Alice nodded. "I would be pleased to help you. Arrive at Almack's as soon as the doors open. We will meet you there."

"Excellent. I must thank you again." After this evening, he had the feeling he would not be the only one wanting to be presented to Theo. "Good night."

"Good night." Their coach drove away.

Hoover opened the door for Leo. "Has my mother returned?"

"No, your grace. We do not expect her for another few hours."

Had she always stayed out late? He took a good look at his aging butler. He was fagged to death. "I insist you go to bed. A footman can wait up for her."

"Your grace. She asked that I be here."

"And I have countermanded that order. Go to bed. I will be up early."

"Yes, your grace." Hoover bowed.

It was a short carriage ride from Harrington House to Worthington House. Theo tried to think over the events of the evening but could not work out what she wanted to know about it. Very strange.

"How did you like the ball?" Grace asked.

"I enjoyed it immensely. I do wish some of the gentlemen were better dancers."

"I predict the house will be filled with flowers tomorrow." Matt groaned.

Why? "I did not stand up with that many gentlemen. Three of them were friends."

"It makes no difference." His lips had tightened. "Several others were introduced to you. They will want to make an opportunity to dance with you at the next ball or take you riding."

"That will be helpful for the flower girls." Someone should profit from Theo receiving flowers.

Grace chuckled lightly. "Then there will be the verses written for you."

Theo had read several of the ones written to her sisters. They were rarely good. She sighed. "Yes. Those."

"Who did you enjoy dancing with most?" Matt asked.

"Chandos." She did not even have to think about it. "He is by far a better dancer than any of the others. He is also entertaining. Lord Holland was interesting to speak with, but he kept stepping on my toes. The others danced competently but had more trouble carrying on a conversation. Well, not Lord Marrow or Lord Rochford, but they are not interested in me as anything other than a friend."

"No doubt, you will receive invitations to dance at the next ball." Grace glanced at Matt as the coach came to a stop. "I am going to kiss the children good night."

"I'll be up to join you." Matt took her hand and kissed it.

That was what Theo wanted. She yawned. The rest of her thoughts could wait until morning. "I am going to bed."

Matt helped Grace out then Theo, and they entered the house. As Theo ascended the stairs, she recalled that her other sisters, with the exception of Augusta, had met after the entertainments in their parlor and discussed the evening. Theo could barely keep her eyes open. Perhaps it got easier during the course of the Season.

The second she put her head on her pillow, Morpheus took her. Her dreams were a strange mix of shopping, riding, and dancing. The only thread was that Chandos was always there. When she awakened, Theo decided nothing was to be gained by paying attention to her dream. After all, Chandos was around her a great deal. That was probably all it meant.

She descended the stairs to find him already waiting for her. "Good morning."

"Good morn to you. Shall we see if Miss Pettigrew and Marrow have managed to rise early today?"

Theo almost laughed. She was fairly certain that both of them had left shortly after her family had. "Yes. We shall tease them if they have not."

Fortunately for the couple, they were ready to depart when she and Chandos arrived at Sarah's house.

"I must say"—Lord Marrow turned to his gelding—"it is a novel experience to have attended a ball and be awake enough to ride the next morning."

Sarah started to laugh. "What did you do before? Stay up all night?"

"Yes." He gave her a wry look. "I would just be going home."

"That would be fun to see!" she exclaimed. "How many gentlemen do you think we will see?"

Theo wondered about that as well. "I suppose we shall find out on our way to the Park."

There were not only gentlemen, but town coaches obviously returning from the evening's entertainments. A few of them waved and greeted their little group.

Lady Cowper's carriage stopped, and she glanced at them. "Ah, the energy of youth. I do not know how you manage to look so fresh on so little sleep."

Chandos approached her vehicle. "We were all in our respective houses, and I dare say, asleep before one."

"That explains it. Go on and enjoy your morning." She knocked on the roof of her coach. "Drive on. These people have too much energy for me."

They waited until her vehicle had turned the corner and started to laugh.

Theo shook her head. "I can honestly say that I do not believe I will ever stay up all night."

"Not even for your come out ball?" Sarah asked.

"Not even then. I enjoy my sleep too much. I will ask Grace to have it end after supper."

Chandos's eyes were sparkling with laughter. "I have no doubt you'll start a fashion."

"That would be interesting. However, I hardly think that is possible. The only thing it will do is enable people to more easily attend another ball."

Another town coach drove by them. "Let us go on. I want to have a good gallop before I have to be home for breakfast."

Later that evening.

"I cannot believe it." Giselle stared at her glass of champagne. Events were not going as she had planned. "I thought the duke would be at Lady Penchly's ball, and he did not attend. Nor did he appear at any of the other balls we went to." She glared at her brother, who was her escort for the evening.

He shrugged. "Don't blame me. I don't keep his schedule. From the looks of it, he didn't go out at all."

"I must find a way to discover at which entertainments he will be." Perhaps she could bribe a servant at his house. But how would she go about doing it? Perhaps her maid if she paid her a few coins, or one of the footmen. That might be a better idea. "Have you been able to speak with him?"

"If I had, wouldn't I have told you? He hasn't been anywhere recently."

"You must find a way. He must be presented to me." Giselle could not very well marry a gentleman she had not met.

Her brother rubbed a hand down his face. "Perhaps he'll be at Almack's. Mama knows some of the Patronesses. She might be able to ask one of them to do it."

"Oh, for the waltz!" Giselle clapped her hands together. "What a brilliant idea. He could be presented to me as a partner for the waltz."

"That's it. Leave it to our mother."

"I shall. She would be thrilled to have me marry a duke."

"As long as she doesn't try to get me leg shackled next."

Giselle ignored him. He would wed when their father ordered him to. She, on the other hand, was looking forward to being the Duchess of Chandos.

CHAPTER TWENTY

The next morning after breakfast, Theo was walking Chandos to the front door when the doorbell rang. "Who on earth could be calling at this time of day?"

He grimaced. "I will wager you that your first bouquet of flowers is being delivered."

"Surely not." That could not possibly be correct. "They should be sent around to the side door."

Chandos's lips twitched. "Not flowers and other trinkets from the gentlemen at the ball."

A footman opened the door, and a lad stood there holding a bouquet of roses that was almost as large as him. He held out the flowers and his hand. "These are for Lady Theodora."

"How ostentatious." If someone was going to send flora, they could at least have been seasonal.

The servant dropped a couple of coins in the boy's hand and took the blooms. "Where shall I put them, my lady?"

"Find Mrs. Thorton and give them to her." At least Theo knew their housekeeper was used to this kind of thing. "She will know what to do."

Chandos's eyes began to twinkle. "There should be a card telling you who sent them."

Theo had completely forgotten about that. "I suppose I should read the card before you take them down."

He plucked a small white missive from the blooms. "Shall I open it?"

"If you would like." There was really no one from whom she wanted to receive flowers.

"It is from the Marquis of Crewe."

"Am I supposed to send him a note thanking him?" Why had no one mentioned how she should deal with this?

"Er, no. The next time you see him, thank him for the gift."

That was easy. "Thank you."

"It is always a pleasure to be of assistance." Chandos bowed. "I must be on my way. I will see you this afternoon."

"I shall see you then. I will be accompanying Grace, Louisa, and Charlotte on morning calls later."

"First time?"

"Other than to friends in the country, yes. I suppose some good will come of it."

He threw his head back and laughed. "You must be the first lady to think that. I look forward to hearing how it went."

"I am curious to see what the difference will be."

That afternoon, Theo was able to renew her acquaintance with Lady Patricia Marrow, the Earl of Marrow's sister and daughter of the Marquis of Carlisle, and Miss Felice Albright, daughter of Viscount Albright.

Theo sat in a chair next to the two ladies. "How are you enjoying the Season thus far?"

"We were just discussing that. Not much has happened," Lady Patricia said. "Except that it appears as if my brother might soon be betrothed."

"Miss Pettigrew is a particular friend of mine." Theo hid her smug smile. "They appear to be well suited."

"They must be," Lady Patricia said. "And to think that my

mother was in despair of him marrying. I wish I could find a gentleman I liked as much."

"I as well," Miss Albright agreed.

These ladies might be Theo's next attempts at matchmaking. "What are you looking for in a gentleman and a marriage?"

"I would love to travel." Lady Patricia sighed. "I so wanted to attend Lady Thornhill's viewing, but my mother thought it might not be suitable."

"She must be consulting with my mother," Miss Albright said. "That was Mama's excuse for not allowing me to attend." She gave a wistful smile to Theo. "I am not interested in traveling as much as occasionally visiting cities such as Paris. I love the country and seeing to our dependents."

Perhaps Lord Holland would be suitable for Lady Patricia. Theo would have to ask Chandos if he knew a gentleman who wanted a wife that would help him keep up the estates. "Will you be at Lady Exeter's ball?"

Both ladies nodded.

"I have heard she gives the most elegant balls," Miss Albright commented.

"My father knows Lady Exeter's father. I am looking forward to it," Lady Patricia commented.

This was excellent. Two ladies of middling age rose as did Grace. "We must be leaving." Theo stood.

"Oh, I am as well," Lady Patricia said.

"Yes." Miss Albright rose. "I see that my mother is ready to move on." She held out her hand. "I look forward to seeing you at the ball."

Theo touched the lady's fingers. "I as well."

Lady Patricia inclined her head. "I shall see you there."

Theo must speak with Chandos about the two possibilities that came to mind for each of the ladies. She joined Grace in their carriage. "Will you invite Chandos to attend the ball with us tonight or invite him to dinner?"

"I am happy to do both." She gave Theo a searching look. "Do I dare ask what this is about?"

"I need his help with something and would like to have time to speak to him."

"I see."

The coach started forward and took them to Lady Bellamny's house, where Theo saw Lady Lana. After greeting the lady, Theo took the chair next to Lady Lana's. "Are you enjoying the Season thus far?"

"Not really." She appeared troubled.

"I am said to be a good listener, and I do not repeat what I am told. What is wrong?"

"I really should not." Her eyes were shadowed. "Yet, I need to tell someone. If I do not make a match this Season, my father will choose someone for me."

"Oh, dear." Theo had, of course, heard of this happening. Thankfully, she did not have to face it. "What is it you want in a husband?"

"The normal things, I suppose." Theo raised one brow. "To be truthful, I have not allowed myself to think about it. Almost anyone would be better than who my father selects." Lana sighed. "I have been half in love with our neighbor's son, but when I mentioned him to my father, he rejected my idea. He said that he was not mature enough to wed. The problem is that I am afraid Father is right. The other problem is that he does not even notice me."

"Will you be at Almack's on Wednesday?"

"Yes. Mama insists that I attend. I am very afraid I will not be asked to dance."

Theo could help with that. Once again, Grace was rising. "I will see you then."

"Thank you for listening."

Theo patted Lady Lana's hand. "It was my pleasure. I enjoy helping others."

They went to one more house before going home. At tea, Grace assured Theo that Chandos had been invited to dine with them. She would mention it to him during their ride. They were once again taking her phaeton. At present, she must send a note to

Dorie Exeter asking if Lords Crew and Holland had been invited to the ball. Theo sent the message via a running footman and received a prompt response confirming that both gentlemen were attending.

At five o'clock, when she descended the stairs, Chandos was waiting for her. He wore a dark bottle-green jacket that made his eyes appear greener, and fawn trousers.

Leo stepped forward and offered Theo his hand as she reached the bottom step. It always amazed him how she seemed to float down the stairs. It was as if her dainty feet never touched the floor. The light bluish-green color of her gown made her eyes even more beautiful. "Good afternoon. You are enchanting."

She inclined her head gracefully and smiled. "Thank you, sir." She took his arm as they strolled out to her phaeton. "I require your assistance."

The last time she said that he was looking into Marrow's financials. "How may I help you?"

"I met some other ladies just out at Lady Bellamny's soirée, and I saw them today during morning visits." She smiled brightly, and he knew exactly what she was about to ask. "I think Lady Patricia Marrow would be a good match for Lord Holland. She wishes to travel, you see."

"I didn't even know his sister and mother were in Town." Yet, if Theo could match Lady Patricia and Lord Holland, that would get Holland away from Theo. "I think your idea is a good one." He lifted her into the carriage and felt her breathing hitch. He went around and climbed in the other side as she arranged the ribbons.

"There is also Miss Albright. She is mostly interested in taking care of a home and dependents. Do you know a gentleman who might be right for her? I had thought that Lord Crewe could work."

Crewe had several estates and would require a wife who was interested in applying her talents in that direction. "We will find out."

Theo had given her pair their office and they were traveling down the street at a good pace. "The last one is Lady Lana Grant. Her father is Lord Grant. She is concerned that if she does not find a husband this Season, he will do it. She is so afraid of that happening she could not even tell me what she wanted in a husband. I have to think it must be someone who is kind and able to support a family."

"Hm. Let me give that some thought." Leo was glad to hear the lady was not like her friend, Lady Giselle. "There are one or two gentlemen looking to wed who might be suitable. Do you know who will be at Lady Exeter's ball?"

"I do know that all three ladies will be there as well as Lords Crewe and Holland. If we could arrange for the gentlemen to ask them to dance, that would start it." Theo's forehead creased. A sure sign she was thinking about something. "I do not think Lord Holland should dance a waltz with Lady Patricia."

Leo couldn't keep from laughing. "He stepped on your toes, did he?"

"He did." They drove through the gate. "It was such a relief to stand up with you."

"I regret to tell you this, but depending on how much Lady Patricia likes to dance, you might have to find another gentleman for her."

"I am afraid you are correct." Theo pulled a face. "Might we ask Lord Marrow?"

"We may." Leo scanned the carriages and those riding horses. "The opportunity should present itself shortly." He drew her attention to a carriage pulled up to one side. "He is there with Miss Pettigrew."

"Excellent." As happy as he was to be able to help her, he was even more pleased when she smiled at him. She expertly maneuvered the phaeton around and stopped next to Marrow and Miss Pettigrew. "Good afternoon." Then she glanced at the landau carrying a younger lady, and an older woman, probably the lady's mother. "Lady Patricia, how delightful to see you."

"Lady Theo, good day." She turned to the other woman.

"Mama, allow me to introduce you to Lady Theo Vivers. Lady Theo, my mother, Lady Carlisle."

"It is very nice to meet you, Lady Theo. I watched you make your way over here. It was quite adroit driving." She glanced at her daughter.

"Thank you. I am delighted to meet you, my lady."

"I understand that I have you to thank for my son's—she cut Marrow a look—"good fortune."

Miss Pettigrew blushed and gazed adoringly at Marrow, who returned the look. Without blushing.

"It was all fortunate happenstance, my lady."

And that was what Theo did. She accomplished whatever she was after, then acted as if it had all simply come to be. Leo had never met anyone like her. She was the most modest force of nature to exist.

Marrow glanced at Leo and mouthed, "Gunter's?"

Leo nodded slightly. "Lady Theo, we should be off. We're in danger of holding up traffic."

She looked around. "Indeed, we are. Lady Carlisle, Lady Patricia, I hope to see you again soon."

Before the carriage behind them could complain, she started her horses. "I take it we are meeting Lord Marrow and Sarah at Gunter's."

"Yes. He has something he wishes to tell me. We are being hailed."

Theo pulled up to the verge and Crewe came riding up just ahead of Hereford. "Good afternoon, my lady. Chandos."

"Good day, my lord." Theo smiled. "Thank you for the flowers."

Leo simply nodded. Then he remembered he'd forgotten to ask her how many gifts she'd received.

"If you are attending the Exeter ball this evening, it would be my honor if you would allow me the supper dance."

"I am sorry, my lord." She gave him an apologetic smile. "The supper dance is taken."

By him. Leo was about to smirk, when Crewe said, "In that case, the first waltz."

The bounder! Unfortunately, Leo knew the man was said to be an excellent dancer. Then again, Theo had already decided to match him to Miss Albright. He watched with interest to see what she would do. A sly smile appeared on her lips. "I would be delighted, my lord." She glanced to the side and behind her. "Miss Albright, how lovely to see you here."

Miss Albright, a pretty lady with blond hair, gray eyes, and an amused expression, was driving a regular phaeton with a groom sitting in the back. "And you."

"May I introduce Lord Crewe to you?"

"You may." She studied Crewe with the same thoroughness one would a horse one wanted to purchase.

"Miss Albright, Lord Crewe. Lord Crewe, Miss Albright." Theo was clearly enjoying herself.

Laughter lit Miss Albright's eyes. "It is nice to meet you, my lord."

"I am delighted to meet you, Miss Albright. We were just talking about Lady Exeter's ball. May I enquire as to if you will be attending."

"I will be."

"May I have the honor of requesting the supper dance?"

"You may. I would be pleased."

Looking very much like a petulant child, Hereford pushed his way forward. Then remembered that he could not speak until Theo decided to acknowledge him. Fortunately, for him, she was all that was gracious.

"Lord Hereford, how nice to see you." Once again, she turned to Miss Albright, who clearly understood the farce and made the introductions.

He asked for her first waltz, which she accepted. Then asked Theo, who gave him the first country dance. After which, Hereford took himself off.

Crewe bowed to the ladies then met Leo's gaze. "It was a pleasure coming upon you."

"We strive to please." Making sure the man knew his intentions toward Theo.

"Miss Albright, might I escort you around the Park?"

"You may, my lord." She drove on with Crewe riding alongside her.

"This has been a good day's work." Theo started the horses.

"It has. Crewe appears interested in Miss Albright. Perhaps you will have as much luck with them as you did with Marrow and Miss Pettigrew."

"That would be satisfying. Speaking of Lord Marrow, I wonder what he wishes to talk with you about."

"Or with the both of us. I gather he didn't want his mother to know whatever it was he intends to say."

"I caught that." The Park had filled, and it was much longer than Leo had expected it would take to get to the gate. Once they drove through, there were drays and other vehicles with which to contend, but Theo handled it expertly.

Marrow and Miss Pettigrew were already at Gunter's when they arrived. He'd parked his curricle off the street and motioned Theo next to them.

They ordered, then he turned to Theo. "I must tell you something. My sister is not a good dancer."

"Is she not?"

"No. No matter how much she practices she is simply not coordinated. Patricia is almost competent, but she's bound to step on some poor gentleman's toes."

"That is perfect." Theo smiled.

Marrow looked all at sea. "I don't understand."

"I want to introduce her to Lord Holland. He is also not a good dancer. But he loves to travel."

"And that is what my sister wants." Marrow grinned. "Excellent thinking, Lady Theo." He glanced at Miss Pettigrew. "Sarah, uh, Miss Pettigrew, knew you would be able to come up with someone for Patricia."

Leo couldn't help puffing out his chest a bit. "I believe she might also have matched Crewe with Miss Albright."

"How wonderful!" Miss Pettigrew clapped her hands.

It was wonderful. Leo was proud of Theo. Now for her to recognize that they were perfect together. Thankfully, he and his secretary had developed a plan whereby Whiting would reply to the entertainment invitations Leo wished to attend, and have the rest of them sent to Mama. Until she came around to having Theo as a daughter-in-law and the next Duchess of Chandos, he didn't want her around to put a spoke in his wheel.

CHAPTER TWENTY-ONE

⊷——⊶

Mary sat on Theo's bed as she was preparing to go to the ball. "With whom are you dancing this evening?"

Theo caught her sister's eye in the mirror. She had already been admonished to sit still while being dressed. "Chandos has the supper dance. Before then I am standing up with Lords Crewe, Holland, and Hereford. I suppose Lord Marrow will also request a set, and Chandos will dance with Miss Pettiford."

"What do you think about the other gentlemen?" Mary asked. "Are they interesting?"

Mary would be thrilled to hear what Theo had done. "I was able to introduce Miss Albright to Lord Crewe and Lady Patricia to Lord Holland. I believe both couples have a strong chance to make successful matches."

"Excellent!" Mary smiled. "I did not know that you had decided to become a matchmaker."

"The idea occurred to me after Marrow and Sarah had worked out so well, I should try to help other ladies and gentlemen. Chandos thinks that I made good choices." Theo grinned at her sister in the mirror. "It even turns out that neither Lady Patricia nor Lord Holland are good dancers."

"Hmm." Mary rested her elbow on her knee and cupped her cheek. "But, Theo, what about you?"

"For the present, I am enjoying Chandos's company." She shrugged. "I overheard two ladies in the ladies' room saying he was looking for a new mistress. When he does select one, I shall not longer have his attention." Theo did not like the idea that he would take a mistress. Yet, she could say nothing about it. It was not as if they were betrothed as Charlotte and Con had been.

"What if he does not? Acquire a mistress?"

"He will." Theo was certain of it. "He said he was not interested in meeting young ladies. Ergo, he is not interested in finding a wife. Which means he will eventually have a mistress."

Payne had a strange look on her face that Theo could not interpret. Should she and her sister not speak about mistresses in front of the maid? She supposed she could ask one of her other sisters if it was improper. Theo knew she could not broach the subject to other ladies, but she had been under the impression that one could speak of all manner of things in front of her maid.

"There you are, my lady." Her maid stepped back.

"Thank you, Payne." Theo waited while a long shawl was placed on her shoulders. "I will see you later."

Mary slipped off the bed and followed Theo out. "I understand Chandos is dining with us before the ball."

"He is." As usual, her family had eaten earlier with the children. But on nights when they attended an entertainment of some sort, a second much lighter dinner was served for those attending the event. Even though Mary was not attending, she dined with them as well. They went to the dining room where their sisters and brothers-by-marriage were already gathering.

The doorbell chimed, and Chandos strolled into the room and came directly to Theo. "I was finally able to convince Thorton that he didn't have to announce me."

"Theo," Grace said. "A few notes came for you. The first one was from Lord Feversham. He approached Matt about an introduction and was approved. He will present himself early in the evening to meet you. He would like to reserve a dance."

"He can have the first country dance."

"The second was from Lord Bolingbroke."

"If he is planning to stand up with me, the only set I have left is the first one. He had best be early."

"I will answer both queries and inform the gentlemen of their dances." Grace went to a small table in the corner of the room. Dashed off two missives and handed them to their butler. "See that these are delivered immediately."

"Now, shall we take our places?"

"It will not be long before you will have more requests than sets," Eleanor remarked.

"You'll either love or hate the moniker I heard today," Montagu said.

It had happened to all her sisters. Theo supposed she should have expected it. "What is it?"

"I was at my club and a gentleman referred to you as 'The Elusive Lady Theodora.' Then another gentleman said 'The Elusive One' is better. They bantered it around for a bit before deciding on 'The Elusive.'"

"That is ridiculous. I am everywhere, nightly entertainments, riding in the Park. I was even at Lady Thornhill's viewing."

"Ah." Con held up one finger. "You are at only one ball in an evening and only until supper." He held up a second finger. "And in order for someone to even speak with you they must find Worthington and request permission."

"That is true. Yet, I hardly see that it makes me elusive." Gentlemen could be so silly.

St. Albans shook his head. "I would wager that all the other young ladies are being dragged around to two if not three entertainments a night. Also, the balls and other things you have attended are very exclusive."

Montagu nodded. "I have visions of gentlemen running around Town trying to discover which ball you will attend."

"That would be interesting," Charlotte said.

"What is, my love?" her husband responded.

"It is usually gentlemen that a hostess wants at her ball. I wonder if Theo will now be the one person ladies will think is the most valuable guest to attend their entertainment." She glanced at Grace. "When you hold your 'at home' it would not surprise me if you have ladies you barely know attending."

"It will not only be Grace, but all of us." Dotty chuckled. "I foresee a great deal of page turning in *Debrett's*."

Theo ate her soup, then took a piece of fish that was brought around as well as haricots verts with almonds. "This is ridiculous."

Next to her, Chandos swallowed. "When has that ever stopped members of the *ton* from doing anything? In my experience, the more outrageous, the more likely it is to occur."

"I suppose you are correct. Still"—she shook her head—"it does not matter what I think about it. That will not stop anyone."

"It will not. But I'll be here to shield you." He sounded completely serious.

Why was he still spending time with her? Charlie was in Town. One would think Chandos would get on with his usual activities. Theo would mention it to him, except she did like his company. If he kept it up, she would eventually say something. Until then, she would leave things as they were.

Beneath his lashes, Leo watched Theo. It didn't surprise him that she would be given a moniker. "The Elusive" was more apt than she realized. Without her really knowing it, she was being closely guarded. He didn't blame her family at all. Over the years, they had experienced quite a bit of drama and danger during their come outs. Charlotte, Alice, and Dotty Merton had all been abducted. A deranged former mine manager had tried to murder Eleanor Montagu. A scion of a wealthy family on the Continent had followed Augusta Carter-Woods on her travels with the intent of forcing her into marriage. It was no wonder at all that Worthington was keeping a close eye on Theo. Leo had even been told that Kenilworth had had a private talk with Thanet, explaining exactly what would happen to him if he was found anywhere near her. The last Leo had heard, the man had taken himself off to France for the next few months.

The clock chimed the hour, and everyone rose to do last-minute preparations before they left for the ball. Leo's valet had brought his tooth power and brush, and an extra cravat if one was needed.

He met up with Theo on the landing between the wings. "I haven't had the opportunity to tell you how beautiful you are this evening." And she was. Her gown was a buttery yellow trimmed with lilac ribbons and small seed pearls. She wore the same strand of pearls she had the other evening as well as matching earrings. Dark curls framed her face. He wanted to take her in his arms and kiss her. Claim her as his own. He held out his arm. "Shall we?"

"Yes, thank you." They started down the stairs. "You do not have to compliment me."

"Oh, but I do." He was afraid if he said more, he'd scare her off. They reached the hall where some of her sisters were already chatting, and he decided to take a chance. "I have just been told that I do not have to compliment Lady Theo on her beauty. What say you ladies?"

Charlotte slid him a sly look. "When a gentleman thinks a lady that he knows is in good looks, it is incumbent upon him to tell her."

"Yes, indeed," Lady Merton agreed. "It is good for one's disposition."

Disposition?

"Yes," Alice said. "Gentlemen should be encouraged in this type of gallantry."

Her twin, Eleanor Montagu, almost rolled her eyes. "I agree. Gentlemen should be rewarded for good behavior."

Madeline Stern stared at her sisters for a moment, then appeared to understand the task. "I must agree with everyone. Accept the compliment and be happy."

"Especially dukes," Louisa Rothwell said.

Theo stared at her sister. "Why especially dukes?"

Leo would like the answer to that as well.

Her sister gave Theo an innocent look. "Because they are notoriously self-centered."

"I heard that," Rothwell said from the stairs. "I defy you to describe me as self-centered."

His duchess reached out and took his hand. "Not you, my darling. Dukes in general."

Leo was about to say something in his defense, when Theo said, "You just insulted Chandos. Louisa, you should apologize."

"I was not referring to him either. Simply dukes in general."

Worthington came out and ordered them all to the carriages. As they were walking out, Louisa Rothwell winked at Leo as she strolled past him. Well, she had made Theo defend him. He'd have to thank her later.

Their party was one of the first to arrive. Still, they received stares of interest, and it was most likely that he was with the family. Nothing said a betrothal was imminent like a single gentleman arriving with an unmarried lady. However, Theo took no notice.

Shortly before the dancing was to begin, two gentlemen made their way to Worthington who, in turn, brought them to Theo and the men were introduced. Leo knew the Earl of Bolingbroke from school. The man was a few years older than Leo. Lord Ashford, a baron, was about Leo's age, but must not have attended the same school. Bolingbroke gracefully accepted the set he'd been given. Feversham had not yet arrived to claim the first set.

Ashford was another matter. "I wish for the supper dance, my lady."

"The supper set is already taken, my lord." Her tone was gentle, but one could feel the steel underneath it. "If my partner for the first set does not arrive in time, you may have that one."

"In that case, I want the supper set at the next ball you attend."

"Oh?" Like her sister, Theo widened her eyes innocently. "And which ball is that, my lord?"

Everyone in the family became silent.

His chest puffed out. "If you tell me which ball it is, I shall be there."

That was enough. "Ashford is it?"

The man turned to Leo. "Who might you be?"

Kenilworth's lips twitched, and all her sisters had raised their brows. "I am the Duke of Chandos. And Lady Theo has already given her supper sets to me."

Theo quickly looked at him. Alice placed a hand on Theo's arm and gave her an imperceptible shake of the head.

"We will see about that, your grace." Ashford glared at Leo before striding off.

"Of all the gall." Theo stared after his lordship, seemingly not knowing what to do. "If either Lord Feversham is not on time, I will dance with him this evening, but never again." Then she turned to Leo. "Why did you tell him that you had reserved all my supper dances?"

"To stop him from harassing you."

"Thank you, but I am not convinced it will work." Her well-shaped brows drew together. "He seems to have a very good opinion of himself."

Unfortunately, the musicians were taking their places and her partner had not arrived. Ashford would return soon. Leo needed to be on that dance floor and in the same set as Theo. He looked around and saw Miss Pettigrew standing with her mother and Marrow. "Excuse me for a moment." Leo approached her. "Miss Pettigrew, would you allow me to have the first set?"

"Of course, your grace."

Marrow touched Leo's arm. "What's wrong?"

"The person Lady Theo is to dance with for the first set. A Lord Ashford. I don't trust him."

Marrow gave a sharp nod. "Let me know if there is anything I can do."

"I will. Thank you."

As Ashford approached Theo, Leo led Miss Pettigrew to the

floor, making sure that they were in the same line as Theo and Ashford. She looked at Leo and smiled. Ashford scowled. Excellent, now to keep her in sight.

"What do you think you're about?" Ashford growled.

Leo gave the man his best innocent expression. "Dancing with Miss Pettigrew, naturally."

Ashford huffed but said nothing more. Leo, though, was going to ask Worthington why he had allowed Ashford to be introduced to Theo. After Leo reserved every one of her supper sets. A sudden chill spiked through his heart. What if something happened, and he didn't win Theo as his wife? What would he do? How would he even live? The music began, and it struck him that he was in love with her. Really, truly in love. Or he thought he was. Leo needed to speak with St. Albans. Or perhaps his mother. No, not her. Maybe St. Albans's mother.

CHAPTER TWENTY-TWO

Theo had never been so thankful that the first set was the minuet. A country dance would have been good as well. But no one started a ball with a country dance. It was either the minuet or quadrille, and the quadrille would have given her too much time with Lord Ashford. She wished she knew why he was so interested in her.

They changed partners, and she found herself with Chandos. "Who is he?"

"I have no idea. He didn't attend Eton. I don't know idea if he is university educated or not."

"I will try to discover more about him." They switched, and she was back with Ashford. "From what part of the country do you hail?"

"My father's family is from Shrewsbury. My mother's family is from Bristol."

Bristol? Theo felt slightly ill as a memory came to her. "Your mother is the sister of the current duke and the daughter of the previous duke."

Ashford's smile was more than pleased that she had placed him than happy that she was dancing with him. "I wondered if you would know."

Of course she knew. She and Mary had looked up Dotty's family years ago. It simply had not occurred to Theo that there was a son old enough to wed. Which begged the question, how old was he? It was hard to believe the Dowager Duchess of Bristol would tolerate Ashford's behavior. "I probably would not have if your cousin, Lady Merton, was not such a close family friend. I have never heard her mention you."

Before he could answer, she was back with Chandos. "He's Dotty's cousin."

"Really?" His eyes widened. "How very remiss of her to have a relative such as him."

Theo almost laughed out loud. "She and Dom will be here this evening. We must ask her about him."

"Indeed, we should. You, however, are dancing every set. Shall I start the conversation?"

"Tell Charlotte. She and Dotty are bosom friends."

"I will do that."

"Good." And once again, she was with Ashford.

"My lady, I have never met my cousin Merton," Lord Ashford said. "Her elder brother and I are of an age, but I was tutored before attending Oxford."

"That would explain it." Yet knowing about the contretemps between the current duke and Dotty's parents, solely because of her father's rank, it made no sense that a baron would have been allowed to marry her aunt. "Is baron a curtesy title?"

He inclined his head. "You are clever. My father is the Duke of Shrewsbury. However, we are residing with my uncle for the Season. There was no reason to open the house for such a short period."

"I hope you enjoy the time you spend in the metropolis."

"I intend to. My goal is to wed quickly and return home." He smiled at her, and she understood perfectly that he meant her.

"How did you convince my brother to allow you to be presented to me?"

"I told him I was Lady Merton's cousin and had planned to meet her here."

The lying snake. "In other words, you lied."

"A slight misdirection," he drawled, sure of himself.

If they had not changed partners, she would have walked off the dance floor and left him there.

The warmth of Chandos's hand engulfed her much smaller one. "What happened to put you in such a temper?"

"He lied to Matt about his intent to meet Dotty and Dom here. He has never even met her." She took a breath. "He admitted it was a lie." She pressed her lips shut for a moment. "He called it a misdirection. When I go back to him, I will tell him exactly what I think of liars and tell him to never approach me again."

"Please listen to my idea first. Pretend to stumble and tell him that you hurt your ankle. I'll tell Miss Pettigrew what is going on, and, if she is agreeable, she can finish the set with Ashford."

"He thinks he is going to wed me! *Me!*" Theo was so furious she trembled.

"I shall escort you back to your family. You will tell your sisters and Worthington. I am quite sure they will know what to do."

That was a much better idea than hers. "Thank you."

Chandos squeezed her hand. "We will take care that he never approaches you again."

She refused to speak to Ashford. Then when Chandos had had enough time to tell Sarah what had happened, Theo pretended to stumble. He was there to catch her, and Sarah smoothly took her place in the set.

"Remember to limp." His warm breath caressed her ear.

"I suppose this means I will not be able to dance for the rest of the evening."

"At least the next set. Your sister will know what you should do."

When they reached her family, Chandos brought over a chair and Theo sat. Everyone gathered around them. Theo told Matt and Grace what had happened and was pleased to see that he was as angry as she was. Dotty and Con had arrived, and they were apprised of what Ashford had done.

"Harry never liked him. I do wish he was here." Dotty pressed her lips tightly together.

"It does not matter," Grace said. "I would like you to accompany us to Bristol House tomorrow. I will tell his mother, and your uncle, if necessary, that Ashford is to have nothing to do with Theo."

"I'll accompany you as well," Con said. "I know Bristol. He is stiff necked and will not like the subterfuge. I should not be surprised if he insists that they return to Shrewsbury."

"While you do that I will—" Theo could not think of what she would do. She had to keep busy.

"You will allow me to accompany you to Hatchards," Chandos suggested.

"Yes. That is perfect." She turned to Grace. "Will I have to sit out every other set this evening?"

"No." She tilted her head. "The next dance only."

The dance ended, and Sarah, accompanied by Lord Marrow, joined them shortly after. "I will never stand up with him again."

Theo knew her own reason, but what had happened to put Sarah off the man? "What did he do?"

She glanced up at the ceiling and huffed. "Every time he opened his mouth, it was to ask a question about you. He seems to think that his uncle will arrange a marriage." Her hands landed on her hips. "Not only that, but he came here this evening to ensure himself that you would be a suitable wife."

Theo almost dropped her jaw. "Grace, are you very sure that I must sit out the next dance?"

"Dearest, I am tempted to allow it, but that would be the equivalent of giving him a cut direct. I am not prepared to allow you to do that at this time."

Dotty gave Theo a sympathetic look. "She is correct. It would reflect badly on you."

"Very well." She could not argue with her sister's reasoning.

Lord Crewe came up to her and raised a brow. "Are you able to dance?"

"Unfortunately, I am not. I must rest my ankle for a bit." He glanced across the room to where Miss Albright stood with her mother. Clearly, he wanted to spend time with her.

"Go on." Theo waved him away. "Chandos will keep me company."

Lord Crewe bowed. "You are all that is gracious, my lady."

He glanced at Leo and winked. It occurred to Leo that Theo had been doing an excellent job of ridding him of his competition for her hand. Ashford, though, would be a problem. He wasn't the type to be easily dissuaded. Still, there might be another solution. "Theo."

"Hmm?" She glanced at him and had not even noticed that he'd used her name.

"If you were to find a lady for Ashford, who would it be?"

"I would not wish anyone on him." Her tone was flat and slightly dismissive.

He agreed with her but needs must. "No, but surely there is someone who would be suitable in both temperament and rank."

"Theo," Miss Pettigrew said. "This is very bad of me, but what of Lady Giselle?"

Slowly, Theo turned her head toward her friend. "That might be an excellent idea. The question is how to arrange an introduction."

The lady his mother had warned him about and who had been staring at them. But who was her family? "Lady Giselle?"

"Lady Giselle Darnel," Miss Pettigrew said.

The woman her brother had been attempting to foist on him. "I know her brother. I will make him known to Ashford."

Marrow grinned. "I sense a scheme coming together."

Leo scanned the ballroom. As luck would have it, Darnel was headed toward the card room. Ashford was standing next to an older lady. Probably his mother. "If you will excuse me. I shall not be long."

He skirted the room and caught up with Darnel before he sat down at a table. "I know you wanted me to meet your sister, but I think I have a better gentleman than I to interest her."

When he glanced at the card table, Leo could see the lust for play in Darnel's eyes. "Who is it?"

"Ashford. His courtesy title is baron, but his father is the Duke of Shrewsbury."

"She does want to be a duchess." Darnel appeared to study Leo's face. "Are you sure you're not interested?"

"Absolutely. I have made my choice." And no one or nothing was going to dissuade him. Especially now that he was sure he was in love. As it happened, he'd worked it out for himself.

"Very well. Introduce me to this future duke."

Fortunately, Ashford was exactly where he'd been when Leo had seen him. He bowed slightly. "Lord Ashford, I'd like to introduce you to Lord Darnel."

The lady next to Ashford poked him, and he looked as if he'd eaten a sour lemon. "Mother, may I present the Duke of Chandos. Your grace, the Duchess of Shrewsbury."

Leo bowed, took her offered hand and kissed the air above it. "A delight to meet you. You look very like Ladies Stern and Merton."

"My sister and niece, as I am certain you are aware." The duchess glanced at Darnel.

"Allow me to make you known to Lord Darnel." He bowed and took her hand as well. "Darnel, the Duchess of Shrewsbury."

"Enchanted, your grace."

"Excellent address, my lord. Your father is the Marquis of Mulgrave."

"He is, your grace."

The duchess glanced at Ashford. "Go meet her, then bring her to me so that she may be introduced to me."

He bowed and went off with Darnel. Leo fell in with them, then turned toward Theo as soon as he could. What he hadn't wanted was to be stuck with the duchess until Lady Giselle was brought to her. He strode as quickly as he could so as not to be waylaid by anyone before he could get to Theo. "Darnel is taking Ashford to meet Lady Giselle." He looked at Lady Merton. "Your aunt is nothing like you and your mother."

"No." She shook her head. "She would not be. My mother says that her sisters and brother wed the people they were told to and are not happy in their marriages."

Leo had heard the story about Lady Stern defying her father to wed Sir Henry, who at the time was a mere mister. "I'm glad for her that she was braver."

Lady Merton smiled. "So are we all."

It was time for the third dance and Theo went off with her partner. Leo stepped over to St. Albans. "When you asked me if I was in love with Theo, I did not understand what that entailed. However, I have since been struck by the almost certainty that I am in love with her. How did you know?"

"What did your mother say?"

"I didn't ask. She wants me to wed a different type of lady." One who would bore Leo to death before a month was out.

"Ah." St. Albans looked over at his wife, who was speaking with her twin. "The first time I saw her I knew I wanted her. The more I came to know her, the more I knew I had to have her in my life. My mother asked me if I wanted to be with her even when we argued. Which she assured me would happen. And when she was out of sorts. I knew that I did." He glanced at Leo. "Is it the same with you?"

He'd wanted her when she poured a bucket of cold water on him. "It is. I can't imagine my life without her."

Alice came up to him and linked her arm with his. "Come with me. Lady Cowper is here. Rather than waiting until tomorrow, you will ask her now."

Leo allowed her to tow him to her ladyship.

"My lady, it is a pleasure to see you here." Alice gave her ladyship a polite smile. "I understand you have already made his grace's acquaintance."

"Lady St. Albans, how nice to see you. I have met his grace." Lady Cowper gave him a look of inquiry. "How may I help you?"

"My lady, I would like to be recommended to Lady Theo Vivers as a suitable partner for the waltz at Almack's tomorrow evening."

Her ladyship's smile was merely polite, but her eyes danced with mirth. "Your grace, how can I refuse. You must want this very badly to have requested my assistance a day early."

"I do." If she only knew how badly.

"Very well. Lord and Lady Worthington always arrive when the doors open. Be there then, and I will make my recommendation."

"Thank you, my lady."

He and Alice were about to leave when Lady Cowper said, "There is one minor thing I will ask of you."

He knew she'd want a pound of flesh. "Yes, my lady?"

She speared him with a look. "I want you to stand up with one of the shyer young ladies."

That was easily done. He bowed. "I will be happy to be of assistance."

"Very well. Until tomorrow."

As Alice led him away, she slid him a look. "You care very much for Theo."

This was the time to let her family know how he felt. "I'm in love with her."

"I thought you might be." They were almost back to their circle, when she said, "Be patient with her. She is extremely canny when it comes to others. I do not believe she knows her own mind yet."

Being patient was the hard part. He wanted her now. "I am trying."

Alice sighed. "You must show her who you truly are. We have all seen the changes over the past year. I do not believe she paid any attention at all."

And that was the problem. "I don't know how to do that except to show her that I want to be with her."

"When you go to Hatchards, engage her in books about your estates. It will make her realize that you are serious about your holdings."

"I was prepared to discuss novels with her. Such as Miss Austen's books." He'd read them while he was up at school and enjoyed them immensely.

"She will be interested in that as well." Alice tilted her head. A habit all the sisters appeared to share. "She will appreciate that."

They reached the family as the set was ending. Only two more before the supper dance, and he could have Theo in his arms.

CHAPTER TWENTY-THREE

During the set, Theo had glanced over to where Chandos normally stood and did not see him. Where had he gone? She was sure he was not dancing, but where was he?

"Lady Theo?" Lord Bolingbroke said.

"I beg your pardon?" She should pay more attention to her partner.

"I asked if you enjoyed riding?"

"Horseback riding or in a carriage?" Chandos was still not there.

"Horseback riding. I wanted to ask if you would like to ride with me in the Park tomorrow afternoon."

"I must ask my sister. Please send an invitation in the morning." He was returning to their circle with Alice. But where had he gone? She gave herself a mental shake. Why should she care? It was not as if they had an understanding or anything except friendship.

"I shall do that." He smiled at her. "Thank you."

He was very nice. "You are welcome."

Why could she not feel anything for his lordship or any of the other gentlemen? Her sisters had all felt something for the gentlemen they eventually married. Even if it was anger. They felt something.

Chandos's eyes followed her as his lordship returned Theo to her circle.

Bolingbroke bowed. "You dance extremely well, my lady. Will you be at Almack's tomorrow?"

"Yes, I will be."

"May I have the honor of a waltz?"

"I have not yet been approved to waltz at Almack's. A country dance?"

"Of course. I wish you a good evening."

"Thank you. I wish you the same." She curtseyed. When she turned, Chandos was there.

He held out his arm. "Were your toes safe?"

"Yes. He is actually a very good dancer." *Not as good as you.* Yet, she would not tell him that. "He has asked me to go horseback riding tomorrow during the Fashionable Hour."

"Will you go?" There was something in his eyes she could not decipher.

Theo shrugged. "If Grace allows it. I told him to write an invitation and send it in the morning."

"It will be a change of pace from the carriage." He still had that look in his eyes.

"Yes." What was wrong with her? Riding would be different. It would probably be easier to go around the Park with all the traffic. She should be happier. "Epione has never been in a crowd before."

"You are an excellent rider. I have faith that you can handle her no matter what happens."

She would also have her groom with her. "Thank you. I should not worry. She is well trained."

"Exactly." He glanced up. "Here is his lordship to collect you."

What was wrong with her this evening? The only thing Theo could point to was Ashford. He had put a damper on her evening. There was no use looking to anyone else. Chandos, for example, was behaving perfectly normally. He had taken a stroll with Alice, but there was nothing in that. He never behaved as if he were more than a friend. Sooner or later, he would find a mistress, and she would find a husband.

She smiled at her next dance partner and curtseyed. Theo could not wait for this night to be over. Finally, it was time for the supper dance, and Chandos led her out.

He bowed. "Are you feeling better?"

"I do not know how anger transformed into malaise." Theo curtseyed, then they took their positions.

"It was probably discovering that he didn't care about you, but what you represent."

"You could be right. I have never had to go through that before." She did not want to meet another gentleman like Ashford again.

"I do think Worthington is going to be even more careful than before."

"I know Grace is so angry that she wants to be the one to deal with him, but do you not think Matt would be the better choice?"

"Probably." They raised their hands and turned in a circle. "But it's up to them to work it out."

"Yes." They lowered their arms. "I hope I do not have to worry about him attempting to abduct me."

"What?" Despite Chandos's eyes being focused on her, he did not miss a step. "Why would you think that?"

"Did you not know? Alice was abducted. St. Albans went after her and saved her."

Chandos nodded. "Yes, I knew about that, but it cannot happen to you. Whoever tried—" As they twirled again his teeth clenched. "I will not allow that to happen to you."

Other than remaining next to her the entire Season, Theo did not know how he was going to accomplish that. "You will not have time to do anything else if you do that."

"I will do what I must." The music ended and he swept her an elegant bow while she curtseyed.

She placed her hand on his arm as he escorted her to the supper room. Simply dancing with him and hearing him vow to protect her had lifted her mood.

Theo's poor spirits had affected Leo. He'd suspected that it had to be Ashford, and Leo had been right. He also knew exactly why the bounder had come to the ball. Ashford had wanted to ensure himself that he could bed her when, in his delusion, they wed. Not that he'd get a chance to have her. Leo would do everything in his power to see it didn't happen.

"You look like you'd like to commit murder," St. Albans said.

"I'm contemplating it." Leo was either going to murder Ashford or ensure he went back to Shrewsbury. Murder would be more satisfying, but sending him away would work. That bounder would never lay a hand on Theo again.

"I was just going to say you don't look like you're doing any better than Theo was," Kenilworth added.

"It's Ashford." If Leo could punch the man, he would.

"If it makes you feel any better, Worthington is furious. He's never made a mistake like that before. He'll make sure it doesn't happen again. He has decided to accompany Grace tomorrow." Kenilworth took out his quizzing glass and polished it. "Bolingbroke approached Worthington about Theo riding with him tomorrow." Leo glanced at the gentleman he hoped would be his brother-in-law. "Worthington asked him if he'd mentioned it to Theo. That was when Bolingbroke admitted that she told him what he had to do. Worthington said that he should do what she instructed." Kenilworth put his quizzer back. "What are you going to do while she is riding?"

"I'll be at the Park on my horse. Theo is a bit concerned that her mare won't handle the crowds well." Leo wasn't happy that she'd be going on a horse ride with Bolingbroke, but it was Leo's own fault. He hadn't invited her himself. It really didn't matter. He'd be there to protect her.

Kenilworth snorted. "There isn't a situation that girl can't handle on a horse."

"So I told her." Leo hoped it had been her way of telling him that she wanted him there.

He had never been so relieved when it was time for the supper dance, and he didn't have to watch her go off with another gentleman and pretend it didn't bother him. Dancing with Theo made him feel as if he'd come home. After what she'd told him about her sister, reminded him actually, he'd keep a closer eye on the bounder.

He brought her back a collection of ices and other foods he knew she'd like. The corner of his eye caught Ashford with a young lady.

"Lady Giselle." It was as if Theo knew what Leo was thinking. "I hope they enjoy each other's company."

"I do as well." He took a seat next to her. "Kenilworth just told me Worthington will accompany your sister to Bristol House."

"I hope they send him back." She dipped her spoon into a lemon ice. "This is excellent. It is not sweet at all."

Movement to his right caused him to look toward it. Ashford and Lady Giselle were staring at them. That pair would definitely bear watching. Leo decided to warn Theo. "I don't want to alarm you, but the nemesis and the dark-haired lady have been watching us."

"Really?" She surreptitiously glanced their way. "I would wager anything that they are plotting."

He didn't understand. "What could they possibly think they could do to us?"

"I do not have a clue." Theo shook her head. "But I recognize that look. We had both better be on our guard."

For a second, he considered asking if he could reside at Worthington House, but that was an unrealistic idea. He would say something to one of her brothers by marriage. "Are we riding in the morning?"

"Of course." She grinned. "I would not miss it."

* * *

They met the next day and rode to Miss Pettigrew's house where Marrow was already waiting. Leo wondered for a moment if she was going to accompany them, when her horse was brought around. A few seconds later, the lady came out of the house. "I am sorry I am late."

"It is no matter." Theo smiled at her friend. "I was afraid that more people would be in the Park, yet it appears that they are spending the morning at balls and sleeping."

Marrow helped Miss Pettigrew mount, and they were off trotting down the street.

They reached the gate and slowed the horses. Theo glanced at her friend. "Last night I had the impression that Lady Giselle and Lord Ashford were plotting something."

"Well," Miss Pettigrew said, "I am not surprised. I was going to tell you last evening, but I forgot. Lady Giselle has decided to be a duchess." Miss Pettigrew glanced at Leo.

It wouldn't be the first time a young lady or any lady had attempted to convince Leo to wed her. "And, of course, Ashford wants to marry Lady Theo."

"This should be fun." Marrow's tone was as dry as dust. "How do we stop them?"

For some reason, they all looked at Leo. "We have to either discover the plan or watch them until they do something. Once a lady sent me a note to meet her." He smiled to himself. "She was more than surprised when another gentleman appeared."

Miss Pettigrew stared at him. "I have read about that in a novel."

"It is effective." He could see Theo thinking. "And easily done."

"I have to know," Marrow said. "Were they made to wed?"

"They would have been." Leo could have laughed at the memory. "But a week later, she was caught in flagrante with another gentleman."

Theo's brows lowered. "What does *in flagrante* mean?"

"It means that I am not going to tell you. Ask one of your

sisters. I'm sure they will. Worthington would have my guts for garters if I told you."

Miss Pettigrew just looked at him. "That is a descriptive way of putting it, your grace."

Marrow burst into laughter. "It might be time for us to have a nice gallop before you get yourself into trouble."

"I believe you're right." Leo glanced at Theo. "Are you ready to race?"

"I am." Her mare started to move forward, and they were pounding toward the tree.

Again, they arrived at the oak at the same time. "What have you decided to do?"

Her smile could only be described as unpleasant. "If I can catch her, and if Ashford is at the same entertainment, I will have the note delivered to him."

"I think it's an excellent idea." Although Leo hoped that by the time that pair got around to enacting their scheme, Theo would already be his. "We will have to be vigilant."

"Yes. We will." She frowned. "I am not looking forward to this afternoon."

"With Bolingbroke?"

She nodded. "I do not appreciate that he attempted to go around me to Matt."

Leo was not going to tell her that most gentlemen would address the lady's father or guardian. To Theo it was unacceptable. "I understand. Would you like me to be there?"

"Yes. If it would not be too much trouble."

"It's no trouble at all." He'd be happy to put a spoke in Bolingbroke's wheel. "I'm delighted to do it."

Her groom cleared his throat. She glanced at him. "We had better be going."

"Yes." He'd become so used to having her groom following, Leo forgot all about the servant.

"Come and break your fast with us." She headed toward the Serpentine where Marrow and Miss Pettigrew would be waiting.

"Thank you, I will." Leo's valet had become so accustomed to taking his kit to Worthington House, he had the feeling the servant kept a bag packed.

He'd just entered the breakfast room when Kenilworth took Leo aside. "You will be happy to know that Theo has had *in flagrante* explained to her. You will be unhappy to know that Worthington will indeed have your guts for garters if you say anything like that in front of her again. Until you are married, of course."

"I understand. I said it before I realized that I should not have." He was so used to being able to speak freely with Theo, that he had not even thought about it until it was too late. "I must remember in whose company I am."

"As long as we are clear about the expected behavior."

"We are."

Kenilworth slapped Leo on the back. "That is what I wanted to know."

Leo suddenly had a thought. "How long did it take Charlotte to agree to marry you?"

"Much too long, but not as long as it took St. Albans to wed Alice. They were almost at the end of the Season."

"Lord, I hope it doesn't take that much time." Leo wanted to groan.

"So do we all. Attending all the balls and other entertainments is exhausting when we're up with the children in the morning."

He couldn't wait until Theo and he had children. First, he had to win her hand. Apropos of that, he should inform the family that he would accompany her on her ride with Bolingbroke. "In the event you were wondering, I will be with her all afternoon."

Kenilworth gave a sharp nod. "That will save one of us from having to go. I'm famished."

Leo was as well. He took his seat next to Theo. "What time are we going to Hatchards?"

"After luncheon." She took a bite of her shirred eggs. "Matt sent a note around last night saying that he needed to meet with the duke concerning his nephew."

Leo took ham and shirred eggs from the footman, then placed a piece of toast on his plate. "That should be an interesting conversation."

"I know." She took a sip of tea as he poured his. "Part of me would like to be there. But even I know that would not be prudent."

He'd like to be there as well, if only to harm Ashford in some way. "We will do much better at the bookstore."

She looked at him from beneath her lashes. "We would only get into trouble."

A footman entered the room. "Lady Theo, flowers have arrived for you."

"Please have them put in water." She rubbed her forehead. "Why do they waste their time?"

Leo had been wanting to send her a bouquet; now he was glad he hadn't. "Perhaps some of them send their valets to purchase them."

"I just want them to stop." She bit her lip. "It makes me feel guilty. I am not interested in any of them."

"Sweetheart," Alice said. "It is all part of the game. Do not worry about it. They are sending other ladies flowers as well."

Theo appeared struck by the information and her brow cleared. "If that is what they are doing, then I will not be concerned about it."

Excellent. Now he could enjoy their time at the bookstore and guard her during the ride. He was starting to feel like Lancelot, until Leo remembered that Lancelot had cuckolded the king. Gawain might be a better choice. Leo almost forgot. Tonight was Almack's. Definitely Gawain.

CHAPTER TWENTY-FOUR

Theo had been surprised that Chandos had asked for advice on estate management. He was really very knowledgeable. What was even more interesting was his love of Miss Austen. Of course, that had given Theo the opportunity to introduce him to some other authors she also read. After they had finished at Hatchards they went to the Burlington Arcade. Theo wanted a new fan for the gown she would wear to Almack's that evening.

"What color is your gown?" Chandos asked as he perused the collection of fans.

"It is a deep butter yellow with Pomona green trim."

"And your reticule?"

"Pomona green." She joined him looking at the fans. "Here is one." It was a very pretty scene of a Georgian couple under a tree. "The only problem is that the colors will not go with the gown I am wearing this evening. It will, however, go with another gown."

"What about this?" Chandos held up a delicate fan of lace with gold trim.

"That is lovely. But I am not wearing any gold."

He stood close to her. "You could wear gold-tipped hairpins."

"Perhaps with pearls."

"Perfect." He went to another area of the store and found the hairpins. "What do you think of these?"

They were small gold-flowered hairpins with pearls in the middle. "They are lovely." She held out her hand. "Once I pay for these we can go."

He held them close to his chest. "I will buy them for you. After all, I haven't sent any flowers, and I guarantee that these ornaments will not cost nearly what some of those bouquets do. You need not worry about the fan and pins being inappropriate."

Theo knew the fan was not inexpensive, but she had no idea what flowers cost. Chandos would be a much better judge of that. "Very well. Thank you."

"It is entirely my pleasure." He made the purchase, and they returned to her phaeton and added the package to the books in the carrying space. "Do you think your brother and sister are back from Bristol House yet?"

"They must be." She looked at her brooch watch. "It has been almost two hours."

He helped her into the vehicle. "I'll be interested in hearing what occurred."

"As will I." She waited until he was seated before giving the horses their office. "You should stay for tea."

"Thank you." He smiled and, for a brief minute, butterflies took up residence in her breast. "I would be delighted."

As she drew up in front of the house, her brother's town coach was being led away. "I wonder what happened to take so long?"

"I suspect we'll find out shortly." Chandos jumped down and came around to her side of the phaeton. When he clasped his hands around her waist and lifted her down, the butterflies returned. It was disconcerting to say the least. Theo sucked in a breath just to make sure she could still breathe.

The door opened as they approached it. Thorton bowed. "Tea will be served in the morning room. His lordship and her ladyship will be there momentarily."

Theo kept her voice low. "That doesn't sound good."

"My thoughts exactly." Chandos took her arm, and they made their way to the parlor. The only ones there were the footmen setting out the sandwiches, tarts, and biscuits.

"I wonder where everyone is?" Surely Grace would have everyone here to learn what had happened.

"We're coming," Charlotte said. "Some of us are just quicker than others."

"Some of you live closer," Eleanor responded.

"That is fair." They took their seats as the teapots were carried in. "The children will have tea in the schoolroom."

"That sounds serious." Madeline said as she and Harry strolled into the morning room. "I am sorry that we missed the ball last evening." She bussed Theo's cheek.

"There is nothing you could have done."

"There is something I could have done," Harry said. "I never liked Ashford. I would have stopped him from being presented to you."

Soon the rest of them had arrived as well as Matt and Grace.

Matt stood as tea was being poured out. "Here are how things stand. I made very clear that Theo would not have anything to do with Lord Ashford. His uncle made clear that Ashford wanted to wed Theo. They even went so far as to make a proposal of marriage. I explained that I had never arranged a match for one of my sisters and I would not start now." He looked at her. "You may treat him as you wish. If he approaches you, tell one of us. If you are with your footman or groom, they will be allowed to take any action they deem necessary to see you are safe."

"I understand." Theo would also start carrying her knife and her pistol.

"I'll send a groom with you this afternoon."

She nodded once.

"I will be there as well," Chandos said.

"I asked him to come." Firstly, because she was not at all happy with Bolingbroke, and second, she did not trust Ashford. "I just wanted a nice calm Season."

"You did not want a Season at all," Mary retorted.

"I might have been better off waiting."

That made everyone groan. "Enough," Alice said. "You are having your Season. It has merely become a bit more interesting."

Theo could do without all the interest. She turned to Chandos. "Shall we send for your hack?"

"If you please. I want to be here when Bolingbroke arrives."

A thought occurred to Theo. "Maybe I can find a match for him."

"Do you have anyone in mind?" He accepted a cup of tea.

"Possibly. Lady Lana Grant." The only problem was that she was Lady Giselle's good friend. "I will think about it."

The other thing Theo had to think about was her recent reactions to Chandos. She could not allow herself to fall in love with him. Not after hearing what those ladies had said. Not after what she knew of his past.

Asclepius arrived at the same time as Bolingbroke. Leo had already assisted Theo onto her mare. Not that she required help. He just liked doing it. Then again, she couldn't use the same technique she used in the country. He mounted his horse.

The other gentleman smiled at them both. "Lady Theo, are you ready to go?"

"In a moment." Mick, her groom, rode up. "I am ready now."

"I'm ready as well." Leo smiled at Bolingbroke. "Shall we?"

"I did not know you were joining us, your grace." He couldn't hide his disappointment at not having Theo to himself.

"I felt like I needed a ride after tea."

"You were here for tea?" Bolingbroke appeared more and more distressed, which suited Leo. Sooner or later, the man would get the hint that Theo was his.

"I frequently drink tea here." He could have added that he broke his fast and dined with them as well, but he'd save that for use if he needed it.

They rode three across until they reached Park Lane, then Leo rode beside Theo, leaving Bolingbroke to ride with the groom.

"You really should not have done that." She glanced at Leo as they entered the gate.

He tried to give her a contrite look. "I couldn't help myself."

"He does seem to be quite deferential to you."

"I am a duke." Not that it mattered to her at all.

She shrugged as Bolingbroke caught up to them.

Unsurprisingly, other gentlemen on horseback joined them. Leo decided to hang back and watch the fribbles attempt to gain her attention. One of them said something she obviously didn't like, and, for a second, she looked as if she'd like to hit him with something hard. The idiot said something else, and she smiled politely. He knew the smile did not reach her expressive eyes. God, she was good at that. Finally, they made their way back to the gate and departed. Leo wanted to ask her if she would like to go to Gunter's, but he'd have to take Bolingbroke, which Leo would not do. He rode with them to Worthington House and waited until Bolingbroke took his leave.

She didn't know that Leo would be dancing the waltz with her. That was a surprise. Would she be hurt if he didn't ask for a set? Or would she work it out? Or had he asked for a set already? He had a vague recollection of doing so, but he usually asked her to stand up with him. Leo had no idea if Worthington would allow him to stand up twice with her, but he wouldn't know if he didn't try. "I'll see you at Almack's. Do you have the supper dance free?"

"My lady, Payne has been asking for you," Thorton said.

Leo raised a brow. "Payne?"

"My maid. I must bathe before dinner." Theo smiled. "I have almost all my dances free. I'm glad you were there today."

He considered giving her a flip response but decided not to. "I am as well. Until this evening."

"Yes, until then."

He arrived home to find a note from Alice St. Albans inviting him to dine with them before going to Almack's.

He quickly dashed off an acceptance, then went to his secretary's office. "Is there anything urgent?"

Whiting shook his head. "No, your grace. Although, her grace left a message asking you to request a waltz with a young lady."

This is what it had come to. Mama writing notes to him. Leo would have to reconcile with her later. After he and Theo were betrothed. "Inform her that I already have plans to ask permission to waltz with another lady."

"Yes, your grace. I wish you a pleasant evening."

"To you as well."

Alice, St. Albans, and Leo arrived at Almack's as the doors opened. He was surprised to see how plain it was. Simply one large open room with long windows hung with blue curtains. There were not even any alcoves.

Lady Cowper was waiting for them. "My lady, your grace, my lord." They curtseyed and bowed. "As soon as Lady Theo arrives, I will take you to her. The first dance will be the minuet. I will introduce you to a Miss Cunningham."

Leo bowed. "It will be my pleasure to stand up with her, my lady."

"I warn you." Her ladyship speared him with a look. "Duke or not, you will not be allowed to avoid dancing with other young ladies this evening. From what I have heard, thus far, hostesses have been far too easy on you."

"Yes, ma'am." He had managed to escape being made to stand up with other young ladies by staying hidden among Theo's family.

A few other people entered the assembly room, including Theo and her brother and sister. She wore the gown she'd told him about. Her skirts seemed to float around her as she strolled in. He was pleased to see that the gold pins gleamed in her chestnut hair. No matter how many times he looked at her, she was still the most beautiful lady he'd ever seen.

"Come along, your grace." Lady Cowper placed her hand on his arm.

Theo was speaking with Alice when her ladyship led him to Theo. "Lady Theo." She turned and her eyes widened in surprise as she curtseyed. "I recommend the Duke of Chandos as a suitable partner for the waltz."

She smiled politely, but there was a look of amazement in her lapis-blue eyes. He had surprised her. "Thank you, my lady, your grace."

For a second their eyes met, and he wanted to tell her how he felt. That he wanted to marry her and for them to spend the rest of their lives together.

Then Lady Cowper said, "Now I will introduce his grace to his first dance partner."

"Yes, my lady." Leo went along with her ladyship to meet a young lady newly come out.

"Miss Cunningham. May I present the Duke of Chandos as your first dance partner?"

Her hair was pale blond, and her skin was like milk. What little color she had drained from the lady's face. For a moment, Leo thought Miss Cunningham would faint. He bowed. "Miss Cunningham, I am delighted to partner with you."

"Th-thank you, your grace." She curtseyed. "It would be my pleasure to stand up with you."

"I will come for you when the opening notes begin." Leo bowed and left with her ladyship. "I am at your disposal for all sets except for the first waltz and the supper dance."

"I am glad to hear it, your grace."

Just then he saw Lady Giselle strolling across the room. "The only lady with whom I will not dance is Lady Giselle Darnel."

"Indeed." Lady Cowper appeared surprised. "May I ask what you have against her?"

"She has been unkind to a couple of ladies I know." Ever since her brother had told him she wished to wed a duke, Leo had decided to stay far away from her.

"Very well. I shall inform the other Patronesses." She curtseyed.

He bowed. "Thank you for your understanding."

"I will leave you here. I wish you a good evening." She strolled up to another gentleman.

Leo immediately rejoined Theo's family, and she came up to him. "What made you decide to ask for permission to waltz with me?"

Because I love you. "I could not allow a lady who dances the waltz so exquisitely to languish by the side of the room or stand up with someone who is not as skilled."

"I am thrilled that you did." Her cheeks colored and her eyes glowed. "There is no one with whom I would rather waltz." There was no other word to describe her countenance than radiant.

If only he hadn't promised not to begin courting her in earnest until after her come out ball. Still, it wouldn't be long now. There was only one more ball before hers.

He led Miss Cunningham, who seemed to have regained her countenance and did not faint, to the dance floor. She was surprisingly graceful as they went through the movement of the steps. Leo was unhappy to see Bolingbroke lead Theo out. "I thought I'd got rid of him."

"Did you say something, your grace?" Miss Cunningham asked.

"No. Nothing at all. From where do you hail, Miss Cunningham?"

"Not far from Harrogate. My father wanted me to attend the Season there, but my mother prevailed and"—she smiled—"we are here."

"I hope you are enjoying yourself." Perhaps she would be a good match for Bolingbroke.

"I am. We have mostly seen the sights, but I attended my first ball the other night. Unfortunately, I have not met many other ladies."

Leo could help her there. "I know two ladies who are also making their come out. They are both kind. Perhaps in between sets I could introduce you."

"Thank you, your grace. That would be very nice."

It occurred to him that a year ago, if anyone would have told him he'd be playing this role and liking it, he wouldn't have believed them.

When the dance ended, he took her back to her mother and went to Theo. "The lady I stood up with, Miss Cunningham, does not know any other young ladies. Would you allow me to introduce her to you?"

"Of course." Theo glanced around. "Sarah, come with me, please. We are going to meet another young lady."

Miss Pettigrew smiled. "I would be delighted. Is she from our part of the country?"

Theo glanced at him.

"No, Harrogate." He held out his arms for them both, but Marrow stepped over to escort Miss Pettigrew. When they arrived, Lady Cowper was presenting another gentleman to Miss Cunningham. Her ladyship inclined her head before leaving. Leo gave a sharp nod to the gentleman. "Miss Cunningham. Here are Lady Theo Vivers and Miss Sarah Pettigrew."

Theo took the lady's hands. "I am very happy to meet you."

Miss Cunningham smiled and curtseyed. "The pleasure is mine."

Miss Pettigrew came up with Marrow. "I am Miss Pettigrew. May I present Lord Marrow?"

"I am delighted to meet you both." She curtseyed again.

Until Leo had begun attending these types of entertainments, he never realized how much bowing and curtseying went on.

As Leo strolled back to Theo's family with her, the first notes of the waltz began to play. "My lady, shall we?"

"Yes, indeed." Her smile almost took his breath away.

They took their places on the floor. "I wish I could dance the Viennese waltz with you."

"What is the difference?" Theo held her arms up as she turned.

"I'll show you one day." After they were betrothed.

CHAPTER TWENTY-FIVE

After breakfast the next day, the flowers started to arrive as well as trinkets. One was a gold heart charm hanging from a gold safety pin. Theo opened the note that had been placed in the velvet pouch.

For the most beautiful lady in England.
With deep respect and regard,
Milford

"I cannot accept this." It must be too expensive.

Grace entered the hall. "What is it?"

Theo held up the pin. "It is from Lord Milford. It must be too expensive to accept."

Her sister took it from her and inspected. "It actually is not. I saw one when I was shopping and almost got it for Elizabeth. My concern was that one of the twins would find it and hurt themselves trying to open it."

So much for that idea. Theo had to keep it. Or give it to Elizabeth with express directions to keep it away from the younger children. "Very well."

Grace began sifting through the other gifts that were on a long side table against the wall. "What is this?" She held up a pouch the size of a reticule. "Open it."

Theo took the bag and took out the fan inside. Even closed one could see it was beautiful. A long narrow note fell out when she opened the fan.

Dear Theo,
I hope you can find a use for this. It's made to fit in a reticule.
I will see you at luncheon.
Yr. Servant,
Chandos

The fan had a pale yellow background with a Georgian scene of children playing. On each spoke was a small amethyst. "How practical."

"I guarantee that fan costs more than the pin," Grace opined.

Theo hoped she did not have to return it. "What does that mean?"

"That a piece of jewelry is not necessarily more expensive than a fan that you would naturally want to keep."

"I understand." Theo picked up the pin again. "It is a pretty trinket."

"Be careful if you decide to wear it. Lord Milford might think that you are interested in him."

It was definitely going to Elizabeth. "I shall." She continued looking through the other presents. She held up a silver thimble. "Whoever sent me this will not be thanked."

Grace looked as if she'd laugh. "I do wonder if it is an indication of what he thinks a lady's role should be, or a lack of imagination."

Mary came from the direction of the music room. "What have you received today?"

"Have a look." Theo showed her youngest sister the thimble. "Do you have any use for this?"

"No, but Nurse might."

That was an idea. "I'll ask her. If you find anything you like, you make keep it."

"Thank you." Mary grinned. "What are you holding?"

Theo had forgotten she had not put the fan back down. "It's a gift from Chandos. A fan that will fit in a reticule."

"I doubt you will find anything you like better than that."

"I think you are correct. What are you doing this morning?" Theo missed Mary. Their lives were so different now.

"French, Italian, and German. Do you want to join me?"

Considering Mary spoke all three languages better than Theo. "No?"

Her sister laughed. "I would not if I were you. I will be discussing political situations in each language."

"With whom and where?"

"With Martha at Merton House. Dom has arranged it." Mary chuckled. "Martha was complaining that we never get any real experience conversing with native speakers."

That made sense. "When do you leave?"

A knock came on the door. "Now. I must get my hat and gloves."

"Theo, I would like you to accompany me on morning visits," Grace said.

"I would like that." Even though morning visits could be fraught, they were also interesting. Theo was glad Chandos was going to join them at luncheon. She would have an opportunity to thank him for the gift.

Lady Pettigrew and Sarah joined them for morning visits that afternoon.

Partway through the visits they came across Miss Cunningham, who motioned for them to come sit next to her. "I have been hoping to see the two of you."

Theo sat on the sofa next to the lady. "Is there anything with which I can help you?"

"Not help exactly. I met a number of gentlemen last night." She smiled. "Thank you for allowing the duke to stand up with me." Theo wanted to tell Miss Cunningham that he did not belong to Theo, but Miss Cunningham continued. "After the first dance, I met a number of gentlemen." Her forehead wrinkled. "The problem is that neither my mother nor I know anything about them. I would like to believe that the Patronesses would not present anyone who was unsuitable, but at the last house, a few ladies were saying that there were some gentlemen whom they would not allow to be presented to their daughters."

That would be a problem. "We can make sure your mother knows my sister, Lady Worthington. She would be able to advise you."

Sarah took a small chair next to the sofa. "Is there anyone in particular you want to know about?"

Miss Cunningham colored slightly. "I was taken with Lord Bolingbroke. He was very nice and conversed with a great deal of sense."

Theo exchanged a look with Sarah, and said, "He is nice. Did he send you flowers or anything this morning?"

"Oh, yes! He sent a bouquet of wildflowers. I mentioned to him that I liked them much better than the cultivated ones."

That was excellent. "Would you like to go riding with me this afternoon during the Grand Strut? It would not surprise me if we saw his lordship."

"If you would not mind taking me." Miss Cunningham's blush deepened. "I would love it."

"Theo, will you take your high-perched phaeton?" Sarah asked.

Miss Cunningham's face immediately lost all color.

Theo took a breath. For the sake of making another match, she could sacrifice driving. "No, I believe we should take the landau. That way we can all go. I will just ask my sister." She looked at Sarah again. "Unless you are already otherwise engaged."

"It is no problem. I will tell Marrow that I am driving with you today."

"Oh, thank you." Miss Cunningham's color returned. "You

must think it very cowardly to be afraid of the high-perched phaetons. I was in one once and experienced vertigo."

Theo had never heard of it happening in a carriage, but she did know that some people got vertigo from being in high places. "Think nothing of it." She took out her notebook and pencil. "If you give me your address, we will collect you at five."

Before leaving the house, she made sure that Mrs. Cunningham was introduced to Grace and confirmed that Theo could use the landau that afternoon.

The meeting that Chandos was in with her brothers broke up at three, and he was invited to remain to drink tea with them.

After he and Theo had their tea and biscuits, they repaired to the window seat. "I saw Miss Cunningham during morning visits today."

"How was she? I hope she had a sufficient number of dance partners."

"She did." Theo grinned at him. "She is particularly interested in Lord Bolingbroke."

Chandos's eyes twinkled as he gazed back at her. "Bolingbroke. That's very interesting."

"That is what Sarah and I thought. So, I decided to take the landau so that we could all go out together during the Fashionable Hour. I know we were to go together, but you do not mind, do you?"

"Not at all." In fact, Leo would be happy to have Bolingbroke interested in a lady other than Theo. "I'll bring my horse and meet you there."

"That is a wonderful idea. I wish someone could tell his lordship that we were going to be at the Park."

Leo could probably help with that. "Let me see what I can do."

Theo's smile made his heart beat harder. It also made his cock take notice. Soon. After her come out ball, he could begin courting her. That reminded him. "May I have your first dance at your come out ball?"

She gave him a curious look. "You usually want the supper dance."

"If you must know, I have been informed that you will be so busy with your guests that I'm better off asking for your first set."

A light tinkling laugh escaped her lips. "Yes, you may have my first dance."

He hoped it was a waltz, but knew it wasn't likely to be." The clock chimed the hour. "I had better go. Are you fetching Miss Cunningham?"

"I am."

"I'll see you here just before five." He rose and bowed over the hand she had held out.

"Yes. I am very glad you are supporting this cause."

"It's my pleasure to assist." She started to rise. "I know my way out but thank you."

Once he arrived home, he gave orders for his horse to be ready no later than quarter to five. Then he called for his butler.

"Your grace?"

"I need to know where the Earl of Bolingbroke resides." Leo could send a note, but a personal visit might be better. If the man was even home.

"Straightaway, your grace." A few minutes later, Hoover returned. "He has a house at number five, Upper Grosvenor Street."

"Excellent work. Thank you."

"It is my pleasure, your grace." Hoover bowed.

Leo went to his chambers to change, and he didn't have much time. It had taken almost fifteen minutes to walk from Worthington House to home.

He found his valet in the dressing room. "I'm going riding."

"Yes, your grace. I will be just a moment."

In the extremely short time of twenty minutes, Leo was descending the stairs.

"Your horse is ready, your grace," a footman said.

"Thank you." Several minutes later, he stopped in front of

Bolingbroke House. As luck would have it, a horse was being brought around. "Is that for Lord Bolingbroke?"

"Yes, sir," the groom replied.

"Tell him Chandos is here and would like to speak with him."

"What do you have to tell me other than to stay away from Lady Theo?" Bolingbroke said as he approached.

"I would like to invite you to join me. Lady Theo, Miss Pettigrew, and a Miss Cunningham are taking a drive this afternoon. I was told you might be interested in joining us."

At first his lordship had a blank expression on his face, then he smiled slightly. "I would indeed. Thank you."

"You're welcome."

Bolingbroke mounted his gelding. "What made you think of me?"

"I was told you danced with her last night, and Lady Theo informed me that she was taking the lady on a ride in the Worthington landau."

"Not her phaeton?"

"Er, no. There isn't enough room for three of them in the phaeton."

They rode toward Berkeley Square. "What are your intensions toward Lady Theo?"

"I wish to marry her, but I promised not to court her in earnest until after her come out ball."

His lordship appeared surprised. "How long have your known her?"

"A few years now. I formed the decision to make her my wife last summer. I've just been waiting."

"I would think her family would be ecstatic at the idea a duke was interested in marrying her."

"That's because you don't know her family. They already have one duke and the heir of a duke, and they don't care at all about a gentlemen's rank. It is his character that matters, and, of course, his ability to support a family. One must also agree to attend family get-togethers."

Bolingbroke's jaw dropped. "You're joking."

"I am most certainly not. At present, I am walking a fine line with her ladyship. Thank the deities that her ball is tomorrow."

"She must be running around like mad. I know my sister did."

"Not she." Which was rather odd. "She's barely mentioned it." Then again, knowing Theo, she had the whole thing planned months ago and trusted her servants to carry out her wishes.

"How did you find Miss Cunningham?"

"Charming." Bolingbroke's countenance softened. "She looks like a fairy princess, but she is extremely practical." They were almost to Berkeley Square when he said, "They are late coming to town because her grandmother was ill. She had a feeling it was the old lady's way of getting attention. She went to her grandmother and told her that if she did not recover soon, she would not be able to have her come out."

Leo barked a laugh. He would have described that as more ruthless than practical. Although, it was quite practical. "I take it there was a miraculous recovery."

Bolingbroke grinned. "Within days Miss Cunningham and her mother were making the trip south."

The landau was out front waiting when they arrived. Theo and Miss Pettigrew were exiting the house, and Marrow was waiting by his horse. Leo dismounted and assisted Theo into the carriage. "I remember the first time I saw this landau. I'd never seen one so large."

"The children begged to come, but they would have to have maids with them, and that would be a distraction."

"I can see how it would be. Let's be off to collect Miss Cunningham."

Theo gave the coachman his leave to start the horses, and they made their way to Green Street where the Cunninghams had leased a house for the Season.

Once they'd arrived, a footman went to the door and knocked.

A minute or so later, Miss Cunningham descended the short steps to the pavement. "Good afternoon." When she saw Bolingbroke, who'd dismounted, she blushed prettily. "My lord, how nice of you to join us."

He offered his arm and assisted her into the carriage. "It is entirely my pleasure, Miss Cunningham."

Leo saw the excited look she flashed the other two ladies as she settled onto the bench. Theo and Miss Pettigrew smiled in response.

They made slow progress around the Park, which was probably intended. Leo would have preferred to have Theo to himself, but he could see that Bolingbroke and Miss Cunningham were quickly forming a bond of some sort.

As they headed back toward the gate, he had an idea. "Would everyone like to go to Gunter's?"

"I would love it," Theo said immediately.

"As would I," Miss Pettigrew agreed.

Miss Cunningham appeared confused. "What is Gunter's?"

"They have the most excellent ices," Bolingbroke said. "I highly recommend them."

"In that case, how can I refuse." She glanced at Leo. "Thank you, your grace."

Leo considered the possibility that he'd have to open an account at the tea shop, then his lordship sidled beside him. "I will pay for Miss Cunningham's ice."

"As you wish."

"Miss Cunningham," Theo said. "I would like to invite you to my come out ball tomorrow evening. I shall have an invitation sent around when I arrive at home."

"I would be delighted." The lady's smile widened. "Thank you so much."

He glanced at Bolingbroke and raised a brow, silently asking if he had been invited as well. Bolingbroke nodded.

Leo shot a grin at Theo, who returned the smile. They worked so well together. He prayed that she saw that as well.

CHAPTER TWENTY-SIX

The next morning when Theo returned from her ride, she was immediately accosted with questions about the final preparations for her ball.

"My lady," Mrs. Thorton said, "the florist said that the tulips he ordered from Holland haven't arrived. He said he can fill in with daffodils, but he's afraid that they won't have enough color by themselves."

"Does he have any suggestions?" This was the reason she had done everything months ago. So this would not happen.

"He said he has some very nice hyacinths. But—"

"I know. Alice is allergic to them."

In the distance the doorbell rang, and Sarah strolled into the room. "I came to help."

"The florist has not received the tulips I ordered. He has daffodils."

Sarah nodded. "But you need more color. What about bluebells? You can have them under the daffodils in the arrangements."

"That is an excellent idea. We could also add rhododendron

flowers around the room." She looked at the housekeeper. "Will that do?"

"I hope so, my lady." She bustled out of the room.

Theo glanced at Sarah. "When is your come out ball? You mentioned it once, but that was all."

An excited smile dawned on her face. "I am not going to have one. I love my mother dearly, but she cannot plan anything more complicated than a dinner. Instead, I am having a betrothal ball at Carlisle House."

"Oh!" Theo hugged her friend. "When was this decided?"

"This morning after our ride. Lady Carlisle and Marrow had been speaking about it. This morning, he broke his fast with Mama and me and suggested that we just have a betrothal ball. Then he went down on one knee and proposed. His mother had even given him a betrothal ring to give to me."

"I am so excited for you!"

"And I have more news!" Sarah took Theo's hands. "Patricia and Lord Holland are betrothed."

"Fabulous! Will they share the ball with you and Marrow?"

Sarah shook her head. "No. They are marrying almost immediately. He must be in Vienna soon. I believe one of the reasons Lady Carlisle was so happy about being able to plan a betrothal for us was that she cannot give her youngest daughter one."

"My lady." Their cook, Jacque, entered the parlor. "It is a catastrophe. The cake we ordered was dropped. It is ruined."

"Who do we know that has a pastry chef? It is going to take more than one person to make everything we need. Instead of a cake we can have an assortment of smaller desserts." She knew Dotty had one, and Louisa. "Lady Merton, our duchess, who else?"

"Lady Montagu. I will think of some more." His countenance brightened. "Lady Kenilworth. *Oui*. That will work. I will explain and send everyone letters."

Jacque left, and a footman ran into the room. "My lady, we don't have enough champagne."

That was not possible. She had been here when it arrived last week. "What happened to it?"

"Someone from Lord Montagu's house came over and needed to borrow some. He took most of it."

"Send however many men you need over there and get it back. Right now. Wait while I write a message to my sister." Theo went to the small desk in the corner, dashed off a missive, sanded it, and sealed it. She handed it to the footman. "Have this given to Lady Montagu." She glanced at Sarah. "I will guarantee you that Eleanor knew nothing about this. I am going to see how the rest of the arrangements are coming along. You may come if you wish."

"I'll go with you."

Theo almost walked into Chandos, who was in the hall. "What are you doing here?"

He spread his hands with his palms out. "I came to see if you needed help."

"The champagne is missing, the order of tulips has not arrived from Holland yet, and the cake was dropped. Our Jacque is writing to the pastry chefs in our family to arrange for desserts."

"Who took the champagne?"

"Apparently someone from Montagu House. I'm going to strangle Montague."

"Recover what you can. I have a good stock of champagne I'll send over. I also have a pastry chef who has very little to do at the moment. Write down what you want, and I'll make sure it's here. I can also ask my gardener about tulips. Several years ago, my mother ordered hundreds of them."

"We decided to use daffodils, bluebells, and rhododendrons, but I would love to have tulips as well." She tugged the bellpull. A footman entered immediately. "If Jones has not returned, please send the missive his grace will write. I also need a list of what Jacque wants done. His grace has a pastry chef as well."

"If you'll point me to a desk, I'll write a missive to my butler telling him to arrange it all."

"Yes, of course." She opened the door to a parlor. "We have at least one writing desk in every room. Even if it is a very small one."

"That's efficient."

"Thank you." She smiled. "It was my idea."

He went over to the small desk and pulled out a piece of paper.

"My lady." The head maid, Simms, entered the room.

"Do not tell me there is something wrong with the table linens." How could so many things go wrong?

"No, my lady. I just wanted to know if you'd like to inspect them."

"It is a little late now."

"Yes, but they are finally all ironed."

That did not make sense. "I thought we were sending them out."

"We were, but everyone at the laundry we used came down with something. They all had spots and some of them died."

That sounded serious. "Please tell me that the linens were not taken there after all."

"No. A messenger came before we sent them."

"That is one good piece of news. Where are they?"

"In the supper room."

"I'll be right down."

Chandos stood and handed her the note as Jones, her personal footman, entered and bowed. She gave it to him. "This must be sent to Chandos House immediately."

"I'll see to it, my lady."

"I must see to the linens." Theo started out the door.

"We're coming with you," Sarah said.

Leo grunted something Theo couldn't understand.

When they reached the room, the tablecloths and napkins were piled on one long table. The head maid and laundress stood by. Theo carefully inspected them. "Excellent work."

"Thank you, my lady." The laundress curtseyed.

"Now we just need the footmen to return so that we can set up the tables," Simms said.

Theo was about to ask how all of them were gone, but of course they were. "I can help."

"So can I," Sarah said.

"I will as well," Chandos added. He looked at the folded tables and chairs. "I never knew that's how they were stored. Tell me where they go."

Simms looked at Theo for permission. She nodded. Simms addressed them. "The important thing right now is to get them all unfolded. Some of them are heavy."

By the time the first of the footmen returned, all the tables and most of the chairs had been unfolded. "My lady, we were able to get a little more than half of the champagne back. Lady Eleanor, er, Lady Montagu rang a peel over his lordship's head for forgetting your ball and taking the champagne."

"As well she should," Chandos said. "Do you know if the champagne from my house has arrived?"

"Yes, your grace. Your footmen delivered it. Your stock made up for what we were lacking and more."

Theo could not believe how helpful Chandos was being. "Thank you so very much. I will replace the amount you lent me."

He shook his head. "Consider it a gift more useful than bouquets."

"Well, thank you again." She smiled at him. Even after unfolding most of the tables, and placing some of them, he still looked put together.

"It's my pleasure."

Theo glanced at Simms. "We will go and see about the flowers. Do you have the men you need now?"

"Yes, my lady."

Followed by Sarah and Chandos, Theo found Mrs. Thorton downstairs in a room near the kitchen with a man identified as the florist's assistant. Among the daffodils, bluebells, and hydrangea flowers, were dozens of red, pink, and deep yellow tulips. "I'm glad everything arrived."

"Yes, my lady," the assistant said. "Do you want to be notified after the first arrangements are completed?"

Not really, but, if nothing else, this morning had taught her that she must. "Yes, please." Chandos, Sarah, and Theo left the room and went up to the morning room where Thorton brought a tea tray. "I thought you might be hungry."

"Thank you." If she was, Chandos most certainly was. She poured each of them a cup and placed the tray of sandwiches near him. "You have saved the day again with your tulips. They are lovely."

"I'm glad you like them." Leo had only planned to stop by to see if Theo required anything. He'd not expected to be put to work. Still, he was happy that she had trusted him enough to take advantage of his presence and accept his offers of assistance. "And I am glad to have been able to help."

Theo glanced at Miss Pettigrew with a raised brow, and she nodded. Then his beloved looked at him. "Sarah and Marrow are to be married. His mother is planning the betrothal ball."

"Finally." Leo had been expecting the announcement for a while now. "My best wishes to you, Miss Pettigrew. Marrow is a lucky man."

She waved her hand. "Please call me Sarah. After all the work we did together, it is proper."

"In that case, I am honored."

"You must also be hungry." Theo motioned to the plate of sandwiches. "Please eat."

These were not the small sandwiches that normally accompany tea, but larger ones filled with various meats and cheeses. "Thank you."

"When do you expect to wed?" Theo asked before she took a bite of a sandwich.

"That matter is currently being debated." Miss Sarah took a sip of tea. "Marrow wants it to be as soon as possible." Leo could absolutely understand and appreciate that. "My mother wants us to wait long enough to have a large wedding breakfast. His mother tends to agree with her. I would like to marry in two to three weeks."

He swallowed. "How long does it take to plan a large wedding breakfast?"

She took a deep breath. "Mama said four to six weeks. Lady Carlisle says three to four weeks."

Theo's expression showed clearly what she thought of a wedding breakfast taking so long to plan. He knew that her sisters had married two weeks after their engagements. "I hate to say it, but I would trust Lady Carlisle over your mother."

"I agree," Sarah said. "I do not wish to hurt my mother's feelings, but . . ."

"She is the one who could not manage to organize your come out ball."

"Exactly. Not only that, but neither Marrow nor I want to wait that long to wed."

Leo was happy to keep his mouth full and hear what Theo thought about all of this. Yet something about Sarah's mother not being able to plan a ball, and Theo arranging her own ball, confused him. "Who is supposed to plan a come out ball?"

She lifted one shoulder in an elegant shrug. "I suppose it depends on one's family. We plan our own. It is a way of ensuring that we have what we want, and it gives us the valuable experience of being completely responsible for the results. It is one thing to help plan a ball. It is another thing to do it oneself."

He could understand that. It was the same with most projects.

"Yes," Sarah said. "Mama has very little experience planning large entertainments. As a consequence, I have no experience. Her ladyship has offered to teach me."

Leo was starting to understand her dilemma. "Ergo, you would rather agree with your future mother-in-law."

"Precisely." Sarah nodded. "It would be of great benefit to me and make Marrow happier."

Theo finished her tea. "If you want my opinion, I support your inclination to agree with Lady Carlisle with one stipulation. Have the wedding no later than three weeks. That really will give you enough time."

"And make Marrow even happier." If it was Leo getting married, he'd want it done as quickly as possible.

"I think you are correct." Sarah's brows drew together. "Mama will have to come around. Aside from that, I cannot see that she will be much help." Sarah glanced at Theo and smiled. "Thank you."

"Anything to help a friend." Theo returned the smile. "I believe everything here is under control. I cannot think of anything else that could go wrong."

"Before I leave"—Sarah looked at Leo then at Theo again—"who will have your supper dance?"

"Lord Milford. Chandos has my first set."

Milford? Really? Leo must set his mind to finding a suitable lady for the man.

Theo and Sarah rose, prompting him to get to his feet. They all walked to the front door together. Sarah's maid quickly joined her.

Once she and the maid left, Leo had the sudden urge to take Theo's hands. "I will see you this evening. However, if you have need of anything else, please call upon me."

"I will. Thank you again."

He didn't want to be thanked. He just wanted to make her happy. "Adieu."

"Until later."

CHAPTER TWENTY-SEVEN

Theo dragged herself out of bed after only four hours of sleep. Her come out ball had been a success. Everyone had commented on the floral arrangements, the desserts, and the champagne. The only part she had not liked was having to stay up until two o'clock. She could have slept longer, but that would put her off her schedule, and there was another ball this evening.

She was surprised to see Chandos waiting as she descended the stairs. "Good morning. I did not expect to see you."

"Unlike some people, I was asleep before midnight. Marrow and Sarah are still abed." He offered her his arm, which she took. "I thought you might be, as well, but I was informed you had called for Epione to be brought around. We still have time for a ride."

They went out and he lifted her to her mare. "How was the rest of the ball?"

"Lovely. Why did you leave so early?" They rode out of the square.

"I'd already danced with you." He grinned at her. "I was extremely surprised and delighted that the first set was a waltz. That was an unusual choice."

She hesitated a moment before telling him the reason. "You waltz so well, that I did not want to waste the supper dance on one."

"I'm glad. There's no one else with whom I would rather waltz." They had almost reached the gate, when he said, "What was the supper set?"

"A country dance."

"Did Milford bring you what you wanted to eat?"

This was the problem with other gentlemen. They assumed too much. "He failed to ask what I liked."

"I'll take that is a no." Chandos grinned smugly.

She should not have told him. "Fortunately, there was not much that I would not eat." That should take the smile off his face.

"It *was* your ball." They began to trot, then moved into a gallop.

It had been her ball. They reached the tree together as they usually did. "Very true. This evening's entertainment will not be."

"I do wonder what it will be like. I've never attended one of their balls."

"You never attended any events that young ladies making their come out would attend."

"Very true." He was quiet for a second. "On the other hand, they would not have been as enjoyable before."

What did he mean by that? "No?"

"No. There was no one who danced as well as you do."

That could not be true. Still, it was nice to be complimented on something Theo knew she did well. Even though they were later than usual, there was no one else around. "It is peaceful here this morning."

"It is." They were walking their horses toward the Serpentine as they usually did. He turned and glanced behind him. "Mick is getting ready to tell us we will be late for breakfast if we don't leave."

She twisted around to look at her groom. "I thought the rest of the family would sleep longer."

"The children, my lady."

"How could I forget?" Theo yawned. "We should be going. I could use a pot or two of tea."

"Coffee. Strong coffee." Chandos kept pace with her as they trotted to the gate.

"Grace will not allow it in the house. The smell. It gets into the wall hangings and other soft furnishings."

"That's a shame, but it makes sense. When you have a home of your own will you do that as well?"

That was an interesting question coming from him. "I do not know. I suppose it would depend on how much I like coffee. I have never tasted it." That still left the smell. "And how often I wished to change the fabrics."

"The wall coverings could be taken care of by painting the walls. A large mural, perhaps."

"An interesting thought." Chandos was acting differently this morning. She could not work out the reason for it. Was it because they were alone? Relatively speaking. "I would have to give it some consideration."

"Were you told that Ashford attempted to gain admittance to your ball?"

That got her attention. "No. When was it?"

"I saw him as I was leaving and gave the footman at the door the information that he'd not been invited."

"Thank you. It saved me from having him thrown out." And the risk of having him make a scene.

"That would have been fun to watch." Chandos's green eyes danced with mirth.

"You are incorrigible." They stopped in front of her house. "Will you break your fast with us?"

"Not this morning. I have several things to which I must attend, and you, my lady, should try to get some more sleep. Otherwise, you won't be fit for Lady Brownly's ball this evening."

Theo yawned again. "I suppose you are right. I will see you this evening."

Chandos smiled. "The supper dance?"

"Yes." She smiled back.

His gaze stayed on her for a long moment. "I should tell you something that I was told."

He looked and sounded serious. "What is it?"

"Apparently, Lady Giselle wants to wed a duke and has decided on me. Naturally, I want nothing to do with her, but because I am attending these balls, I could be at risk of being compromised."

Theo did not like the lady, but that type of behavior was beyond the pale. "I will think of something."

"Thank you." His eyes searched hers as if he was looking for something. "I knew I could depend upon you."

By the time she and her family were ready to leave for the ball that evening, Theo, with the help of Mary, had devised a plan. When they arrived at Brownly House, Theo gathered Chandos, Sarah, and Lord Marrow. "Did Chandos tell you about Lady Giselle?" Sarah and Marrow nodded. "The only way I can think of that she could possibly compromise him is to send him a note to meet her."

"It probably would not be signed with her name," Sarah said. "She will use your name."

Theo had not thought of that. "Indeed. Still, we must give her the opportunity to have him receive the note."

"What if some other gentleman received the message?" Lord Marrow said.

"That would involve an innocent." That was the hard part. If Chandos just did not go, Lady Giselle would try again. Therefore, someone had to meet her.

"She has been seen with Ashford lately," Chandos commented.

"That would be perfect." Sarah grinned. "They can have each other. She wants a duke, and he will be a duke, and it would keep him away from you, Theo."

"I'll have to appear as if I'm available to receive a note." Chandos glanced at Lord Marrow. "We should take to strolling the ballrooms."

"I agree." He nodded. "I think this will work."

"Do not look now, but Ashford has entered the room."

"What I do not understand is why he seems to be assisting her." What did he have to gain?

"And there is Lady Giselle with her mother," Sarah said.

"Very well." Theo's shoulders tightened as if she was about to do battle. Or how she thought that would feel. "Let us begin our scheme."

If Leo hadn't already been in love with Theo, he would be now. Seeing her take charge of keeping him safe from being compromised was incredible. As to Ashford, she might not know why he would help Lady Giselle, but Leo did. The bounder obviously thought that with him out of the way, he'd have a chance with Theo.

He glanced down at her. "Are you obligated for every set?"

"No." Her lips curved up. "You were right. I did require more sleep. I received requests but turned down some. I am only dancing four sets, to include the supper dance. I have my first dance with Lord Milford. The second with Lord Bolingbroke. Then I am free for one set. Another dance, and so on."

"While you are dancing, I will stroll the room with Marrow." As long as Marrow wasn't standing up with Sarah. They would have to coordinate this plan for the next entertainment and the ones after until the lady played her hand. "I have to say that this takes the enjoyment out of these events."

"Do you really think so?" Sarah frowned. "For me it makes them more interesting."

Marrow huffed. "That is because you, my love, are not the potential victim."

She shrugged. "You are right, of course. I would not like it at all if someone was attempting to compromise me."

By the end of the evening, Leo was frustrated. "Lady Giselle and Ashford are both spending a great deal of time watching us, or rather me, but they did nothing."

Theo put her hand on Leo's arm. "This is the first time you have given them a chance to approach you. It might take a few nights."

"I suppose it will." He wanted this over. "I just do not like waiting around like a bird to be shot."

"Hmm." She gazed up at him. "*Do* birds just stand around waiting to be killed?"

"No, it was a bad analogy. Animals have more sense than to make themselves vulnerable."

A few evenings later, Theo, her family, and Chandos arrived at the ball being given by Lady Smythe and her sister-in-law Mrs. Smythe. It appeared as if every member of the *ton* had been invited and it was still early. Generally, Grace and Matt preferred smaller balls. Tonight, Theo and her family were only here because her mother was friends with Lady Smythe and had promised Theo would attend. She scanned the crowded ballroom. Near a set of French windows at the other end of the room, Lady Giselle was in conversation with Lord Ashford, then he left. Considering that Lady Giselle attended very few of the same balls as Theo, her presence could not be good. Lord Ashford was, unfortunately, invited everywhere. Except for Theo's ball.

"What or who are you looking at?" Chandos twined his arm with hers.

"Lady Giselle. Lord Ashford was with her, but he left."

Chandos took a deep breath and grimaced. "It does appear that the Smythes decided the larger the ball the better."

Theo averted her eyes when Lady Giselle glanced in Theo's direction. "Do not look."

"I'm not." Ever since one of the gentlemen Chandos knew had added to the warning his mother had given him about Lady Giselle, Theo and he had been on their guard. "Do you think it will be this evening?"

Theo shrugged. The few times Lady Giselle and Lord Ashford were at the same ball, she and Leo had been prepared for something to happen. They had even taken to strolling separately just to encourage the couple to do something. "I have no idea. We must not let down our guard." She had been working on a plan that would not involve an innocent victim and finally decided that Sarah was right. It must be Ashford. He could in no way be considered an innocent. "If I can reroute the note, I will send it to Lord Ashford. He is the right height and hair color to be mistaken for you."

"That is not a compliment." Chandos had a disgruntled look on his face.

"No, but it is helpful." Theo would send his lordship to Lady Giselle and whatever she had planned would happen with Lord Ashford.

"And you know that I would not send you a note at a ball." There was no reason Chandos should. Except for the time they circled the room with another person, he stayed with her family. "But as with Ashford, Lady Giselle has dark hair and could be mistaken for you."

Perhaps they were overthinking this. "Do you really believe they could be that prepared?"

"Remember, it was in a novel. All they'd have to do is follow the plot."

Sarah and Marrow joined them.

"I see they're both here," Marrow said.

"Yes." Theo nodded.

"Who is your first dance with?" Sarah asked.

"Lord Bolingbroke. I forgave him for his remark after he became interested in Miss Cunningham."

Sarah laughed lightly. "I am sure he will think that having to dance the minuet is still punishment."

"But not as much as being made to dance it with a lady he does not know. My second set is free. We can stroll the room." And hope to see something occur.

"I'll take our duke for a walk as well." Marrow flashed Chandos a smile.

"She has done it!" Sarah said excitedly. "She gave a note to the footman with heavy dark eyebrows."

Chandos glanced at Marrow. "It is time for us to go look at the rest of the ballroom."

"Do you want to remain here with Theo's family or come with us?" he asked Sarah.

"That is a hard choice." She looked around the room. "I shall stay here. I am safe enough, and if the footman has been told to come to our circle, I will be able to misdirect him. I just wish I was tall enough to see him coming. It was amazing that I saw the note being passed."

The crowd parted as the orchestra began to prepare for the first set, and Theo could finally see something other than people milling around. "He is headed toward us but has paused."

"He'd have to, wouldn't he," Marrow said. "He can't very well give Chandos a note from you if you're standing with him."

"That's the part about all of this I do not understand." Theo shook her head. He was always with Theo. Except when she was dancing, or they were strolling separately. How did they think to fool him?

Sarah placed her hand on Theo's arm. "It does not make sense." It was as if her friend had read her mind. "Except that Lady Giselle believes that everyone will behave as she does. Without regard for others."

Lord Bolingbroke came to Theo and bowed. "Good evening, my lady. I believe this is our dance."

She curtseyed. "It is, my lord."

They stepped onto the dance floor and took their places in the set. Yet, Theo could not concentrate. Fortunately, she knew the dance well enough that she did not need to mind her steps. Lady Giselle joined the set with a gentleman Theo did not know. At least it was not Lord Ashford. Lady Giselle would have had to have planned to meet Chandos sometime after the dance. Theo kept an eye on Lady Giselle, who glanced around the room regularly looking for someone. Then Theo saw it. The footman. Of course it was. How else would she have known the note had been delivered? The first part of the set had ended, and she left the dance floor. Theo glanced to where her family was gathered. Sarah had a smug smile on her face. From the corner of her eye, Theo saw Lord Ashford leave the room. Her only regret was that she would not be there to see whatever happened.

"Lady Theo, are you all right?" Bolingbroke sounded concerned.

"Perfectly." She smiled at him as the music began again. "Are you standing up with Miss Cunningham?"

"I am." The corners of his lips rose. "She has agreed to dance the supper set with me."

"Excellent."

A few minutes later there were loud gasps and exclamations. The music stopped. A footman went to Lady Giselle's mother, and the lady left the room. The servant then went to the Duchess of Shrewsbury, and she followed Lady Giselle's mother.

"Something's going on," Bolingbroke said. "Allow me to return you to your family."

Oh, thank God. Theo did not think she could have continued to stand here with all the commotion and not give in to the temptation to follow. "Thank you. What are you going to do?"

He gave her a slightly guilty look. "I'm going to see what happened."

She could not think of anything to say, other than she would like to go as well but could not. So, she nodded. By the time she returned, Chandos was there with Sarah and Marrow.

"Where is Bolingbroke going?" Marrow asked.

"To see what the fuss is about."

"I wonder how they will handle it," Sarah said, staring in the direction that several of the guests were walking.

"I suppose we will find out soon." Theo could not look away either.

Not many minutes later, Lord Ashford, his mother, and Lady Giselle, and her mother reentered the ballroom. Lady Giselle had a shawl tied around her shoulders.

"Good Lord!" Sarah gasped. "Did she actually rip her bodice?"

"It appears like it," Chandos, who had been silent, commented drily. "Stupid chit."

Lady Smythe and Mrs. Smythe reentered the room, both wearing happy smiles. They went to the couple and their mothers. The room fell silent as the ladies clapped their hands. "We have some excellent news, Lord Ashford and Lady Giselle Darnel are to be wed."

Footmen came around with champagne. Leo took two glasses, handing one to Theo. "I suppose we must toast to the happy couple." He gazed across the room to where they were standing and raised his glass to them. He didn't care that they knew he was happy they'd failed.

"That was exciting," Kenilworth said. He stared directly at Theo. "How did you manage it?"

Leo resisted a laugh as she opened her eyes wide and gave her brother-by-marriage an innocent look. "Manage what?"

Kenilworth fixed her with a firm look. "Do not try to bamboozle me, my girl. I've known you much too long."

"We were all in on it." Leo indicated Theo, Sarah, and Marrow. "We had a feeling Lady Giselle and Ashford were up to something."

"We did." Sarah smiled. "When the footman came looking for Chandos, I directed him to Lord Ashford."

Kenilworth glanced at Theo again. "You, I take it, came up with the plan."

She had the grace to look at least slightly guilty. "Mary and I, but only the outline. Everyone had a hand in working out the details."

"But truly," Sarah said, "Theo and I were not sure it would work."

Theo nodded. "I do not understand how they did not figure out what our response would be."

Leo wanted to take her in his arms. "It was as Miss Pettigrew said, Lady Giselle believes everyone is like her. And she does not have the intelligence to realize that someone would plan against her." He glanced down at Theo. "It was a good scheme."

Marrow nodded. "And it succeeded perfectly."

"The four of you are making me feel old." Kenilworth sauntered away.

It had been successful. Lady Giselle was no longer a threat to Leo, and Ashford could no longer attempt to court Theo. The only problem Leo could see was that women like Lady Giselle did not take losing well. If she found out Theo had anything to do with foiling her plan, the damned chit would find a way to get back at her. Perhaps it was his turn to save Theo. He'd have to stay even closer to her.

Several of the guests had left. It was probably so that they could go to other entertainments and tell people what had occurred. The music began again. This time it was a country dance. Leo had been told that the supper set would be a waltz, but he did not know how many waltzes there would be, and he dearly wanted to dance with Theo more than once this evening. "Would you like to stand up with me for the country dance?"

Her eyes were wide with confusion. "Two sets?"

"As a celebration of sorts. We won." Hopefully, as an excuse, that would do.

"Yes. I have never stood up with you for a country dance."

Because given a choice, he'd rather waltz with her. He took her hand and placed it on his arm. "Now is the perfect time."

CHAPTER TWENTY-EIGHT

Several minutes after the announcement had been made, and Giselle had had to paste a smile on her face as best wishes were offered to her, she was taken out of the ballroom by her mother.

"I cannot believe you tried such a trick." Mama glared at Giselle. "You are very lucky Ashford acted as he should. If he had not, your reputation would be ruined."

"You did it. You told me you did." It was not fair that Giselle was being blamed for the same behavior her mother had engaged in. Strangely, Ashford was not that upset. He knew they had been played and did not seem to care. But she did not want to live in Shrewsbury or be buried in the country.

Her mother's lips flattened. "My father was going to marry me to an ogre more than twice my age. Your father and I planned to be compromised."

That Giselle had not known. "I am sorry, Mama."

"We will arrange the wedding to be soon. Not immediately. That would cause too much talk." She adjusted her shawl. "Well, my dear, you got your wish. You will be a duchess."

But not for years. Who knew how long Ashford's father would live? Chandos was already a duke.

"We will have to make an appointment with our modiste." Mama frowned at Giselle's bodice and shook her head. "That bodice is ruined, and I will not replace it."

She waved her hand dismissively. "I suppose it does not matter. You will require different gowns for when you have wed. Until then, you will simply have to make do with what you have."

She did not have that many ballgowns. The idea had been to have enough that she would not have to wear a gown more than a few times. Yet, there was no arguing with her mother. "Yes, Mama. When will I marry?"

"The duchess said she thinks in three weeks' time. That way no one will believe you could be with child. You did not—"

"No!" Giselle would have with Chandos, but not Ashford. Although, she would have to when they wed. She hoped he knew what he was doing. Everyone knew Chandos did.

A footman assisted them into their town coach. Giselle sat back against the squabs. She knew, she did not know how, but she knew Lady Theo was responsible for this debacle because she wanted to wed Chandos. Giselle had heard the story that he was a family friend. But she had seen the way Lady Theo looked at him. Somehow, Giselle would get back at Lady Theo. Giselle would make sure that Lady Theo disgraced herself so badly that Chandos would not want to marry her. At the moment, Lady Theo thought she had won. Yet, if Giselle could not marry whom she wanted, then Lady Theo would not either.

The next morning, Mary came into Theo's room. "I thought I might find you here."

Other than when Mary had helped Theo think of the scheme to stop Lady Giselle, Theo and her sister had not spent much time together this Season. Mary always seemed to be busy with her studies, and Theo, of course, had things she must do during her come out. She grinned. "As you see."

Her sister sat on the chair next to the desk where Theo was reading. "I heard that the scheme worked."

"Yes." As Mary had played a part in the idea, she deserved to know the result. "Lady Giselle is now engaged to Lord Ashford."

"I am glad to hear it." Mary tilted her head to one side. "But what about you? Who will you marry?"

Theo closed her book. "I do not know."

"If you continue to find matches for the gentlemen who are interested in you, there will soon be no one left." Mary paused. "Except for Chandos."

"He is turning out to be not at all what I expected." Theo was torn about him. He still did not have a mistress. He had taken control of his estates, and he was attending the Lords. He was also extremely kind to her. The only question was would his behavior last. "But still. I do not know if I can trust him."

"It appears to me that he is in love with you. You were greatly attracted to him at Christmas. Are you still?" Mary kept her gaze fixed on Theo.

"Yes." She rubbed her face. "No. I do not know. I am trying not to think about Chandos. I do not want to fall in love with him."

"I seem to remember Madeline not wanting to fall in love with Harry because her mother would not approve. It did not work. She fell in love with him anyway."

"The heart wants what the heart wants." Theo had heard that often enough. "I will not have my heart broken when he takes a mistress. I cannot. I do not trust easily as it is."

"What will you do if he declares himself?"

She stared at Mary. It was almost as if she knew something Theo did not. "Will he?"

"He has asked for permission to court you," Mary confirmed.

"I thought he was spending time with me because of his friendship with Charlie." Theo did not understand. He had not been particularly lover-like. "I do not know what to do." She did not even want to think about it, and she did not believe he was serious. "He already said that he was not interested in meeting young ladies."

"Very well, then. Perhaps I am mistaken." Mary rose from

the chair. "I must go. I will see you later." She leaned down and bussed Theo's cheek. "Good luck."

"Thank you. But I think I will not wed this Season."

"As you will." Her sister smiled as she walked out of the room.

Theo glanced at her brooch watch. She had a few minutes more before she had to leave to meet her friends to go shopping. They were gathering here because Worthington House was the most central place to meet. She finished the chapter and donned her bonnet, gloves, and spencer. The doorbell chimed, and she went downstairs. Sarah, Patricia Marrow, and Felice Albright had arrived along with their maids.

The doorbell rang again, and Sophie Cunningham entered. "I am sorry to be late."

"You are not." Theo smiled. Jones, her footman, entered the hall. "We are ready to depart." They had decided to walk to Bruton Street, and she had arranged for the town coach to pick them up at Hatchards in three hours. That would give them time to visit the shops and browse books.

"I have news," Felice said as they walked down the steps. "Crewe and I are engaged to be married."

"That is wonderful." Sarah smiled widely. "Best wishes to you."

"Yes, indeed." Patricia grinned. "I will tell you my news as well. Holland is meeting with my father today to ask for my hand."

They congratulated her and looked at Sophie.

"We are not quite as far along, but Bolingbroke's mother has arrived in Town and my parents and I have been invited to dine with her. I believe it is important to meet his family before any decisions are made."

"A very smart thing to do," Sarah said. "Although, if I had to depend on my parents to be part of Marrow's decision, we would not be getting married."

She was probably right, Theo thought. Especially her father.

"Has everyone heard that Lady Giselle and Lord Ashford are engaged to be married?" Sophie asked.

"I had not," Patricia said. "When did that happen?"

"Last night at the Smythe ball," Felice said. "Did you not attend?"

"No. My mother is not on good terms with Mrs. Smythe. We received an invitation, but Mama sent our regrets."

"Theo, what of you and Chandos? Have you decided to wed?"

What was it about today that she was being asked about marrying him? "We are just friends."

Felice raised a brow. "How can you believe that? He has been dancing attendance on you since before the Season began."

"Indeed," Patricia said. "He has eyes for no other lady."

"He is not looking to marry. He said he was not interested in meeting unmarried ladies."

"Why would he want to meet other ladies when he has decided on you?" Sarah added. "Theo, you cannot actually believe he only wants to be your friend. I have seen the way he looks at you. He does not even notice other ladies. Even Lady Giselle who was attempting to trick him into marriage. He never could remember what she looked like or even her name. Do you have no feelings for him at all?"

Theo did. That was the problem. The heart wanted what the heart wanted, and her heart wanted Chandos. Still, she would keep it to herself. "I do not wish to talk about it. Truly we are no more than friends."

"Very well," Patricia conceded. "Are we all going to Lady Howe's ball this evening?"

Thankfully, talk turned to the ball and what everyone was wearing. They all decided to go to Burlington Arcade for various things they needed. Yet, when they got to the shop with the fans, all Theo could think about was Chandos selecting the fan for her, and the fan that he sent to her house. Was he, could he, be in love with her? How would she even know if he did not say anything? If only she was not falling in love with him. Who was she trying to fool. She was already in love with him.

* * *

When Theo arrived at the ball that evening, Sarah came up to her. "Will you go with me to the ladies' room?"

"Yes. I need to visit it as well. Do you know where it is located?"

"Up the stairs and to the right. I hope it is not crowded."

Theo did too. When they arrived a maid directed them to the screens that had been set up. Theo was glad that the chamber pots were incorporated into stools. The door opened and two women were talking. She recognized the nasal tone of the first one.

"Have you heard that Chandos finally selected a mistress?" the lady asked.

"My brother told me that he held a contest to pick the one he'd have for the Season," the second one said.

"A contest?" Theo could hear the lady's eyes widen. "What did they do?"

"They had to perform certain acts on him. Something no lady would do, I am certain."

"Do not be a prude. Those acts are what make relations so pleasurable," Nasally said.

The other woman sighed. "I only wish my husband would ask or even suggest that we do something other than doing it in our nightclothes."

"Do you really want to see him naked?"

"At least it would be different." Another sigh. "Perhaps I should take a lover. I hear Lord D is amenable to bedding married women."

Theo could not believe what she was hearing. Hot tears sprang to her eyes. Just as she had decided she was in love with Chandos, he did something like this. She had been right all along. He had no desire to wed. She had to leave now. But how could she when those ladies were still talking?

"Excuse me, but do you really think you should be speaking about such things where others, especially young ladies, can overhear you?" Sarah said.

The door opened and shut as if they had run out.

"Thank you." Theo wanted to leave the ball, leave Town, and never see Chandos again.

"They should be ashamed of themselves having that sort of conversation where anyone could hear them. If that one lady does take a lover, I hope her husband finds out and banishes her to the country."

Theo stood and shook out her skirts. "I agree."

When she came out from behind the screen, Sarah looked at her with compassion. "Are you all right? I would not believe a word they said about Chandos."

"It is fine. I knew it would happen at some point." Theo just wished it had happened sooner. Before she had fallen in love with him.

"Would you like to take a stroll? We can ask if Patricia and Felice would like to come with us."

"I would like to get some air, but we will be safe by ourselves. I shall tell one of my sisters or brothers where we are going."

"As you like." Sarah linked her arm with Theo's.

They saw Charlotte and told her what they were going to do. "Do not be long."

Fortunately, Theo did not have another dance scheduled. She had refused all of them because she only wanted to stand up with Chandos. What a mistake that was. As soon as Theo could calm herself, she would tell her sister that she wanted to go home.

Even though it was still light, the gardens were decorated with lanterns. A great many people were strolling around. Lady Giselle was there with one or two of her friends. Chandos was speaking with St. Albans. She did not want to see him before she had got herself under control. Especially now. She took a step forward to turn down another path, when she felt a shoe on her leg. The next thing she knew she was falling forward, then strong arms caught her, bringing her to a hard chest. A scent of clean man and lemon filled her senses.

Chandos! No! This could not be happening.

Gasps sounded from ladies who must have been nearby.

He shifted her so that she was by his side. His arm still tightly around her. Binding her to his side. "Excuse us. Lady Theo has just agreed to become my wife." She tried to wiggle free, and his breath caressed her ear. "Stop. We don't want a scene."

He was right. The only thing to do was to come up with a way out of this. Theo stood straighter, turned toward him, but could not look at his face. She patted his chest. "Do not worry. I know you do not wish to wed. I will think of a way out of this."

CHAPTER TWENTY-NINE

Not wish to wed! All Leo had been doing this Season was trying to work out a way to marry Theo. Any brief thought he'd had that this would make taking Theo as his wife easier died a swift death. Bloody hellhounds. He'd been certain, more than certain, convinced that Theo loved him. He was going to ring Lady Giselle's neck. First, she tries to compromise him, now this. What he didn't understand was why trip Theo? Didn't the stupid chit know he would save her from falling? Or hadn't she seen him? "We can discuss this later. Let's go back inside."

"I want to go home." Her tone was suddenly shaky, as if she was close to crying.

Something was wrong, but what? "We must wait. Let's go find Worthington and your sister."

Theo nodded. He led her back to the ballroom. As soon as he joined her family, he told them what had happened. "Naturally, several ladies came upon us just after I caught Theo. I declared that we were engaged to be married."

"She tripped Theo near the fountain?" There was a sense of urgency in Worthington's tone.

"Yes. If I hadn't been there, she could have been badly hurt." Leo swore to himself.

"This is not the way I wished for this to happen." Worthington's countenance was a mask of politeness.

"You're not the only one." He glanced at Theo, who was with Charlotte and Alice. "She told me that she would think of a way for me not to have to marry her." Leo had to find a way to change her mind.

"Of course she did. She doesn't think you want to wed," Kenilworth said.

"It was that stupid remark I made about not wanting to meet young ladies." Leo had been berating himself for saying that ever since he'd done it. "I think she had been crying. But I don't know why or actually when, except that it was before she was tripped."

"We're going to have to find out what, if anything, is wrong," Worthington said. "Theo rarely cries."

"She wants to go home." Leo wanted to accompany her, but she did not want to have anything to do with him.

"I doubt she's going to be able to do that now." Worthington raised a brow. "We're about to have company."

Leo glanced in the direction in which Worthington was looking to see Lady Howe bearing down on them. "Damn. She'll want an announcement."

"She will," Worthington agreed.

"I'll get her." Kenilworth turned and walked to where Theo was with her sisters.

"My lady"—Sarah Pettigrew, who had been standing nearby, drew Lady Worthington aside—"there is something I must tell you."

"Come over here and we can speak," her ladyship said as she and Sarah started to walk away. "In the ladies' room there were two . . ."

Sarah's tone dropped and Leo couldn't hear anything else. He would have to discover what she'd said to Lady Worthington. It might have something to do with Theo's reaction to him just now.

Kenilworth returned with his wife, Alice, and Theo.

"My lady." Lady Howe smiled broadly at Theo. "And your grace. I understand there is an announcement to be made."

Theo assumed a polite mask. Yet, Leo could see the tension in her shoulders.

"There is." Worthington smiled easily.

The rest of her family gathered around them. Lady Worthington finished speaking with Sarah and joined the group. She also wore a polite mask.

Leo stood next to Theo. He tried to hold her hand, but she pushed it away. Something was definitely wrong. But what? And who would tell him?

Lady Howe made the announcement that he and Theo would wed. And then they had to stand there acting as if they were happy while people congratulated them. Several of the ladies opined that they knew this was coming. He had been so devoted to her all Season.

When they were ready to leave, St. Albans came up to Leo. "I'll give you a ride home."

"I need to know what happened. Something did. Before she was tripped." He wanted to follow Theo and ask her. But St. Albans was right. This was neither the time or the place.

St. Albans nodded. "I'll try to discover what it is."

Leo passed a fitful night trying to work out why Theo didn't want to be around him. He went to Worthington House the next morning only to be told that Theo wasn't riding that day. Leo was grateful when two days later a missive from Worthington came during breakfast demanding Leo's immediate presence. He sent up a prayer that this would finally be resolved.

When he arrived, he was taken to the large drawing room. All her brothers and sisters were present, and not one of them was smiling. The ladies had their brows raised, and the gentlemen looked ready to run him through. He wasn't even offered a seat.

It was like being an accused in the dock. What the devil had occurred?

Leo wanted to rail at them, but at least a semblance of civility was needed. "Will someone tell me what is going on? Why won't Theo see me?"

Stanwood speared Leo with a hard look. "You said that if you were allowed to court Theo you would not have a mistress."

"Yes." What the hell had happened? "I do not have a mistress."

"Then why did Theo overhear two ladies talking about your new ladybird?" St. Albans asked.

Leo gave himself an inner shake. He couldn't believe this was actually happening. "I have no idea why anyone would think I have engaged a courtesan."

"Really?" Charlotte asked in a deceptively sweet voice.

"Yes, really." He was starting to become angry himself.

"You mean to say that you did not have a contest to choose a mistress by having them perform acts upon your body?" Lady Montagu's tone was just as saccharine, but barely concealed anger could be heard beneath the sweetness.

Leo didn't mind being accused of what he'd done, but he'd be damned if he'd be blamed for something he did not do or even thought of. "One, I do not have a ladybird and have not for a year. Two, even at my most depraved, I would not have had women demean themselves by trying to cap one another in public." He felt like he was about to explode. Leo took a breath. "I have no idea who those *ladies* are. Nor do I have any idea where they came up with such a debauched description of how I would select a mistress. I have done nothing but to do my best to remain by Theo's side." He paced, wishing he had a brandy. "If I knew who these *ladies* were, I'd wring their necks. Or, better yet, make them publicly admit they were lying."

Suddenly, the tension in the room had broken, and everyone let out their breath.

"I told you so," St. Albans said. "It was pure gossip. Probably based on his past behavior."

"Although," Alice mused, "it might be an excellent idea for unmarried ladies to test out prospective suitors to see if they do indeed want to marry them?"

Every gentleman in the room dropped his jaw. Only St. Albans spoke. "Sweetheart, is there something we need to discuss?"

"About us? Goodness no. However, after listening to so many ladies complain about their husbands, I have come to the conclusion that some sort of assurance should be given. As you know, proof of prowess can be done without taking a lady's maidenhead."

"Hmm." Eleanor had a thoughtful look on her face. "That is an excellent idea."

Then the rest of Theo's sisters joined in the conversation, which quickly devolved.

St. Albans handed Leo a glass of brandy. "Sorry to have put you through that, but we had to know. Theo was devastated."

"Wait." No! It couldn't be possible. "Do you mean to tell me that she was the one who heard the ladies?"

St. Albans nodded. "In the ladies' room at a ball."

Bloody, bloody hellhounds. "That's the reason she's keeping her distance from me. She wouldn't even ride in the mornings. Or see me. I need to talk to her."

Alice joined them. "She will not speak with you. I suggest you find a way to do it at the ball this evening. She cannot lock herself in her room there."

That was an excellent idea. "And she won't make a scene at the ball."

"She will not," Alice confirmed. "You will have to find a way to make her listen to you."

"At least she can't put her fingers in her ears and sing la-la-la." That's what his youngest sister used to do.

Alice chucked. "Not at the ball."

The rest of the day seemed to crawl by. Finally, it was time to leave for the ball, but this time, he would not be accompanying

Theo and her family. Even though it was early, a good many guests had already arrived. Leo just had to find a way to get her alone so that they could talk. Or he could talk and make her listen.

Leo scanned the ballroom and couldn't see his betrothed. Where the devil had she got to? He grabbed Stanwood's arm. "Theo, do you know where she is?"

He glanced around the room. "No. The last time I saw her she was with Milford. I don't see him either."

"I'll find her." Before Worthington could answer, Leo headed for the terrace. Milford had been interested in her before she'd been compromised into marrying Leo. It wouldn't surprise him at all if the man hadn't given up. After searching the terrace, he went to the ornamental green house. She was there, sitting on a bench staring straight ahead. Milford stood before her. Theo must be more upset than Leo realized to have gone somewhere alone with a gentleman. He opened the door and stepped in.

"I say, Lady Theodora, surely you don't mean to wed him," Milford said with certainty. "What kind of husband would he make? Everyone knows his reputation. When you finally throw him over, I want you to know I will be waiting for you."

The bounder moved closer to Theo and appeared as if he would try to embrace her. Leo had never wanted to murder anyone as much as he did Milford right now. Not least because she had used the same argument when explaining why they should not wed. Striding forward, Leo picked Milford up by his cravat and shook him. "Lady Theo is betrothed to me, and she is going to marry me." Leo tossed Milford away, clutched Theo's arm before she could run off, and started walking out of the conservatory almost dragging her behind him. He couldn't believe a gentleman would attempt to propose to Theo when she was still betrothed to him. Alice was right. It was time they straightened a few things out. "I suggest you ask Lady Lana Grant to dance."

"I don't know Lady Lana," Milford protested.

"Find someone to introduce you. Theo is taken." *Forever.*

"Chandos. Stop." Theo's voice was tight and angry. "You do

not need to pull me along like a recalcitrant child. I will come with you."

He did as she commanded and offered her his arm. "Very well."

Casting him a strange look, she placed her fingers on his sleeve. "That is better."

He'd been in this garden many times in the past since he'd been on the town, but never with someone he loved. Unerringly, he led her to a small fountain with a stone bench and turned her to face him. "Theo, I love you. I think I fell in love with you when you threw that bucket of water on me. I have spent all my time since then becoming the man I should be. Not just for you but for me and the dukedom as well. I have not drunk to excess since last June. I have stopped gambling."

"Women?" She raised her stubborn chin. "What about your mistress? Everyone knows you have one."

He stared into her eyes. "Then everyone is wrong. I have not touched a female"—God knew she would parse words with him if he wasn't clear—"since I left Town last June. I did not attend the Autumn Season because I knew you would not be there." He dragged a hand down his face then took her hands in his. "I have never before wanted to wed. I have never wanted a wife, but I want you. I want you in my life. Nay, I need you in my life. As my helpmate, the mother to my children, and my duchess. I've been trying for weeks to convince you that we would make an excellent match. That we would be happy together." He searched her eyes for some indication she understood and believed what he was saying. And he finally saw her lapis-blue eyes warm for him. "Theo, please marry me."

The next thing he knew she was in his arms. "I never could allow myself to believe you had changed. I wanted to. Then I heard about your mistress."

"And you had to harden your heart toward me?" Leo finally had the missing piece. The reason she'd been cool, almost cold to him. "If I thought it would do any good, I'd announce to the world that I don't have a mistress."

"Kiss me." Theo raised up on her toes.

"Kissing you is the least of what I want to do with you." He brushed his lips against hers. "I dreamed of you in my bed." And on his desk, and in the garden, and anywhere else he could make love to her.

Her lips formed a perfect O. "You have?"

"It has practically killed me to watch other men dance with you when all I wanted was you in my arms. Theo, marry me, please."

She pressed her lips against his jaw. "I will be extremely happy to marry you. I love you. I think I fell in love with you when I first waltzed with you."

"At Christmas?" That was a surprise.

"Yes. But I was not out, and you had such a bad reputation."

Damn him and his reputation. He claimed her mouth and stroked his hand down her supple back over her tight derriere. "Two weeks. I know your family will not agree to less time."

"You have already spoken to Matt?"

"I talked to Stanwood first. I spoke to Worthington after he arrived in Town." Leo grimaced at his memory of the conversation. "Naturally, he said it was your choice. I was to be given no special consideration for being a duke."

Theo chuckled lightly. "It is what he always says." She pressed against Leo and drew him into a searing kiss.

Their tongues danced. He'd spent months wondering what she would taste like. Finally he knew. Parsley and bergamot. Light and fresh. He cupped her breast and caressed it, causing her to press more deeply against him. He wanted her, but he knew he had to stop soon.

"If I thought I could get away with it, I'd take you back to my house and ravish you tonight. Although, I have a feeling, I'd soon be missing a few body parts." The thought of losing her had undone him. He'd known her for years, but he'd never *known her*. Who she was.

"I have no doubt." She pressed her lips together and shook her head, but her eyes were laughing. "Come." Theo took his hand. "Let us tell them that we have decided on a wedding date."

They strolled hand in hand into the ballroom, skirting the dance floor. "I want all your waltzes."

"I gathered you would." She squeezed his hand. "What about the other sets?"

"We can stroll the room or the garden or find an empty chamber." His imagination was boundless when it came to having her.

"That last one sounds a bit risky."

Only because she didn't know what could be accomplished in a garden. "Gardens are fascinating places."

As they approached her family, Rothwell was standing next to Kenilworth and their ladies.

He met Leo's gaze, then turned to Rothwell. "We are going to have a wedding."

"He could not have convinced her so quickly," Rothwell retorted.

"Would you care to wager a monkey?" Kenilworth drawled.

"Very well," Rothwell grumbled. "We're having a wedding."

Theo started to laugh.

It *was* funny. "Do they do this often?"

Her face was alight. "All the time, and Rothwell always loses."

That didn't surprise Leo. "I wouldn't wager against Kenilworth. He usually knows what he was about."

"He does." She smiled up at Leo. First his heart seemed too large for his chest, then his cock started to rise. Soon. Very soon.

Leo and his love strolled up to Worthington.

"We're getting married in two weeks." Theo grinned.

Worthington inclined his head. "Two weeks it is. In my office tomorrow after breakfast to review the settlements."

Leo thanked his future brothers-in-law for advising him as to how the settlement discussion would go.

"I'll send my information over first thing tomorrow."

"Excellent." Worthington glanced at Theo. "Are we staying for supper?"

"We are. I do not want to miss waltzing with my affianced husband." Something caught her attention because she stared across the room and to the right. "Is that Milford with Lady Lana?"

Leo looked in the direction Theo was staring. It was. "Good man. He took my advice."

She gave him a disgruntled look. "Not an hour ago, you wanted to murder him."

"That was because he wanted you." He might not have actually killed Milford, but Leo would have beaten him badly.

Behind them, there were soft chuckles. He was looking forward to being in this family.

CHAPTER THIRTY

Theo was ready to go a good half hour before Chandos was due to arrive. She had never been so happy. She had been so afraid of being hurt, that she ignored her common sense. The only explanation for him "living in her pocket," as her friend had said, was that he wanted to marry her. Finally, she heard a horse stop in front of the house, and she almost flew down the stairs but waited as Thorton opened the door.

"Good morning, your grace." Thorton bowed. "Allow me and the staff to congratulate you on your pending marriage."

Chandos glanced at her over the butler's shoulder. "Thank you, Thorton. May I take my betrothed for a ride?"

"You may, sir." The butler stepped aside, and Theo stepped into Chandos's arms.

"I love you." She gazed into his warm green eyes.

"I love you too." He held out his arm. "Shall we go, my love?"

My love. Theo had waited so long to hear those words. "Indeed, we shall."

He lifted her onto her mare, and stroked her leg before letting go. "We have something to discuss on our way to the Park."

Chandos sounded serious. Could it be about the marriage settlements? Matt would not budge on them. They rode out of the square. "What is it?"

"We have no place to be private except for a house that I own."

That was a strange way of putting it. "Not Chandos House."

"Not with my mother there. She had her heart set on me marrying a lady who is malleable and would bore me within a week. The chance that she would give us any time alone is nonexistent. She's already asked when you will visit to inspect the house. She plans to take you around herself."

"Oh, dear." Theo had not wanted a difficult relationship with her mother-in-law. Yet, she would not be the first one. Louisa had had a problem with hers. What was it about the mothers of dukes? Only Alice was lucky in St. Albans's mother, then again his father was still alive. "Very well. What do you suggest?"

"As I said, I have a house." He seemed hesitant. "It is where my mistresses lived. One at a time. I never had more than one at a time."

If Chandos was not so solemn, Theo would have laughed. "Yes, I understand." This might be interesting. "May I see it?"

"Yes, but there are plans to be made before you go. You'll need to wear a bonnet that covers your hair and a veil."

How strange. "I do not understand."

"The area is generally known as the part of Town where courtesans live."

"Ahh." That was something Theo had not known. "So, if I am seen there, it will, naturally, be assumed that I am your mistress."

"Exactly." His mouth was set in a stern line.

The idea of going to a house and an area that housed mistresses appealed to her sense of adventure and curiosity. "Very well. Make the plans."

His lips curved slowly up. "If you're sure you want to be with me before we have the ceremony."

"I am. As long as you promise not to die." None of her sisters or her brother Stanwood had waited.

His eyes twinkled. "I will do my utmost to include purchasing a special license so that the service may be performed on my death bed if necessary."

"Let us hope it does not come to that." Although Theo could imagine her family rushing her to him. "What will you do with the house after we are wed?"

Chandos shrugged. "Probably sell it. I've already had some offers."

It spoke well of him that gentlemen knew he would not keep a mistress after he was married.

Marrow and Sarah joined them as they reached the Park.

"I am so glad everything turned out well," she said, then glanced at Marrow and turned a deep red.

"She told me what you heard." His lips were pressed together as if he was trying not to laugh. "Don't you think it odd that the same two ladies entered the ladies' room after you entered and discussed Chandos?"

Theo had not even considered it. She had been too upset. "It could be. On the other hand, many of us are invited to the same balls, and it might be coincidence."

"Hmm. That's exactly what Sarah said." Marrow glanced at Chandos. "What do you think?"

He scowled. "I think that if I ever find out who they are I'm going to publicly embarrass them."

Well then. Some part of Theo hoped they did discover who the ladies were. "Let us race to the tree."

"Let's just gallop." He smiled. "We've won our race."

"We will meet you by the Serpentine," Sarah called after them.

They got to the tree and Chandos reined his horse in. "Why do we still have your groom?"

"In the event anything untoward occurs. Matt is very careful. Aside from that, he is my groom and will come with me when we marry."

"I'm not going to pretend to understand, but I will accept it. How many more servants are you bringing with you?"

"Only my maid and my footman." Theo was not surprised that he was confused. Most ladies only brought their maid, if that.

They reached Sarah and Marrow, who were discussing their wedding. Sarah turned to Theo. "When is your ceremony?"

"In two weeks." Chandos's jaw firmed. "We would like you to be able to attend our wedding."

"I agree," Marrow said. "However, we don't want to change whatever you have planned for afterward."

Theo would like to be at their wedding as well, and Patricia and Holland's, and Felice and Crewe's. "Do you know if the others have dates for their ceremonies yet?"

"I do not," Sarah said. "We should all get together and discuss it. Luncheon or tea?"

"Brandy," Marrow muttered.

Chandos barked a laugh. "If you ever want to leave Town after you're married, you had better go along with them."

Sarah had had an excellent idea. The discussion might be rather lengthy. "Luncheon." It would be easier for Theo to arrange. "We can have it at Worthington House. I shall send out the invitations this morning."

"After the settlement agreement meeting?" Chandos asked.

"Yes." She had a feeling he knew what would occur.

Mick cleared his throat.

"We must go, or we will be late to breakfast." She shot her betrothed a smile. "And for time keeping."

They rode to the gate, then on to Worthington House. Thorton opened the door and bowed. "Your valet is here, your grace."

"I will see you soon," Theo said as she ascended the stairs. Chandos handed his hat and gloves to the butler. As usual, her maid had a bath ready. "When would you like to meet the staff at Chandos House and inspect your quarters and my chambers?"

"As soon as possible, I should think, my lady. There is a great deal to be organized."

Theo soaped up and stood to be rinsed. "I will discuss it with Chandos at breakfast."

"Yes, my lady." Payne handed Theo a warmed towel.

She finished dressing and arrived at the landing to find him waiting and took his arm. "When do you suggest I meet with your mother to inspect the house? I must bring my maid, footman, and groom as well."

"This should be interesting." He pressed his lips together. "I want you to know that the second, the moment we are wed, she will no longer control the house or any of the estates. She has her own dower properties."

"What about any changes I wish to make to the decorations or the nursery?"

"You may start on them. She has her own apartments. I suggest we leave them as they are until she moves from the house."

"I agree. I assume you will join me when the ladies, and, hopefully, their gentlemen, meet to discuss the wedding dates."

"I will. I'll warn you I am not putting off our date for any of theirs."

Theo looked at him and raised a brow. "In order to have a date, you must first go to St. George's and speak to the rector. He must be reserved, and it *is* the Season."

Chandos opened his mouth and closed it. "I'll take care of that immediately after the meeting."

"Good. While you are securing a date, I will send the invitations. What are our plans for this afternoon?"

The corners of his lips rose slowly. "Visiting a house. Do you have a veil?"

"No." She had never had need of one. "You should buy one after seeing the rector." She also needed to speak with one of her sisters to gather more information. Theo had the feeling it should be either Alice or Charlotte. Both of their husbands had been men like Chandos before marrying.

They arrived in the breakfast room to find everyone smiling. Chandos was heartily welcomed. The children shot questions at him about his estate, horses, and whether there was a lake or river. He glanced at her. "Why does that matter?"

"Because," Gideon said. "We'll be visiting, and we must know what to expect."

"So far, the best one is Whippoorwill Manor," Hugh added.

"But Uncle Charlie has a real castle," Elizabeth objected. "That should be the best one."

Leo swallowed a sip of tea. "I see. Is this a competition?"

"No." Constance shook her head, causing her braids to swing. "It is so that we know how much there is for us to do."

"Understandable." Apparently planning was ingrained. "Well, my main estate has an old castle. It will take some work before you can play in it. Although, that shouldn't take too long. I'll get on it immediately." He was glad to see that met with their approval. Worthington gave him a look and tapped his watch, and Leo applied himself to his food.

Not long after that, Worthington rose. "Chandos, Theo, with me."

The meeting was short. He immediately agreed that Theo would keep all her personal and real property that was currently in her possession or that she might acquire during the marriage. In the event of his death, she would have guardianship of any children they might have. That if his mother was still living at the time of his demise, that Theo would have her own house in which to live if they did not have children. A suitable allowance and widow's portion was agreed to. One section of the agreement was a bit different than what her brothers had told him was that Theo wanted complete access to all the estate's financial information. Leo had no problem agreeing. She actually had more experience in dealing with estate matters than he did.

Worthington handed him a pen. "Now you may sign it."

The whole thing took just under than an hour. Thus, giving him time to go to St. George's before luncheon. He kissed Theo. "I hope to return soon with a date."

He arrived at the church only to have to wait while the rector spoke with another gentleman. It turned out the person was

Crewe. Leo slapped his friend on the back. "I'm glad to see you. Were you able to get a wedding date and when it is?"

Crewe appeared confused. "Why?"

"The ladies are going to get together and attempt to coordinate the dates so that we can all attend each other's weddings."

"Excellent idea." Crewe's brows drew together. "When do you want your wedding?"

"In two weeks." Leo would not put it off.

"We really need Marrow and Holland here." Crewe glanced at the piece of paper he held.

"Do you have a date and time?" Leo had assumed the man did. He'd just come from the rector.

"I was sent to get possible dates and times."

The cleric signaled to Leo that he was to go in. "Wait here, would you?"

Crewe nodded. "I'm not expected back for a while."

Leo knocked on the door and was told to enter. "Good morning. I'm the Duke of Chandos. My betrothed is Lady Theo Vivers. I have been told to get a date for two weeks from today."

"Your grace." The rector stood and bowed. "Please take a seat and allow me to look at my diary. I would like to perform the service myself. You see, I have married all of her sisters." Leo had to stop himself from fidgeting. Something he hadn't done since he got his knuckles rapped when he was ten years old. "Ah. We are both in luck. I have a space two weeks from today."

An idea that had been forming came to him. "We have three friends who wish to wed close to our date so we can all be at one another's weddings. Do you think that can be arranged?"

The rector glanced back at his diary. "Yes, if they decide on the dates within the next day or two, I can reserve the following three days." The rector glanced up at Leo. "You did not want the same day, did you?"

Leo had no idea, but it would not make sense to all get married on the same day. "No, I believe four consecutive dates would be best."

"In that case, I will write down the days and times that are available."

"Thank you." He hoped this would make Theo happy. He rose and held out his hand. "I look forward to seeing you again."

"I look forward to it as well. I assume the whole family will be there. They usually are."

"They will be." Leo left and went to the waiting room. "Crewe, I have dates for all the weddings to be held on consecutive dates."

"In two weeks?" He looked amazed.

"Yes." Leo felt like a boy getting away with something.

"Thank God." Crewe let out a breath. "Our mothers want us to wait until a large wedding can be arranged, and Felice's mother is being difficult."

"We are meeting for luncheon at Worthington House at noon tomorrow. Theo is sending the invitations as we speak. When we meet, we can work out the days for our ceremonies."

"That sounds like the best idea I've heard lately." He clapped Leo on the back. "Thank you. And Theo."

"Until tomorrow. I have some other errands to run." Leo put on his hat.

He'd left his carriage at the side entrance. When he reached it, he tossed the boy holding the horses some coins and drove to Burlington Arcade. They must have veils there. If not, someone would know where he could find one. It was a straightforward enough drive, but traffic was heavy, and it took him much longer to arrive than he'd planned. He left his horses with another lad to watch. "I'll just be a few minutes." Leo carefully scanned the stores and found one with a good selection of veils. He selected two, one in lace and the other in netting. Both were black. He also found a bonnet that would work perfectly with either one of them. The clerk wrapped them separately as he'd asked. Once outside, he paid the lad and put the packages in a box under the seat. He should probably take his town coach instead of the curricle when he went to the villa. Leo decided to ask Theo when he returned to Worthington House. The only thing he hadn't done was to notify the caretakers that he'd be bringing someone to visit. Damn! He pulled out his notebook and wrote a quick message.

"I would like you take this to 10 Waverley Place, St. John's Wood, if you will? I'll pay for the hackney."

"How much?" the lad asked.

He had to make this worth the boy's trouble. "A quid. Half now and half later. Give them the note and tell whoever answers the door to sign it."

"Do I hafta pay for the hack outa the quid?"

"No, here's enough to get you there and back. Take the note to Worthington House and tell them it's for Lady Theo."

"Yes, sir. I'll take it now."

"Good lad." Leo watched the boy take a hackney and leave. It would take him close to an hour for the trip. He hoped there wasn't too much to prepare. As for now, he had to go back to Worthington House and find out the status of the luncheon tomorrow.

CHAPTER THIRTY-ONE

After Chandos left, Theo went to her parlor and wrote letters to each of her friends who were marrying soon, suggesting they meet for luncheon tomorrow at noon. She gave them to her footman to deliver. "If anyone wants to write an answer, please either wait for it, or return for it."

"Yes, my lady."

Now it was time to write to Chandos's mother. A task to which she was not looking forward.

The Duchess of Chandos
Chandos House
Park Lane
Mayfair

That might be a little too much considering that the missive would be hand delivered. Yet, better to be overly formal than not.

Your Grace,
I have been given to understand that you would like to escort me to inspect Chandos House. I would like to suggest that we meet the day after

tomorrow at ten o'clock. If that time does not agree with you, please send alternative dates for the inspection to take place that will occur within the next five days.

Yrs sincerely,
Lady Theodora Vivers
Worthington House
Berkeley Square
Mayfair

Theo read it over twice before she sealed it.

Jones returned with the first of the acceptances for luncheon tomorrow. "I'm to go back in an hour to Miss Pettigrew's house. She's at a fitting."

"Thank you." Considering the meeting was Sarah's idea, Theo did not expect any problems. She handed him the letter for the duchess. "Please take this to Chandos House."

"Straightaway, my lady. It'll be nice to see a little of where we'll be livin'."

"Have fun then." She shooed him away.

The first note she picked up was from Patricia.

Dear Theo,
I would be delighted to join you to discuss the timing of our weddings. I had already thought that there might be some conflicts if we did not make a plan.
Yr. friend,
P.M.

The second one from Felice merely stated that she would attend.

"Theo." Grace entered the parlor. "You have a fitting tomorrow as soon as we finish breakfast."

That was unexpected. "How does she work so quickly?"

"It is an illusion." Grace smiled. "I sent her the measurements a few months in advance. She knows what you look like, and which colors and styles would suit you the best. That is for the come out gowns. I suppose she and I could be accused of being too optimistic, but then she begins work on the garments you will require after you wed. We have never had one of our sisters fail to marry."

"But I had said that I did not care about that this Season."

"Ah, but you see, we all know you. None better than Mary. She was certain it would be Chandos."

Theo did not understand. "She knew I would not wed a rake."

"She also knew he was making improvements in himself. Perhaps you should consider that when it comes to ourselves, we are not as clear-eyed as we can be for others. She saw what you could not."

Theo had to think about that for a while. What Grace said made sense. When Theo and Mary decided to help St. Albans, they had seen what Alice had not. That he was trying very hard to give her what she wanted and needed. "I understand. Although, it is extremely disconcerting to know that I can guide others and have no notion what to do for myself."

"We all go through it." Grace chuckled. "Even me. If you remember, I was certain that I could not marry Matt, but you and the others convinced me that I could and showed him the way."

Theo almost wondered what people without large families did, but she knew. At least if those people knew someone in her family. They assisted everyone they were able. One of the things she liked best about Chandos was that he helped people as well. She looked forward to being his wife. Which reminded her that she must speak with one of her sisters. "Is anyone joining us at luncheon?"

"Not that I know of, why?"

Theo did not want to hurt her feelings, but she had discovered that Grace was not good at explaining things of an intimate nature. "I wanted to speak to my sisters today."

"Ah. In that case, I will see what I can do."

She left and a footman came in. "My lady, you have a letter from Miss Pettigrew."

"Thank you." Theo broke the seal.

Dear Theo,

I am delighted to join you for luncheon. I am in desperate need of assistance.

Yr. friend forever,
S.P.

Theo wondered what had happened now.

Jones knocked on the open door. "My lady, an answer from the Duchess of Chandos has arrived."

Theo took the note and opened it.

My dear Lady Theodora,

Unfortunately, I am unavailable for the next week or so. I suggest we meet in three weeks' time. I will write to you when I am free of other obligations.

Sincerely,
Amelia, Duchess of Chandos

This was a problem. Did she not know when Theo and Chandos were getting married? She might not. He and his mother were not on good terms at the moment. He would just have to deal with the timing.

She rang for tea while she tried to work out a schedule for the next two weeks, but it was useless until Theo knew when she would be able to tour Chandos House.

She was staring out her window when another knock came on the door. "My lady," Thorton intoned. "The Duke of Chandos."

"I am so glad you are here." Theo stood and went to him.

His arms came around her, and he held her against his chest for several moments. "What is it?"

"Did you not tell your mother when we would wed? I received a response from her to my letter asking if we could meet within the next week. She wrote to me saying she was not available for about three weeks. That will not do at all."

He pressed his lips together and exhaled. "She knows. There's only one thing to do. Plan around her. If she's not present, then she cannot complain."

"I suppose this must be her way of attempting to put off our wedding."

He touched his finger to her nose. "I think you're right. She obviously does not know my almost duchess."

The tea tray arrived with a large pot, and substantial food. Jacque must believe that all gentlemen require sustenance. They sat on one of the small sofas and Theo poured. "What shall we do?"

"We will go to my house after our tea." He picked up a sandwich.

So sudden. "It might be better to go after luncheon. That way you can warn your housekeeper."

Chandos shook his head. "I don't want anyone to know, with the possible exception of my valet. However, considering the time, after the midday meal might be better. Can you gather your servants by then?"

"Yes, Jones just returned. I will send messages to my groom and maid telling them to be ready at one o'clock." This was a bit sneaky, but needs must. "When does your mother go on morning calls?"

"About that time, I believe. I'll write a missive to Matson to come here in the town coach. Then we can give him instructions."

"It might be easier if I have Jones take our small coach and bring your valet back with instructions to send your town coach here." Theo grinned.

"That would be more efficient." Leo went to the desk and wrote the letter to his valet.

Theo handed the note to her footman. "This is for Mr. Matson, his grace's valet. Do not give it to anyone else. Take the small, unmarked coach . . ."

"Yes, my lady. It shouldn't take long."

A few minutes later, Theo's lady's maid and her groom begged entrance.

"Come in. After luncheon we are going to Chandos House. Payne, you must look over our quarters and make a list of what we will need."

"Yes, my lady. I will be prepared."

Theo nodded and the maid departed. "Mick, make sure the stables are in good shape. I want to know about anything that is awry. Not that I think there will be, but one never knows. There must be sufficient room for my mare and carriage."

"I know what to look for, my lady." The groom left as well.

Chandos put down his cup. "This ought to be interesting."

She gave him a curious look. "How so?"

"I have not even visited the stables since I've been here." Stupid of him really. "I assumed everything was fine."

"I am doing it because when Alice went to inspect St. Albans's stables, they were a disaster. That situation was different. The heir's stables had been closed for years, but she also discovered that the grooms and other stable servants were not being paid enough."

Theo made him think about the boy who was delivering his message to St. John's Wood. Thanks to his mother, he wouldn't make it there today. "There is a lad that I employed to send a message to my other house. If he does a good job, I would like to hire him."

She gave him a broad smile. "What an excellent idea."

Matson arrived shortly before luncheon. "I came as quickly as I could, your grace. Is anything wrong?"

"You might say that. Her grace is not available to escort Lady Theo around the house for at least three weeks."

"I cannot say that I am surprised. Her maid was in a taking that a new mistress would be there."

"Lady Theo, her personal servants, and you and I will go this afternoon and start the inspection. I did not notify Swisher because, quite frankly, I don't know where her loyalties lay. Can you recommend a maid that could accompany us?"

"The under housekeeper, Jaynes."

"When we arrive, please fetch her to us." Leo glanced at his betrothed.

"Do you know where her grace will be this afternoon?" Theo asked.

"I do not. However, she has ordered the small carriage to be ready at one fifteen."

Leo glanced at her. "We should arrive just after she departs."

"I agree." Her stomach rumbled. "It is time for luncheon." She turned to Matson. "If you wish, you may join our servants. It would give you a chance to meet Payne and Jones, my other personal servants who will come with me."

He bowed. "Yes, my lady. I would like that."

It was not until they were ready to depart an hour later that the boy arrived asking for Theo. "The gentleman that gave me the note said to ask for you. He owes me half a pound."

"The gentleman is here and there is your payment."

The boy handed the missive to Theo. "Here, me lady."

"Thank you. Can you wait for a moment?"

"Aye." He held his battered hat in his hands in front of him and stood still.

After reading the letter she handed it to Chandos. "There are apparently several problems with your request."

He took it from her. It was on a much larger piece of paper than he'd given to the boy. Apparently, they needed to provision the house before he brought a lady to it. Tomorrow, he was told, would be much better, but any time after that, all would be in order. "It's a good thing we made other plans for this afternoon. They are not prepared."

Theo appeared slightly aghast. "I beg your pardon. Did you not instruct them to keep everything in readiness for an immediate arrival?"

He appeared chagrined. "To be honest, I don't remember. I didn't think I'd need the house again."

She glanced at him, then at the boy. "What's your name?"

"Clyde." He gave her a curious look.

"Clyde, it is nice to meet you. Would you like a job as a running messenger?" He was too young to be a footman, but there were times when one wanted to send a message and not have the servant delivering it in livery. "You would also have the opportunity to learn how to read, write, and add numbers."

He cast a suspicious look at Leo. "How much ye payin' me? I got to make sure it's more than I'm makin' now. Me ma's sick."

Damned if he knew how much to pay the lad. He didn't even know what his valet received. He glanced at Theo and raised a brow.

She nodded and addressed her attention to the lad. "Clyde, you will be paid twenty pounds a year, in addition to meals, a room if you need it, tea and ale."

His eyes widened at the amount of money and stayed that way.

"Is that acceptable to you?"

"Aye, me lady." He nodded enthusiastically. "I can take care of my ma real good."

"Perhaps we can also do something to help your mother." Theo gave him a warm smile. "I will make plans to visit her."

As fast as he'd nodded, he shook his head. "In St. Giles, me lady? It ain't safe."

"We will work something out. Now then"—she turned and looked toward the door to the servants' area where Payne, Jones, and Matson were waiting—"we must be going, but if you come here . . ." She glanced at Leo with a question in her eyes.

"Have him come to my house. I'll tell Whiting to take care of it."

"Very well." Her brows drew together. "He might as well come with us. That way it can be done today. And he can sign it."

"Don't know how ta write," Clyde said glumly.

"That is all right. It will be explained to you." Theo gave him a kind look. "And you will soon learn."

It occurred to Leo that, unlike Worthington House, and in the homes of the other family members, he didn't have a schoolroom set up for the younger servants. He couldn't even remember the last time he'd seen the schoolroom or nursery floor. He did know that it looked nothing like the ones here. The children had given him a tour one day when he was waiting for a meeting to start and Theo was out.

Mick entered the hall. "My lady, your grace, the coach is ready."

This was it. Leo held out his arm for her. He wondered what Theo would think of his home. He also wondered who he'd have to remind that they worked for him. Not his mother.

Mama's coach passed as they turned into Park Lane. That was one problem resolved. He felt like a child trying to sneak around so his parents couldn't find him. It was time to recall that he was the one in charge.

CHAPTER THIRTY-TWO

Theo and Chandos held hands in the coach on their way to his house. Her initial impression was that the grounds were in good order. The drive was well kept with no potholes. The hedges were trimmed. It was all neat and tidy, but there was nothing to add a spark of interest. She would have to think about that.

They pulled up in front of the house, and the door opened. A slightly bemused footman stood there. "Your grace, Mr. Hoover did not expect you."

"That's fine." He climbed the steps, still holding Theo's hand. "Annott, is it?"

He bowed, "Yes, your grace. Should I get Mr. Hoover?"

"Not yet. This is Lady Theo Vivers. She will be my duchess in two weeks. She has come to inspect the house."

He appeared panicked. "Mrs. Swisher isn't here, your grace."

Theo patted Chandos's arm. "Is Miss Jaynes here?"

"Yes, my lady."

"Please have her join us." The footman took off as if he was glad to leave them.

The butler and a woman in her early thirties strode into the hall. *Jaynes*. She had a pleasant countenance. Though, again, she appeared confused.

The butler bowed. "Your grace. I was not informed you would be bringing Lady Theo to the house. Nothing is prepared."

"I didn't expect it would be." Chandos motioned to Theo. "My love, I would like to present my butler, Hoover, and I presume this is Miss Jaynes." They bowed and curtseyed again. "As you know, this is Lady Theo Vivers. We will be married in two weeks." Chandos apparently wanted to ensure the servants knew the date. "I gather that information has not been given to you."

"No, your grace." Hoover appeared grim. "I and the staff wish you congratulations on your pending marriage."

Theo looked at Jaynes. "I would like to inspect the house. Can you show me around?"

She seemed hesitant. "Usually, Mrs. Swisher would perform that task."

"We have been told she is not here." Theo gave her an encouraging smile. "I am sure you are eminently capable to take over for her. Am I correct?"

The servant straightened. "Yes, my lady. You are correct. Would you like to begin at the top and work your way down, or the other way around?"

"Let us start at the top." She turned to her maid. "This is Payne, she is my maid." Then she motioned to her footman. "This is Jones. He is my personal footman. Both Payne and Jones answer only to me. Is that understood?"

"Yes, my lady," the butler and housekeeper said at the same time.

"Very good. Let me see what we have."

Chandos led the way up four flights of stairs to the schoolroom and nursery. They were filthy. That really did not surprise Theo. Once the children were grown and no young ones were around, these rooms frequently became areas for old furniture to be stored and were not kept up. They also needed to be renovated. "First of all, they must be cleaned." She turned to him. "I will send a note to the architect and decorator my family uses to remodel these rooms. I would like something akin to what we have at both Stanwood and Worthington Houses."

"I've seen them, and I agree." All the darkness would depress a child. "The broken furniture will have to go as well."

He seemed to have the same impression of the rooms as she did. "Indeed."

Jaynes and Payne were making notes.

"Are you ready to go down to the next level, my lady?" Jaynes asked.

"Is that where the servants' quarters are?"

"Er, no, my lady. They are on the other side of the house on this floor."

"I would prefer to see that first." Theo wanted to ensure that all the servants were comfortable, especially hers. "Where are my maid's rooms?"

"There is a small apartment that is attached to the mistress's suite," Jaynes said.

She glanced up at Chandos. "How often did your parents come to Town?"

"Twice a year until my father's illness. What I don't know is when it was last refreshed."

Theo was not any more impressed by the servants' quarters. "It all needs to be painted, and they need new soft furnishings." She looked at the windows. "Since the windows on the other side will be changed, the windows here must be redone as well. Otherwise, the house will seem odd."

Chandos glanced in the rooms and frowned. "The chambers seem too small."

That is what was bothering her about the space. "They are smaller than the ones in Worthington House."

"And at Kenilworth House where I was trained," Payne said.

"It's because the floor is shared with the nursery," Jaynes commented.

They looked at Chandos, then Theo. "We will have to give this some thought."

He nodded, but did not respond.

"Let us move to the next floor." She hoped the more lived-in areas would not be nearly as bad.

As with the nursery and servants' quarters, the stairs had no landing but descended directly from the middle of the floor. The furniture was all covered; still, it was clear that the rooms and windows were larger. "This is what I expected from the children's level. Who stays here?"

Jaynes wrote something in her notebook. "No one, my lady."

"Odd." Theo did not understand the arrangement of this house.

"It is." Once again, Chandos glanced in each room. "What if we were to make over this floor into the nursery and schoolroom? That would give us the space to make the servants' chambers larger."

"It would also allow us to separate the male and female servants, which is not the case now." She looked at Jaynes. "Would that make it more comfortable?"

"Yes, my lady. The women always have to be fully dressed when we leave our chambers, but the men don't always remember."

Theo could well imagine that. "We could also add a bathing chamber to that section."

Chandos nodded. "We have pipes going to a bathing chamber on the family level. I assume they could be run up to make additional bathing chambers. It was not something I ever thought to do. We could also put one on this floor."

"That is a very good idea." There would be plenty of room. "We may discuss it with Mr. Rollins, the architect, when we meet with him and his wife."

They descended to the next floor and continued the inspection.

"This is the family level," Jaynes said. "Her grace's apartment is down here." She pointed to the right. "The master chamber is on the other side of the floor."

"We do not have to look at her grace's rooms at the moment." The time for that would come later. She smiled at Chandos. "I am very interested in seeing our chambers."

He appeared a bit disconcerted. "Frankly, I'm not certain you'll approve of the arrangement."

What could be wrong with them? "Why?"

"You'll see." He led her to a set of rooms at the end of the corridor in the back of the house and opened a door. "This area contains my apartment. As you see, it opens up onto a parlor, the bedroom is to the right, and my valet's rooms are to the left." He grimaced. "Your rooms are at the other end of the corridor."

"You were correct. I do not like it at all." Theo turned on her heel, strode past other chambers to the other end of the wing and opened the door. It was the same plan. There was not even a way for the duchess to conveniently access her husband's bedchamber or vice versa. "Am I correct in thinking that your mother's rooms are next to your chambers?"

"Yes. We could combine those two areas for our apartments."

That would work with one possible exception. "Do you not intend that we sleep together?"

He stared at her for a several seconds. "Is that what you want?"

"I do." Theo realized that many couples did not. Yet, all her sisters shared a bedchamber with their husbands. "I desire to sleep with my husband. Not alone."

Chandos smiled. "I would like that as well."

"In that case, we can have Mr. Rollins design the rooms accordingly."

"Excellent." Leo breathed a sigh of relief. He hadn't thought at all about where Theo would sleep. He was ecstatic that she wanted to be with him. "The rest of chambers on this floor are for family, and the few guests that must be accommodated overnight."

"With your mother here, we will not be able to reorganize the rooms until later." Perhaps they would both stay in his rooms until hers were finished. She would be sleeping there in any event.

"We still have my rooms." If he had his way, he'd move his

mother into her own house immediately. He wanted to show her his bedchamber, but all she'd be able to do was look at it. His villa in St. John's Wood was a much better place to introduce her to lovemaking.

They went on to view the other rooms on that floor and descended to the next level. He shouldn't have been surprised by her attention to each little detail, but he was. Leo thought she would become bored long before they reached the kitchen and cellars. Once they reached the main areas, she made a point of greeting all the servants she saw and asking their names. To a one, they appeared to be genuinely surprised to see her and discover that she and Leo were to be wed. It was probably his fault. In truth, he'd not been home much at all since they'd become engaged. He hadn't even told his secretary. They had reached the servants' hall when they ran into their first bit of resistance. Swisher had returned.

The second she saw him, her jaw dropped, and an unpleasant expression entered her eyes. "Your grace, why are you down here?"

Normally, that would have been a fair question. He'd never been below stairs before. He turned to Theo. "My love, allow me to present Swisher, our housekeeper. Swisher, my betrothed, Lady Theo Vivers."

Theo held out her hand. "It is a pleasure to finally meet you. Do I take it that you were not aware of our engagement?"

Swisher just looked at Theo's hand for a moment before taking it. "Her grace mentioned something about it. I didn't expect to see you for a few weeks."

"I understand. Her grace wanted to wait for some time before escorting me herself on a tour of the house. However, the wedding is in two weeks. There is too much to do to wait to perform such an important task."

"Yes, my lady. If I'd known you were coming, I would have been here."

"I appreciate that. Jaynes has done an admirable job taking

notes, as has my maid, Payne." Theo inclined her head to the housekeeper.

Leo was certain there was some sort of female power struggle going on that he didn't understand. As his duchess, Theo would be in control of the house. Wouldn't the servants understand that and obey her?

After several moments, Swisher dropped her gaze. "Very good, my lady."

Theo smiled, but the expression was one that left no doubt she would be in charge. "I do not have time at present to inspect the linens. You should know that I will be changing several things in the house. We will begin as soon as we are able. While I am at it, is there anything in your quarters that you would like to refresh?"

For the first time, the housekeeper relaxed. "Yes, my lady. The curtains and bed cover are very old."

"Excellent. When Mrs. Rollins comes with her fabric books you may choose what you like."

"Thank you, my lady." The corners of Swisher's lips rose slightly.

"You may also join us as we discuss what else should be done."

Swisher finally decided to curtsey. "Would you like me to show you around these rooms and to the kitchen?"

"Yes, please." This time, Theo's smile was warm. "I would appreciate that."

They toured the servants' hall, and she met his chef de cuisine, André, who as far as Leo was concerned was being far too charming. He'd be glad when they were done. He was getting hungry, and he'd been invited to her house for dinner.

They returned to the hall. "Are we done?"

"Almost." She kissed him on the cheek. "I would like to meet your secretary, I also have not seen my footman recently."

"I know where they are, my lady. I'll go get him," one of the younger footmen to whom Theo had spoken earlier said.

"Thank you . . . Paulie, is it not?"

The lad blushed. "Yes, my lady."

"Come." Leo took her hand. "I'll make Whiting known to you."

"I have been looking forward to meeting him."

Thus far, Leo had shown her all the rooms with the exception of his study and his secretary's office. And his bedchamber. Two more weeks, and she'd be living there with him. Unless they took a honeymoon. The only questions were if to take one and where to go. Her brothers suggested that if he wanted to go to Paris to wait until autumn. What Leo really wanted was to have her to himself for a while.

They entered Whiting's office. "Good afternoon."

He immediately stood. "Your grace. Lady Theo, I presume."

Her eyes danced as her lips tipped up. "Mr. Whiting. A pleasure to meet you."

He bowed. "The pleasure is all mine. I take it that you are now betrothed."

"We are." Leo never thought Whiting could be so charming. "The wedding is in two weeks."

"Shall I ask Mrs. Merryweather to prepare a list of the guests her grace will wish to invite to the wedding breakfast?"

"Yes, please do," Theo said. "If she tries to put you off, you may explain to her that if you do not receive the list within the next few days, it will be too late for her grace's guests to attend."

"I understand." Whiting gave Leo a curious look. "Does her grace not wish for you to marry?"

"She had been urging me to do so for the past year. I have the strong feeling that she had a young lady in mind. I knew who I wanted to wed."

Theo's cheeks became pink. He'd like to see how deep her color could be. "In any event, she put Theo off on inspecting the house and failed to tell the staff I would wed soon."

A thoughtful look appeared on Whiting's mien. "Just yesterday Mrs. Merryweather mentioned a problem with the dower house."

That made no sense. "The main dower house is in Bath, and the last report I had was that it was in excellent condition. I also went there to inspect it just before coming to Town."

"When was the last time she visited the house?" Theo asked.

"I don't know if she's ever been." Something was going on with his mother. He'd have to find out exactly what. "Do you know if she is going out this evening?"

"To the best of my knowledge, she is not. Hoover would know for certain," Whiting said.

Theo looked worried, then glanced at Leo. "Perhaps you should speak with her after we dine this evening."

"I'll do that. This strife between us must end." He'd always been close to his parents, and she was the last one he had. "Speaking of dinner. We should go." He glanced at his secretary. "Is there anything of which I should be aware?"

A small smile dawned on Whiting's face. "I am to be married at the end of June."

"Excellent!" Theo beamed at him. "Congratulations."

Leo wasn't convinced that was wonderful news. "Does that change your employment here?"

"No, your grace." His secretary stared down at his desk for a few moments, then glanced at Theo. "My lady, are you in need of a secretary or companion?"

"I will need a secretary. I thought to wait until after I was married, however, I will happily meet with her to see if we suit."

"Thank you. She likes to keep busy."

"Next week, I think. I will have to look at my diary."

"My lady," Payne said, "you could plan to meet with the lady on the same day you consult with Mrs. Rollins."

"That is an excellent idea. Thank you." Theo held out her hand to Whiting. "I shall see you again."

"Yes, my lady. It was a pleasure to finally meet you."

When they reached the hall again, Hoover and Jones were in conversation. "Your grace," Hoover said. "Her grace informed me that she was going out tonight. She will be at home for a short while before she leaves again."

"Thank you." Leo wouldn't be meeting with her this evening. "Do you know what her plans are for tomorrow?"

"She has nothing scheduled in the morning."

It would have to be then. "I'll be at Worthington House."

"Yes, your grace."

Leo was glad he'd brought Theo to his house today. He'd had no idea how much needed to be accomplished. Although he should have. His almost brothers-in-laws had all mentioned improvements her sisters had made to their houses.

CHAPTER THIRTY-THREE

The next morning, after riding with Theo and breaking his fast at her house, Leo went home to speak with his mother. His betrothed had reminded him that he must listen to what she had to say, and he would. But no matter what else happened, his mother was not going to talk him out of marrying Theo.

He found Mama in the breakfast room, sipping a cup of tea. He bussed her cheek. "Good morning."

"You are in a good mood." She, clearly, was not.

"We must talk. I understand that when Theo wrote to you asking for a date to tour the house, you suggested she wait for a few weeks."

Mama assumed a sour look. "And I understand that she completely ignored me and was here yesterday with her *personal* servants."

This would not stand. Theo wouldn't be blamed. "She was, because I insisted on bringing them here." He resisted drumming his fingers on the table. "There is a great deal to do before our marriage."

"I do not know why this must happen so quickly." His mother's tone was tense.

"No, you don't know why it must happen at all." Leo was forcing himself to be calm. "You wanted me to wed. I'm doing just that. Why are you upset?"

She put down her teacup. "When you were young, around eight years old, my closest friend gave birth to a lovely little girl. I tried to convince your father to enter into a betrothal contract for you to marry her. He would not do it." Mama screwed up her lips as if she had eaten a lemon. "He asked me if I never wondered why the duke and duchess's apartments were so far apart. I admitted that it had crossed my mind, and he told me that it was because until you, every marriage had been arranged, and that several of the couples actively hated one another." She lifted her empty cup and put it down. "Despite that, my friend and I never gave up hope. Clarissa came out this year. But you would have nothing to do with her. You would not even meet her. It was embarrassing for me."

Leo had been so focused on marrying Theo, he'd never mentioned it to his mother, until they arrived in Town. "I told you before the beginning of the Season that I knew who I wanted to wed."

"Yes, yes, I know you did. I do not understand how you could have made your mind up so quickly, and to a lady with whom you would clash. Suddenly falling in love does not make for a stable marriage."

"I wasn't sudden. I have known Theo for almost four years as my friend's sister. Last year I realized that she might be the perfect lady for me. I spent a great deal of time visiting whichever house she was at to make sure she was the right one." He wished he'd rung for tea. "Mama, Theo is kind, intelligent, funny, the best whist player I've ever met, and knows how to run estates better than I do, and grand houses. She will also not put up with anyone, including herself, being treated badly." And beautiful. "Even if you had told me about this Clarissa, it wouldn't have mattered. I had made my decision."

"You could have told me." There was weary anger in her tone.

"I didn't tell anyone. Not even her brother, who is one of my best friends, until I asked for permission to court her." There was no point in telling his mother that he'd had to prove himself to her family or they wouldn't have allowed him near her. Mama would never have understood.

"I suppose they gave it right away. They must have been very pleased."

"Actually, no. I was told it was her decision to make, and she took a lot of convincing." His mother still didn't look happy. "I do not want this to continue to cause a rift between us. That said, Theo is the lady I will have for my wife. It would make me very happy if you could bring yourself to accept her."

"I suppose she is going to make a lot of changes."

He had no doubt Mama had insisted on reviewing Jaynes's notes. "Yes. First of which will be the location of the duchess's chambers. She is contacting an architect her family works with, and his wife, who is a decorator."

Her eyes widened. "You are going to remodel the house?"

"We are. One of our proposals is to move the schoolroom and nursery and expand the whole top floor into servants' quarters." That would be enough to tell her at present.

"Goodness. I never even thought of that. Not that your father would have agreed." She frowned briefly. "Where will everyone live while this is going on?"

"We'll discuss that when we meet with the architect." Then Leo realized she wanted to know where she'd live. "I will give all of this serious thought. If you have any ideas, we would like to hear them. Before the final plans are made."

"Yes. This certainly is not the situation I had imagined it to be." She stared at him for several moments, then reached out to him across the table. "I apologize for not welcoming Lady Theo. I wish to make amends. Perhaps she could join me for tea this afternoon."

No, no, no! He had plans for her after luncheon. And he'd be there when she had tea with his mother. "I'll ask, but I believe she has something she must do. Tomorrow?"

"Yes, that might be better." Mama appeared more resigned than pleased.

He glanced at the clock. How could time go so quickly? "I am meeting Theo and some of our friends for luncheon. I'll see you later."

"Yes, dear. Have a good time."

"I will." If they could get all their weddings arranged to everyone's satisfaction, it would be a miracle. Leo made sure he had the dates the rector had given to him.

After giving orders for the unmarked town coach to be at Worthington House just after one and to wait for him, Leo decided to walk to Worthington House. As he was passing Grosvenor Square, he saw Crewe and Felice descending the steps from Crewe House. "Good day."

"It will be if we can get these weddings arranged," Felice said in an exasperated tone.

That didn't sound promising. "How has your morning been going?"

She came as close as a lady could to rolling her eyes. "Our mothers are about to make me mad."

Crewe gave a sympathetic look to his betrothed. "If they get everything they want, we won't be wed until next year."

She nodded. "I would dearly love to put my foot down. The problem is that I risk stepping on someone's toes."

For the first time, Leo realized how lucky he was in Theo's family. They knew exactly how to plan a wedding and hold it a couple of weeks later. "This seems to be a common difficulty."

As they reached Worthington House, Marrow, Sarah, Holland, and Patricia were going up the short walk.

The door opened, and Theo was there waiting for them. "Come with me, I have had our luncheon set up in one of the parlors in the event we take longer than an hour." She waited until the gentlemen had given their hats to the butler. "Follow me."

The parlor was a smaller room tucked away next to the large drawing room. There were windows onto a side garden. They all took seats, and Jones led two other footmen bringing soup, various meats, salad, cheeses, bread, and wine.

"Now then." Theo looked around the table as her guests served themselves. "Chandos has a list of dates that are contiguous with our wedding day. I would like each of you to pick one."

He passed the paper around, and the couples did as she had asked, then passed the paper to her. Marrow and Sarah had chosen the day before Theo and Chandos's wedding. Patricia and Holland had chosen the day after, and Felice and Crewe took the day after that.

Theo looked at Marrow, Sarah, Patricia, and Holland. "Have you thought about having a double wedding?"

"No." Sarah glanced at the other three. "We have not. That is an excellent idea. It would save time and preparation."

Patricia nodded. "It would allow us to depart earlier. Holland wants to show me some of Europe before we take up our posting."

"I like the idea as well," Marrow said.

"Me too," Holland agreed.

Theo raised a brow at Sarah. "How will you deal with your mother?"

"I honestly believe that once the four of us present Lady Carlisle with our decision, she will make it happen."

"Mama can be very forceful," Patricia said. She glanced at Sarah and pulled a face. "She is also a little tired of your mother changing things all the time."

"She is not the only one." Sarah groaned. "The sooner everything can be taken out of Mama's hands, the better."

Theo looked at Crewe and Felice. "What about the two of you?"

"I have been threatening to elope," Felice said. "Not that I would, but this is all too much to bear. I understand Crewe is a marquis, but there has been much too much fuss."

"I agree with Felice." He glanced at Chandos. "If a duke can wed in two weeks, so can a marquis."

Theo made the changes to the dates. "Witnesses. Since the four of you are marrying first, Chandos, Felice, Crewe, and I will stand up with you and be your witnesses."

"Wonderful!" Sarah said. "Then Marrow and I can stand up with you and Chandos."

"And," Felice said, "Patricia and Crewe can stand up with us."

"Now that that has been decided," Patricia said, "how do we get our mothers to agree?"

"Are your settlement agreements signed?" Chandos asked.

"Crewe and I have agreed to our settlement. We are waiting for the solicitor."

"Give him a firm date for within the next week," Chandos said.

"I should have thought of that." Crewe pressed his lips together. "I allowed myself to be distracted by the less important parts of the wedding."

"Papa gave Mama a list of what he wanted, and authorized his solicitor here to sign it for him," Sarah offered.

Marrow made a moue of disgust. Theo wondered if it was because of what Lord Pettigrew wanted. "I'll tell our father that if he wants to avoid delay, he should hurry our solicitor along. But why the rush?"

"Because." Theo could not resist a slightly smug smile. "Once you have the settlement agreements signed, you can wed by special license, and no one can contest it on the grounds that we ladies have not yet reached our majorities. The contracts are clear evidence that permission has been granted."

"Ohhh, that is devious." Sarah grinned. "All we have to do is insist that we marry on the dates we picked."

Crewe looked at Theo with approval. "You could have been a lawyer, my lady."

"Much better for her to be a duchess." Chandos poured everyone glasses of wine. "My duchess. Is there anything we haven't discussed that we need to?" They all looked at each other around the table and shook their heads. "Excellent. Tell either Theo or me if anyone has a problem they cannot resolve by themselves." After they toasted to their respective weddings, and finished eating, he rose and offered Theo his hand. "I have something extremely important to show my betrothed."

"Really? What?" Theo could not think of a thing. "I must leave word for Grace so she will not worry."

"Tell Thorton. He'll inform her."

"That will do. We cannot leave before our guests."

The gentlemen took their ladies' arms and quickly strode to the door.

Crewe flashed Chandos a devilish look. "Shall I guess?"

"No." He narrowed his eyes. "You may keep your suspicions to yourself."

Theo did not understand why they had to rush. "You can at least tell me."

Crewe barked a laugh and pulled Felice out the door. "Come, my love. We do not want to be run over."

Theo only had a chance to wave goodbye before Chandos lifted her into the coach. Once he entered and sat next to her, Theo had had enough secrecy. "Tell me now where we are going."

"To my villa in St. John's Wood."

Theo almost dropped her jaw. "But the note said it would not be ready."

"I had the forethought to send Jaynes, with two footmen and two maids, there early this morning. They will ensure it is up to your standards and mine." His green gaze caught hers. "Are you sure you want to do this? We can wait."

"I am certain." She pressed her lips to his. He would have to show her how to go on.

Once they were past the Park, he handed her a bonnet and veil. "Put these on so that if anyone sees us, they will not recognize you."

She removed her hat and donned the new one. It had a wide brim that curled down in the back, hiding her hair. Theo decided to wear the net so that she could see a bit at least. The veil covered her entire face, neck, and shoulders. "What about my gown?"

"The villa has a solid gate. No one will be able to see you depart the coach and enter the house."

That was discreet. They made the drive mainly in silence as she sat back and looked out the window. She had never been on this side of London before. Finally, they entered a leafy area with charming free-standing houses and town houses. Tall walls with entry gates surrounded the houses. The coach slowed and turned into one of the drives. The house was three stories in white brick with long windows. Behind them, the gate closed. "It is beautiful!"

Chandos jumped down and held out his hand for her. "It's one of my favorite properties. In a way, it's a shame that the area has become synonymous with courtesans."

Thus, making it more easily sold than kept. "Is the inside as lovely?"

He grinned. "I think so. You will have to tell me."

Theo had images of naked people painted on the ceilings. "I am looking forward to seeing it."

He used his key, and they entered a small mostly marble hall with scantily clad, Greek-looking statues placed in nooks. The walls were painted azure. The ceiling motif was mostly naked bodies, but they were cherubs. A curved staircase rose to the next level. "It is beautiful." She glanced around. "Will no one greet us?"

"Uh, no. We will serve and wait on ourselves today." Chandos twined his arm with hers. "Come with me."

As they ascended the stairs, she was becoming a bit nervous. Theo supposed that was normal. After all, she had never been intimate with a gentleman before. He opened the door to a parlor decorated in various shades of medium to light green, with windows and a French door leading to a small balcony. "This is like a fairy-tale house."

He tilted his head. "I suppose in a way it could be seen like that. Would you like a glass of wine?"

That was when she noticed a round cherry table and two chairs. On the table were covered plates and a bottle of wine in ice. "Yes, please." She had pushed back the netting over the bonnet when they had entered the house. Now she removed the hat, took the glass of wine, and sipped it. "This is excellent."

"I found it during my tour at a vineyard in France and arranged to have several cases shipped home."

Theo wandered to the French windows and peered out to the garden beyond. For almost the first time in her life, she did not know what to do next.

CHAPTER THIRTY-FOUR

Leo watched his beloved Theo standing at the window. If anything was going to happen today, it would be up to him. He smiled to himself. This was one area where she had no experience, and he did.

Setting down his wine, he strolled over to her. "Do you like the view?"

He took her glass as she turned, and set it on a small table. She gazed up at him with her lapis eyes. "It is wonderful."

He framed her face with his palms. Her eyes drifted shut as their lips met. He'd only really kissed her once before. She opened her lips for him, allowing him to taste her. Soon her arms were around his neck, and her tongue tangled with his. He quickly unmoored the buttons on the back of her gown. As it slid down, he feathered kisses on her neck and shoulders, then removed the pins holding her hair. The chestnut curls poured over her body almost to her waist.

"More." She squirmed in his arms.

"More is coming, my love." Next her stays dropped away, and all that was left was her chemise. She untied the bow at the neckline, and he followed with his lips. Twirling his tongue around one nipple, then the other, they came to stiff peaks under his ministrations. Her clothing pooled around her feet, and he swept her into his arms, opened the door to the bedroom, and placed her gently on the bed.

She was beautiful, staring up at him. "You have on too many clothes."

"That is easily rectified. Do you wish to watch?"

Her cheeks and neck pinkened. "Yes."

Slowly Leo removed his clothes, watching her eyes as he did. He was concerned about her reaction to his cock when he removed his trousers, but she appeared more fascinated than afraid. That was a very good sign.

"Come to me." Theo held out her hand.

He climbed carefully onto the bed. "Now what?"

A line formed between her brows. "I am not sure. More kisses?"

Their lips came together again, but this time he stroked one finger over her cheek, down her neck, and cupped her ample breasts. She pushed up into his hand, and he bent his head, taking one nipple into his mouth before kissing his way down to her mons. Settling between her legs he licked.

"Oh. Oh, Lord! That feels so good!" Her body pushed up, wanting more.

Leo claimed her mouth again and he inserted one finger and lightly rubbed with his thumb. Theo threw her head back as she spasmed around him. Then he entered her. She gasped as he breached her maidenhead and clung to him. "Are you well?"

"Yes." Her voice was shaky. "I knew it would hurt."

He stilled, then when she relaxed began to move again, and, thankfully, she moved with him. It wasn't long before she convulsed around him and he allowed himself his release. She was his. Leo hadn't expected this, with Theo, to be so different. Yet it was. Love made the difference. He reached over to a bowl he knew contained water and a small linen cloth to clean them. Even though he'd expected the blood, it was still shocking somehow. He cuddled her, holding her in his arms. He'd been with many women, but it was never like this. His love grew even stronger for Theo. From this day forward, she was his wife. She would be the mother of his children. And he'd protect her with his life.

Theo lay in bed, curled next to Chandos. In his arms. Savoring the fading feelings of his lovemaking. She had known it would be good. She had not realized how wonderful it would be. Aside from the bite of pain, the experience was like no other.

His chin nuzzled her head. "How do you feel?"

"Perfect." It was true. She had never been so content, so happy. "We really are one now."

"We are. Forever." A smile played around his lips.

She rolled onto her side, then threaded her fingers through his soft, black chest curls. "I am very glad we visited this house. In a way, I wish we could keep it."

Theo could feel him looking down at her. "Do you?"

"Yes." She moved to be able to see him better. "I do. It is comfortable, quiet, and very pretty."

"The reputation of the area doesn't bother you?"

"Not really." She kissed his chest. "After all, you will not have a mistress here."

"That's true."

"And now that we have done this, it is an excellent place to do it again." She couldn't keep from grinning. "I would ask to do it again, but I know I will probably be sore."

"A warm bath would help." He cuddled her closer.

"But we have no servants. You would have to carry up the water."

"Ah, you have yet to see the bathing chamber."

"I will definitely enjoy that." She started to push herself up, and he covered her again and kissed her. Theo still could not believe how erotic a kiss could be. As their tongues danced, she grew hotter, her desire building faster than it had before. She spread her legs to encourage him, but instead, he caressed and kissed her breasts, then stroked between her legs until she saw bright lights and stars.

Chandos caressed her back as she recovered. "There are many ways to make love."

"You did that so I would not be too sore." She knew she sounded like she was making an accusation.

"I did that because I enjoy the way you look when you come for me." His warm green gaze moved over her body. "You don't know what you do to me. I've dreamed of this for months." He kissed her again. "Just looking at you makes my cock come alive."

Theo glanced down. He was right. At least one part of him wanted to take her again. "I suppose we should bathe. Who will go first?"

"We'll bathe together. Wait here." He rose from the bed and disappeared through a door. When he returned, he lifted her into his arms. "Your bath awaits, my lady."

The tub was massive. It could easily fit three people. Then again, water did not splash out nearly as much as it would if it had been smaller. She had the foresight to put her hair back up before getting into the water. "You must have put a good deal of thought into the size."

"I did." He lifted her from the bath, placed a towel over Theo's shoulders, and began to dry her. Pleasant shivers speared through her. She might like to stay here for a much longer time. "A friend had a vessel that was too small. He hit his head when he slipped getting out of his bathtub."

"You could put towels down around it."

He shrugged. "This seemed easier and less work for the maid cleaning up." He poured an oil onto his fingers and stroked between her legs and into her passage. "That should help you feel better."

"What is it?" Theo really did have a great deal to discuss with her married sisters.

"Almond oil. I have a small vial for you to take home." Chandos kissed her neck.

If he did not stop, she would never leave. "What time is it?"

"We need to dress if we are not going to be late for dinner."

They had been here for hours? It did not seem that long. They went into the bedroom, and she was surprised to find her gown hung over a chair along with the rest of her clothing. When had he done that? "Lift your arms." She did as he asked and he dropped her chemise over her head. Theo quickly tied it, and donned her stays, which Chandos tied. Before she knew it, she was dressed. "Someone will have to look closely to see anything amiss."

Soon he was dressed. He tugged a bellpull, and they went downstairs. A few minutes later, the coach came to the front of the house, and she donned her bonnet and veil. "I am sorry to leave."

"I am as well." He lifted her into the coach and followed after, putting his arm around her. "When we're wed, we can do this as much as we like."

Theo tried to bring her diary into her mind, but she was having a little trouble concentrating on it. "How soon can we return?"

"When you are ready." There was a distinctly amorous look in his eyes. The problem was that she was responding to it. "A day or two. I'm glad you enjoyed yourself."

"More than you know." She felt sorry for the ladies whom she overheard talking. "I think I am lucky. I could not imagine being married to someone who did not know what they were doing."

Chandos settled her closer to him. "Are you speaking about the women you overheard talking?"

"Yes." She craned her neck to see his face. "One of them has never seen her husband naked, nor he her. You seemed to enjoy seeing me, and I liked seeing you."

The corner of his lips rose. "You are the most beautiful female I have ever seen."

"You remind me of the statues I saw, but with more hair. And larger. Much larger."

He tossed back his head and laughed. "That is the best compliment I've ever received."

Theo leaned her head on his shoulder. "I wonder who they are."

"Considering they almost drove you from me, if I found out,

it would not go well for them." The crown of her bonnet pressed down. "I don't like that hat. I can't kiss your hair."

Theo laughed. "I'll be able to remove it soon."

"Good." He turned his head. "What can you tell me about them?"

"Not much." She shook her head. "One has a husband whose name is Gerald. One spoke in a nasal tone. Oh, and there is a brother who purports to know you. That is where most of the information came from."

"The erroneous information." Chandos's voice was hard.

"Yes." He had a right to be upset. They had almost lost each other because of the gossip.

"Do they sound like anyone you know?"

He shook his head. "No." He glanced out the coach window. "It's time to change hats."

Theo quickly donned her own bonnet. "That is better. I can see everything now." Including someone staring at the coach. "Who is that, I wonder?"

"Who?" Chandos leaned forward. "We must have passed them."

She shrugged. "I suppose it does not matter. I am allowed to be here with you."

"When is the next ball?"

"Why?"

"Because every set is mine." He cut her a look. "If you agree, of course."

"As long as we do not have to stand up for every dance."

"Only the waltzes." The amorous look was back in his eyes. "We can explore the grounds."

"That sounds delightful." Now that she knew what he meant to do. "It is tomorrow evening."

When they arrived at Worthington House, there was a note waiting from Mrs. Rollins informing Theo that the Rollinses were available the next morning. "We have an appointment with Mr. and Mrs. Rollins tomorrow at ten."

"Excellent. The sooner we can have what we want done in the house the better."

"I will write back to her, accepting the time." A few minutes later, Theo sent Jones off with the message. "Do you know if your mother will be there?"

"No. I do know that she plans to invite you to tea. I shall be there as well."

"Perhaps she is ready to accept our marriage." Although, she would not mind Chandos being present.

"We had a discussion, but I'm still not certain about her feelings."

They were in a small parlor when the door opened, and she heard Charlotte's voice. Chandos turned to Theo. "What do we tell them about where we were?"

"Nothing. I doubt if anyone will ask." She reached up and stroked his cheek. "We are betrothed. We can always tell them about our luncheon."

He took her hand and kissed it. "We are indeed."

CHAPTER THIRTY-FIVE

The next morning, they were greeted with a message from the duchess that she would be available to discuss the changes in the house at eleven thirty.

The Rollinses arrived promptly at ten o'clock. After Theo introduced Mr. and Mrs. Rollins to Leo, they went to the attic then to the next floor down. "What would you think about moving the schoolroom and nursery to this level and expanding the servants' quarters? I want to keep a wall between the male and female areas and add a bathing room to one end of each part, and heating."

Mr. Rollins spread out the architectural drawings of the house on a bed. "There are fireplaces in the nursery and in the schoolroom. It would not be difficult to build another fireplace in the other side of the floor."

"Excellent." That was one problem resolved. "We then need to add a schoolroom, nursery, and other rooms for art, music, and rooms as the children grow older."

"Such as at Worthington House," Mr. Rollins said.

"Precisely. I have no idea how many children we will have." Hopefully, not eleven. Then again, that was two families combined.

"That will be the easy part. You will want the nursery some distance from the schoolroom area. So as not to disturb sleeping babies."

"Yes, indeed." That was something no one had considered when the Worthington House children's floor had been renovated to match the one in Stanwood House. When Gideon had come along, they had to rearrange some of the area.

"What happened?" Leo asked.

"The children were too loud, and they woke the baby." Theo shook her head remembering the first time they had awoken the baby. "Grace moved Gideon down to be near she and Matt until the Season had ended. Then they renovated the floor."

Mr. Rollings tapped the drawing. "Did you know that you have a staircase leading from the floor below to this one?"

"I did not." Leo leaned over the plan. "Theo, look at this. It makes no sense. The stairs go from the room my mother is using to"—he stepped over to a part of the wall that bumped out—"here."

Rollins went over and tapped on the wall. "I believe you've found it, your grace."

It all made sense now. "I knew something was wrong with the way the rooms were arranged. The room your mother is in must have been the original duchess's chamber."

Leo nodded. "And, at some point, after one of those infamous arranged matches, it was changed."

"Do you want to open it up again?" Mr. Rollins asked. "Its original use would have been to allow quick access to the children."

"Yes." Theo liked the idea a great deal. "Are there any other tunnels or passages in the walls?"

"I don't think there are. The house was built in the mid-eighteenth century. Most of the tunnels existed before then. I'll take another look when we go back downstairs, and I have designs for the other floors."

"Just what we need. Secret passages," Leo mumbled.

They would be exciting, but Theo had to concede they could be problematical as well. "It is better to know than not."

"You're right, my love." He put his arm around her waist, drawing her closer to him.

"Speaking of decorating." Mrs. Rollins grinned. "Let us discuss a color scheme for this level. It will probably be finished before the attics are."

"I am quite partial to the colors at Worthington House." Considering she had helped to select them. "I would like this to be the same."

"Easily done. If you will show me the other rooms, we can discuss them as well."

"Yes. We do not want to unnecessarily take up your time." Theo led Mrs. Rollins to the stairs. "The main entertaining rooms are in good shape. But in other areas of the house, almost everything but the furniture must be refreshed." Theo glanced at her brooch watch. "We must hurry. We are due to meet with the duchess in an hour. She would like to see what we are doing."

Mrs. Rollins gave Theo a sympathetic look. "It must be difficult for you and for her. Your sister Rothwell's mother was not happy over the modifications she decided to make."

"I think she is resolved to the change. Chandos is making new living arrangements for her."

Mrs. Rollins had left the fabric books she had made, in the family dining room where they were to meet with the duchess. The only real problem was that her grace desired to remain in Town for the rest of the Season, and Theo and Leo wanted to start the renovations as soon as they left for their wedding trip. That was not an easy task in the middle of the Season. He took her hand when they reached the hall.

"Have you found a house for your mother?"

"I believe so. Marrow told me that Lady Pettigrew is returning home after Sarah's wedding. As long as we pay her for the amount of the remainder of the lease, Mama can reside there."

"And then she will remove to Bath?" Bath could be a very busy place. She should have a great deal to divert her.

"That is the current plan." He sounded so uncertain.

"Something is the matter. What is it?"

"I have just the past year taken full control of the dukedom and the holdings. As you know, until Whiting came to work for me, I was having trouble with some of the tenants at my main estate. I must leave Whiting here to oversee the construction and the estates until we return."

Theo understood his concerns. They and their friends had formed a scheme to travel with Holland and Patricia to Vienna. Perhaps Theo and Chandos could come home earlier than planned. "We could arrange to be gone for two months instead of four months. We will simply travel with everyone until it is time for us to return. Will that work?"

"Yes." He let out a breath and smiled. "That will be perfect. Thank you for thinking of it."

Theo returned his smile. Planning was her most useful skill. "Excellent. Now let us try to intrigue your mother with the plans."

"Instead of scare her?" He grinned.

"Indeed." Even though the duchess would no longer reside in the house, she was uncertain about what they wanted to do. "You will have to find her a house to lease for the next Season."

"If she likes the one I've arranged for her, perhaps I can buy it or lease it again."

"That is a good idea." She took Leo's hand. "Come. We must finish so that the Rollinses can get to work."

The duchess joined them with a look of trepidation. Theo poured her a cup of tea, and her grace smiled her approval. "That was lovely, my dear."

"Thank you, ma'am." It was nice to have one's soon-to-be mother-in-law's praise. "Let us show you what we planned."

When Theo was done, the duchess frowned. "I understand the

reason to move the nursery and schoolroom, but why do we need to improve the servants' quarters?"

"To make it more comfortable for them." It struck Theo that the duchess had not really considered the comfort of those who served her. "As you know, many households have great difficulty in keeping their staff for any length of time. My family has been successful, by treating them better. This involves higher pay, better living conditions among other things. I read recently that one lady gives the maids an option of gowns to wear for work. Not a livery. Gowns in the same color but to the maid's design."

Her grace appeared interested. "I have never considered it. Although, I should have."

"Now to our most interesting discovery." Theo exchanged a smile with her betrothed. "There is a staircase from your chambers to the next floor. We believe that your rooms were the original duchess's chambers, and the staircase was to the nursery."

She appeared stunned. "Do you mean to tell me that the duchess's rooms were not always at the other end of the corridor?"

"Exactly." Theo nodded. "That must have happened due to discord between one of the ducal couples."

"Good Lord. I never would have supposed." The duchess looked at both Theo and her son. "Congratulations on discovering that piece of information."

Leo went on to tell her about the house he was leasing for her so that she could remain in Town while they made their wedding trip and the construction was underway. "Does that suit you?"

"It does, indeed. But what about the house in Bath?" Creases marred her smooth forehead.

"Mama, I visited before coming to Town. It is in perfect condition. Who told you otherwise?"

Mrs. Rollins was packing her books. "We must go," she whispered. "Send a message with the date we can begin work."

Theo rose while Leo spoke with his mother and walked the Rollinses to the door. "I will. As you can see, we just need to relocate the duchess."

"I understand. We will see you later."

By the time she returned to the dining room, Leo was angry. "What happened?"

"The caretaker of the Bath house told my mother that it needed extensive repairs."

Theo took a breath. "It appears as if he and his wife have become too comfortable living there. We will have to let them go and replace them."

Leo nodded. "I believe you are correct."

The rest of the morning was spent deciding which servants would go with the duchess and which would remain at Chandos House. Leo, though, had no idea how many servants were needed to run a town house.

Theo finally interrupted the conversation that he and his mother were unable to resolve. "Excuse me. I suggest we make up a list of what we each require in the way of servants. Then we shall ask them who would like to remain here and who would like to move with your mother." She looked at the duchess. "Your grace, you will not require nearly as many servants in the smaller house as you do here." Then she looked at her husband-to-be. "Chandos, you need more than you think you do." Theo picked up her pencil. "I shall make a list. When I have finished, we can discuss this with the senior staff first."

The duchess appeared disgruntled, but Leo threw her a thankful look. Theo glanced at her brooch watch. "I must be going. I have a fitting."

He rose. "I will take you to the modiste."

"Thank you." She turned to her future mother-in-law. "Your grace, I will see you in a few hours if you are available."

"I might not be here, dear. You may make the arrangements."

"Thank you, again." Theo curtseyed.

They waited outside for his curricle to be readied. "She is still not pleased with our marriage."

"She is going to have to accept that I will not wed anyone but you." He glanced at the door. "We will find a way."

They would. Theo turned at a sound. "Here is your carriage."

After her fitting Chandos took her home and joined them for luncheon. Later that afternoon, they took her phaeton to the Park.

"Theo!" Sarah hailed from Marrow's curricle. "We have news!"

Theo pulled off to the verge and Marrow brought his vehicle beside hers.

He exchanged a glance with Sarah. "We discovered why Lady Pettigrew was attempting to put off the wedding."

She nodded. "Mama does not want to leave Town until the end of the Season."

Chandos did not look pleased. Theo leaned toward her friend. "What happened?"

"We did as you suggested. As soon as the settlement agreements were signed, the gentlemen purchased the special licenses. Then we gathered our parents together and told them that neither we nor Patricia nor Holland would wait to wed and gave them the date and the plan for our double wedding. Mama burst into tears, and it all came out."

Theo glanced at Chandos. "Does she plan to remain in the house?"

Sarah shrugged lightly. "That remains to be decided. Fortunately, both Lord and Lady Carlisle agreed to a wedding on the date we want."

A few moments later Felice and Crewe rode up on horses. She smiled at them. "Theo, your idea worked. We will wed the day after you."

Crewe glanced fondly at his betrothed. "We may now plan our departure to the Continent."

"Perhaps another luncheon is in order," Patricia suggested with a grin. "I must say, I feel as if a weight has been lifted from my shoulders."

Felice nodded. "I completely understand. A wedding is supposed to be a time for happiness, not full of stress."

Chandos's lips quirked up. "Indeed. I'm glad everything is working out the way we want it." He slid Theo a look. "Gunter's?"

"Yes." The only thing left was to make plans for Chandos's mother.

They all left the Park and arrived at the tea shop together. There was a great deal of discussion and merriment in selecting the ices. It turned out that, like Theo, Felice did not enjoy sweet ices.

"Shall we depart for the ship the day of our wedding or the day after?" Crewe asked.

"My father offered us the use of his yacht. It has extremely comfortable cabins," Marrow said.

Chandos nodded. "That sounds much better than taking the packet."

"He will have the yacht brought up to the docks here, which will save us the journey to Dover," Marrow added.

Felice, Patricia, Sarah, and Theo exchanged glances. It was as if they were all thinking the same thing. "In that case, we could board her that evening and depart on the next tide."

Her friends nodded. "Depending on when it arrives," Sarah said. "We could have most of our luggage sent to the ship early."

"Efficient." Leo gave her a fond look. "Shall we plan to do that?"

They all agreed and were preparing to leave when a curricle driven by Lord Bolingbroke and carrying Lady Lana drove up. Both of them seemed to be in excellent spirits.

"Do you think they will make a match?" Sarah whispered.

"I certainly hope so," Chandos drawled. "It was my suggestion to him that he ask her to dance."

Crewe barked a laugh. "Just think about how many more matches you could arrange if you remained here for the rest of the Season."

Chandos shook his head. "I accomplished what I set out to do. That's enough."

"I for one am very glad you thought to introduce me to Sarah." Marrow smiled at his affianced wife.

"And I'm grateful you thought of Patricia," Holland said.

"I hadn't actually thought that you two had something to do with me meeting Felice," Crewe said. "But now that I consider it, I believe you did."

"How are we to travel when we arrive?" Felice asked.

"We must make arrangements for coaches and hotels," Chandos said. "I can recommend some good hotels."

"Did not my brother Worthington make the coach plans?" Theo was certain that he did.

"Yes. Do you think he would mind helping us?"

"Not at all. We can ask him at dinner." Speaking of that, she glanced at her brooch watch. "We must go. Is everyone attending Lady Carlson's ball this evening?"

They all agreed to meet there.

CHAPTER THIRTY-SIX

Once again, Leo was more than happy to be joining Theo's family. Worthington agreed to assist Theo with hiring coaches and horses. Grace said that she would call on her cousin about hotels across the Continent and contact her friend Lady Evesham about the possibility of using her house in Paris. By the time the light meal before the ball was consumed, everything, including the coaches—through an agent in London—had been resolved.

Leo placed the light silk cloak over Theo's shoulders. "Every dance."

"Yes." She turned her head to smile up at him. "Every dance."

"I wonder if those ladies will be there." Leo would love to be able to discover who they were. He was still angry about their role in his almost losing Theo.

"I do not know. Perhaps."

Just in case, he decided he'd follow her to the ladies' room and wait in the corridor. "It's time to go."

As usual, her family was present, then their friends joined them. The talk centered around their pending marriages and honeymoon travel. He had to address his concerns about the time. "Theo and I have decided to remain with the rest of you for two months. I don't feel as if I can leave my estates for much longer than that."

"I understand," Crewe said. "It took time for me to establish myself as the new master when my father died."

"Will you stay at the main estate?" Patricia asked.

Theo glanced at Leo. "I think we will go there first. But I would like to see the other properties and see what needs to be accomplished.

He nodded his agreement. "Something I have not had the opportunity to do yet."

"Lesser estates must be kept up," Marrow agreed. "We will live at the estate where my parents resided when my grandfather was alive."

Patricia's eyes sparkled. "I am so happy to be able to travel."

There was something Leo didn't know. "Holland, do you not have an estate?"

"I do." He nodded. "My mother lives there with my younger siblings. The eldest of my brothers manages it. It will be a long time before we will reside there."

"When we do come back home for visits, we will stay in the town house," Patricia added.

They strolled and talked through the first two sets, then all of them, with the exception of Holland and Patricia decided to join the first waltz. This was the first time Leo had danced the waltz with Theo since they made love. It made it more special. He held her closer than before, and she seemed even more comfortable in his arms. That had never happened to him before. "Is it different for you?"

"Yes." Her eyes warmed him. "I can almost feel your hands stroking me."

Leo almost groaned, and his cock stirred. "Perhaps I can find an empty parlor."

Her lips curved up in an almost sly smile. "That would be interesting."

Lord, he was going to enjoy being married to her. Fortunately, he knew exactly where to take her. "I believe it will be."

By the time the set ended, he was ready to drag her away, but he'd have to be discreet. They and the others rejoined Patricia and Holland, who didn't dance.

Sarah glanced at Theo and leaned closer. "Would you accompany me to the ladies' room?"

"Of course." They linked arms and strolled toward the stairs.

Leo started to go after them, but Marrow placed his hand on Leo's arm. "Wait a few minutes. If those females do plan to follow them, they won't if they see you."

"You're right." That could be the reason Theo had not heard from them recently. He'd been too quick. He waited until he deemed enough time had passed, then went to the parlor that had been set aside for the ladies and waited.

When Sarah and Theo reached the ladies' room, they went immediately behind the screens. She had just stood and shaken out her skirts when the door opened and closed.

"Did you hear that Chandos's mistress has been seen?" the low-voiced lady said.

"No! In the Park? That's where he usually takes them," her nasally friend responded.

This should be interesting.

"No. With him on some street. I cannot remember the name. In the area where most of the gentlemen house their ladybirds," the lady with the low voice said as if she was certain.

It was all Theo could do not to laugh. Had someone seen his coach?

"Do you know what she looks like?" Nasally said.

"My brother said that she had red hair. Curly red hair and blue eyes," low voice responded.

"I suppose she is beautiful." Nasally sounded jealous.

"That is what he said. She is a great beauty. Her skin is like milk, and she speaks with a slight burr. As if she is from Scotland or maybe from France. There are quite a few of the Scots still in France."

Now that was a lie. How could they attempt to tarnish his reputation that way?

"I feel sorry for poor Lady Theo. Having to wed the duke. Even if he is handsome," Nasally responded.

That was kind of her. Unless the lady knew Theo was present.

"And rich. I've also heard he is very good in bed." The lady's voice was different. As if she was imagining it.

He was that. Theo was going to burst out laughing if they did not leave soon.

"Still, to have a mistress when he's engaged." Nasally sounded offended.

Maybe too offended on Theo's behalf.

"I heard that after the wedding he's taking her to his castle where they'll remain until Christmas. And you know he only has a mistress in Town." The low-voiced lady's tone was crisp, as if she did not care.

This was all very strange.

"If that's the case, who cares if he has a ladybird now. She is going to be a very lucky young lady."

Yes, she was. But first, Theo would find out why those ladies were lying. She came out from behind the screen. They were both middle-aged. One was taller than the other, with an elaborate purple headdress with silver feathers. The other was blond, dressed in a white gown with silver netting. "I must say, that was very interesting. It was also a complete lie. Chandos does not have a mistress. He has not had one for a year. Well before he began to court me. Both of you owe him an apology for maligning his name."

"Well," Nasally said. "We had no idea anyone was eavesdropping."

Theo speared them with what she knew was a hard look. "I do not believe you. You have done this too often for it to be an accident."

"I do not believe you either," Sarah said. "I think you are doing this on purpose for some reason."

Theo agreed. "Why do you not tell me what it is?"

"You are a very bold young lady." The low-voiced woman raised her chin. "We do not have to tell you anything."

The other lady opened the door to Chandos lounging against the wall. "You might not want to tell my affianced-wife," he drawled. "However, I think you'd better tell me. Otherwise, I might be tempted to inform the rest of Polite Society that you are malicious gossipmongers."

"Her grace is going to be so disappointed," Nasally muttered.

One of his dark brows rose. "Her grace? As in her grace of Chandos?"

"Yes," the low-voiced lady said. "If you must know, she wants Lady Theo to call off the wedding." The lady cast a disappointed look at Theo. "Apparently, she has no intention of doing so."

"Very forward young lady," Nasally said.

Chandos's lips rose. "Exactly how I like my future duchess to be. Now." He stood and beckoned for Theo. She joined him, taking his arm. "What does my mother have against my betrothed?"

The ladies exchanged a look, and the low-voiced lady said, "She is not ready to leave. She thought that if you had a more malleable wife she could remain as mistress until she was ready. That is what happened to her. She had been very grateful to your grandmother for her help. She wanted to play the same role."

That was the reason for all the talk about a wife who would not be so strong. "I should have thought of that."

The other lady glanced at Theo. "It is not as if she does not like you. She thinks you are an exceptional young lady."

She stared at the woman. "She simply does not want me to marry her son."

"Yes."

"She almost got her wish." Theo squeezed his arm. "I was

ready to break it off with him until he convinced me what you had said were lies."

"I want an apology. Or I will do my best to blacken your names." He glanced at the low-voiced lady. "Perhaps I will also tell your husband about your fantasies."

The woman blanched. "I do apologize. I am very sorry to have agreed to interfere."

He speared Nasally with a hard look. "And you?"

She was much better at keeping her countenance than her friend. "I apologize as well." She took the other lady's arm.

"Before you go, where else did you spew your lies?"

"Only where Lady Theo could hear them," Nasally said. "As much time as you were spending with her and her family, we knew no one else would believe it."

Theo watched them depart. "Now I feel like a fool. Even Sarah and the others told me how it was."

"You were hurt." He gently rubbed her back. "Come let us go." He held his arm out to Sarah as well.

"Do you know who they are?" Sarah asked.

"I haven't a clue." He shrugged. "Although, I suppose I could find out fairly quickly if I wanted to, but why?"

"Why indeed." Theo sounded weary. "We still have your mother to deal with."

He was relieved to know what his mother's real problem was, but he had to support Theo. "I'm going to tell her to remove to her old chambers. That way we can start refreshing the chambers she's using, for you."

"Thank you." She gazed up at him. "Do you trust her not to attempt to interfere?"

"No. While we're gone, I'll leave Whiting in charge. He can tell the Rollinses that if Mama attempts to change anything they are to inform him immediately."

"That would be for the best."

Leo abandoned his plans to get Theo alone and make love to her. "Let's rejoin the others."

"Yes." She smiled. "There are at least one or two more waltzes left."

"And supper." He grinned. "I hope they have ices."

"I do as well." She stepped a little closer to him.

They returned to their friends and relayed what had occurred.

"Does it seem to you that mothers appear to cause the most problems regarding marriages? Or rather who their son or daughter weds?" Felice asked.

"It could be because they become powerless." Patricia's brow creased. "My paternal grandmother once told me that although she pushed my father to wed, she wanted to select his wife. She knew it would be the new marchioness who would take over her duties, and that she would have to find a new life."

Leo nodded. "That is the case with my mother." Mama had handled things badly. "However, if she had been honest with me my feelings toward her would be much different. I no longer feel as if I can trust her."

"I do not know what I can do to make the transition easier for her." Theo closed her eyes for a second.

"I don't see a way either." His mother had managed to alienate both of them.

"It would have been different if she had embraced Theo and your marriage," Felice said. "That is how Crewe's mother has treated me. She even agreed with us wanting to marry sooner." She pulled a face. "Unlike my mother."

"Well, it's spilt milk now," Crewe said. "Perhaps after you have a child it will be easier."

Leo glanced at his betrothed and rather doubted that would be the case. Still, they could hope. "At this point, I am just looking forward to being married."

Everyone agreed on that point.

In the coach on the way to Worthington House, he and Theo told Grace and Worthington what they had discovered. "I think we should both speak with her."

"I would rather that Theo did not engage with her," Grace said.

"The wedding is only days away, and after that, she will not see her again for several months. Depending on what happens then, you could, if you like, visit her before going to your estate."

Theo nodded. "I agree. I am so tired of the contretemps. I do not want to think of it for a while."

She was right. Leo was the one with the problem parent. Not his betrothed. He was glad he hadn't told her about his mother attempting to introduce him to another lady. "Very well. Maybe it is best if I don't mention it either. Her friends probably will."

"Most likely," Worthington said. "My stepmother wasn't at all sure about my decision to wed Grace. She thought my sisters would become lost in the Carpenter family children."

"But it did not happen that way." Theo's lips rose. "We all decided to become brothers and sisters and be one family."

Leo had heard that. It was one of the things that made them all so special. "And now you'll add one more person."

"We are." She leaned against his shoulder. "You will be a perfect addition."

The talk turned to their wedding trip. Neither Grace nor Worthington had traveled overseas much, but friends had. Theo decided Leo and she should visit her cousins who had taken her sister Augusta to Europe.

When they arrived at Worthington House, he kissed Theo goodbye and walked home. Fortunately, his mother was still out. He really didn't know how he would react to seeing her after the events of the evening. He had been furious with her and nothing had changed.

The next morning, after Leo returned from breaking his fast with Theo, a message arrived from Marrow informing Leo that Lady Carlisle had invited Sarah's mother to reside with them for the remainer of the Season. Lady Pettigrew would remove from her leased house to Carlisle House before Sarah and Marrow's wedding. Sarah would stay with Theo. He suggested that her grace could view it in three days' time.

Leo wandered into Whiting's office. "The house I will lease for her grace will be vacant in a few days. I would like you to take her."

"Certainly, your grace."

"I am expecting letters from some hotels in Europe." Leo had given his address for the hotels in Calais and on the route to Paris. The rest of the responses would arrive at Lady Evesham's Paris home. "Please make sure all the post comes to you first."

"I will." His secretary gave him a concerned look. "Is there anything else I can do?"

"No, thank you. You will be quite busy enough while I'm on my honeymoon." Aside from his wedding, that was what he was looking forward to most.

CHAPTER THIRTY-SEVEN

Theo woke early as usual, but today she would not be riding. Today was her wedding day. Yesterday, Chandos, who had taken possession of the family jewelry and brought over a collection of rings. She selected an emerald ring in a wide gold band. Her trunks had been sent to the yacht. Then they attended Sarah and Marrow's wedding and the wedding breakfast. After two weeks of planning, it seemed to be happening so soon. Which made no sense at all.

Payne entered the room, and Theo donned a simple day dress for breakfast. It was strange not to have Chandos there, but her sisters insisted that he not be allowed to see her before the ceremony. While she dressed for the wedding, a knock came on the door and Mary, Elizabeth, Constance, and, Louisa's daughter, Alexandria entered.

"We have gifts for you," Mary said. "Well, three gifts and one on loan."

The little girls nodded. Mary stepped forward. "I have something new." She held out a rectangular box covered in silk.

Tears sprung to Theo's eyes. She remembered all the times she and Mary had done this on their older sisters' wedding days.

"Thank you." She opened the box. In it was a gold bracelet set with emeralds. It looked as if it had been made to match her ring. But how could that have happened? "It is beautiful!" She hugged Mary. "Thank you so much."

Next Elizabeth came to Theo. "I have something old." She handed Theo a velvet bag. In it was a delicate necklace with an emerald shaped in a teardrop. It was as if they all knew which ring she would choose. "It is lovely." She hugged her niece. "Thank you!"

Mama helped me," Elizabeth said.

Constance was next. "I have something borrowed." She handed Theo a gold hair comb. "Mama said not to lose it."

Theo chuckled wetly. "I will not lose it, and I will return it immediately after the ceremony."

Alexandria blushed as she handed Theo a packet wrapped in paper. "This is something blue. I hope you like them. I embroidered them myself."

Theo unwrapped the gift. In the paper were three handkerchiefs embroidered with three different blue flowers, a forget-me-not, a bluebell, and a delphinium. "These are extremely well-done!"

Her niece blushed again. "Thank you. Mama said that the same thing."

Mary patted Theo on her back. "No crying."

"I know. Is it time to go yet?" As Theo spoke a knock sounded on the door.

Grace opened it. "All right, everyone. We need to be off."

Sarah stood behind Theo. "I am so happy for you."

"One more to go." They would all attend Felice and Crewe's wedding tomorrow. Theo linked arms with Sarah. "I am so excited I can hardly breathe."

"That sounds like me yesterday." She smiled. "I can tell you that thus far, married life is wonderful!"

They drove to the church with Matt and entered through the side door. All Theo's brothers and sisters, including the ones by marriage, were already seated. Then she saw Chandos. He was magnificent. He wore a black jacket and trousers, with a snowy white cravat. His waistcoat was green paisley with silver thread. He had never looked more handsome. He turned from speaking to Marrow and smiled.

Theo took Leo's breath away. Her gown was of salmon-colored silk with gold netting. The neckline of the bodice hinted at her lush breast. It dropped almost to her natural waistline showing off her small waist. The skirt, narrower than in previous years, flared out over her hips. He couldn't wait to get her alone. But first the wedding and the breakfast afterward.

The rector took his place as Theo moved toward him, Worthington by her side. "Dearly beloved, we are gathered together here in the sight of God, and in the face of this congregation, to join together this man and this woman in holy matrimony . . ."

Having just witnessed a marriage ceremony, Leo knew he couldn't take Theo's hand until after her brother allowed it. Finally, the rector asked who would give Theo to him.

"I will." Worthington glanced at Leo. "Take good care of her."

He nodded and the rector continued. Gazing into each other's eyes, he and Theo continued their vows in strong voices. Marrow gave the ring to the clergyman. He blessed it before giving it to Leo. Despite knowing what he'd say, Theo blushed when he promised to worship her body. Then they were pronounced man and wife. He felt as if he'd run a marathon and had won.

After signing the registry, he turned to Theo. "Are you ready, wife?"

"As ready as you are, husband." Instead of merely placing her hand on his arm, she twined her arm with his. "Let us go."

They strolled up the aisle, accepting the congratulations of their relatives. Even his mother appeared happy. Hopefully, her attitude toward his wedding had changed.

February 1825 Stallwart Palace, Northamptonshire

"This baby can come anytime." Theo rubbed her stomach. "I wish I knew what was taking it so long." She and Leo had arrived back in England in time for the family get-together, then traveled up to their main estate and immediately wrote to the Rollinses. While the master apartments and the nursery and schoolroom were being refreshed and remodeled, they continued on to the rest of their estates. They had returned to Stallwart Palace just after Christmas to await the coming of their first child. But the dratted thing was refusing to make a showing. Theo was almost two weeks late.

"This is quite common with firstborn children," the midwife said reassuringly.

"No one else in my family has been this late." Why her?

"Theo." Grace's tone was gentle. "Most of your sisters have had twins. They always come early."

"Yes, but Louisa, Madeline, and Augusta were not this late." Theo prayed there was nothing wrong.

"That is no indication of your pregnancy and the birth of your child."

Grace was right. All of her sisters by blood had experienced morning sickness, and she had not. "I suppose you are right."

Leo knocked on the door and entered. "Is there any news?"

Theo shook her head. "Your son is apparently as stubborn as you are."

"Oh, no! I think it's your daughter." He kissed her. "I so want a girl."

"You are perverse." Theo could not not sound a bit crabby. "Most gentlemen want boys."

A slow smile grew on his handsome face. "More fools they. Having a girl means we will have to keep trying."

"You are impossible."

He took her hand and kissed it. "True, but you love me anyway."

"I do love you." Theo drew him down for a kiss.

"And I love you." He searched her eyes before kissing her again.

"How is your mother doing?" The dowager duchess had arrived two weeks ago and made a point of keeping to herself until Grace and Louisa had also arrived.

"She wants a boy." Leo's tone was dry and dismissive.

"Everyone will get what God gives them," Louisa commented. "Come, Theo, you should walk."

"I know."

Leo helped her up from the chaise. She took two steps and almost doubled over in pain.

"What is it?" He held on to her until she could stand.

"I believe her grace has got her wish," the midwife said as she moved around the room gathering her things and going into the birthing room.

"I need to walk."

Leo wrapped his arm around what was left of her waist. "I'll be right here with you."

"I've sent for small bites of food to be brought," Louisa said. "You must keep up your strength."

Before Theo could reach the door, another pain struck.

"These are close together," Grace said. "Do not go far." She glanced at Leo. "Up and down this corridor. I do not think it will be long now."

"You see what you did?" Leo said teasingly. "You complained so much, the baby gave up."

"Good. Hopefully, this means he or she will listen to me."

They made it to the corridor and fluid flowed down her legs. "I think my water broke."

The midwife came to the door of the birthing room. "I think it's time you got in the chair."

The chair was the birthing chair that all her sisters had used. Its strange shape was supposed to help with the birth. Theo's maid removed her robe, leaving her in a chemise. Pain speared through her again. "That was close."

Leo helped her into the chair, and the midwife took a look under her shift. "I can see the head."

Until last week, they had been concerned that the baby would be breech, but it turned. Since then, Theo had had more trouble pushing it down so that she could breathe. She caught her breath with the next pain.

"Push hard," the midwife said. "That's excellent. Once more and we'll know what we have."

Theo pushed with the pain and the baby seemed to pop out. "What is it?"

"You have a boy, your grace," the midwife said as the baby screamed. "He has a good set of lungs. Once more for the afterbirth, and they can clean you up."

Theo bore down as hard as she could. The afterbirth had to come out whole.

"There you are. Excellent job." The midwife grinned.

One of the nursemaids handed the baby to Leo. "He's beautiful. Wrinkled, but beautiful. And bald."

Payne cleaned Theo and helped her to the bed. "There you are, your grace. I shall order something for you to eat."

"Thank you." Theo gazed at her husband and baby. "I would like to see my son."

Leo came over and sat in a chair next to the bed, then handed her the baby. "We must decide on a name." Their son started to root around and she put him to her breast. "We could name him after your father and Matt?"

"Bartholomew? Douglas, my grandfather's name, might be better."

"What do you think of Douglas Harold, after my grandfather, Matheus?"

"Douglas, Harold, Matheus, Marquis of Stratton. I like it." He grinned and stroked one finger lightly down her cheek and over their son's head.

AUTHOR'S NOTES

I hope you enjoyed reading Theo and Leo's story. Leo was already a friend of Charlie's when he suddenly became Theo's love interest.

Words are always changing but imagine my surprise when I discovered the word *ambivalent* was not in usage until around 1912. That made me take a deeper dive into the OED where I found *pococurante*. Also, *midmorning* wasn't used until the end of the nineteenth century, therefore, I used ante-noon. However, hooray! Ladies' room was finally in use.

As with words, fashion was changing as well. Sleeves grew larger, skirts narrower, and waists were coming down.

Walter's book is next. He will return from Spain with orders to wed.

I hope you loved Theo and Chandos's story.

Until the next book,

Ella

ACKNOWLEDGMENTS

Anyone involved the publishing process knows it takes a team effort to get a book from that inkling in an author's head to the printed or digital page. I'd like to thank my beta readers, Jenna and Doreen, for their comments and suggestions. To my agent, Jill Marsal, and my wonderful editor, John Scognamiglio. To the Kensington team who do such a tremendous job of publicity and to the copy editors who find all the niggling mistakes I never am able to see. Last, but certainly not least, to my readers. Without you, none of this would be worth it. Thank you from the bottom of my heart for loving my stories!

I love to hear from my readers, so feel free to contact me on my website or on Facebook if you have questions. Those links and my newsletter link can be found at www.ellaquinnauthor.com.

On to the next book!

Visit our website at
KensingtonBooks.com
to sign up for our newsletters, read more from your favorite authors, see books by series, view reading group guides, and more!

BOOK CLUB
BETWEEN THE CHAPTERS

Become a Part of Our
Between the Chapters Book Club
Community and Join the Conversation

Betweenthechapters.net

Submit your book review for a chance to win exclusive Between the Chapters swag you can't get anywhere else!
https://www.kensingtonbooks.com/pages/review/